ROMAN CIRCUS

A NOVEL BY

FRANK O'NEILL

SIMON AND SCHUSTER

NEW YORK   LONDON   TORONTO   SYDNEY   TOKYO

Simon and Schuster
Simon & Schuster Building
Rockefeller Center
1230 Avenue of the Americas
New York, New York 10020

This book is a work of fiction. Names, characters, places and incidents are either the product of the author's imagination or are used fictitiously. Any resemblance to actual events or persons, living or dead, is entirely coinciden-tal.
  In particular, no reference is intended to United States diplomats stationed now or in the past in Rome. Indeed, if any of these excellent public servants were to attempt to take up their work inside the embassy within these pages, they would quickly be baffled by a layout quite unknown to them.

SIMON AND SCHUSTER and colophon are registered trademarks of Simon & Schuster, Inc.

Designed by Levavi & Levavi
Manufactured in the United States of America

10 9 8 7 6 5 4 3 2 1

Library of Congress Cataloging-in-Publication Data

O'Neill, Frank.
  Roman circus: a novel/by Frank O'Neill.
    p. cm.
  I. Title.
PS3565.N495R66 1990
813'.54—dc20   89-37784
                                                CIP

ISBN 0-671-68336-5

*A BIANCA, CONTESSA LOVATELLI, SENZA LA
QUALE A QUESTA STORIA MANCHEREBBE IL
CUORE.*

P·R·O·L·O·G·U·E

The General's hands and feet were bound. Though he was wedged between the Italian driver and the Libyan gunman, he had to brace himself as best he could when the headlights picked out a curve ahead. The bandaging around his body was greasy with sweat and hurt him under the armpits. He willed himself, not quite successfully, to disregard it. The lights of Naples had been cut off by the headland. There were fainter lights by the gulf below. Salerno, he decided, already passing behind them. He checked his bearings. He saw the lights of an aircraft cross the gulf low above the sea. Military. Navy F-111 fighter-bomber, ours, thought the General automatically. But to count on the American warships and the air squadrons and the missile bases and his own command, all on his team against the five pious totalitarians in the van, seemed in his present situation to have passed into the field of fantasy, to be rejected. The van was carrying him south, already well beyond Vesuvius, but this hill road meant nothing to him. He could remember no installations here that he commanded.

Since the Italian Red Brigades had no combatant status, he

was not a prisoner of war and, as far as he was concerned, he was still Commander of U.S. Army Forces, Southern Italy.

His hands and feet were tied, not cuffed, a single tie that suggested a provision for quick release. He had noted that he was in the front seat, close to the widest door; not the obvious position for a prisoner, even bound, and at night. The man to his right, the Arab, his personal jailer, held a knife close to his ribs. He sensed that the rancor between the Italians and the Libyan was sharpening but also that it was restrained by discipline and not usable by him. He also sensed that the four men and one woman in the van were going into combat that they knew was dangerous. He had not seen their weapons, but the concealed space available would not hold any larger than anti-tank rockets. The heat and the pinch around his chest forced him to think about the bandage, and thinking about it wrung his gut with cold.

So he made his mind keep taking fixes. A woman was a new element. He had not seen her or heard her voice until two hours ago, when they had taken him out of the tent of black cloth inside the room where he had spent the last two weeks. They had put him back into his uniform, newly pressed and with the three stars polished, after wrapping him with the bandage though he was neither wounded nor sick. When they put it on, the bandage had been cool, heavy, and smooth. Still blindfolded then, he had been startled when he felt a woman's hand straighten a tuck on his chest. Later he had seen the sexless clothes and severe handkerchief around the head of a good Red Brigades bitch, but then he had smelled a wraith of perfume, not quite scrubbed off. She had authority here.

The General studied this as he had studied the voices of the two terrorists behind—both of which sounded young and pushed to the breaking point with resolution. Any characteristic of his guards that might be in conflict with their present actions repaid study. Study had kept him functional for two weeks behind his blindfold in his circular dark tent. He had studied the Book of Psalms, the maintenance manual for the M-1 tank, four plans of action at divisional level in the case of an outbreak of conflict with the Warsaw Pact, and the episodes of *Don Quixote,* all from memory. It had made the space behind his blindfold as neat and stacked with data as a chart room.

He did not have to study the nature of the bandage coiled around him. Its filling was as heavy as tar. Though he had been blind when they put it on, he had recognized it suddenly by its smell. Any doubt remaining was removed by the observation that his jailer held a knife against his side, not a gun.

It was plastic explosive.

General Curtis Leipzinger once again recited the Twenty-third Psalm in a firm, though silent, voice.

Since the American guidance station did absolutely nothing but emit a gentle humming sound, the only local beings still interested in it were some sheep who coveted the uncropped grass inside its chain-link fence. Because it was night, even these were asleep. The station was a concrete bump supporting a stubby antenna on top of a brushy hill near the village of Sagatto, about eighty kilometers southeast of Naples. It was manned at all times by one U.S. Army Corporal-Technician and two armed sentries. They came and went through Sagatto in shifts by Jeep, One of the sentries tonight was PFC Frank Caprocore of Buffalo, New York. His grandfather had been born three villages away from here, but this coincidence had ceased to be of much interest, even to himself. Caprocore paced outside the blockhouse watching the smoke from his cigarette move unhurriedly away through air that still smelled of wild thyme and sheep shit. His nose ignored the trace of oil and metal from the M-14 slung on his shoulder as his ears ignored the station's peaceable hum. From time to time he heard a Vespa wind up through the streets of Sagatto and every now and then a voice. On most evenings he was able to very faintly hear the television in the café, but not tonight. He could pick up the telephone on the blockhouse wall and be let back in, but there was not much point. Amos Jones, the technician, who was black and ambitious, was studying for a technical exam, and Wade, the other sentry, was reading a paperback.

Since the station was fully automated there was absolutely nothing, absent breakdown or attack, for any of them to do.

Caprocore, rather abstractedly, thought of a girl he had seen from the Jeep in Sagatto and whether it would be possible, he being Italian, for him to pick her up without being killed by someone. The station sent out a variety of unremarkable signals to do with location and navigation. In darker circumstances, it would provide an early fix for Cruise and Pershing missiles on their way from Sicily to Soviet targets. That was why it rated a specialist and two guards.

The van with the General in it slowed and turned onto a narrower road. It was a shabby Fiat minibus with the markings of a godly but obscure charity connected with the Carmelites. The driver missed the gear change and the engine faltered on the grade. *"Porca miseria!"* he swore, but absently, and clanged the shift. Then he said clearly, "Now the weapons. From now on we go armed." He spoke in Italian. The General, who liked to read d'Annunzio, had no trouble with it.

The woman said, alone on the middle seat of the minibus, "We have not been followed. There is no doubt of that." But she reached under her seat, as did the others, and there were noises of metal in the truck. The two youths in the backseat murmured to each other. One of the voices had become familiar to the General in his prison. The woman was called Rosa and the driver, Alfredo—though the General doubted that either name was real. One of the youths in the back went as Roberto; the General had not caught the fourth name.

"Maybe so," said the driver. "But on this road at night there would be no traffic. We must assume that any vehicle now is the police or the Americans. If we are stopped, we fight."

The woman said, "I do not think it will happen. He says there has been no unusual movement up here at all."

General Leipzinger thought, *They know each other well, these two.* He added to himself, *But he doesn't screw her. Not him.* The driver was angry and slight with a spiky beard like a pinko schoolteacher and Rosa was just noticeably soothing him. But Alfredo had been tensely polite to the General during his captivity, and the General saw now that the boy was afraid, but controlling it.

Ever since the General had smelled the explosive coiled around his chest he had known in his head that he was going to die tonight. Now the knowledge had settled into his bones, and he no longer fought it. He felt cold and clear to a degree that hurt, as though his nerves had been scraped and then touched with ice. He had not had to face death directly since a moment in the Korean War, and on that occasion he had had a great deal else to do.

He saw that Alfredo was looking at him. Alfredo said, either struggling with English or hating to pay a compliment, "You should not think your people abandoned you. Not since our brothers took Aldo Moro has there been such a stir. Some good things were said about you. By Italians also. We do not hate you personally. You should have stayed in America."

The Libyan, his jailer, said, "To destroy the nest of vermin who guided the American terror bombers to Tripoli, I would swim through this man's blood."

And even situated as he was, General Leipzinger thought, *Asshole!* before he thought, *But he's talking about the target. That's the first clue.* He said nothing aloud.

From the corner of his eye, he saw the woman look significantly at him and say to the driver, "When?"

"Very soon," said Alfredo. "There's a place up here to stop." He said it seriously, as though of a delicate topic. He added, "We are also a few minutes ahead of time."

General Leipzinger felt the bandage lick him with his own sweat. Hang on, he told himself, it's yours now. He had been a one-star combat General in Vietnam and many of his men had died for him. He was not an insolent man.

The lights of a small village showed ahead and then were cut off again by the mountain. A little way on, there was a deep curve with a flat space beyond the road. The driver let the van roll into it and stop. It rolled silently, for the place was overhung by chestnut trees and the ground was matted with husks.

"Now?" said the woman.

"Yes," said the driver.

She took a case out of her pocket and opened it. It contained

a syringe already screwed to a hypodermic. She made as though
to pass it to the driver.

"You do it," said the driver. "You have better hands." The
Libyan laughed theatrically. His teeth were crooked but white.

The woman hesitated and then leaned over and caught up the
General's cuff and pulled it someway up his arm. It caught on
the elbow. She put her hand against his skin, not harshly.

"*Mi dispiace,*" she said. (I am sorry.)

The General thought, *So this is the last thing I shall ever
know. This is the last. At least it's a woman.*

The prick was sharp. The Libyan said, "He does not deserve
apologies."

Late though it was, the owner of the café of Sagatto served
his guest with deference and pleasure. He had known at first
sight that he was not a northern Italian, still less a foreign tourist, but a gentleman of the Mezzogiorno and a man of refine-
ment. He had come several times to the village and, eating once
before at the café, had complimented the owner discerningly on
a dish of kid that was very good but also very simple.

Now the owner knew that his guest was a famous man, for
tonight he had seen him reading through a long article in a newspaper from Turin, of which, according to the little photograph,
he was evidently the author. The gentleman came to these hills
for his rest and relaxation, which apparently took the form of
wandering around chipping off little bits of rock with a hammer
and taking them home to collect. The owner had long ago been
a valet in Naples and thought that the more psychotic a pastime
would be for ordinary people, the more it distinguished a gentleman. He had turned the television right down, in deference to
an intellectual, although his one regular customer still at the bar,
Angelo Grusti, looked sulky, for he would have liked to have
heard the late soccer results.

The guest finished his coffee, finished his *grappa,* seemed to
consider and reject a second glass, and called for the bill. Standing by the tin table at the gentleman's shoulder, the owner wrote
it out carefully in a limp little notebook covered with squares.

"The gentleman drives back to the city so late?" he said
politely.

"Indeed," said the gentleman, "it is only an hour." He smiled pleasantly. "Work calls for both you and me," he said. The owner acknowledged the condescension with a simpering bow.

The guest left the proper tip. He picked up his dusty pouch full of rocks, which clinked. It occurred to the owner then that the pouch must be heavy for such a small man, and with a limp, to carry all day in the hills. The gentleman pushed through the bead curtain in the door and looked down the street toward his car. Insects bumped in the lamp above his head. Angelo Grusti got up from the bar and turned up the television ostentatiously loud. The gentleman turned a moment in the door.

Just then there was a noise in the street and a van came driving moderately fast. The gentleman looked at it with surprise and the owner looked at it with even more. It wasn't a local car, and the only other thing in that direction was the American place that hummed. It was odder yet that the van belonged to a pious organization connected with the Carmelites.

Later, when the night had gone berserk, the owner had no hesitation in telling the police that his customer had simply driven off toward Naples, had never looked at his watch, had certainly not seemed nervous, had openly displayed and left behind a newspaper with his name and photograph, and had been as surprised by the truck as he himself had been. Grusti resentfully confirmed this. This carried conviction, for Grusti was clearly a hostile witness, what with the television.

The General's mind was clear. His body was numb as meat. His muscles were dead. His lungs had stopped and he was suffocating slowly.

His bonds had been cut. He had watched the Libyan cut too close to the wrist and take off a piece of skin, impersonally. It hurt. Evidently, he was not dead. The Libyan was propping him up. On a bend, his unbound hand flopped over into the Libyan's crotch and was pushed away with a curse. His eye was not yet dulled. They drove through a village. A man came out through the bead curtain of a café carrying a small bag. "It's all right then," said Rosa and her voice was suddenly husky with excitement. The driver swallowed hard. A sudden loud voice gave the soccer score, Palermo versus Lecce. The Libyan let him go and the General toppled forward and saw the dashboard come toward him and felt his head hit it. The Libyan swore and then pulled him upright and took a revolver out of his pocket.

The village ended and the road became rougher and steep. The driver had the van in low gear at full throttle. Various parts of the General hit parts of the van and the Libyan held him by his hair. He saw a blockhouse ahead and knew what the target was. He saw a sentry outside it. *Poor kid,* he thought; *get inside, you idiot.*

The woman was carrying a machine gun at her breast and was breathing deeply as though in lust. Her eyes were raptly on the target. She looked at the General briefly, then looked him suddenly in the eye. She said to the driver, "He's not out. He knows what's going on."

The blockhouse was coming closer. Alfredo said in a small voice, "It doesn't put him out. It stops him moving. He's meant to look conscious but he can't talk. It's called *curare*." He didn't look at the woman.

"You can't do that," she said. "That's filthy. You can't shoot a man like that."

"He said to do it," said the boy. "It was his orders." The blockhouse was now very close. There was a light fence with a gate in front of it, but they were clearly not stopping. The young sentry, with a horrified look, had unslung his rifle.

The Libyan pointed the revolver carefully at the General's belly, well below the bandage. *I cannot even flinch,* thought the General.

The woman said, "You bastard!" and reached toward the Libyan. The Libyan pulled the trigger.

The two youths in the back of the truck had opened fire through the windows. The sentry fired on automatic, and bits of glass and metal whined through the truck. One of the youths, Roberto, gasped. The other fired through a disintegrated window and the sentry fell. The driver stopped the van by the blockhouse door. He was cursing in fear. The iron door slid open a little way and a gun barrel came out of it. The Libyan, either snarling or moaning, opened the door and threw General Leip-

zinger out. The driver got the van moving again. A rear window blew out and a bullet went through the roof.

The driver stopped the van abruptly again a hundred meters from the blockhouse, outside the smashed gate. The fallen sentry was on his knees and looking at the General on the ground. The driver took a small black box with a button on one side out of the glove compartment. His hands were shaking. The box was a remote detonator.

The Libyan looked at the woman in fury. "Bitch!" he said. In the Libyan's case, it was his voice that shook.

All of them watched the blockhouse door.

Just before the attack, PFC Frank Caprocore had heard the café television come on louder than usual. When he heard the engine noise, it occurred to him that it was already close, beyond the village. He was suddenly uneasy. Since General Leipzinger's kidnap two weeks before, everything had supposedly been on top alert, and for several days the Lieutenant had made surprise visits. Naples was still crawling with MPs. Out here, a state of alert had gotten to seem too dumb to keep up, but he remembered it now, alone, outside, in the night.

Perhaps this was the Lieutenant, he thought. He picked up the telephone and called inside in a casual voice, "We expecting anyone?" He discovered that his other hand was on the M-14.

No. The engine was now close, though he could see nothing. Then blinding headlights went on, coming straight at him. He picked up the telephone again and yelled, "We're under attack!" Then the fence gate had crashed open and people were shooting at him. He was nineteen and nobody had ever shot at him before.

He had a second of satisfaction when it seemed that he had hit the truck. Then something kicked him in the hip and he was on the ground, hurting. The truck drove right up to the door with everybody firing and something got thrown out of it. He thought maybe it was a bomb and he cowered and closed his eyes.

Then the truck went away. He opened his eyes. On the ground was a man. It was an American uniform. Maybe it was

Wade, the other sentry. He crawled toward it, making crying noises that he didn't hear. It wasn't Wade.

Then Frank Caprocore thought he had gone wrong in the head because it seeeemed to be a General lying there on the ground. And not just any General, but General Leipzinger, with his three stars and all, whom all of Italy had been looking for for two weeks. He looked away and shook his head.

But it was General Leipzinger and he was still lying there bleeding terribly and looking at him with desperate eyes, though saying nothing. So Caprocore lunged for the telephone again.

PFC Wade Thompson thought his buddy had been knocked silly, but he was a good soldier and when he opened the steel door he moved fast. He reacted first to the fact that the two men on the ground were wounded Americans exposed to enemy fire and only then to the fact that one was General Leipzinger, who had dropped out of the sky. He pulled first the General and then Caprocore into the blockhouse. Caprocore turned white when he pulled him over the ground. The General was limp and his eyes were fading. Thompson left them on the blockhouse floor and turned to the armored door. Amos Jones, the Corporal-Technician, had been on the emergency channel. He was sitting at the console with his back to all this. When he turned around he looked at the floor, paused a long moment, and said reverently, "Motherfuck."

Wade Thompson closed the blast-proof door. He stretched his hand toward the medical kit.

C·H·A·P·T·E·R   1

Giovanni Sidgewick Stears examined the guidance station where a senior General and three inconsequential young men had died together. The concrete was intact. The steel door bulged out from a gash down its middle as from a clumsy can opener and had had to be removed later with oxyacetylene. Inside, instead of grand annihilation, plastic explosive had played a round of nasty jokes: Here a set of electronic switches was in excellent repair amid the general ruin; just above it, someone's jaws had been driven through a dial. Much of a leg, with neatly tied and unscuffed shoe, lay by itself in a corner. A medical kit, no more than scorched, sat precariously on an incinerated chair. Open me first.

The leg, the eager jaws, the other unusual features of the station's interior, gained in clarity from being displayed as black-and-white photographs. Stears passed them back to the Lieutenant of U.S. Army Intelligence. Outside the blockhouse, in natural color, a score of cars—Italian, American, military, diplomatic, police, and presumed civilian—had by now assembled. A U.S. Army helicopter fidgeted noisily some distance away on a flat piece of ground.

"You want to go inside, sir?" said the Lieutenant. "You can go in when the Eyeties finish."

"No," said Stears. "Thank you."

The Lieutenant put his thumb by the leg. "All that stuff's gone by now," he said.

"Even so," said Stears. "Thank you."

"I meant that the remains have been removed for analysis, sir, which is partially complete. I was instructed to keep you up-to-date. And give you full cooperation." The Lieutenant was a tall youth with serious eyes who gangled in sections, stiffly, and seemed embarrassed to have tricked the CIA into a confession of unmanliness.

"I should only be in the way," said Stears. "I'm not forensic or anything like that."

"No, sir," said the Lieutenant, accepting with wariness any information whatsoever about someone who had arrived with the United States Military Attaché and the CIA Chief of Station, Rome.

A puff of morning breeze came up the hillside. Stears breathed more easily. From the doorway of the blockhouse, a bitter breath of explosive fume, mixed with seared flesh and plastic, still leaked into the air but was no longer strong enough to prevail over earth and herb and dung. Inside the blockhouse, which was now brightly lit by tripod lamps, the backs of technicians, presumably Italians, moved back and forth. Outside, among the cars, a number of groups in a variety of uniforms or none tried to seem needed. A combined Italian-American road-block had been set up between the station and Sagatto, but its criteria must have been liberal since Stears had already recognized, acknowledged, and evaded a *New York Times* reporter. The major American television news teams had lingered for some days after Leipzinger's abduction but had since left Rome; no doubt they were now hotfooting it back across the Alps. Stears also saw two stray Italian politicians. Scouting parties of sheep had penetrated the broken fence and were cropping the fresh grass. The impression was of a booth at a country race-course, not well organized.

Discreetly to the side yet firmly in the foreground sat a solemn black Oldsmobile with diplomatic plates and both rear doors open. Stears had driven down from Rome behind it and it now almost hid his own more frivolous Jaguar. Two young men in business suits stood twenty feet on either side of it and their eyes moved ceaselessly, without expression. He turned toward it now.

He said in parting, "Thank you, Lieutenant. I will stay in contact with the Italians myself and your people will be reporting to the attaché. When I leave here, I'll be going back to Rome. Let me know of anything that comes up on site, though I doubt there will be much. Do you know Italian?"

The Lieutenant did, though only at attention. He said in three violent bursts. *"Lo parlo un poco, signore, ma non perfettamente."*

"Just try and listen," said Stears. "Stay around the Italians. They got here first. And call me personally."

"Yes, sir," said the Lieutenant.

In light-gray suit, Stears walked across the grass. Though the first week in June had come to the Mezzogiorno, there was still the soft green of spring here in the hills, and wildflowers lingered around the outcropping stones. Inspecting them made Stears seem bowed in thought. He had customarily the look, reflective but not entirely serious, of a man who might well have lived as a scholar had he not drifted into something weighty and frivolous at the same time—political advice, perhaps. In Stears's own case, it had been Middle-Eastern finance on his own account, followed by intelligence for the CIA. He was a man of about forty; he had the real youthfulness preserved by a pastime of slightly serious alpinism and the more questionable youthfulness of someone who has never accepted the conditions of life as binding. The eye of one of the business suits passed over him and moved on. The two men in the back of the Oldsmobile watched him approach and stopped talking as he sat down in the front seat. Stears twisted around toward them. One of the two was in Army uniform, with a single general's star.

The other looked at Stears. "Well," he said.

"There is very little we did not know in Rome," said Stears. "The inside of the station must have been horrible. The Carabinieri confirm the communiqué from the perpetrators, the Aurora Rossa, the Red Dawn. Our people tentatively confirm identification of General Leipzinger. As expected. That's by telephone. The police have found the attack vehicle damaged and abandoned on a hill track not far away. They are examining it now. The terrorists must have transferred to another one. There are spent bullets to be analyzed and things like that. That is all police work, and I have pulled every string I know to be sure we'll be kept fully informed. Nothing more, sir." He spoke to the Chief of Station of the CIA, Rome. Randall Quincy Beebe III.

Stears went on. "I don't know the Aurora Rossa," he said. "Does anyone?"

"Now we do," said Beebe. "We also know the Red Wind, the Red Wave, the Red Flame, the Red Spirit, and the Future Path." He spoke them precisely and as though their cases were in hand; in fact each name represented a single pustule of shrewd and sordid violence against Americans, American friends, American facilities, American dignity. Stears looked at Beebe's graying temples, the fine, guarded eye, the crisp blue polka-dot tie, and the Tripler pinstripe. *He must have copied a doctor in the family,* Stears thought. *A terrifically grand ladies' doctor in Boston. He even leans forward a little when he speaks.*

General Larsen, the Military Attaché, said, "Curtis Leipzinger was as fine a man as ever wore this uniform. He even loved the goddamned Wops. This stinks. This one truly stinks."

Beebe put on the approved labels. "Vicious. Cowardly," he said.

The identification of General Curtis Leipzinger had been partly confirmed by a photograph sent before dawn to the *Osservatore Romano* with the communiqué from the Red Dawn Liberation Faction, which came off better as Partito Liberatore Aurora Rossa; it had shown the General dressed, or at least bandaged, to kill, with a note on what was in the bandage. The identity had now been confirmed by the U.S. Army through "dental work" in a plastic bag. And the last word heard from Amos Jones on the radio from the guidance station had sounded much like "General."

Brandt Larsen said, "It doesn't add up. Taking Curtis is the biggest thing those bastards have ever done. Shit, he was a harder target than Moro was. I could even have respected them." He spoke sadly, a decent farmer speaking of a boy's prank turned ugly. "You don't kidnap a general and use him for a shotgun shell. It didn't even hurt us, blowing up that thing. Navy had some aircraft off course for ten minutes. That's all it did."

He picked up the Red Dawn's communiqué and poked it with a finger. He read:

> The Chief Gangster of the Fascist Occupying Forces, General Leipzinger, was appropriately employed to destroy an element used in the American Air Murder-Raid against the People of Tripoli and the Libyan Revolution. The Italian Proletariat will continue this counterattack in ever growing force.

"We didn't even use that fucking station when we hit Tripoli. It's not on that range."

Beebe murmured, "You know that, Brandt. But who else does?" He lifted an eyebrow at Stears. It said, *Your thoughts?* Stears was still the newcomer, imported for situations of just this sort but as yet unproved.

"Contempt," said Stears.

"Yes," said Beebe. "I think so." He looked gravely at Stears. Superior to Beebe as Chief of Station, Rome, were the Chiefs of Moscow and Bonn, perhaps, and then only the tribal elders in Washington. Beebe might be sitting uncomfortably in one of twenty cars on a stony pasture around a squalid atrocity, but he filled it with an aura of rich reflection. Nor had technical opulence been neglected. The Oldsmobile carried a formidable antenna; Beebe had a telephone by his hand and a computer screen in front of him. No one was calling on the telephone and the screen was blank.

"Leipzinger was loved," said Stears. "I hear that from all my Italians. He was the best thing we had. That he was kidnapped was an unspeakable humiliation for us. If the thing had become heroic, if these people had made great demands and we had refused them, if it had become apparent that Leipzinger had refused to make a plea for himself, if he had then been executed, there would have been tragedy and courage. That makes dignity. Instead he was used here like toilet paper. We get nothing back out of it. It is difficult for Italians to respect a man who is humiliated and cannot protect his own family, and that is the position the United States has been put in. Especially here in the South of Italy, which is where our facilities mostly are. We are dealing with great intelligence.''

Beebe said sideways to General Larsen, "Stears is here because he understands the natives." He smiled. "In fact, he is one." But his eye tentatively received Stears, the newcomer, into the CIA's fellowship of guile.

"What are your Italian friends doing?" he said. "So far? I know it's a quick start for you. You've only been in Italy ten days, but then, of course, this sort of thing is why you're here. It's a piece of luck you're here already."

"Eight days," said Giovanni Sidgewick Stears.

Which was accurate, though making no allowance for the years of his adolescence and youth. His father had been an expatriate New England poet whose amalgamation of snobbish fascism and angular verse, safely practiced during the war in Vichy France after a retreat with picnic hamper from Paris, had brought him close to treason in the eyes of his victorious country in 1945. In happier, pre-war days, he had eloped with the sweetly unruly daughter of a Tuscan count who had begun her development into Stears's scatterbrained, unsuited mother somewhat before the marriage. Tuscany had given Stears his oval face, light-brown hair, and an arrogance of attitude that he did not recognize and which consequently brought him constant surprise from others' reactions to it; New England had made it all a bit lankier. After the war, Stears had been raised in a degenerating exile in neutral Switzerland—shrinking apartments with photographs of his parents behind Dali and the Fitzgeralds and John Dos Passos on the walls and unpaid bills in the drawers.

But his mother had a prodigious uncle, the Marchese Ugolino-Ferrara, who had covered himself in the latter half of the war with partisan glory at the same rate as Stears's father had de-

scended into shame. When his father died, the boy found himself
disputed between the warrior and Eugenia Semple Stears, an
astonishingly tall maiden aunt in Boston with a nose almost as
cold as a dog's. He had been sent to Choate and then to Yale
but spent his vacations in a Roman palazzo. There had been a
time when he had thought himself Italian. There had been a time
when an Italian life, with its own logic, had seemed to lie before
him. So he looked now at the roofs of Sagatto, the road crawling
downhill through stands of chestnuts, the Italian uniforms, the
little train trundling over the river on a stone bridge below and
tried more directly than ever before to mediate between his
mother's disheveled and abiding country and the urgent and
disorderly machine he served.

"The Italians are acting quite efficiently," he said. "But they
are acting against considerable resources. This is the new Red
Brigades." He leaned forward and picked up the communiqué
from the top of the seat where Larsen had laid it down. "If there
ever was any doubt where their new support is coming from,
there isn't now. Qaddafi. Qaddafi, if you recollect, promised to
drive the United States first out of Lebanon, then out of the
Middle East, then out of the Mediterranean. He has succeeded
in the first. Taking this operation from Leipzinger's kidnap up
to last night, you would need forty or fifty people, several surveillance teams, undercover people of every kind, good information, operational experience, safe houses, vehicles, lots of
money."

He saw impatience on both faces and said, "I know that's
obvious. I am only reminding you of what our Italian allies are
up against. And that all these horrors are caused by the American presence. That's what they are meant to think, and they
know they are meant to think it. They are intelligent people. But
from time to time they think it anyway. They can't help it. Let
us be clear that we are drawing the Italians into a species of war
with Libya in a cause that is not theirs. And a lot of Italians
thought that bombing Tripoli was neither justified nor smart.
There will be a little bit of sympathy there."

"In other words," said Larsen, "the Italians know who did it
and they got no suspects. As usual."

"That is not how I would put it," said Stears. He was so crudely the outsider now that Beebe rescued him with open condescension.

"But you are developing contacts, of course," said Beebe.

"Yes," said Stears.

But a composite image came to Stears of the Italians whose liaison with the Americans he had been summoned rather apprehensively to improve. He had his work cut out. There was co-operation, there was ability, there was sympathy to spare, there was still loyalty; and in the back of every eye, looking forlornly beyond all these, was a look as to an elder brother beset by ill luck and going downhill too fast to come back. And who had done some serious sinking in the last six hours.

"It will help you to be seen in our company," said Beebe. "Breaks you out of the pack." He leaned forward as though offering Stears a well-chosen gift. "It's one of the reasons I made time to come here myself."

"Curtis Leipzinger deserved more time than we've got between us," said General Larsen.

Randall Beebe's vigilance did not falter. "There's something up with the Italian police," he said. Stears followed his eye. And indeed a hedge of senior uniforms around a crisp-white van had begun to ripple as he looked. Beebe's finger jabbed commandingly at the telephone buttons, which caused a series of yelps ending in a monotonous wail.

"I'll go and see," said Stears.

He looked at the grass again as he returned and at the stones covered with lawns of moss the size of a hand's palm; crimson and violet flowers grew there as big as pinheads. A yellow ladybug perched, unwieldy as a vulture, on a bud of sempervivum. This time he looked for relief. Stears lived a great part of his working life around the battlefields of ideology and he had never been able to accept the human remains there as a neutral part of the landscape. He sat down in the Oldsmobile and spoke to the opposite window.

"We have some more analysis," he said. "Very quick of the Italians. It explains why the perpetrators attacked a target they couldn't have blasted their way into without a tank. Among the bullet holes in the terrorist van was one fired downward through a seat from inside the van itself. It passed through someone at point-blank range on the way. There was a lot of blood and some other matter. The victim was alive in the vehicle for at least a minute or two after the shot. The blood is Leipzinger's. The area the bullet passed through is his lower intestine. It was a .38, which makes a big hole. There are traces of the same blood on the ground in front of the blockhouse and they indicate that Leipzinger was shot in the van to produce a slow mortal wound and then thrown out alive onto the ground there. Which is doubtless how the perpetrators knew that, standing orders to the contrary or not, those three kids in there would bring him inside.''

"That is really grotesquely unattractive," said Beebe. "I do not think it will do their cause any good." He paused and collected himself and continued with a grand and somber cadence, "We have a fleet in Naples which is one of the greatest forces on the planet. We have bombers here that could make a good start on blowing the world apart. We have satellites of awesome power, and all this is in a cultivated allied nation. It is a bitter irony that a man who commanded much of this and whom we respected, even loved, should have died helpless among human animals." He looked at both of them in turn to confirm it.

"God couldn't stop them killing his own son," said Larsen. "And He was right at home." Stears looked at him in surprise, but there was no expression on his face and he had said it to his lap.

"Perhaps there is no point in staying here longer?" said Beebe and seemed actually to ask advice.

"Very little, I think," said Stears.

"Our people know their jobs? The Italians are in order?"

"Yes, sir," said Stears.

"The U.S. Army knows its job," said Larsen.

"Then we agree our duty is in Rome," said Beebe. "That is, General Larsen and myself. You should do as you think best, Stears."

"Yes," said Stears. "And this evening?"

Beebe shifted in his seat. "The Ambassador had not canceled when we left this morning," he said. "You are still expected for dinner if you are not told otherwise."

"Yes," said Stears. "Protocol?"

"The Ambassador no doubt feels that we should not appear panicked. It is a legitimate decision. No protocol. No one but Americans or regarded-as-Americans. The personal dining room at the residence. Six-thirty. Come to my office first. I'll walk you over and present you." He settled back and Stears saw for a moment past the peremptory eye into a man aged beyond his best and hoping without conviction for an aide's support.

"This is not a happy day, Stears," he said. "Do your best. And would you please call the driver and the guard?"

"Yes," said Stears.

He watched the Oldsmobile turn and teeter down the track toward Sagatto. Under the uncurbed sun of the southern hills it was fiercely black and its smoke-gray windows were dense as smog. It also looked heavier than Sagatto, no doubt an illusion.

He considered his own duties. He had been summoned from the London station to Rome with vertiginous speed, seemingly as the result of someone's remark in the Cosmos Club in Washington, three days before General Leipzinger's kidnap. He had arrived four days after it. He had been immersed at once in every vat of panic, spite, recrimination, indecision, and jealousy stored in the Roman embassy and station. His comments had been solicited, usually in bad faith, on ideas he found for the most part grotesque, on How to Deal with the Italians; he had come to sound to himself like something made up of a Fielding guide, an anthropologist, and a picturesque movie peasant. Meanwhile time, which had no known boundaries, for the unknown kidnappers had not set any, had ticked on toward catastrophe.

Catastrophe had exploded last midnight and, like other explosions, seemed to have left the bystanders dazed, hard of hearing, and loud of voice. Certain things were nonetheless, if not clear, at least becoming visible: the attack of the new Red Brigades on the American position in Italy had reached a focus and intensity not to be endured; to defeat it would require an American-Italian operational liaison that did not exist except in splinters of reality and vapors of rhetoric; and this cooperation would not only be between two nations but between police work, intelligence, and military and geopolitical action. This would be exceedingly difficult to achieve under a single government, much less two. It was also clear that Giovanni Stears, who had been sent by the tribal elders as an expert on Italian liaison, though with no very precise position, was responsible directly to the Chief of Station, Rome, and was standing at the scene of the crime.

This scene had not much changed. It was close to noon. There was no haze; most of those present who had nothing particular to do seemed to drift insecurely on the grand geometry of the hills. Some sort of mobile police laboratory had arrived, bearing the heraldic arms of the City of Naples. Italian police technicians were still photographing, measuring, and placing fragments into bags with tweezers. They worked slowly and with rapt precision. Stears watched them while he pondered whom to see first in Rome. He watched them with envy and then with a pleasure he did not at first understand. To live in a country is to work there. Now that the catastrophe had come and he was at its center, he had his hand again on the root of a life severed two decades before. He was at work in Italy.

C·H·A·P·T·E·R 2

For the terrorists at Sagatto most, though not all, had gone well. When the General had been dragged in and the steel door closed and the van driver pressed the button on the little box, everybody had watched the blockhouse. The door blinked blood-orange once, like a hooded, hellish eye; this was followed by a perfunctory lick of flame. There was a dull thud. There was no grand, consummating destruction. The village of Sagatto, which the terrorists had no choice but to return through, already seemed a good deal livelier and noisier. The Libyan and Rosa said nothing more; it was difficult to manifest outrage when running away to hide, especially sitting doubled over so as not to be seen through the window. At least the van still worked.

It roared and swerved down the village street, bullet-marked, with ragged windows, but still painted with a crucifix, the name of a godly charity, and a pious motto. An elderly stonemason, long ago a Sergeant of the Bersaglieri, achieved several days of fame—and, since he wore a nightcap, a striking picture—by firing a shotgun at it from a bedroom window, but he achieved no real effect. The van tore off into the night, a piece of metal flapping behind it. The one representative of law in Sagatto, a simple *vigile,* wisely remained inside and called the real police, twelve kilometers away. Thus the terrorists had a good start.

Inside the van, it was not pleasant. General Leipzinger's heavy, intestinal blood was all over the middle of the front seat, and there was an unattractive cloacal smell. Happily, blood was not on the gear lever. The Libyan had smeared himself with it while throwing the General out and he was beginning to take account of how indelible it would be and of how it endangered him over the next few hours. It could have been avoided merely by a tablecloth or a towel, and it occurred to him to resent the woman even more for failing to supply such a simple, womanly touch. It was clear that Roberto, one of the two youths in the back, was badly hit in the head and bleeding heavily. The driver had now left the road and was driving very fast up a mountain track. The van lurched and bucked and seemed to be coming apart below. At each buck, the wounded boy gave a high, piping cry. He was meanwhile hugged and comforted by his frantic comrade in a manner that embarrassingly suggested a different sort of liaison. After they cleared the village street, the Libyan looked behind him, saw this, and loured. Rosa now sat up straight and held herself so even as the van pranced. She looked out of the broken window with the blank, suspended look of a woman whose lover has quickly rolled off her and gone to sleep.

The van stopped abruptly under an olive tree. In the shadow was the shape of another vehicle with large, dead eyes, which turned out to be a Land Rover. A driver emerged from it. The terrorists hastened out of the van into the Land Rover—and here the woman took charge of the wounded Roberto. She held him kindly and firmly. She called his friend Maurizio. The Libyan, whose loins were wet with blood, appeared to have acquired the General's wound, as though mystically.

The Land Rover started fast on a track that led steeply up a ridge and was probably a goat track. They drove without lights, following the silver trace of bared rock through the mountain grass. There were sparse olive trees, also silver. The present driver spoke only then to the first driver.

"So, Alfredo, all right?" he said.

Alfredo said, "We have a wounded man. But operationally

perfect. Perfect.'' His voice, which was barely under control, did not confirm this.

"The wound can be seen to in due time," said the new driver, who had achieved composure. "It is the operation that counts."

The woman occupied herself with putting the hurt boy's head back in the best position each time it was sent flying by the motion. She had stanched the bleeding somewhat, but his face still looked like a Halloween mask. The skull seemed irregular. Roberto still screamed, but it was higher now and birdlike. The pupils of his eyes were tiny.

From the top of the ridge they saw a procession of headlights and police lights beginning the climb toward Sagatto.

"Shit," said Alfredo. "Not already."

The new driver said, "It's a completely different road the other side. You know that. They won't even have thought about it. We'll be there in four minutes."

The Land Rover descended insanely. This side of the ridge smelled of pine. It was doubtful that they were now on any kind of track at all.

Then the Land Rover pitched almost onto its nose, slithered ten meters, rocked through a shallow ditch, and righted itself hard on a paved road. The driver barely took his foot off the throttle and they shot off at once downhill.

"Nearly there," he said.

Soon he turned left up a gap-toothed avenue of cypresses where there was an old stone building, a barn or stables. He turned off the engine. "Quiet now," he said.

The night did not menace. Very far away, a train screeched on a curve and gave one penetrating toot. A dog farther up the valley barked, but politely. The Land Rover ticked. The shoulder of the mountain cut them off completely from Sagatto.

"Okay," said the driver. "No one coming. But there's no time to waste."

He went to the barn. It had tufts of plants growing out of the stonework and the big door was balky. Alfredo helped him drag it open while the Libyan lit a cigarette. A bat flew out, not much bigger than a moth. The unwounded boy, Maurizio, looked piteously at them both and dabbed Roberto's bloody forehead with a handkerchief.

The barn smelled bitterly of moldy stone and sweetly of departed horses. In it were two vehicles: a glossy, urbane new Lancia, and a police car. The Lancia was in front. The driver called to Rosa, "Hey, sweetie, you're ready to go. You first and then these policemen three minutes later."

Rosa looked at Roberto and walked over slowly to Alfredo. She stood in front of him. She seemed to be coming out of a state as though rising through still water. She pointed to the Libyan.

"Never him again," she said.

Alfredo began, "The doctor said . . ."

She said, "It is for me to tell the doctor what I will do and how. But you remember, never him again." Her voice was low. Alfredo had no answer. The Libyan smoked his cigarette and looked elaborately away.

The Land-Rover driver stepped forward. He unlocked the Lancia and felt around on the seat. He withdrew a dark bundle which turned into a jacket. He held it for the woman. She unwrapped the scarf from her head with one hand, took off her denim jacket, and dropped them both on the ground. The new jacket was dark, tailored silk. She put it across her shoulders. From the waist up, it turned her into a plucky, prosperous wife on her way home, protected from the dark highways by her nice new car.

The Land-Rover driver said, "Pretty car. Pretty jacket. You are a lucky lady. You can pretend you are rich for a while." He sounded only as though he were to trying to distract time.

He gave her the key. She took it without looking at him and got into the car. She said to Alfredo, "You must take care of Roberto. He's badly hurt. You must call a doctor as soon as you are safe. A real doctor." She added quietly, "He was a brave boy."

Alfredo nodded. She found the ignition and started the engine and then quickly felt her way around the gearshift. The Lancia popped awkwardly out of the barn but then moved smoothly. Its tires creaked on the drive. It was swallowed up by the cypresses. She did not turn the lights on until the road.

In the police car were uniform jackets and caps of the Carabinieri. Alfredo got them out while the Libyan went for the two boys. They each put on the uniforms and at last put a cap over Roberto's bloody face. Even in near dark, the effect was of a death's head, a mask to terrify children.

"Oh, Christ," said Alfredo. He did not even try the jacket on the boy.

The Libyan went silently to the back of the car and opened the trunk. He gestured to Roberto and his friend. The hurt one seemed to realize what was being asked of him but also to be too disoriented to respond. He stood shifting his weight and saying, "Oh, no. Oh, no," as to a puzzling misstatement.

Then Maurizio grasped the Libyan's idea and cried, "No! You can't. You can't do that."

The Libyan pushed him away and led the other toward the trunk. "Be sensible," he said. "Otherwise we'll all be caught." He somewhat urged but mainly pushed Roberto into the trunk, where he could lie only doubled up with his head against the jack.

"Give me some water," Roberto said. "Just some water, please."

The Libyan shut the trunk. He said generally, "Anyway, the police drive three in a car sometimes. Almost never four."

Beside the Libyan, who seemed made up of muscle and indifference, Alfredo looked frightened and ashamed. The other boy, Maurizio, was now pure and almost incorporeal hate, but when the Libyan pushed him toward the backseat of the police car, he did not resist. The Libyan would have made an impressive real policeman.

"I'll drive," he said.

They passed one other police car in the night, going the way they had come. Thirty kilometers farther from Sagatto, they changed cars in a wood in favor of a middle-aged Alfa-Romeo sedan. Roberto was hastily transferred from trunk to trunk. It was becoming clear that the situation with him was both alarming and critical. The Libyan's solution of it occasioned a dangerous delay before their next stop, but it left Roberto silent forever and impossible to identify by standard police means. It also caused the near disintegration of Maurizio, Roberto's friend, though he was not made to help the Libyan, and caused Alfredo, who was, to vomit. In the end, however, the Alfa was driven to the market town of Muro Lucano, still farther east and well outside of the area of intensive search, as confirmed earlier by the radio in the police car.

Here the terrorists' individual cars were parked, by no means together. Alfredo walked to his. Farm traffic had just begun to stir. Roberto and Maurizio had come as a unit, thus there was no problem of a supernumerary car, Roberto or no Roberto. The Libyan drove the Alfa to his own car. He was able to park directly behind it. This was fortunate, considering the state of his pants; though, in real necessity, the Libyan would have been in a position to claim diplomatic immunity.

Neither he nor any of the others had a criminal record, nor were they police suspects as far as could be known. Though each could possibly have found the identity of at least one of the others, they knew each other by false names and knew little else about each other. The organization was skillfully constructed. It was therefore not surprising that they all drove quite uneventfully home. Those who went to Rome arrived about midday.

Alfredo lived in Rome. Under another name, Guido Callucci, he taught geography and economics at a working-class school. It was in a formless district toward the east of the city, where small factories and four-story workers' flats had been littered around railroad yards and the entrails of *autostrada* interchanges. The school served principally the children of detribalized Calabrians festering with odd insect bites and social neglect.

It would be rash to suppose that Guido Callucci was his "real" name, though his mother would have thought it so, or that schoolteaching was his "real" job, though he did it most of the time. He saw himself as "Alfredo"; in the classrooms, the ideological brawls that he constantly ignited were only dull, smoky sparks substituting for the pyrotechnic bangs of his better life.

This evening he sat in a dirty kitchen, one of his three small rooms. He was not in good heart.

Alfredo could find no argument. The individual must be sacrificed for the group. Therefore he was ashamed of having inwardly protested against the Libyan.

Except that the spare Carabiniere jacket could have been wrapped around the boy's head, keeping it company in the dark trunk, keeping it from smiting the hydraulic jack, thus avoiding the awful moment when the car had romped over a spine-wrenching bump and Alfredo had tried to ignore what was clearly happening back there in the locked dark. After that, it was probably true that the boy would have died before they could have taken him safely to a doctor. He had seemed to be dying when he was transferred to the Alfa. The way the Libyan snapped his neck was efficient and might have spared him pain. It was true enough that when Alfredo had held Roberto still for the Libyan to use the paving stone and the cigarette lighter on him, he had been holding only a corpse.

But it also occurred to Alfredo that not only would any woman have thought of the jacket but that, conversely, so would have any real man. Therefore he was ashamed of having been oppressed by the Libyan's manly self-possession to a degree that had caused him to take part in spiteful and callow negligence.

The boy's head had displayed purple, coagulated blood between the broken skull and the skin, the color of aubergine but also much like a blood sausage. He disguised that memory by reflecting upon the operational liability occasioned by having to make an unreconnoitered detour followed by a struggle across rough ground to throw the body into a building site. It is on such uncharted rocks that operations founder. And the revolutionary morale of Maurizio, who had been bound to the boy by ties against which there should be no prejudice, was now in doubt.

All of these things, as well as weariness rubbed raw by two weeks of strain and fear only just laid by, contributed to an oily sweat stretching from his armpits to his bowels, a deep headache, and a feeling of great aloneness now that the band had dispersed. The last, in the kitchen of his unshared apartment, was objectively justified. The gallant, iridescent enterprise of the Fascist General Leipzinger's abduction and exemplary punishment had rocketed off into history and left behind a soiled and empty nest.

Alfredo also hated Rome.

He was from Turin. In the Roman summer, his spirit pined for Turin's gray, straight streets splashed with the colors of German industrial trucks, for the cold winter fog of the Po Valley flavored with astringent fumes, for the early-morning dark at jostling factory gates, for the armies of morose workers in cheap leather coats, for rain shining in the tram tracks. Or so he saw it. For all places where the sky is leaden and ideology can crackle brightly in the heart.

He sat now at his kitchen table eating salami, which was hard for he had rewrapped it badly; and bread, which was both damp and stale, for his refrigerator sweated. Although he had not been concerned with the abduction itself of General Leipzinger, he had been in charge, with the Libyan, of hiding him for two weeks and then of executing him in a very dangerous way. It had gone almost flawlessly. He had struck a terrific blow. It is no small thing for a young man prone to dejection and sad bowels to make the American war machine tremble, however slightly. He was to report to the doctor in the morning and he could claim achievement then with legitimate pride.

But it sat in him like a worm that his neglect of the boy had been the clumsiness of cowardice. And that faced with shooting a man paralyzed but fully conscious, it had been the woman who said what he himself had thought, not him.

But his shame ashamed him, for it was bourgeois and romantic.

The Libyan, whose name was Yussuf ben Baghedi and who was Cultural Attaché at the Libyan embassy, did not share Alfredo's distaste for Roman life. He loved to be in any great Western city almost as much as he reviled those cities in the abstract. Though he cultivated a surly manner, the spirit behind the face pirouetted in amazed and childlike delight while his shoulders brusquely pushed through crowds of Americans, French, or Swiss. He was here in these fabled, haughty cities. Any shop, any banker, any leggy, blond, expensive whore would serve him. He was remarkably dangerous. He was often rude. It was tremendous fun.

Especially in Italy. Especially in Rome. Here in the peninsula, he had the feeling that Libyans at home could actually see him: that he pushed through a bunch of nuns, or let his cigarette burn the tablecloth, or complained loutishly about a shirt surrounded by a vaporous, dark-eyed, and acrid-smelling claque.

He was far better positioned than Alfredo to enjoy a morning walk through Trastevere. He passed lustrous vegetables piled in a barrow, a caged canary singing in the shade. He stopped and listened, for he liked many simple things. To savor the world's unaffected offerings seemed to him a proper gratitude for the complete success of yesterday. Yussuf wore a flower in his lapel. It was a great improvement over his bloody trousers of the day before. Yet, as with Alfredo, there was a surly worm within him that stirred itself to feelings of anger and abuse.

When he got to the Piazza Santa Felicità, he sat down at a café. There were two *trattorie* and an old church in the square, which attracted a certain number of foreigners. It was early; the tables outside had the superb whiteness of tables not even approached by customers and the waiter was annoyed to be asked to serve. Both of these circumstances pleased Yussuf. He ordered a fizzy orange juice and stirred a great deal of sugar into it. He was waiting for the doctor.

He saw the doctor coming around the church. Since the doctor wore a stone-gray suit, was small, and limped, he looked as though one of the gargoyles might have gotten down and gone for a walk. Yussuf had set up the meeting with due regard for secrecy. The doctor mocked this by changing course abruptly and walking straight across the square to his table. The doctor walked as though he were a respected academic, a known journalist quite unwanted by the police, keeping a private appointment with an accredited diplomat of a power friendly to Italy; it irritated Yussuf even more to reflect that all this was precisely the case. The doctor sat down at once but with no emphasis, like a moth settling. Since he was annoyed, Yussuf began, "My success was absolute," knowing as he said it that it was an unwise entry.

Dr. Calvetto looked at him closely and said, "I am so glad to hear it. What success?"

Yussuf's mouth locked with confusion and wrath and he was able to get out only, "Leipzinger. The operation."

"Ah yes," Dr. Calvetto said. "That. Alfredo told me the details this morning. I watched it on television last night. But there were many people involved in that. I thought you meant something of your own."

"Without me there would have been nothing," said Yussuf. "The others were a woman and and cowardly boys."

"Cappuccino," remarked Calvetto mildly, but this was to the waiter. "Also another orange pop for my friend."

"A woman and two sodomites," said Yussuf. "You force them upon me. A warrior does not have such for comrades."

"She is a very brave woman," said Calvetto. "A superb fighter. She is very lucky as well. A little confused, of course."

"She insulted me, an Arab."

"But that would be so little," said Calvetto. "I have heard her succeed in insulting a Swiss." Yussuf knew that his utmost center was being laughed at, and that if he showed he knew that it was being laughed at, then the laughter at it would be success-ful. He therefore sat poker-straight. Calvetto looked at this with amusement. These were the sort of horrible alternatives that Yussuf associated with interrogation rooms, and he resented them at a café.

"But it was successful, Yussuf," said Calvetto, as though to the painfully modest. "You and we together toward our com-mon goal. Success is all around us. The Americans have lost a notable General. Their nerve is shaken. It is very easy for the Italian left to say that American power in Italy is a provocation that can not even protect itself. To take America out of Italy is a journey of a thousand days, but yesterday was a good day. All for only two casualties. It must not be wasted. You owe us quite a lot of money."

"Libya does not ask gold for its blood," said Yussuf. "Why does Italy?"

Calvetto wasted no time on this. "But I do not expect you to pay me here," he said. "This week there should be a meeting at your embassy. I shall have more plans as well as our bill. We do nothing without the customer's agreement.''

''There was only one casualty,'' said Yussuf. ''One of the two little buggers.''

''And you handled it badly,'' said Calvetto, ''as everyone agrees. Because of that, his friend is probably dangerous. I could note that at your embassy or I could give you the friend's real name and whereabouts and leave it up to you. Since I have no doubt of your choice, I say, 'Two casualties.' Would you like the information?''

''Yes,'' said Yussuf.

''It has to be you,'' said Calvetto. ''My troops are a little too chivalrous.''

Yussuf left moodily soon after Calvetto. He felt that he had been abused and by one to whom he had gone with an honest grievance. But there is good in all adversity and he took pride in his willingness to offer his blood to his country's service and then to accept the second sacrifice of mockery at the hand of little foreign apes. God had not seen fit to make him clever and God knew this.

As to the boy Maurizio, who turned out to live in Naples, he barely thought about him and then only in the flattest detail.

Yussuf was by any reckoning vicious, a hoodlum, a pair of fists let loose upon the world, an enemy of every cultivated value. He was dangerous because he was, by every value he had ever understood, a man of simple virtue, humble before God.

His loyalty to the Qaddafi regime was unquestioning. It was born of modest gratitude and approached true love. His forebears had trod through time a path of obscure misery until Yussuf had entered the new Libyan army, become a Sergeant, and had by chance caught the Leader's eye. He had been made an officer. He had been tried in certain special things. These had required intestinal fortitude, which was all but universal among his people, and physical courage, which was not so very rare. And here he was, a weapon of Libya beyond the seas, a diplomat, a gentleman, an Attaché. Never again would his family be despised. He knew the simplicity of his gifts. He did not understand why God had looked with such grace upon him.

C·H·A·P·T·E·R   3

Italy, into whose ankle Stears now stuck a red-tipped pin, commanded the Mediterranean, split East from West. From a Sicilian airfield, within a NATO power, an F-111 could bank within thirty minutes over Qaddafi's tent. For the fleet, if it hurried, there were thirty hours between missing a wallet in a Naples bar and standing antiaircraft duty off Egypt, with venereal reassurance available along the way. The United States embassy on the Via Veneto, the often quite real governmental amity between Americans and Italians, the airfields, and the port of Naples carried the United States halfway into the Middle East, the reality behind diplomacy. Through this same geography the Knights of Malta had stood in the jaws of the Turk, and Carthage had departed history. Pushing the little red pin into the village of Sagatto drained a drop more blood out of this strength.

The pin joined a family, mostly Neapolitan with Sicilian cousins. A United States Navy staff Captain shot in his car as he drove from his house in Naples. A Sicilian politician, friendly to the American military, found murdered with a small American flag coming out of his throat like a pocket handkerchief. A fire bombing, as nasty as could be, of a brothel dance-hall catering to Americans on the outskirts of Naples. Some machine-gunned airmen, a Mayor in a garbage can, an Editor thrown out of a window, a bomb thrown into a wedding. Stears, leaving his office, switched off the light above the map. Sticking in the pins served no purpose he could think of but was an approved activity.

All this was designed to intimidate by insolence and brutality, as Stears's growing collection of posters and transcribed graffiti showed. *"Ehi, signor Prefetto, chiamate i vostri amici americani"* (Mr. Mayor, call your American friends) had been the advice given to the Mayor in the garbage can and served as a model—though not for the abominably obscene suggestion given to the poor girls carbonized in the brothel. General Leipzinger had yet to receive posthumous advice but Stears expected it to be on the walls by morning.

There was unity of style in the posters, but not in the operations. Some could have been done by one psychotic. Others, especially this last, absolutely needed a force of disciplined, resourceful, and remarkably brave troops. But there was a cadence to the attacks that made direction behind them almost inarguable. And now there was crescendo. It was, Stears thought, as though someone had drawn to himself all the sundry demons in Italy and unleashed them upon the Italian-American alliance.

Putting in the pin had been the symbolic end to his working day, though dinner at the embassy was unlikely to be a frolic. He had forty-five minutes between now and the Ambassador's odd choice of six-thirty as an hour for assembly. There was no time to see an Italian official, if he could have thought of another one to see. There was time to have a drink informally with some useful person, but though the reknitting of his old Italian connections was a necessary part of his plan, he had not yet had time to do much of it gracefully. There was time to go to his apartment by Jaguar and find a parking place if he could, but barely time to change his shirt there.

So he sat alone at a café near the embassy on the Via Veneto.

Viewed as work, this was a window upon the population whose cooperation Stears was called upon to retain. Viewed otherwise, it put him midway between his Roman past and his Roman present.

Downhill and some distance to the right, behind the Piazza Navona, was the Palazzo Ugolino, a severe stone box where dark corridors opened suddenly into rooms full of the sun and roofs of Rome. It was the foster home of his youth, where his great-uncle, the warrior-Marchese, had first searched him without pity for his father's cowardice and then given him his love. A floor of it had very nearly become his lifetime home. Still, it had remained the headquarters of his young adulthood, the address on his fondest letters other than erotic, an invariable, though wistfully painful, stop on his vacations. He had brought his bride there—though for an endorsement, as it had turned out, less than unreserved. In the palazzo now, an old Marchese with rheumy eyes and wet chin, all wrapped up in dressing gowns, drifted between consciousness and fog on tiny bowls of broth and held Stears's hand, when Stears could be there, in a hand as light as a bird's foot, cool as glass.

Uphill to the left was Stears's spanking-new apartment in modern Rome, where he had picture windows, a microwave oven, and an unshared bed. The sheets had been chosen for him by Marie-Sophie, his wife in London, over the telephone to the maid, had been well laundered, and carried no scent real or imaginary. The maid had packed them. Marie-Sophie had not been at the London flat, still less at the airport, to see him leave for Rome. Marie-Sophie existed now in an elliptical orbit, brushing the poles of marital reserve and formal separation; for the last six months he had never seen her less than fully dressed.

As for the place where he now sat, the Via Veneto, his memories of it were from the sixties and of film stars, silk shirts, and cafés whose umbrellas projected a specially cool and flattering shade. The impressionability of youth, no doubt. He had been much at home here when his future was Italian. Until the genial heat of youth had suddenly produced a horror: a loved girl's near suicide, her disfigurement, his certainty that all of Italy blamed him, his flight back into his father's exile. Geneva, the Middle East. And finally, by chance and recoil, the holy grail of his dubious Americanism, the CIA. A life, in fact, in which velocity had substituted for mass. If he thought about it, the Via Veneto could give him the shakes. Anyway, his memories were overwhelmed by a present of car exhaust, postcard kiosks, and airline offices of a Middle-Eastern sort. His Campari was badly mixed and the ice had melted.

Ambassador Buxhalter, who in his past had been a Senator for thirteen years and the current President's choice of Attorney General for three days, took Stears's hand in his and looked into his eyes. He said, "So you're Randall's undercover terrorist man with the Italians? You come at a sad time, Mr. Stears." He paused. "A day of infamy." Ambassador Buxhalter looked one straight in the eye and projected himself, but what he projected was puzzling. It was like a salesman's face with an elderly beaver's looking through it.

"That's not in public, Ambassador," said Beebe. "Stears is overt CIA, with publicly listed duties connected with NATO. That is for the American news media as well. America does not interfere with Italian internal affairs and we are not going to give anybody a chance to say otherwise."

"No," said the Ambassador, "and I would not wish to interfere. Are there new developments?" He still held Stears's hand, though with no apparent need for it, and Stears slightly flexed his fingers in reminder.

"The Navy has sent a picket ship to the Gulf of Sidra, with some vessels to guard it. It can listen to telephone conversations in Tripoli," said Beebe. "That is all I know at present."

"Ah," said Buxhalter. He released Stears's hand and then stroked Stears's sleeve as though Stears were a large dog. "Welcome aboard," he said. "Would you like some milk?"

"Not just now, sir, I think," said Stears.

"It builds nervous endurance in time of stress," said Buxhalter. "I am very partial to it. My state is a dairy state. But there is also wine. You may have heard of a saying, Mr. Stears, 'In Rome do as the Romans do.' Wine is a part of the Italian culture and encourages the Catholic, anti-Communist segment of it. Have some wine if you are a drinking man, and then come meet Mrs. Buxhalter. We are all a family in this embassy."

"Thank you, Ambassador," said Stears.

A waiter extended to him a silver tray on which were large glasses of milk, some small glasses of wine, and a huge hairy flask of Chianti.

"Grazie," said Stears.

The waiter, who was dressed for some reason as a gondolier, looked at him suspiciously.

Stears muttered quickly, *"Sarebbe possibile avere un Campari?"*

The waiter brightened. *"Per Lei, certamente, signore. Subito."*

"O forse whiskey?" said Stears hopefully.

"Questo no," said the gondolier, with a terrific and conspiratorial sneer at the ambassadorial couple. *"Non sarebbe tipico, capisce."*

Randall Beebe, still near him, said to a woman, "Certainly not, Edna. The terrorists can no more grab any of us at will than they can play the Superbowl every day. They will have spent months and great resources preparing this and they are now exhausted."

Ambassador Buxhalter said to her, "This is not Beirut, dear." And with more conviction, "This is Mr. Giovanni Stears. Mr. Stears, this is my wife, Edna."

Mrs. Buxhalter also took his arm, but more practically, to pull him closer to a small, padded face where bright-blue eyes held acumen surrounded by perfect ingenuousness.

"Oh, Mr. Stears," she said. "Were you at that place this morning? It must have been unbearable."

"It was not nice," said Stears. "But for them it was very quick. They would never have known what happened."

"Even Curtis Leipzinger?" she said. "It seems he would have known quite well."

"Mr. Stears is a CIA statistical analyst attached to NATO," said Beebe firmly.

Mrs. Buxhalter looked at him with bland surprise and then said rather crisply, "Oh, all right, Randall. Statistics. Anyway, you're welcome, Mr. Stears. We are all a family in this embassy." Then to her husband: "The Princess will be late. She's only coming for coffee. She called our butler."

"She called just now?" said Buxhalter. "I hope nothing is wrong with her."

"I doubt it very much," said Beebe. "There rarely is."

The dinner was not large. Whatever its original purpose, it was now for reassurance, which could not be asked for shamelessly, and information, which could not be given out freely. It was consequently awkward. There were a Director of the American Academy, a pudgy and placid Rear Admiral, an American with industrial interests in Italy, an Italian with perfect English and banking interests in America, and a long-silent American novelist, all with their wives or husband. No press had been invited. The party ate in a beige and airy room with nice chandeliers but still much like tourists in the old pensions sheltering from an alarming native festival. Iced tea was served as an alternative to milk, though the bristly Chianti could be obtained. Two more gondoliers assisted, one of them female. They circulated in front of the masterly Western bronzes on pedestals—*Let Him Buck!, Tired Cowpoke, Dead Indian*—for which the room was famous.

"Ever since my husband attained diplomatic rank," said Mrs. Buxhalter to Stears, "we have been prone to internationalism as a way of thought. That is why he is so interested in your role here. How did you immerse yourself in the Italian culture? Are you from Brooklyn?"

"No," said Stears, "but it was easy enough. My mother was Italian. I spent quite a lot of my youth in Rome. Especially school vacations."

To his right, the Director of the American Academy said, "And what is your role, Mr. Stears?" She was a tall woman with black hair that fell like a stage curtain over silver-framed spectacles and who wore a magnificent silk shawl of dragons.

"Statistical analysis," said Stears.

"Is that what one has an Italian mother for?" said the academician. She waggled a bright-yellow finger at him and added, "I don't believe a word of it. My husband is a novelist but I can also suspend belief. At first sight I would have taken you for English, except for the tie."

"Boston and Florence, ma'am," said Stears. It was true that his suit was English, but his tie reveled in glossy simplicity, midnight-blue with one burgundy medallion.

The waiter passed him a mound of spaghetti topped with flecked meatballs and stabilized by a crimson sauce.

"Now take cuisine," said Mrs. Buxhalter. "Much of it in the world today is quite without its national character. The Ambassador and I love Italian cuisine, but most of what you get in Rome is fried fish and lamb, just like in Maryland or Kansas City. We try to keep a real Italian kitchen here. At home we hosted several Mexican soirees after our vacations there."

Stears prevailed against the suction of the sauce and looked significantly to the waiter at his empty glass.

"Perhaps you know the Princess?" said Mrs. Buxhalter to Stears, and then to the waiter, *"Gracias, Stefano. Es todo. Ogni."*

"Yes, Ambasciatrice," said the waiter.

"Which Princess?" said Stears. "Princess who?"

"Do you think they'll be bombing the Academy?" said the academician. "We're in a lovely palace full of Yanks right in the middle of Rome. Seems tempting enough to me."

"I think they would bomb other things first," said Stears. "And I think they will be stopped before they get to you. This new bunch is stronger in the South, anyway."

"Oh, that's what you are, is it?" said the academician. "Well, it's an honest answer."

"Which Princess?" said Stears to the Ambassadress. For—if this dinner was for Americans and the Princess had to be American too—the thought of a ghost had cut through the cheerless room and simultaneously chilled his heart and flushed his loins.

"I talked to Leipzinger three weeks ago," said the academician. "He wasn't any drill Sergeant, you know. He was up for a lunch in Rome and he came around for tea. We talked about minor poets of Dante's era. Frederick of Hohenstaufen in Naples. Guittone D'Arezzo in Florence. It was fun." She kept her voice to the same level but looked straight at the table. "I suppose he was tortured?" she said.

"It would be impossible to say," said Stears. But he liked the academician and she seemed worth the truth. "Yes," he said. "At least he was treated very badly at the end."

She pulled her shawl tightly around her and did not speak at once. "We are all quite ordinary people," she said. "Not superpowers. Not heroes. Not even very young. I kissed Leipzinger when he left. Just socially, we were friends. But it is an odd feeling."

Randall Beebe said loudly from close to the Ambassador, "The point, of course, is not to make terrorism impossible, for that is impossible itself, but to relay the true cost back to the true perpetrator. That, the United States is able and prepared to do. Our Italian friends know it."

"The President has said the same to me," said Buxhalter and said more, but his voice receded into the general talk.

"And I think our country is like us," said the academician to Stears. "We can put together a considerable amount, we are not insignificant by any means whatever, but we can no more deal with mania, whether good or evil, than a weak husband can deal with a rabid wife. We just can't. How do you face occupying yourself with this sort of thing all the time, Mr. Stears? What sort of life is that?"

"I wouldn't know," he said. "Because it isn't mine." And then, echoing himself: "One in which velocity substitutes for mass, I would think. But I do very little of it."

"Or perhaps even . . . oh, never mind," she said. "I will resist saying something both cute and trite. At all events, you seem to have more lettuce than you really need to hide your spaghetti. Perhaps you could lend me some for the same purpose? There seems to be a moment of confusion developing. I imagine the Princess has arrived."

"Princess who?" said Stears.

But at this moment the gondoliers became suddenly at attention and the chancery doorman was found to have thrown open the double doors and inflated himself to say, *"La Principessa Gabriella Harriman-Farnese."* A woman with chestnut, sumptuous hair, a nice black dress, and an expression of mild apology came into the room. Stears breathed deeply and unknowingly said, "Oh, God," for the operation of time insisted simultaneously that the same chestnut hair was still across his shoulder, his face buried in the Princess's breast, her scent and legs around him, and that she was unapproachable across eighteen light-years of memory and a nightmare guarding the bridge.

Princess Harriman-Farnese said to the Ambassador, who rose up on his toes toward her, "I am most terribly, dreadfully sorry, Ambassador. You understand these things. It simply wasn't under my control." And the Ambassador said, "I understand completely, Princess," which was imaginative of him. She smiled at the novelist, the academician, and a gondolier who bowed, and, by now close enough to Stears that his senses once again inhaled her skin, spoke ruefully to the Ambassadress. She came to Stears as evenly as the movement of the planets and put out her cheek to be kissed and let her arm fall on his. "Nanni," she said, using the extreme familiar of Giovanni, "this is perfectly lovely. I had heard vaguely you were back in Rome," while her eye said, *You will apologize later when you have lots and lots of time.*

Everyone sat down, the Princess beside the novelist. Everyone got up, for the Ambassadress haltingly announced coffee and ice cream in the salon.

The academician said quietly, "You are either abnormally impressed by rank, Mr. Stears, or Gabriella is not just any Princess to you. You even forgot my lettuce, though hiding things must be second nature to a spy."

"I am sorry," said Stears.

"Not at all," said the academician. "It was rather fun to watch, on such a depressing evening. But if you like our Gabriella so very much, perhaps I understand better now why you adopted mayhem as your career."

Her English was no longer absolutely a native's; Harriman had weakened, Farnese had prevailed. It disquieted him. *We float down time on the same current as our friends; the little sideways movements, a change of accent, are more than the progress from eighteen to forty.* She could not have been in America much. He knew that already.

The plastic surgeon must have been superb. He had known

that too—but it had been hard to be sure from photographs. Now his eye could rest on her face without remorse; it rested there with awe.

The image of her face and body had been the unpredictable visitor of any lonely night for nearly twenty years, bringing a moment's warmth and then chill. He noticed a peculiarity: he had remembered her as a girl; she was a woman now and yet his memory was not far from the present truth. *Perhaps,* he thought, *our fantasies age with us.*

The dinner was over. He walked up the Via Veneto to the corner of the embassy and felt for his car keys but then walked on. He left the Jaguar in the embassy lot. It was not late. The Buxhalters' dinner party had ended at about the Roman dinnertime, for which the Princess Harriman-Farnese, he had no doubt, would somewhere be only slightly late. He found a space in his mind and realized he did not know whom she was dining with.

"Were you really not going to call me?" she had said. This was at a coffee table across the room where they had talked.

"Yes, I was," said Stears. She raised an eyebrow in question. The vibration of time gave him again a mistress, on whose bosom his eye might rest, and a virtual stranger.

"Not a call from the airport," he said. "The right time. I would never treat you as a detail."

Her mouth twitched as he remembered. "Thank you," she said. "Why did you not come to see me in the hospital? I never forgave you that."

"By the time they would let anyone see you, I was in America. I was American. I remained one, though not in America. And I never excused you. One doesn't use a Ferrari to settle arguments." But her flawless face drew his eyes back as to an old and happy home and he disliked his own tone. "You healed," he said. "You healed."

"The Ferrari worked in its own way," she said. "But I would have healed better if you had come. But that is not interesting anymore. Now that you are a Roman again, do we avoid each other? That is what I came to United States territory to find out."

"I am not a Roman again," he said. "We need do nothing so dramatic."

She touched his hand to put an end to fencing. "Giovanni," she said, "do you want to see me again?"

He gave no haste to his answer. He thought of himself after Yale, the American more than half Italian installed at the Palazzo Ugolino. And Gabriella, whom he first had taken almost for a pretty child, a month out of convent school, spoiled by rank, by money, by vacations in Palm Beach, by anything else one could easily think of, festering with small intense rebellions like a babe with measles, and using a vocabulary like a dutiful fishwife. He had—twenty-one years old, a Marchese's nephew, just back from Yale and with a snorting sports car—presented her with the favor of seducing her. In the middle of the act he had located, within the American ways and blistering mouth, an authentic, though not dedicated, Catholic virgin.

And found himself with a girl who took to coitus like a Scotsman to drink and, what was more, turned out to be chivalrous, bottomlessly loyal, very soon intensely jealous, and who measured the dignity of anything exclusively by its risk. The intensity of her passion, which she seemed to take for granted, had forced him to grow from a pleasant youth into a man.

Italian noble society could have handled with gentle ease a pair of children with a penchant for each other's beds. What Gabriella had devised—a crimson progress through borrowed castles, an address card she had printed up actually with both their names, an appearance in *Paris Match* discoursing on free love in its more carnal aspects (quashed at the last moment by Prince Farnese at great expense)—was a lot too much.

Hysterical arguments, accusations—usually unfounded— from her of cowardice, of disloyalty, of hypocrisy, of affairs. Then the horrible day when the child rushed off in the Ferrari a demented aunt had given her.

No brake marks at all.

She was a good driver. She barely drank.

She had put a skull into his life. By her disrespect for limits she had turned what in its essence was the brightest of things, a loving game, into horror. He could not bear to look upon the pain she had inflicted without cause upon herself. He had never forgiven her for it, or himself for not forgiving it.

She had never otherwise done an ungenerous or a graceless thing.

He looked at her now. "Yes," he said. "I do."

He reached the crest of the hill and crossed the Porta Pinciana into the Borghese Gardens. There was a streak of pink still in the sky, a light that gave the Roman pines a look of Chinese fancy. The gardens were empty, but not ominously so, and he cut straight across the grass toward his neighborhood, Parioli.

Walking calmed him, faster than he expected or quite wished. Touching her flesh had turned Gabriella from his myth back into his woman. A woman. A resplendent girl had become a resplendent woman; his desire, which had taken her virginity and then first grown fully in her, swung to her as to a childhood home. His "yes" to her question had had a sudden quiver of sex.

Just as quickly and just as well preserved came a resentment of the antic caprice that seemed still to be her stock-in-trade. The thought came to him that if she were still carrying around her old flawed drama, unrevised, and it still had a part for him, the thought did nothing but depress him.

He apologized immediately for the thought.

Still, he had much to do in Rome. Much that was of great importance, required great skill. And the next line came to him straight from Gabriella's school of drama. He had a brave man's murderers to destroy. He corrected it at once. He had a craft of intelligence to pursue.

At the end of the Borghese Gardens he was nearly home. Good deserted Parioli streets with trees and street lamps and apartment doormen. He walked down his own street. From time to time an Alfa or a Lancia came up from an underground garage like a careful rabbit. His doorman let him in. The lobby's marble shone like varnish and the elevator bore him upward to his four neat rooms with a barely audible sigh.

C·H·A·P·T·E·R 4

General Brandt Larsen, the Military Attaché, shone like a russet apple. Randall Beebe's collar glowed with authority and starch. They were on their way from the United States embassy to the Quirinale Palace to see the Italian Deputy Minister of the Interior, the Head of the Italian internal security service, SISDE, and perhaps a senior General of the Carabinieri. Both behaved to Stears with encouragement, but watchfully, as though considering asking him to turn out his pockets for contraband inspection now that they were going with him among the Italians. They went down the Via Veneto and past Triton on his fountain in the Piazza Barberini. They went up the Via delle Quattro Fontane and the *putti* on the four fountains waved them Godspeed as they turned onto the Via del Quirinale. The palace appeared beside them, feathered with Roman pines and gay with tricolors and riot police.

This was in the Oldsmobile. The three were in the backseat. A Marine driver's head was segregated from them by heavy glass.

Randall Beebe said, "The Italians are in a defensive posture. This is their country and Leipzinger was taken off base and on their watch. So when we offer clandestine intelligence we can damn well expect cooperation in exchange. Are you on board there, Stears?''

"Yes," said Stears. Beebe spoke with some discomfort. He was squeezed into the extreme back left corner of the seat—a security precaution additional to the blue fog of the windows. To see the Chief of the imperialist CIA actually penetrate the Quirinale would be as exhilaratingly awful to any hawk-eyed local leftist as to see the devil scrape sparks with his hooves on St. Peter's Square. Stears was given the middle, as being the least recognizable, even to the CBS camera that had swept the Oldsmobile as it left the embassy.

Beebe said, "The Navy now has an intelligence ship in the Gulf of Sidra monitoring every telephone in Tripoli. The Italians do not have that capability.''

"No," said Stears.

General Larsen said, "We're building up a file of Libyan offi- cials calling their drivers. Problem is, since we've been monitor- ing it, that's all they use the telephone for.''

"At least we have a prominent-person traffic profile," said Beebe. "It may be a powerful tool. And not using the telephone must be crippling Qaddafi's government. Think of Washington without telephones. Quiet now.'' They had arrived at a gate of the Quirinale and the car was surrounded by Carabinieri. The gate grandly opened.

Grandly, too, the Deputy Minister's double windows brought in a view almost prodigally august: the Vatican, cleansed by distance of nuns' buses and rosary touts and looking surprisingly spiritual; Castel Sant'Angelo, golden, gallant, and serene under its pines; the Tiber and the wooded hills beyond. A garden for an elderly God. Stears thought that he could see a corner of his uncle's little Palazzo Ugolino down by a tight bend of the river. It was true that the Minister's window was covered by a metal grille, perhaps against bombardier anarchists with pitching arms of steel, perhaps against pigeons.

The Deputy Minister sat on a pretty sofa to show that this meeting was between friends, global if not personal. Nearer the window sat General Della Cappella of the Carabinieri, rock-faced and totemic in a hard armchair. Francesco Croce of SISDE had adopted an easy pose at a small writing table, a pose vaguely reminiscent of Scarpia during his more urbane moments in *Tosca*.

The Deputy Minister, whose name was Fausto Tasso, spoke like a reasonable man whose umbrella has been taken. "But Italy enjoys excellent relations with Libya," he said. "Perhaps I should say, 'enjoyed.' We shall continue to enjoy them if we still have them."

"The United States understands this," said Beebe. "However, there are realities."

"But there are so many realities," said Tasso. "That is the problem with realities. It is where they are so different from principles. Surely you come upon this continually in the CIA . . ." Tasso paused to seek a title for Beebe and came up rather wildly with "Commendatore?"

"We are not asking for major overt changes in the Italian posture, Minister," said Beebe. "Rather, covert."

"But those are so often the noisiest," said Tasso, "like whispers in church." Tasso's English had the frolicsome symmetry of language very well learned and not worn with use. This was provoking to Beebe, as Stears could see, and even to himself. And the view from the ministerial window suffered from the problem of politics practiced in Rome; it was like visiting the Great Pyramid with an interior decorator.

"I do not mean to be unresponsive, Commendatore," said Tasso. "The situation is repugnant. Every decent Italian knows this." General Della Cappella's head nodded three times like an upheaval in a ponderous old clock. A Captain standing behind his chair nodded exactly twice as fast.

What was more, thought Stears, Tasso's sympathy was baffled, painful, and real. Tasso had a reputation as one of the most able and honorable of the younger Christian Democrats; an intelligence in his eyes and a sensitivity in his olive face suggested that this might be true. (In a group by Raphael he would have been the wise subaltern behind the braggart at center stage.) And Francesco Croce of SISDE had made an admirable job of taming the more than seven hundred homebred Italian terrorist gangs he had inherited from the seventies. When Randall Beebe of the CIA spoke, Croce bowed minutely with professional respect. General Della Cappella had risen from the ranks and had crippled the real Red Brigades by hunting down their three most dangerous gunmen. General Larsen had been wounded three times as a Colonel of air cavalry in Vietnam. General Della Cappella had given General Larsen's hand a single, wrenching shake. There was not a buffoon in the room.

Beebe said, "I come with more than you may expect, Minister. I am authorized to open American electronic and satellite intelligence on Middle-Eastern rogue states to the top level of Italian security. You will be informed of their intentions and you will have less need for a posture of appeasement. Meanwhile the Sixth Fleet and its air power will unobtrusively increase its surveillance of your southern coastal waters. In distant waters, the Navy will take a positive interest in the safety of Italian shipping. We have a job to do together, gentlemen. Let's do it. The Sixth Fleet will be by your side." The motion of his hand suggested that he had brought the fleet with him and that it was a very big dog.

"That is generous," said Tasso, "and a little worrying."

"On our side," said Beebe, "we ask for access to Italian security files on terrorist activity, especially activity with an Arab or Eastern-European tinge. We would like you to begin tight surveillance of Libyan and Iranian embassies and consulates and restrictions on their personnel. We request intensive surveillance of passenger lists and manifests from Arab points of origin. It is quite a lot, Minister, I know that."

"Oh, yes," said Tasso.

"And then a less embarrassed attitude to open cooperation with our uniformed personnel. America and Italy are intimately allied nations and our forces are here to strengthen Italy, not to undermine her. Most Italians know that. There is no reason why our military police and the Carabinieri should not operate jointly when that would offer benefits. That is what I am here for, gentlemen, a request which my offer should make painless and in a situation that threatens Italy as much as the United States."

"Or more," said General Larsen. "This is where it's happening." General Della Cappella, who seemed at least to understand some English, smote the arm of his chair, but it was Croce who spoke.

"There are great difficulties with this," said Croce. He lifted the pen with which he had taken notes. "Since 1977, we have very strict laws governing privacy and rights. If I were to open now one of the files you speak of, I would have to send even General Della Cappella out of the room. He is Carabinieri, you see. It is sometimes quite difficult."

"Difficult," said Tasso. "But not impossible between close friends. I see what is wanted very clearly." He went on, but spoke to the air now, as though recollecting the contents of a drawer.

"It would all be very possible," Tasso said. "There will be teams of Americans and Italians sorting through the data that the spy ships and satellites pour out. Since each knows what the other knows, there will be inducement to react. Italian teams will fan out here and there. There will be headlines and arrests. And meanwhile embassies in Rome will be surrounded with binoculars and machines and vans full of police. There will be demonstrations, of course, and then more arrests. I have seen it in Paris. Italy has crack troops, too. We will rush them into action when Italian airliners are kidnapped somewhere and blown up, a thing that has never occurred so far. If matters become intolerable, your carriers will move out from Italian ports and give Tripoli another brutal beating—quite a deserved one, certainly.

"Here in Rome, bodies will be tossed around the streets. It is so much easier to take revenge on people standing at a railroad station than on aircraft carriers. General Della Cappella's men will be all over the place with their submachine guns. Especially at the trials that follow the bombings. We shall survive. Once there were more than a thousand armed outrages in Italy every year. Now it is not so bad. I am sure that Croce can deal with anything the Arabs can hand out, even if they ignite the Red Brigades again. We can put sandbags out all over Rome—they endured that in London.

"And out of all this smoke, there will come victory of sorts, someday. I am quite with you there, Commendatore. Libya and Iran are not much compared to Italy and the United States, are they? A global justice will have been done.'' Tasso's eye had sunk toward the end of the sofa, where a shepherdess skulked behind a cushion. Now he looked at Beebe.

"It is not much to ask between close friends," he said. "But do you see the difficulties, Commendatore?"

Beebe did not move in his chair. He said, "Should I assume that that comes from the Minister himself?"

"Not in nearly so many words," said Deputy Minister Tasso. "But yes."

"A clandestine involvement merely," said Beebe. "At the highest levels of our governments."

"Then I would make you a clandestine bet," said Tasso. "Would it come to light first in the American Congress or in the Italian press? You may take the bet on either side. It will keep us both interested."

"CIA access to your security intelligence files, with a guarantee of no uncoordinated action," said Beebe.

"It would be discovered in the end and it would add ten percent to the Communist vote."

General Larsen said, "General Leipzinger was kidnapped, mutilated, and killed on Italian soil because he embodied the American-Italian alliance. That alliance is being targeted. Italians who honor it are being murdered and intimidated by other Italians in league with an enemy alien power. Do you disagree with that, Minister?"

"No," said Tasso. "It is not tolerable, is it?"

There was a sound like a stove being dragged across a basement; General Della Cappella had cleared his throat.

"Worst of all things is a sniper," said the General. "A sniper is death itself. To kill death is hard. I have seen a tank make of a building nothing but rubble and flame and the sniper is still there, turning a platoon into a coward. So you do not use a tank against a sniper. You use two men and an officer who will go to where the sniper is and kill him. A young officer who may die himself. No more than three men. That is the case with a sniper. I speak in metaphor, perhaps, but it is apposite to the case."

This was in Italian, or in a Piedmontese version of it, made with an admixture of cement.

Into the ensuing silence, Beebe said, "There could be a possibility of NATO channels being used. Very discreetly. No direct interface between CIA and SISDE."

"Yes," said Tasso. "I think we need to consider all this more deeply. We are talking in an atmosphere of crisis. The abomination to do with General Leipzinger is history now, I fear, and we must look to the future calmly. Naturally our forces will be alert. I am sure that your base security will be so too. We must all reflect on the political realities and the state of opinion. Those are the important issues, not what some madman does with a gun. Italy and the United States are great nations. We cannot change our policies every time a pistol fires."

Signs of departure were manifested. Beebe rose in hopeful regret. Tasso stood and vibrated with sympathy. Croce folded his notes. General Della Cappella, who had not moved, gave voice. He spoke to Stears.

"This is Captain Mascagni," said the General. "He will cooperate with Mr. Stears. He will be available when Mr. Stears requires him. He will continue to report to me."

Captain Mascagni ventured from behind the chair. He was a lanky man with eyes wide apart and his jowls and throat seemed to secrete a darkish color, like a squid. His collar jutted away from his throat. He was not young to be a Captain. He came to Stears and shook his hand. He seemed discouraged and to defy Stears to be otherwise. He murmured, "Captain Rodolfo Mascagni, First Regiment of Carabinieri, Rome." On his chest was a medal, that of a Grand' Ufficiale dell' Ordine Militare d'Italia. It was the highest award likely to be given for courage in peacetime.

General Della Cappella said at large, "The Captain and Mr. Stears make already two of the three men required." And then to Stears, "Is your uncle, the Marchese, well?"

"He is old," said Stears.

"I know that," said Della Cappella, "and it is not what I asked."

. . .

On the drive back, Randall Beebe said, "Between us and the Italians there is certainly a mutual appreciation of the problem, even if there remains a division on solutions."

Brandt Larsen said nothing.

Beebe leaned back in the seat and stretched, a Boston lawyer just arrived at the Maine fishing camp, dropping his suitcase on the bunk. "It's pissing in the wind, Brandt," he said. "Pissing in the wind."

"Affirmative," said Larsen.

The entrance of the Palazzo Ugolino was a scuffed door in a blank stone wall; the wall remained blank until the second floor, where some severe armorial bearings, including a Cardinal's hat over a frightful bludgeon, found a purchase, and gave way to ladies, bare-breasted but bored, on the third. All this could be seen only if one stepped far back into the Campo dei Fiori, looking under one's heel at every backward step. Right up against the door, one smelled the furniture finisher's shop in a small rented cave below and to the right of it. There was a large electric bell, more mammary than necessary in shape, and, beneath it, a name handwritten in smudged ink: "A. Ugolino." This represented Colonel the Marchese Alessandro Ugolino-Ferrara, Knight Companion of the Order of Malta. The bell only worked if one stroked its nipple beguilingly to the left and then bore down on it fiercely. Stears did this.

The door was opened, by no means at once nor after any sound of feet approaching, by Luigi, his uncle's man. Luigi greeted him, *"Signor Giovanni!"* and Stears replied, *"Buon giorno, Luigi!"* Luigi wore a sort of military coat, though with a valet's stripes, for he was to some extent a soldier-servant and was also permitted a mustache. His feet might have caused concern; they were wrapped up in rags and stained through with crimson, as after a picturesque military disaster. But it was only his day for waxing the tiled floors by shuffling on them.

"How is my uncle?" said Stears.

"The Marchese is well today, Signor Giovanni. He is awake. He remembers that you are coming." Luigi performed a complex gesture in which he somewhat bowed to Stears, somewhat ushered him in, and somewhat turned his back to return down the corridor. He was unsure of Stears. Stears was of the blood; he was a foreigner; his great-uncle loved him; he had abandoned his great-uncle for too long; and when he was young he had made such an ass of himself over the American princess that he had had to leave Italy altogether. In fact, the feudal bond was weak. Stears did not much like Luigi.

So he walked past him up a staircase into a hallway where the ceilings were painted with murky battles given new perspectives by bulging plaster. It was a small palazzo, pre-baroque. Two doorsills let forth cracks of light and clues to the luncheons of the tenants, a retired Major and a lady dress designer with her daughter, all of good family. This could once have been Stears's own floor and he hurried through it, before Time pounced.

Up to the noble floor, where sunlight sat by the stair.

Ugolino-Ferrara's eyes were blue. On the bad days of his old age they were stained and clouded like an infected pond; on the good days they were clear as a boy's. Stears found his uncle propped in an armchair in the salon nurtured by a beam of sun fresh from the Pamphili Gardens and by the limbs of the nymphs dancing on the wall beside him. This was a good day. His uncle took his hand. Italian Stears had learned to surrender it for minutes at a time, though Boston Stears objected; his uncle seemed to draw as much from it as from the broth he ate.

"This is very nice," said Ugolino-Ferrara. "I had looked forward to your coming. On the days when one wakes up with a memory it is nice to have something in it. Will you even stay for lunch?"

"Definitely," said Stears.

"Heaven knows what there is." Ugolino-Ferrara still had his hand and tapped his wrist with a sharp-nailed claw. "You have not been to Caraceni yet, have you?" He meant his tailor. "I even had Luigi call to tell them to expect you. You should not go around Rome in those American clothes. Not you."

His uncle sat in a cocoon of dressing gowns, mostly tattered. On bad days, the effect was in fact depressing. On good ones, there seemed an element of burlesque.

"I am only supposed to be a little bit Italian," said Stears. "Really very little. If I wore Italian suits, I should have to carry an American flag. Besides, I've been busy."

"Ah," said his uncle, "Giovanni Sidgewick Stears. Do you know how funny 'Sidgewick' sounds? Like a small firework on a damp night."

"I had always thought a garden insect," said Stears.

"That also. Go and tell Annunziata you are staying for lunch, my boy. She should run to the butcher on the corner. Otherwise you get my damn broth."

"I spent the morning at the Quirinale," said Stears.

"Bad luck," said Ugolino-Ferrara. Stears had been served on a small *faux marbre* table with a beefsteak and lettuce and a bottle of Ligurian wine much too good for lunch. Now the western shutter had been closed against the afternoon sun and the French windows opened to the roof garden. Two grapefruit trees were in flower and the figs had begun to blush.

"A Deputy Minister named Fausto Tasso."

"They say he is better than most," said the Marchese. "But it is all politics, and that is a poisoned stream. No poison is as hard to clean as cowardice." But he said it by rote, and Stears, who had surprised himself of late by watching his uncle's face as closely as he had ever watched a woman's, saw a trace of staleness invade his eye. Though he needed urgently to go through his uncle's pockets for contacts at high level, he dropped the subject for the moment and said, "The fruit trees are doing well."

"Yes," Ugolino-Ferrara said. "It is the last thing I miss, being able to wander around out there. It was nice to feel the leaves and know they would bring fruit from nothing. I own a great deal of land still, but this roof has become my *patrimonio*."

"You could still go out there," said Stears. "I could carry you to a chair."

"It is not the same when one cannot move. Better to see it from here." And then: "I hear you have been seen again with the American Farnese."

"No," said Stears. "Once. At the embassy. Gabriella was a guest and I was a guest."

"Gabriella, yes. I got very tired of that word once. I agree, the embassy is hardly cause for scandal. Though they say that this Ambassador is a greater fool than his predecessor. Drink some more wine. Luigi will only guzzle it if you don't."

"It's excellent," said Stears.

"Prince Colonna sends it to me. Not once since you arrived in Rome have you mentioned your wife."

"Have I not?" said Stears.

" 'Have I not?' What answer is that? Are you more senile than I am? Is she dead or something?"

"No," said Stears. "Not dead at all."

His hand was claimed again but this time with nails that scored his wrist. His uncle said, "Don't dare be an American with me, boy! Is she betraying you?"

"I have no knowledge that she is," said Stears. "I don't think so. Her intellectual development has progressed to the point that she finds my calling inhumane. She has 'educated' me upon this point. She observes that wherever I go there is blood even if I do not shed it personally. She says she finds it immoral to solace me. The truth is she has left me. I find her in the house from time to time, but she has left."

"So what? One ignores that sort of asininity in a woman. Or one deals with it. She is still your wife." The claws undug and lay on his hand.

"I never faulted your taste with the Farnese. I don't mean her body—no man would have faulted you for making a fool of yourself for that. But there is a certain nobility in complete recklessness and I liked you for falling for it. But once is enough. It is not a good sign that she never married. Even recklessness needs form in the end, and a formless woman spoils. Her mother and father should have lived longer—I was worried about that girl when Fabrizio died. She should have had brothers. I was sorry for her, even if she had been more trouble to my house than a neighbor's bitch in heat. Once is enough, Giovanni."

"Exactly," said Stears. "I saw her once. At the embassy."

"And I am a silly old man? I don't think so. If your wife is not betraying you, then bring her to Rome. Then she will be less likely to."

"I have written to her to persuade her to come," said Stears. *And having locked the letter in a drawer does not make that a lie.*

"Good," said his uncle. "What was balls when you were twenty would be folly now. It would be caprice. Nothing more."

"I understand you," said Stears.

"Good. Though perhaps that means that you have thought about it already, which is not good. And it has always disturbed me that in all the years that have passed since you had to do with that girl, you have never talked about it. It suggests something that I do not like. Still, I will not persist. Now that we have dealt with the important things, I will allow you to ask me questions about the politicians. Though I only waste a day when I have a brain on such a topic because I love you. Who else was at the Quirinale? You have a need to talk about it, I know."

"General Della Cappella."

"He is not a politician; he is a man. I know him."

C·H·A·P·T·E·R 5

Stears's servant usually left before Stears returned home. The mail was put on the hall table under one of the glories of the furnished apartment, a brightly varnished oil painting of a traffic jam of gondolas near St. Mark's, considerably after Canaletto. This evening, the envelope on top had been placed at an angle that represented the discreet cough of a servant seriously impressed. The paper was the gray of a freshly bathed dove and had the creamy weight achieved only by Pineider's on the Via dei Due Macelli. There was a coronet on the back. Stears opened it.

The note read:

Villa Pamphili-Farnese

My dear Giovanni,

I am having a very few of the nicer Americans in Rome out for supper at the villa on Thursday. I think you would enjoy meeting them now that you are here. We shall be outside the seahorse pavilion if it doesn't rain. Do hope you will come. Eight o'clock.

Affectionately,
Gabriella

The full crest above the name was new; in the old days a simple coronet had sufficed. Her letters were taller and more beetle-browed; once her *i*'s had had the vestige of a child's big dot, now the upstrokes were like poplars in a wind. The Villa Pamphili-Farnese still neither had nor needed an address.

The "sea-horse pavilion" no doubt still possessed the freak acoustics that permitted an approaching step outside to be heard over the most engrossed cries of love within in time for a sporting chance at getting dressed again if one was used to one another's buttons and snaps. He was sure it still had tritons by Bernini.

He could not know whether Gabriella still thought coitus as deficient without hazard as without display, though he had been her consort while she discovered both. The more intimate she had become with love, the more an innocence in her had come out like a peeled twig, until Gabriella in the afternoon, spread gloriously on an Abruzzi hillside (grass and thyme beneath her, a yellow butterfly on her toe, a tourist path barely out of sight behind a modest rock) made the night he took her awkward virginity seem lewd. The memory of this, and of the pavilion, and of Gabriella in a hundred poses and morning lights, drove a shaft of lust and loss into him.

His apartment offered no defenses. He therefore read the letter several times during the evening and, just before bed, replied.

> My dear Gabriella,
>   How very nice to have a chance to meet your friends. I accept with great pleasure. Thursday, eight o'clock, at the villa, the sea-horse pavilion.
>   Affectionately,
>   Giovanni

He copied it out again in the morning, sober.

Stears had called Captain Mascagni, who existed at the far end of a telephonic network patched together with sergeants who claimed no knowledge of him, operators who let calls ripen on hold, and colleagues who doubted that he could be found. He had offered to go to Mascagni's office. Mascagni had answered darkly, "That is not very nice for you," but Mascagni had chosen to answer in English and his English was certainly not good. At all events, Mascagni preferred to come to the embassy the next day.

And was late. He explained this, shifting his feet uneasily. "The bus from there is not so good," he said. Meanwhile he put his hand in his pocket in such a way as to give Stears the terrifying thought that he might not have bus fare home.

"It is very kind of General Della Cappella to permit us to call on you," said Stears in Italian.

"Is all right," said Mascagni vaguely in English.

"Parliamo italiano," said Stears. *"Sarà più facile."* Things improved a little. A decision had been made.

Mascagni looked around Stears's office. It was almost a basement and at the far end of the embassy, though a high window revealed a slanting strip of the Via Lucullo, peopled with legs and ankles. It excited Mascagni's admiration nonetheless. His eye fell upon a watercooler, placed there because unwanted somewhere else. "Private," he said. "Very nice." He looked at Stears's map of Italy. "Poor Italy," he said. "She is always full of pins. Just like a woman. Still, I have known her worse." He looked around Stears's collection of terrorist posters and graffiti. "That is all meaningless," he said. "Something there will maybe turn into a clue for a policeman one day, but the names mean nothing."

"That is my opinion, too," said Stears.

"Do you know exactly what I am?" said Mascagni.

"I know that you are a brave man," said Stears, looking in the general direction of the medal. Mascagni looked in agony at the floor. "And an officer of the Carabinieri."

"Ah," Mascagni said, "not that exactly. I am a Carabiniere seconded to SISDE—Servizio dell' Informazione e Sicurezza Democratica."

"So much I had assumed," said Stears.

"Under the law since 1977, I have none of the judicial powers of the Carabinieri now that I work for SISDE. Although I work against terrorists, I am not allowed to obstruct a terrorist who is aiming a gun at someone. That would be wrong. I should call a policeman. On the other hand, if, during an investigation, I find evidence of some ordinary crime, I cannot keep this to myself. Never tell me that you have parked your car too long—I must run to the policeman on the corner. If, while I am talking to the policeman on the corner about your parking, he sees a terrorist aiming a gun at me, he should not divulge this to me before he consults a judge. The terrorist has his right to privacy. That is the situation."

"I see," said Stears.

"It is completely impossible. I find it very pleasant here. You must have air-conditioning."

"All over the embassy," said Stears. "Even the kitchens."

"Ah," said Mascagni. "Nicer than with us. Although the situation is completely impossible, there are far fewer terrorists now. It is a contradiction."

"Intelligent men adapt. It is the measure of their ability," said Stears. "Particularly in Italy."

"Very often, yes. But it really is almost completely impossible for SISDE to cooperate with the CIA. You saw that at the Quirinale."

"Alas, yes," said Stears.

"At the highest level. So there we are. Not many years ago there were ten thousand terrorists in Italy. Ten thousand who were actually sometimes armed. About a thousand who lived in hiding and were always armed. At least we think so. Maybe there were more. That is not even to count the 'sympathizers.' I expect you know this?"

"Yes," said Stears.

"Nearly all of them liked to hate America. They hated the American military most of all. Many of them seemed to like the Arabs. I wonder how many of them have really changed their minds. I wonder where they all are, each of them, at any time of day. Some are in prison, of course. But think of all the rest. There will be hundreds that we never knew about at all. Thousands more who no longer give us an excuse to watch them. Some of them were killing poor General Leipzinger last week."

"One was apparently a woman," said Stears. "That must help."

"Very little. In the old days there were lots of women. That is why nothing serious ever happened in August. The terrorist mothers made their men take their families to the beach. Probably very often the same beach as the Carabinieri families. That there is a woman hardly helps the search at all. I know you get the police reports. And you have American soldiers here and there all across southern Italy. Sailors in bars, officers in their houses, wives shopping, airplanes sitting on the ground, little establishments like that one at Sagatto that nobody had ever heard of. I cannot tell you how worrying it all is."

Mascagni fell silent at this and rubbed a large and bony-knuckled hand over his other wrist. Then he said, "The CIA believes that there are Arab paymasters, am I right?"

"The CIA believes it and so do I myself," said Stears. "I think it is almost certain."

"I would not say that that is wrong," said Mascagni. "There are many Arab embassies and many strange people in them. Very many. But not nearly so many as the legions of Italians we were speaking of or the thousands of Americans. It would be much easier to watch the Arabs. But SISDE cannot do that. Absolutely not. That is the real problem."

"Why would that be?" said Stears. In the desolate atmosphere that Mascagni emitted it had been impossible for Stears to sit firmly behind his desk. He had sat on a corner of it and now found himself leaning forward.

"We must not annoy Arab governments. That has been decided at a very high level. It is a real order. If only some organization existed that could bring us that information. Suppose then that SISDE were to share with that organization all the things that only Italians can find out in Italy. Then some progress might be made. But that can never be. Think of even saying such a thing! Think of saying it at the Quirinale! And if that could not be said at the Quirinale between Deputy Ministers and Military Attachés, how could it possibly be said here? Even in Italian with no English ever. Even never written down. Do you understand just how impossible it is, Mr. Stears, in all its aspects?"

"I believe I do," said Stears with growing interest, "though perhaps not entirely. Perhaps not enough. More meetings between us may be necessary for me to see it fully."

"I should go now," said Mascagni. "My barracks is not in a convenient place. General Della Cappella thought that you might understand." He stood up and for a while investigated with his fingers the space between his collar and his neck. "I must go," he said again, but without confidence.

"We shall quite certainly talk again," said Stears. "You have given me some hope."

"Ah," said Mascagni. "Speaking of police reports, did you get the report about the boy with no face? I think you did not. Two days after Leipzinger, a body was pulled out of a building site in the countryside. A young man's body. His face had been crushed with a paving stone and the skin of his fingertips had been burned off with a cigarette lighter, so nobody yet knows who he was. Also his neck had been broken. It seems that he originally had a bullet wound in the head. It was really not his day. But that was just a ricochet. Not the sort of thing that kills all at once. And in fact it did not kill this boy at all. This was near Sella di Conza, not very near Sagatto but not extremely far from there, either, on the other side of the mountain. If by any chance he had something to do with all that, he was probably killed by his friends because his wound had become a nuisance. One does not like to think about that."

Mascagni reached the door and shook Stears's hand.

"Remember that the worst of these people hated all sorts of things," he said. "You could write their political ideas on a postcard, but what they hated was quite impressive: America, Italy, probably their own fathers. But please remember that they hated one thing most of all. So much that they could not stop talking about it."

"What was that?" said Stears.

"The CIA. It is better that we are not seen too much together. Good-bye."

He left Stears conscious of an incongruity that he did not resolve until later in the day. It came to him that he had expected Mascagni's handshake to be clammy. The truth was that it was firm and dry.

.   .   .

On Thursday evening, Stears drove the Jaguar to the Villa Pamphili-Farnese. A huge new *ipermercato,* a supermarket in the mind of Beelzebub on the outskirts of Rome, wiped the past cleanly off the slate. He nearly lost his way. But Rome has almost no suburbs and a kilometer farther on, the Campagna came back to life. The country road complacently unpacked the remembered little hill with olives and a sheepcote near the top where the wattle gate still hung one-third open. Down the hill, in a canal full of reeds, the half-sunk rowboat sat at its dock— but with the mooring rope changed from the left-hand to the right-hand bollard, just to send memory sprawling. The road tried to present itself as an erotic echo. Stears stepped on the gas to give the road something else to think about.

And so he very soon arrived. The villa was a toy, built by one of the family popes for a summer respite an hour or two by carriage from the city. It was not a serious estate. Agriculture here stopped at a few vines and figs.

There were four cars visible. He parked without thinking right under the statue of Diana and thus right on top of the fifth car, an invisible, now incorporeal, red Alfa Romeo coupé he had bought the summer after Yale and had always parked in that very place. He swore at himself mildly for doing so.

He listened for voices. He was a little late. It was after eight. The Roman pines wore golden crowns but they sat on ebony trunks. If Gabriella had changed her mind about the pavilion, he knew that she would use the *orangerie* or the terrace and voices would carry through the opened panes or past the pretty Graces grooming Virgil in the rotunda. There came a voice but it was in anger and Neapolitan and rose from the kitchen-cellar deep below and offered to stuff a chafing dish up another person's anus. He doubted that either was a guest.

He was not the only late arrival, it appeared. Another car, a middle-aged large Fiat, came circumspectly up the drive, then stopped in the circle of parked cars as though perplexed. The head of what must have been a very small man looked out in no good humor. Stears, acting before he could stop himself as habitué of the house, walked closer and asked if he could help. From this distance the man might have been deformed and

Stears did not look closely. And he was certainly ungracious. His baleful face was no doubt due to the setting sun being straight behind Stears—but still he muttered something about "wrong house" and put the Fiat hard in gear. One would have thought the dun of duns if one did not know better, thought Stears without great interest.

So the sea-horse pavilion it was. He walked down the avenue of cypresses. Swallows soared and plunged like souls of doubtful status; in the darkening grass glowworms tentatively lit. It was blacker where the steps went down to the pavilion; there were lanterns outside it and they sparkled on the water jets thrown up by chalcedony carp. He saw seven people there and a footman behind. Gabriella looked up to the steps as he stood there in the twilight and she followed him down with her eyes. It came to him that they owned the rarest choice: a new and warm and trusting friendship or a delight of body still familiar though completely new.

Her kiss was not stately as at the embassy but firm and matter-of-fact. "I thought you'd like to find your own way again," she said.

"I did," he said. And so he had. She kept her arm around him as she brought him into the light. "I believe you have met Mr. Stears already," she said, presenting him to a lady. "Mrs. Quist."

"Good heavens, yes," said Mrs. Quist. "I believe it is the spy who would have lent me his lettuce. How charming to see you again, Mr. Stears."

"A great pleasure for me," he said, bowing to the academician, whose shawl tonight had sea serpents and flying horses. Her cigarette holder was amber, the color of her fingers.

The academician's novelist husband extended a hand from the shadow. There was also an American Archbishop on loan to the Vatican Library, a woman painter fresh from a licentious exhibit in New York, and an Italian Admiral with his American wife. Gabriella stood close beside him while he spoke to each. He listened with care while his attention, though still under control, amended the map of her shoulder and neck according to new data. He smelled nerves beneath her scent, but they could have been his own. He deferred Champagne in favor of a martini.

A team of grilled lobsters arrived, bringing with them a fragrance of burned apple wood, olive oil, and lemon. Gabriella shooed the servants away. "Let's be American," she said. "Pretend they're hamburgers. Everybody serve themselves and make a mess." A night breeze now made the crests of the water jets quiver at their edges and Mrs. Quist had drawn her monsters tight around her neck. Goose pimples formed on Gabriella's outer arm but lay down when she moved. The Archbishop put a lobster on a plate for the painter and a selection of tools from a heap beside them. The painter was a woman with a solid jaw, a corded neck, and a haircut hard as a helmet.

Mrs. Quist motioned Stears to join her. "Is your business progressing?" she said. "Are we all becoming safer by the day?"

"Very slightly," he said.

"Which is all you can say, of course," said Mrs. Quist. "When Gabriella promised a mysterious old friend, I rather thought it might be you."

Stears heard an interrogative noise from the shadow and realized that Quist the novelist had spoken Stears's father's name. He acknowledged it with surprise.

"Your father was an underrated poet," said Quist. "You probably think that he was a good minor poet, or at least a good stylist, and that it is a shame that nobody remembers anything but his fascism. But the fascism was the point, you see. He was on to something for his time. Organized violence in this century always overpowers art unless art joins the council of organized violence. Which could be a courageous thing to do. It's a precipitous thought, but it wouldn't surprise me if Mailer had read your father, in his own way."

But Gabriella indicated her empty glass to Stears, driving off the footman with her other hand, and he rose to fill it. As he stood over her she said, "Why don't you get us each another lobster and come back to me? They're tiny." And so they were, but sweet as apples. She lifted her plate for him a millimeter from her lap. Mrs. Quist looked at her sharply.

The Archbishop answered Quist. "That is the evil of the twentieth century," he said. "There is not more evil done today, but there is much more done consciously. Maybe even temptation has become as obsolete as a hair shirt. We have evil as an aesthetic instead. Or perhaps as a sport. I hope you were not speaking with approval. It is caprice prancing in the face of God." But he said it evenly; he did not presume to instruct. It was daring for a priest to be at the Villa Pamphili-Farnese without a Cardinal's hat and he was enough of a churchman to know it. Especially with the Princess looking swiftly at him and then indifferently away.

Gabriella motioned to servants to collect debris and plates— American unpretentiousness would not embrace disposal. She smiled frequently but rather blankly at all her guests in turn. Peach Melbas took the field. A flutist and a cellist arrived; they were heard with wary respect for several minutes and then ignored. By the side of Gabriella, Stears abandoned himself to the thought that a woman known long ago would be entering a house by moonlight, the corridors followed without stumbling or hurt, the doors quietly opened—but one would never know the color of the walls until morning. The Princess served excellent Champagne.

"What about that Leipzinger stuff?" the woman painter said. "I was in New York when it happened and I haven't opened a paper since I got back."

It blew an ill wind. The dark of the garden turned to blackness and shoulders drew toward the light. The Italian Admiral said quietly, "Pigs. Arab filth. Slime of the Naples gutters."

His wife said brightly, "It upsets Paolo terribly."

"It damn well should," said Mrs. Quist. "It upsets me, too."

Gabriella put her head to Stears's. "Leipzinger was a soldier," she said. He felt her breath in his ear. "He expected to fight. He wasn't a clerk. That's what made him a brave man. People talk about him as though he was a poor old woman."

"He didn't expect to fight like that," said Stears. "Not shot in the belly by a vanload of hoods. He wasn't fighting. He was mugged." In turning to answer he almost brushed her mouth.

"Of course," she said and lightly touched his arm. "How stupid of me."

The musicians drew attention to themselves by stopping.

"It doesn't seem such a hell of a topic," the painter said.

"Nobody's been caught, if that's what you mean," said Mrs. Quist.

Gabriella was joined by the Admiral and his wife, who gave signs that they felt neglected. Stears walked toward a pulsing spark where the parapet faded into the night and confirmed that it was Mrs. Quist. "Ah, Mr. Stears," she said, and exhaled a cloud of smoke that drifted into the ivy.

"We would like to see more of you," she said. "New faces in Rome do not usually amount to much anymore. And Wesley really does have some interest in your father."

"What is your husband writing now?" said Stears.

"Wesley has become a minimalist. He feels that plot and dialogue destroy the simple beauty of a contract. That is a joke, of course. He has been working on something rather knotty. It may come out next year. I would like to show you around the American Academy myself. We have some lovely things. A lovely palace."

"I would like that very much," said Stears.

"As for this evening," said Mrs. Quist, "I started with the strangest feeling that I was here as somebody's duenna. Which would be more improbable, do you suppose, Gabriella's or a spy's?"

"Mrs. Quist," he said, "you really should not call me a spy."

"But now," she said, "I have the even stranger feeling that I am a bridesmaid. You have a rather odd effect upon her. Gabriella's usually quite jolly with her lovers while they last. Remarkably numerous and generally unsuitable as they are." She looked at him with a sociable smile, which faded. "Damn!" she said. "You actually are not going to bridle and get indignant, are you? Oh dear, this is very complicated."

The musicians played a coda and then packed away their instruments. This got them applause at last, but in the beleaguered circle of light the sound was piteous. The Archbishop discovered that it was late. A switch turned on strong lamps and the pavilion suddenly joined the steps, the cypress avenue, and even the driveway, where a chrome bumper came to life. After many regrets, the Archbishop receded. The Admiral showed signs of restiveness. The painter sought attention to an empty glass, which suddenly became invisible. Stears found himself corralled by Gabriella's side and had difficulty deciding whether to smile vaguely as a new acquaintance or shake hands heavily as a new host. Being of an American party, departure was a long, agonized indecision that broke suddenly into a rout. The Italian Admiral led.

The Quists lingered. Wesley Quist made grateful sounds. His wife said, "Very nice as usual, Gabriella. Is it the new etiquette to have a lesbian as a Bishop's date?"

"I don't really know," said Gabriella, "but it makes sense, don't you think?"

The Quists continued to walk beside them, as though they were indissolubly a group.

"Mr. Stears will not know the way back at night," said Mrs. Quist. "Perhaps it would be better if he followed us."

"I wouldn't think so," said Gabriella. "I should think anybody could find Rome." She stopped abruptly as she spoke and held Stears back by his coattail. The Quists went by on their own momentum and she fluttered a hand at them and said, "Good night, Deborah. I'm so glad you came." She pulled Stears closer and as he acknowledged Mrs. Quist's tart goodnight he saw again Gabriella's old entranced smile at getting her own way. It was still shameless, unmitigated cheek.

They leaned against the parapet and watched the Quists tramp up the foreshortened steps and be stalked by funny shadows down the avenue. He breathed peaceably the scent of her arm and breast. Time still stood guard between them and he ignored the fact that it was a quickly fading wraith.

"I wasn't quite sure you'd come," she said. "I was afraid you might change your mind."

"That would have been *incivile*," he said, using the Italian, much stronger, sense unwittingly.

"I'm glad you think that," she said, and took his hand and ran her fingers between his. "I'll bite my tongue before I say, 'How long are you in Rome?' but you're not leaving soon, are you?"

"No," he said, and thought of Mascagni and the map with pins and the burned blockhouse waiting on tomorrow's planet. "Not very soon at all." She squeezed his hand in answer.

The Quists' car started. "Let's hit the lights," said Gabriella. They walked across the terrace. "*Questo è tutto, grazie, Giuseppe,*" she said to a servant collecting glasses. He bowed, said, "*Principessa,*" and left by a back path.

She turned a switch in the ivy. The world retreated to the terrace with its six brave lamps, though there was a glow within the pavilion. She put her hands on his shoulders and they stood like dancers waiting for another tune until her hips moved him toward a seat.

She sat beside him. "What are you doing here?" she said. "In Rome?"

Her voice had a discordant haste. It startled him and he answered shortly, "Liaison." Each looked at the other in dismay. She turned around and rested her back against his chest.

"I'm shy with you," she said. "And that's silly." He felt her ribs breathing and saw with affectionate surprise a tiny orange mole rise and fall between her breasts. He had forgotten all about it.

He said gently, "It seems that American liaison with the Italians has gotten notably shitty. The terrorist business is escalating, as you very well know, and we are the targets, and some acute person thought that an American with a nickname like 'Wop' might help the flow of information."

"I never let anybody call you that," she said. And then: "Have I changed very much, Giovanni?" There was a tenseness in her shoulders that he wanted either to soothe or push away. He put his fingertip on the little mole and said, "I'd forgotten all about that."

She gave a short laugh that came from her stomach and growled in her throat. That was an old friend too, though its timbre had deepened. "You were supposed to say something encouraging about my face," she said. She took his hand and laid it on her right breast and put her own hand over it heavily. "*Ecco*," she said, and her voice settled with equal decision upon Italian.

Time had fled its post. He had nothing in his arms but woman, though he kept the savor of the choice upon the steps. Gabriella said, "If you're dealing with things like poor General Leipzinger, it worries me."

He said, "You shouldn't ask me any more." He sounded pompous to himself—more so as Gabriella's hand led his around her breast.

She said, "Of course. But I have not forgotten how to worry about you." She laughed suddenly, this time rubbing him cozily with her side. "It was fun sitting politely with you and all those people just outside the sea horses. I knew it would be." She looked up at him. He felt himself smile back. Lifting back her head had formed a dim passage through her bosom into the dark beneath her dress. She said, "And I thought putting the invitation that way might cheer you up in your little apartment. Was I right?"

"More or less," he said, remembering two uneasy nights.

Light glowed in the entry of the pavilion, but memory was just as bright. Inside, battalions of sea-knights, riding dolphins, raised their tridents to Bernini's *Neptune*, who burst in swelling menace from a pool. One of his fiercest memories was of Gabriella stretched out beside the pool with her hand trailing back behind her in the water, of her breast higher than his face, which lay on her taut belly, of the copper like autumn beeches between her thighs. It made him catch his breath, and for the first time tonight he felt lust.

"So," she said. "You came." Her voice held so much relief that he looked down surprised, but she smiled and said softly, "Marble seats get awfully hard. Perhaps we should move on." He let her coax him up and stand close beside him. Her pelvis snuggled sweetly in his groin.

He murmured, "Gabriella, we were a long time ago."

"Oh, I don't think so," she said. "It doesn't feel like that at all."

Crude carnal merriment was pure Gabriella. If it hadn't been for the trick in her voice he would have thrown himself upon her then and there. But in a dingy corner of his eye he could see her as a frayed neurotic grubbing in a ragbag of a life and coming up with him.

But she was also still his Gabriella and he gently said, "This might not be a very good idea."

She stroked his arms for a moment. Then her body changed. This time her voice had a dull edge when she said, "What was that?"

"We should not start over," he said.

She pulled away from him. "Then you should go home," she said.

"The past is the past," he said. She walked ahead of him. They were soon upon the steps. He took long strides and caught up with her. He said beside her, "And when I leave Rome again, which I will, what then?"

She spoke straight ahead. "If you call changing your mind and not coming tonight *incivile*, would you like to tell me what you call this?"

Moths circled around the top of the steps in the cold moonlight of two marble lions. They passed them.

"A fucking little bureaucrat?" she said. "Is that what you've become?" At the far end of the avenue, a glow from the villa lay upon the roof of his car. But shelter was not at hand. Gabriella came close. "Yes," she said. "You should run now. You ran from me when I was in the dark in the hospital and you would have lit up the room for me. Maybe you would be wise to run now."

"That is completely wrong," he said. So wrong that he walked briskly from her. So wrong that it was like the faintest growl from a tiger far out in the darkness and which certainly could not be there. They came to an archway in the avenue, leading out to gardens beyond. "Stop," he said.

"So?" she said. But she did stop. He was in a state with her that he recognized from long ago; he was angry, baffled, and rather warm. She must have seen it too, for she gave an unintended smile. But not for long.

"You have something to say before you go?" she said.

"Yes," he said, and said nothing. For what he had been about to say led out into the dark toward the preposterous tiger. The avenue seemed open as a beach. He took her arm where it was clenched beside her body and pulled her through the archway. This brought her close to him. He looked her in the eye. He expected to see her old devils, temper, cultivated *amour propre*, and whim.

What he saw was grief, a woman crushed and holding it back by a curled lip. What he saw was woe. He was not quite vain enough for that to make much sense, not in a grand and experienced woman, not after eighteen years; but he knew also that this was his Gabriella, that their flesh had once become welded for all time, that he had spent nearly twenty years fleeing from the sight of what she had done to herself and that he could not see her now with a cut finger. He took her very gently by the waist and held her against him as though she would collapse like down if he pressed.

"You don't want me," she said in a dry small voice. He held her without moving, waiting for his loins to warm his blood so that his touch would know how to cheer her. "I don't want to be fucked for sympathy," she said. "That does not amuse me at all." But he held her tighter and moved his chest until her breasts were sharp against it and kept her still when she made a twitch of rejection. He murmured to her hair, "I haven't stopped wanting you for twenty years," and, when she neither spoke nor pulled away, relinquished her shoulders and let his hands slide down her back. Her ear was near his mouth and he whispered, "For the last two days, I've almost died thinking about you." The ear sank a little on his shoulder and he said, "All night, I keep seeing us making love. I remember more and more. I almost cry."

"Really?" she said, as at a birthday card unexpected but received.

"Yes," he said. "Do you remember the meadow in the Abruzzi?"

Her chin made a doubtful movement and then her voice gave a sudden happy mew. "Oh, yes, I do," she said. Her face emerged from his shoulder and her eyes looked at him under the splendid modeling of her brow. "Then what was all that nonsense about?" she said.

"It doesn't matter now," he said. She shrugged and put back her head and he relinquished her back and lifted her breasts gently up between them. He felt at the top of her dress and she said indistinctly to his collar, "It's in the back. You have to pull it sideways," and bent her shoulders forward for easy reach.

He found the catch and then silk buttons. Her dress hung on one determined button and then fell with a sigh into a ring about her feet. She wore no bra. He bent to her breasts and tasted and kissed them slowly; he knew again that he loved them dearly, loved them as precious children lost and now regained, loved them so that to move from one to the other was a difficult choice, as causing jealousy. In the light of the quarter moon, her colors had a marvelous simplicity: dark mass of hair, only the edges auburn; shadows sharpening the architecture of her face; shadows rippling down her ribs and playing on her belly; nipples dark and shining from his tongue. He sank down on his knees, passing the white unders of her breasts, and sent her panties quickly off to join the dress. Even in moonlight, the chestnut flame glowed between her thighs and he bathed his face in its warmth and rediscovery. Gabriella bent down and touched his shoulders, kissed the side of his head. He looked up into the whole bowl of her above him, tingled with joy and pulled her belly against his face. His knees had sunk into pine needles, insistent but not harsh. He said, "We can lie down here, can't we," and felt her nod. So, putting one hand up to the middle of her back and cradling her hips between the other and his face, he laid her gently on the ground.

"All right?" he said.

"Yes," she said, moving her shoulders a little and stretching her arms out to hold him. "Quite all right. Come here." He lay against her, kissing and stroking her up and down. His body hunted memories of her ways and angles and found them softened and sweetened by a full-grown woman's flesh. He entered her finally by accident and would have changed to delay it still, but she said in a conclusively firm voice, "Don't go!" So he abandoned himself, flying on her scent and sounds with her ebb and flow about him, feeling rapture swell and hang, feeling as his head rose above the waves at last that his voice was surprisingly high-pitched and realizing dimly that it was hers.

Her lips played with his fingernail and lapsed into a beatific smile. The moon, moving for another shot, came straight underneath the pine tree and turned her hair almost to its daytime color. A small pair of eyes watched them from well beneath the tree, but the sound when they moved was reassuringly furry. It was not altogether warm, at least on places where they were not together. He groped blindly among clothes, retrieved several yards of Balenciaga, and dragged it on top of them as best he could. There were goose pimples growing on her behind and he found something for that, which turned out to be his tuxedo. It was now quite comfortable, if one dealt with individually offending pine needles one by one. She drew his face between her breasts, where it was like perfumed bread, and wrapped her arms around him. "That was so nice," she said, "Giovanni." And then, "That's so much better. I do hate things halfway."

C·H·A·P·T·E·R 6

The Cultural Attaché at the Libyan embassy, Yussuf ben Baghedi, lived in a world in which a great deal was expected of men largely unqualified and culturally negligible. Libyan diplomats lived at a dangerous and visible height of national life. Antic and savage penalties rewarded fumbles. A Libyan embassy was expected to be a dignified, seemly place one week—like a British embassy in a movie—a den of seething dervishes the next, and even, if required, a beleaguered guerrilla blockhouse, though this had not come to pass in Italy. There were crimes to be committed at all times, from hooliganism to murder. Life in the embassy—or "People's Bureau," as it was now called—was secretive, privileged, intense, and was lived scared.

As Cultural Attaché, Yussuf was obliged to attend operas, gallery openings, and even dress shows. All of them were incomprehensible to him and most of them were shocking, but he was expected to display a suave and knowing manner; it would have been ill received in Tripoli if word had come that its Cultural Attaché was a clown. Yussuf had some help in this from an ancient clerk, Dr. Basenji, who had been a Councillor in King Idris' old Libyan service. Dr. Basenji had the sort of noble,

timorous face that sensitive schoolmasters acquire after forty
years of school food and frayed cuffs. His family had been rich
in pre-Qaddafi times; he had gone to Italian schools. As late as
the sixties he had known Roman society. For this reason, he
was still kept around. Also because it was funny to see Basenji's
shame at his beautiful old suits' fraying and even parting at the
seams—for he had neither money, servant, nor wife.

Over Yussuf's desk also passed all the paper connected with
keeping the many indispensable Italian technicians in Libya at
least slightly entertained; failure here would have been a national
catastrophe. He was also responsible for what passed for Libya's tourist operations in Italy. None of this was his real job,
which was terrorism, subversion, and a crude kind of espionage.
He had an affection for this work because he understood it.

In the last few days, the telephone to Tripoli had become
unusable, because of the Americans. This made everything
twice as difficult. It made Yussuf especially irritable since his
clerk, though the old man trotted back and forth with papers as
fast as he could go, was allowed no access to things to do with
subversion or crime.

On top of that, the Italian Calvetto had made it clear that he
would have to murder personally the boy in Naples, the friend
of the wounded fairy Yussuf had been obliged to kill. Yussuf
understood the urgency, but was simply not able to fit it in until
six days after his meeting with Calvetto. Even then, since he
could not easily explain an absence, he would have to be at a
performance of something called *The Master Singers* by the
Bavarian State Opera that same evening in Rome. He could
manage it, but it would be a long day.

He went down to Naples the night before, taking a bag of
necessaries. He arranged for the false-name rental of a medium-
sized Fiat. He went to Maurizio's neighborhood and began to
look.

Because of this delay, Maurizio had had a week to become
unhinged by grief and terror. Dr. Calvetto, who was Sicilian,
would have predicted this, but Calvetto did not expect the Libyan to let time slip.

Maurizio had written a letter to the police. He had done this because he was afraid.

During the getaway from Sagatto, he had clung wretchedly to his moaning friend and lover, but his distress for his comrade's wound was no greater than his very natural fright. At the stable beyond the mountain, he had even had a season of relief while Rosa, whom he admired deeply, had seemed to take charge. When Rosa had gone away and the Libyan forced Roberto into the trunk, his feelings for Roberto, by then despair and anguish, had still been mixed with rage against the Libyan and shame at his own weakness.

The Libyan had killed Roberto in the cold first light.

The Libyan had stopped the car. He had pulled on at leisure a pair of gloves. "Out," he said and did not wait for Alfredo and Maurizio to obey before walking composedly to the rear of the car. He opened the trunk, bent to collect his strength, and jerked from the trunk the poor light body. Roberto's head was covered with blood and suffused with blood inside the skin. The face rotated toward Maurizio; it might have been the random motion of the skull upon the neck but, for Maurizio, the eyes had seen and spoken. The Libyan broke the neck with a snap and afterward there was a sound of grating when it was moved.

The sky, the piles of rubble by the building site, were cold and gray. Maurizio huddled by the car. Alfredo and the Libyan carried Roberto away, but not far. He saw the Libyan pick up the paving stone and chop with it on Roberto's face. This was in silhouette, like a horrible puppet show. He saw Roberto's hands, in which he had known some meager happiness, splayed out, saw the lighter carefully adjusted and the flame suck the fingertips. He had smelled it. He saw the body thrown into a shallow ditch and quickly hidden with stones.

Maurizio had a room in Naples near the university. When he got back, he stayed in it for two days, leaving it only for the lavatory downstairs. This was noticed by no one, for at the best of times Maurizio rarely attended classes, wandering instead around protests and "meetings." He did not have the stomach for these just now. He grieved for Roberto. He woke up at night in agonies of knowledge of the suffering that his friend must have known. He quivered with hate and shame against the Lib-

yan. But what grew most terrifyingly in him was the image of
the faceless corpse, lonely and dishonored and familiar with
him.

Maurizio was a homosexual, an urban *guerrigliero,* a Marxist,
and a university student. All this, while strictly true, was also
strictly misleading. His grandfather was a Calabrian peasant; his
father, postal clerk. His uncle, the family's great success, was a
village lawyer. Maurizio, whose learning was trivial, was able to
be at a university because the universities of the Mezzogiorno
had all but abandoned standards a decade before. Though hys-
terically self-important and corrupted by texts that he barely
understood, Maurizio was a very simple boy. Given more sense
of the world and some skills, he could have been a young peasant.

The sense of the corpse, restless and misused, haunted the
corners of his mind. By any standards, he had been Roberto's
friend; he should have been his champion. Roberto knew very
well where to find him, he knew his bed at night. In his clammi-
est moments, Maurizio, who was a deeply confused boy, saw
the dead also as having guilty lusts.

After five days of this, he wrote anonymously to the police.
The letter had read simply:

> The man whose body will be found in the building site two
> kilometers west of Sella di Conza is Guido Mattone from Lecce.
> His father is Giuseppe Mattone, the grocer. He was murdered by
> the American Fascists. Long live the Proletariat!

The objective part of this information was accurate and suffi-
cient to bring about Catholic burial and peace.

Without the flourish at the end, which Maurizio had put in to
salve his revolutionary conscience, the police, who already had
the unknown body, might possibly have taken the matter as the
end of yet another obscure Calabrian gang murder. The flourish
tied it almost beyond doubt to the events at Sagatto. This was
the first constructive discovery in the case.

Writing a letter to the police had opened a chink in Maurizio's
mind. To some small degree, they were now Maurizio's police

and he had an interest in their zealous performance of their duties. It had impressed him that simply by writing a letter to them he could set events in motion. Though he was far from being able to envisage any shape for himself but that of a leftist *guerrigliero,* he was enough of a Calabrian to think instinctively of picking up advantage where it lay. He began to wonder if he could use the power of the police to take care of other things, such as his inadequacy in front of the Libyan.

These thoughts, while elaborate and not entirely unrealistic, were also childish and compulsive. They led him to leave his room, buy a better meal than usual, and begin hanging around the central police station. The next morning, he even walked twice up and down its steps.

It was very, very unlucky that this was the morning the Libyan followed him.

When the Libyan saw Maurizio stand on the police steps and look up them with a face of irresolute cunning, he felt an explosion of exasperation and contempt. Contempt was normal for him in Italy, a cageful of dirty monkeys whose tricks were quicker than his eye. Exasperation, because he had come down simply to kill Maurizio, for which he barely had time, and now would have to do much more. Fortunately for the Libyan, his thoughts were nothing but practical and he almost immediately had a plan.

He walked quickly back to Maurizio's neighborhood. On the way, he went into a cheap store and bought a plastic raincoat in a pouch and then visited a grocery and bought—offering a short prayer against the impiety—a liter bottle of wine. He reparked the Fiat twenty meters from Maurizio's door. He left the doors unlocked. The neighborhood was in no way picturesque—it was a street of cheap four-story apartment buildings built through a government program twenty years before. This being Naples, however, it had a busy street life; close to the Libyan's new illegal parking place were a wagon selling crisp fried dough with a smell of sugar, a rack of used clothing, and an open van selling stolen radios and televisions and a line of electric clocks with paintings of the Virgin. The apartment building was a warren, and there was plenty of traffic around its door. The Libyan took a small object from his case of necessaries in the car. Then he stood in a shadow by the wall. He waited.

He knew quite well from Maurizio's posture on the steps that the boy had not yet visited the police. He thought it likely, however, that he had talked to people or had taken some preliminary step. A less honorable man than the Libyan would have let the matter drop—it all reflected badly on him. Yussuf, however, had the probity to obtain needed information even if it worked against him. Having worked all of this out within a hundred meters' walk of seeing Maurizio on the steps, he waited for two hours and thought of almost nothing.

When Maurizio was almost at his door, the Libyan moved quickly out of the shadow and walked straight up to him. Under the circumstances, Maurizio could have been more aghast only if it had been Roberto in front of him, without a face. The Libyan spoke in a peremptory tone about "orders." Maurizio was halfway to the Fiat before the Libyan sensed that he was about to run. He clapped him on the back in a friendly manner. Since his hand held a hypodermic, it required all the Libyan's strength of arm to put Maurizio smoothly into the car.

Yussuf knew Naples well. He drove onto the Via Don Bosco, switched onto the Corso Garibaldi, circumnavigated the busy piazza, and swung to the south side of the central railroad station along the Via Galileo. He had taken the opportunity of the first quiet street to tie Maurizio's neck loosely under the collar to the head support and to fasten his right hand to the door pull. After that, Maurizio flopped about much less than General Leipzinger had done under the curare. From the Via Galileo, the Libyan took more obscure streets flanking the railroad tracks until he reached a section partly waste, partly the far outskirts of a switching yard, which he followed until it narrowed under vaulting overhead as the main line entered the hills. There was a place here in deep shadow about forty meters from the tracks and very rarely visited. Here he parked.

Yussuf had not come to Naples expecting to engage in interrogation, but he had all he needed in the way of means. The Libyan quickly took thin wire, intended as a garrote, out of his case and used it to bind Maurizio's feet unbreakably to the seat frame. He took the boy's trousers down and rolled up the shirt, searching the clothes for wallet and papers. Then he twisted the body enough to tie the arms doubled around the steering column. Maurizio had begun to snuffle and stir.

Yussuf quickly opened the door and took jumper cables from the trunk. He worked quickly to strip cable and make connections secured by tape. Very shortly, he had the cables wired into the ignition. He led the cables back through the window on Maurizio's side, rolled up the window as tightly as he could, and stuffed his shirt of yesterday into the remaining crack. He put the raincoat on and buttoned it up tight. He took one of the alligator clips of the jumper cables and fastened it to Maurizio's scrotum. This fully woke up Maurizio and the Libyan switched on the engine and touched the other clip to Maurizio's nipple to show him how it all worked.

The Libyan switched off the engine, stuffed a good deal of Kleenex into his ears, and checked with some apprehension the solidity of the steering column. He opened the door and made sure of their isolation. This done, he sighed, and shut the door. He liked cleanliness and had no illusions about the ordeal before him. He switched on the engine and began.

At the end, he was left with full knowledge of Maurizio's letter to the police and a certainty that there was nothing more. He had had the former within ten seconds. He had done all that could be asked. His head ached, he was sweating furiously inside the raincoat, and the car was full of smoke, which was the least of it. As a man who prayed daily, Yussuf had some feeling for the harmonies of the world; it made him uneasy to use this method on a man. Maurizio was not, to Yussuf's mind, a full man, which removed some of the moral repulsiveness of the process but did not change the nature of its physical results.

He opened the car. He got out with some difficulty, for the steering column had been bent toward his knee. He removed the raincoat with squeamish fingers, and threw it in. A freight train passed a hundred yards away and he let the locomotive rumble out of sight while he opened the bottle of wine and emptied it on the ground. It ran in a gritty stream toward the railroad tracks. He knelt beside the car, pushed a tube into the tank, and sucked to begin the syphon. He spat, and put the tube's end into the liter bottle. When it was full, he let the gasoline run onto the ground beneath the car. He went quickly back, took his shirt out of the window, splashed it with a little gasoline, and stuffed a sleeve into the bottle neck. He put the bottle between the seats and spread the shirt. He saw that Maurizio's eyes had reopened.

Yussuf said gruffly, but not unkindly, "The worst's over. You won't feel much." He stood outside the door, lit a match, tossed it onto the shirt, and ran. The car burst into a bowl of orange flame which strove toward the vaulting and carried away with it Maurizio's spirit, which issued as a shriek.

By the time the first police car arrived, Yussuf was waiting peaceably at a bus stop in an industrial neighborhood outside the tracks. In such a part of Naples, neither his features nor his cheap but sober suit were in any way remarkable. The car was not traceable to him. What had been done inside the car could not be disguised, but Maurizio was almost certainly beyond identifying. The police would not quickly assume a political motive. Naples suffers greatly from the barbarities of organized crime.

In spite of his best efforts, the Libyan Cultural Attaché was late for the German Ambassador's invitation to the opera. It had been necessary for him, as befitting his station, to change out of his cheap Western suit into appropriate Bedouin evening wear. The Germans had issued edicts and late-comers were obliged to sit in the echoing foyer, where the seats were few and very hard, until the end of the first act. It turned out that this was interminable and Yussuf was appalled to learn that there were two more.

During the intermission, he perceived Dr. Calvetto talking to a German diplomat. The German was straight and tall and beside him Dr. Calvetto looked like a comma beside an *l*. At such a gathering, there was no objection to Yussuf's openly encountering the doctor if it were done with prudence. It was an elegant assembly and Yussuf was almost certainly the only person there who had spent part of his working day in a Fiat filled with smoke, vomit, feces, and urine while a man screamed a foot from his head. Yussuf found a moment and gave Dr. Calvetto the news, including that of Maurizio's letter and the fact that it had been sent two days before. Calvetto's expression of wise mischief did not change, but when he said, "A pity that you waited," an inner facet of his eye flashed up toward the Libyan. Yussuf carried it with him all night and saw it frequently during the next day at the embassy.

Giovanni Stears, who believed that performances of *Die Meistersinger* should alternate nightly with *The Marriage of Figaro* in all great cities, had gladly accepted Beebe's suggestion that he should attend like any other diplomat. Stears was in far better humor than Yussuf and needed only the glass of Champagne even now being put into his hand from behind the bar to be in an all but perfect one. Barely twenty hours before, he had walked hand in hand with his partially rewrapped Gabriella from the pine needles to her door, kissed, and said good night. Today had gone well in other ways. Nonetheless, Stears's pleasant day, like Yussuf's disagreeable one, was spoiled by Dr. Calvetto, whom Stears by no means knew.

Looking up as he took the Champagne he at once forgot all about his thirst for, at the far end of the foyer he saw, not Gabriella in memory, but Gabriella herself. It passed through his mind that she had not said that she would be there, then that he had not told her that he was going, then with warm pleasure that this might be one of the last evenings that such surprises could be the case.

She had not seen him. He moved with difficulty away from the bar. It seemed that she had just separated herself from a small group and was on her own. Her face turned toward him.

And changed at once from the lingering smile of leave-taking to a look startled, uneasy, and covering distaste with a pretense of hurry. He felt his own face freeze. Then he saw that she was still not looking at him at all but at a small, twisted figure moving toward her with a sprightly smile from a point about between them. The man took her hand and kissed it. They spoke a few seconds. In that time Stears saw his Gabriella become a big, confused girl in the presence of a sarcastic superior. She seemed to pull herself together and speak a pressed farewell. All this, Stears soon told himself, would have been seen by no eye less hungry than his own and only then because he had first taken her expression as caused by him. She went quickly to a door which, as he remembered from the two footmen beside it who now opened it for her, led to a private lounge and then to the boxes. Her friend turned in Stears's direction now, with a smile still in place but crooked at the edges. He was no object of jealousy. Alberich the Nibelung, thought Stears, not needed on stage until tomorrow. He could see why a girl might not fly toward him.

Back in the auditorium, Stears searched the boxes for her like the best Victorian romantic. The lights went down without her. The pleasure of the evening curled at its edges. In the next intermission, he looked for her without success while at the same time he talked to a man he had been pursuing for three days, a distant acquaintance of long ago now in the Ministry of Justice.

The acquaintance was developing a weighty train of thought. In the middle of it, it came to Stears that if Gabriella's friend was Alberich the Nibelung, then Alberich was remarkably like the driver of the car that had arrived at the Villa Pamphili-Farnese last night.

The acquaintance achieved the train of thought. "Yes," said Stears. The acquaintance looked at him closely. "Did you hear anything I said?" he asked.

Stears made an enthusiastic gesture. In the course of it he saw that the unattractive friend had at least not disappeared with Gabriella; he was by the staircase right now, in conversation with Cardinal Vestrelli.

C·H·A·P·T·E·R 7

The day that ended at the opera had begun for Stears in the Borghese Gardens. He walked to work most mornings. Fifteen minutes on foot straight across the gardens had attractions over twenty minutes of elbowing the Jaguar around them on the Via Pinciana through morning traffic. Some gardeners smiled and said good morning: he had not observed this in the traffic police. This morning he had gotten home at 3 A.M. in the state of merry, yawning, self-congratulatory disorder that he recalled from nights much earlier in his life; he had even sat on his bed a while picking pine needles from his clothes, not particularly to spare his servant trouble but because the clothes held fragrances of Gabriella.

Even so he walked this morning. The smell of sprinklers on warm grass prolonged the effect of the florist's shop he had stopped at first, the pleasure of the enormous bouquet of roses glistening under a last fond spray, and the deep bow of the shop woman when he gave the address, Villa Pamphili-Farnese. The prick in his thumb, where he had plucked out a blemished stem and drawn a bulging drop of blood, covered any presentiments of perfidy or disarray.

So he arrived at the embassy exhilarated. Even the duty clerk seemed in tune with it as he wished Stears a cheerful good morning. Then he handed him a summons from Randall Beebe and a letter from Marie-Sophie, Stears's absent wife.

Randall Beebe said, "So you are proposing that you and this Puccini character run around as General Della Cappella's private army? Or as a supranational authority, perhaps. Is that the general idea?"

"Mascagni," said Stears. "Captain Mascagni."

"Mascagni, then," said Beebe. "The one who doesn't shave."

Randall Beebe sat behind his desk and used Stears's tentative typed rendering of Mascagni's offer to swat Mascagni's name.

Beebe read aloud, " 'These exchanges of information should be regarded as reserved to the field officers concerned and as outside the general command structure in the near and medium terms.' What in hell does that mean?"

Very nearly nothing, I should have said, thought Stears, as Beebe fixed him with a crystal eye. But Beebe supplied the answer. "I think it means that in your opinion that ice-cream man who doesn't shave is going to tell you things I can't be trusted with. Is that correct?"

"No, sir," said Stears. "Certainly not. Only things you might not wish to have to say you know. Or how you knew them."

"That's certainly very kind," said Beebe briskly.

Yet he was not, thought Stears, as nettled as he wished to seem. Considering the bile that Beebe had been fed over the last two weeks, that did him credit. The pin-striped jacket hung from the back of his chair and certain papers on his desk gave signs of breaking rank. Beebe's manner was troubled, not truly bleak. Beneath this, he looked at Stears with faint hope. Beneath hope, Beebe looked spent.

"General Della Cappella," said Stears mildly, "initiated this idea in front of the Deputy Minister and in front of Croce, his own nominal boss. Up to a point, at least."

Beebe said nothing. Stears said, "And in front of you, who are my boss."

Beebe said, "Della Cappella told a lackey behind his chair to return your phone calls."

"This is Italy," said Stears.

"Yes, it is," said Beebe. "And what are you?"

"An officer of the CIA serving at the post he was ordered to," said Stears, but he did not say it glibly.

"Yes," said Beebe, "so you are. An officer of the CIA is an American, Stears, for better or worse, like me. I wear a belt on my pants in London. In Paris, I do not carry bread under my arm or work a vineyard. In Peking, I am not the first cousin of the Minister of Pensions. In Vienna, I do not represent the Hapsburgs on alternate days of the week. I belong to one hierarchy and I have one set of loyalties and I am a bureaucrat. There are people who work for the CIA during the day, after they get out of bed with the Soviet Ambassador, or who are Polish fighter pilots, or who play bridge with the President of France. They are called agents, Stears, not officers, and they are treated as very different fish. Do you have anything to say to that?"

"I was in London," said Stears. "I was working on German material. I was nearing the end of the analysis of an operation I had run myself. I was sent here. I wasn't even asked."

"That's perfectly true," said Beebe. "I know your boss in London, Brindle Woods. He said he was sorry to lose you. Whether I'm sorry to get you, I'm not yet sure."

"What Mascagni proposed is trade," said Stears. "That's basic to running intelligence. We do it all the time. And there's nothing unusual about a government's operating a policy under the table that it won't look at on top."

"There's nothing unusual about a government's buying a double agent, either," said Beebe. "Don't fire up. I'm not saying you'll even know the day you're bought. General Della Cappella spoke to you, not to me. The ice-cream man came to you. You will receive all sorts of little privileges and confidences from the Italians, Stears, because you're not some blundering Yank. Because you're trustworthy, you've got some Italian loyalties, some special sensibilities. You can see their side too. They're allies anyway. You're the honest middleman. And at that point, Stears, you're nothing. Do you understand?"

"Yes," said Stears.

"How good are you, Stears?"

"Good enough to listen," said Stears. "Good enough at least for that." And then he spoke meticulously, for his first impression of Beebe as a stuffed puppet had already begun to seem incomplete. "That we are dealing with native enemies in an allied nation is a fact, not my sentiment. That it is a good deal more nebulous than a KGB confrontation and requires other tactics is my deduction, but one that I will hold to." But Beebe's air still had power to rile and he added, "My purpose, incidentally, is to assist you in hindering people who shoot Americans in the stomach to use them as bait. Perhaps that is a legitimate use for contacts. Since I was sent here."

Beebe looked him in the eye and took two unhurried breaths. Then he nodded slowly and said, "I am authorizing you to use resources to raise the level of surveillance on Arab embassies and associated targets, as you request. I am informally permitting you to exchange information with Captain Mascagni of the Carabinieri so long as American interests are given strict priority. You will report to me frequently on this. I will allow you limited discretion to withhold from the log information that Mascagni gives you when it relates specifically to criminal or subversive conduct by Italian nationals in Italy. You have no authority to initiate action with the Italians without consulting me. I do not like any of this and I would not do it if your Italian friends were not stonewalling me on every front. Do you understand, Stears?"

"Yes, sir," said Stears.

"The CIA may look a horse's ass from time to time but the power we represent is real and great. I have seen it used badly. I have seen it used in personal rivalries. I have seen it used by people who had slithered around so much they'd forgotten which way their heads were pointing. The results were never pretty. I've given you most of what you want, Stears. Don't get seduced."

"Thank you," said Stears.

Marie-Sophie's letter bore Swiss stamps. It was from Huissier-sur-Cosson, just outside Geneva. So she was staying with her friend Mathilde. Indeed she was. She wrote:

Dear Giovanni,

I am writing because you would not have found me on the telephone and I do not want to seem to have vanished, especially because of what I am about to say. I am staying with Mathilde, of course. At least, I am staying in Mathilde's house and she is here sometimes. I was lonely in London. I was often lonely there, sometimes most lonely when I was there with you.

But I have made myself not be lonely for you, Giovanni. I say "made myself" because I could be, I know. But I know I would be sorry, too. I hope you are all right in Rome, but when I think about it, I know that I do not want to be with you there at all. I drove by my old house on the lake here last week. Yes, we did have some very nice times once, but it only made me realize that it is not like that between us anymore. So I am saying that one day I think I will do something with the lawyer about a real separation and then a divorce, because life should go on, shouldn't it?

But I do not want us ever to be anything but friends and able to call on each other in case of need. Would you send me some sandals from Franceschini? Maybe two pairs. You know how I love them and I can't get them here or London, only in Rome.

Anyway, you know Mathilde's number if you should need to call me and talk about all this and I have written it on top anyway. I may go to Morocco next week but I will let you know if I do. Otherwise, I will go back to London, probably. Maybe you would call me anyway about where to send the sandals when you find them.

Love. I hope you will be happy.

Your (until I post this, I suppose) Marie-Sophie

P.S. Don't forget to call about the sandals.

When the letter had been unopened in his pocket he had felt it, in this morning's circumstances, as materialized guilt. It seemed to have changed substance all at once; Marie-Sophie's letter had been postmarked before he had even accepted Gabriella's invitation to dine. Guilt, he knew now, had also been a restraining gate, something to lean against while he looked at the shadows on the path back to Gabriella. No sooner had he leaned against it than it had opened, even if on a squeaky hinge.

Two mornings later, Mascagni came.

In Stears's office now, the map of Italy had been joined by a plan of Rome, just as big and also acquiring pins, and a smaller plan of Naples, which had just been hung. On his desk were profile sheets of surveillance operatives whom the Company had used before in Rome. He knew in advance that the surveillance obtainable would be inadequate; the Libyan embassy alone would take most of his resources. Families of spies could not be installed with cameras in every apartment building overlooking a Middle-Eastern embassy; most Arab personnel would never be watched. Most were not worth watching. Many, unfortunately, were; Libyan sympathizers could well be found in the embassies of Syria and Iraq or even as far afield as Algeria, anything to do with Lebanon was open game for anyone—and there was always Iran. His task was to find connections, however indistinct, between Arabs who could serve Qaddafi and Italians who hated America enough to commit the acts of the last few months. Constant interchange of intelligence with Mascagni would narrow the search until finally one target would stand out in perfect clarity with a bull's-eye pinned to his chest.

At least if one could omit certain difficulties. Interchange with Mascagni was likely to be so hampered as to be almost useless. If his surveillance were discovered and connected with the CIA, the surveillance would be discontinued amid loud protests from the Italians and shocked apologies from Beebe. One operative's unreliability could suffice for this. The best surveillance he could possibly effect might never turn up a target. The target, if found, might be politically impregnable. These objections were depressing.

Mascagni had called in advance. He entered Stears's office more briskly than before, not as though he had intended to come there, but at least as though he would be able to leave. Nonetheless, he shook Stears's hand quite warmly. He carried a manila envelope.

"I should not leave this here," he said. "It is quite confidential. You must remind me when I leave." He looked swiftly around Stears's office.

"Certainly," said Stears.

Mascagni said, "There is very little since I saw you last. One thing of interest. You remember the poor man I told you of who was shot and had his neck broken and was thrown out into a building site with no fingertips or face? You do? We know who this man is now. Somebody in Naples wrote the police an anonymous letter. The dead man is a boy from Lecce but he studied at the university in Naples. He was known among the radicals there. He was also a homosexual, it seems. The police are looking for his particular friend. They have not been looking for very long, of course. Maybe he is on the run. Maybe he wrote the letter—that should not be very difficult to find out. The letter was certainly written by a radical and there were foolish remarks in it about the Americans. So we are almost sure now that this is connected with Sagatto. It is perhaps a beginning.''

"It certainly is,'' said Stears.

"But it is still almost nothing. We know of seventy radical groups among the Naples students and I imagine there are many more. I doubt if this was organized in Naples. Maybe this boy had some very simple task and, of course, now he cannot help us. Still, it might make a pin for your map collection. Many of these Neapolitans are described in that folder that I really must not forget. It would be interesting if you yourself had come in contact with any of them. The body was at Sella di Conza. Shall I stick a pin in there for you?''

"Please,'' said Stears.

"There. Now you have a pin farther east than any you had before. Perhaps that is important. How does it go with you? I see you have new maps.''

"My superiors have given me an additional role,'' said Stears. "I am to initiate special surveillance of certain Arab embassies and things like that.''

"Is that so?'' said Mascagni. "Just as we talked about the other day? That is very interesting. Are you making progress?''

"It is early days,'' said Stears. "I am still choosing surveillance personnel. A mistake would be dangerous there.''

"Yes, indeed,'' said Mascagni. "One case of mixed loyalty could be the end of that. Many of these people would probably be Italians. Is that the case?''

"All those in here,'' said Stears. He held up the envelope with the profile sheets inside. "We have detailed information on

them but it is hard to be sure of its accuracy." He laid the
envelope beside Mascagni's. "At our next meeting," he said,
"could I not at least offer you lunch? The Casina delle Rose is
not far away. I could reserve there the day after tomorrow."

On Mascagni's face there was a spasm of actual longing but
Mascagni sadly banished it and said, "It would not be wise. You
should not be seen with me. Especially now that you have these
duties against the Arabs, who can be so extremely lawless. But
the day after tomorrow, certainly, I am at your service. I am at
your service more than ever now."

When Mascagni left, Stears found that the worst had hap-
ened. In his confusion, the man had taken the CIA's material on
Italian personnel. This was material that Italians who had hon-
estly aided the CIA had every moral right to consider sheltered
from their own government, since they had in many cases broken its laws to do so. Stears discovered this loss when he opened
the envelope Mascagni had left behind and found it full of material on radicals, subversives, and terrorist suspects in the Naples area—just that kind of thing most heavily protected by
Italian law and the charter of Mascagni's service. He settled
down to read.

The next day, just before he left for lunch, the telephone rang
on his desk. He picked it up and recognized the voice of Teresa,
one of the two Italian receptionists, the one with the tinkling
bracelets and the downy lip. Teresa said formally, "The Princess Gabriella Harriman-Farnese is here to see you, Mr. Stears.
She says that she has no appointment."

Stears, out of pure surprise, said nothing. Teresa switched to
confidentiality. *È una nobildonna romana, Signor Stears, ma
è anche cittadina americana. Qui, la si considera una veep.* He
translated the last word correctly as VIP.

So Stears said politely, *"Grazie mille, Teresa. Vengo subito."*

Gabriella was in the small front waiting room to which important guests were guided. Under her hair she was pale gold, the
effect of an ostrich-leather suit light enough for the skirt's hem

to tremble against the fan. The First Secretary, Henry Halston, was arranging the furniture around her, not for much reason. She was talking to him with the deep, concerned attention that she gave to everybody, including waiters. She smiled pleasantly at Stears.

"We have an arrangement for lunch, Mr. Stears," she said. "Do you remember?"

"Of course we do, Princess," he said. "But how nice of you to come here."

"Thank you so much, Henry. I am sorry to have wrecked your morning," she said to the First Secretary. The First Secretary, who was accomplished, smiled socially for the Princess and looked acidly at Stears. He left.

"Come on," said Gabriella. She took his hand. "Lunch is in the car."

"You still drive these damned things?" he said. Her car was a white Ferrari, and it was parked in the shade around the corner. It was also in the middle of the entrance to the embassy parking, but the line of trapped cars was not yet very long.

"They're really quite nice cars," she said. "Anyway, if you fall off a horse, you're meant to get back on."

This Ferrari seemed cushier than the first. It had puffy buckram seats. Just now, it had a picnic hamper with bright brass buckles in the back. It had Gabriella's legs, below the molding of the golden skirt, directing the pedals with swift authority.

"Where are we actually going?" he said.

"Your apartment. You're having me for lunch there."

"Of course I am," he said. "It's Via Paisiello. Just off Parioli."

"I know where it is, idiot," she said and sounded actually annoyed. And then: "Those were lovely roses."

"Weeds compared to their recipient," he said.

"Oh," she said, "that's nice."

"I saw you at the opera," he said. "*Die Meistersinger*. I think you left early."

She looked away from him, quite reasonably, at a traffic light. "It's disgustingly long," she said, "that one. Isn't it? Puccini is more my sort of evening.'' Separated from her in a bucket seat, he touched no part of her; he simply could not tell if there was constraint there or not. Then she turned to him. "Did you sit through it all?'' she said. Her eye was candid to a degree that, in such a trivial question, might have been inquest or a challenge or a plea or nothing of the sort at all.

"Yes," he said. "I did."

She walked through his apartment, room by room, pausing thoughtfully at the shiny painting of St. Mark's; she examined the portentous coat of arms imposed by the apartment's owner on a skimpy modern hearth; she picked up the strange little box made out of a deer's skull. "This is all extravagantly awful, Giovanni," she said. He nodded. He noted from the kitchen the lingering smell of a freshly pressed suit, but Eduardo, his servant, had evidently left. Two hours before his time. Stears was never home by day. He had left the picnic hamper in the hall.

He followed her to the small dining room. On one wall, some peasants frolicked with completely rigid legs. On the opposite wall, two cardinals drank wine. Stears had eaten in this room once. "Not here, I think," said Gabriella.

"No, indeed," said Stears. He followed her to the bedroom, where all was stripes and clever wardrobes. But there was a view over a little church to the Borghese Gardens. "This will have to do," said Gabriella decorously. "Go and get the hamper, my dear."

He did. She had opened a closet and hung her jacket neatly. She had closed the blinds, so the sun entered now in rays. "There is plenty of Champagne," she said, "but there is no ice for it, or glasses, so you should get those now, since you seem to have no servants."

He did, came back, and found the bed embellished with a pretty wicker tray.

"Now," she said, "go and get undressed comfortably in your bathroom. I shall be perfectly all right here."

When Stears came back she was sitting on the bed with her legs curled under her. Her skin was not a very different color from the dress. He kissed her and held her, but she put her hand against his arm.

"We are having lunch," she said, "exactly as though we were at a table at the Bolognese. In which case, you would not be holding my breast like that so enthusiastically, I should think. Lie back on the pillows like a gentleman, my dear. The tray goes there, you see, and I shall tuck up my legs and sit beside you here. You may look all you wish, of course. In fact it would be rude not to. It's nice you've kept your figure. The white sandwiches are *foie gras* and the brown ones are smoked salmon. The peaches, of course, are peaches, and from my lands in Apulia at that. You will have to sit up a little higher to pour the wine without spilling it, since we have no waiter here. There, bravo, Giovanni. You really should say something. It is usual at lunch."

"Open your mouth," he said. He gently put in it a square of bread with a tongue of salmon licking out of it, much like the color of her own. She lowered her head a little as she took it. He watched her throat move and the outermost strands of her hair turn from chestnut to fire in the window light and her breasts rebalance themselves with careful serenity. "What was in you came true," he said. "If I closed my eyes I would still see you when you were eighteen and when I opened them I would only see you complete. I'm so happy that I did."

"Are you really?" she said. "It's easy to say now."

"Yes," he said. He stroked her flank but she took his hand and kissed it lightly and put it on his lap where it stayed, even though as against magnetism. "Wait a little, Giovanni. You have not even had a sandwich. My turn to serve. *Foie gras,* I think." He felt it melt upon his tongue, a soft cloud of richness rinsed with tart Champagne. The sun was on his shoulder. Her perfume, the warmth of the day upon her skin, the scent of her loins like the first smell of the sea beyond a cliff made glorious the air he breathed. Somewhere, he was half crying out with lust, but she was right, it could mature.

"Close your eyes," he said. "My choice." He thought, and placed smoked salmon in her. She kept her eyes shut. He refurbished her with *foie gras* and held the icy bottle a millimeter from her nipple, then took it back again—a small event that she would never know. He held a glass to her mouth. She bent forward a little more and he watched her belly float beneath her ribs and pucker in its middle. A sunbeam had put its hand upon her haunch's outermost curve and was moving stealthily. *That is as fast as time should move,* he thought. *That is all the time we need.* When next he brought the glass to her mouth he did it awkwardly, on purpose, watched the Champagne dribble down her chin, then wiped it gently.

Then she opened her eyes and said quietly, "Why did you not come and see me in the hospital? Even if we were very young and stupid, we had been each other's life for a while. You wouldn't disagree with that." He felt a wave of cold from far away wash over his chest and down his thighs.

"There were no skid marks," he said. And: "We had been each other's life and you wanted to take it to the grave. That's what I thought then. Later I decided I was probably wrong, but that was later. I was very angry. Now you know it."

"You were wrong," she said. "You were. You left me alone with the devils." She put her hands palm-open on his chest. He raised an eyebrow and she said, "These are my rules and I can break them." That came with a little smile but it faded quickly and she looked down a considerable time like a thoughtful child. She said, "I wanted to show you how far I would go, and when I had once thought of doing it like that with the car, it seemed cowardly not to. It was very stupid. On the other hand, it wasn't very easy either and it was a lot worse than I expected. Afterward I began to have nightmares about the fire. I mean the fire that didn't happen and that I had never thought about. I used to see myself in it. I haven't had that for quite a while."

He looked up at her in silence; for a moment, as in the garden, he was beyond concupiscence and with the same thought that he had been welded to her forever. Finally he said, "How far you would go where? To what, Gabriella? Why?"

"Away from the dead brambles."

"What?" he said.

But her eyes were not on him at all. They were to his side, as though some other person had come into the room. She said,

"The things that want to pull you down. The dried-out things that want to drink your blood and see you die among them and stay with them. The things that have time and time and time. You know." She spoke as though the new person were of known and obstinate indifference. "The old women with little bowls of soup, the men who stand at the same bus stop every day, they hate us, my love, they want us cold and finished. Because then they're right, you see. We were getting ordinary, you and me back then. The brambles were coming. The car was better than that. Maybe even the fire. But you did not understand, Giovanni. I did it for both of us and then you left me. You left me in the dark. After the hospital my parents sent me away, you know. Out of Rome to an old aunt's castle up in the Adige. You were gone. A lot of people thought I was crazy. I became very obedient; why not? A lot changed after my parents died, of course, but for a long time I seemed to be living in a narrow corridor with empty rooms on both sides. I think I got into the wrong set of rooms in the end."

The cold had intensified and was drenching him. From a corner of his imagination a little twisted figure with a sprightly grin burst out of the shadows and capered a few steps before vanishing. He said as lightly as he could and fastening his eyes upon her breasts for comfort, "Nobody seemed to think us very ordinary then. We seemed to be about one step ahead of the police, as I remember."

At that she laughed and focused on him again, but she made a gesture of indifference that was not convincing at all, and when she put her hand back on his chest her fingers were tense. "I was wrong," she said. "I was actually and genuinely wrong to do it. I was a pain in the ass, but I was very young." Her fingers began to knead his chest, less clearly in affection than to relieve some affliction in themselves. "But the dead brambles are real, Giovanni. They love to wrap you up. You only know you're fighting them if you bleed. That's what I was running from. I couldn't make you understand."

"All you did was take everything away," he said.

But she leaned forward so her breasts brushed against his chest. She reached out and took a peach and held it meticulously halfway between their mouths. "Dessert does not really have to be so formal," she said. "We shall eat this together, half and half, like this. All that other stuff was a very long time ago and I should not have talked about it. I decided that you would have me to lunch because you must spend many hours alone in this dull apartment and now you will have something to remember here. But when we have finished the peach, please make love to me very thoughtfully and kindly because I am not always as cheerful as I seem. No, don't do that yet. First the peach."

aptain Rodolfo Mascagni sharpened each morning the alertness that becomes an officer of the Carabinieri. He sharpened it on his mother-in-law. His wife's mother lived with them and their five children in an apartment that incorporated four boxy bedrooms, a living room, a kitchen, a balcony tangled in clotheslines and scraggly plants, and one bathroom.

Therefore when he heard a grunt followed by shuffling, bumping sounds come through the wall from his mother-in-law's room, he tore himself from the bed, as usual, and hobbled on morning-stiff legs to the door. If she got the bathroom, she kept it.

Outside the door, he fell over a train. The train was shiny wood with a bright-red smokestack, and he had bought it for his youngest son, whom he adored. He kicked it down the hall. This wasted a crucial second and he saw that his mother-in-law, approaching from the left, was closer to the bathroom door than he, approaching from the right. Captain Mascagni employed a ruse. He pointed at the carpet in front of the old woman's feet and shouted, "Watch out!" She did not wear glasses in the morning and she stopped. Captain Mascagni, who had hurt his bare toe, hopped past her and slammed the door. Alone in the hall, she raised her fist at the door, then turned and shuffled, muttering, back. Her curses did not go unanswered. Within, Captain Mascagni had discovered toothpaste in his shaving cream.

He was really no ogre. At breakfast he fixed the train. This was kind, for the kitchen in the morning did not induce leisure. His eldest daughter, Adriana, ten, had just come back with the morning bag of *panini,* sticky rolls, and was arguing with her mother. His wife had made coffee. His youngest daughter, Roberta, four, was standing around stark-naked. The middle children were smearing chocolate-nut paste over bread slices and their faces, all of which were about to leave for school. His mother-in-law had the only convenient chair, where she held a bowl of coffee under her chin and made rootling noises in it while one eye looked at him over its edge with mean and mysterious triumph. The shaving cream? Or just the chair? His little boy, who had a cold, held a railroad car with a broken coupling in each hand, and whined. Mascagni mended the screw.

Though he loved his children, he was not usually this amenable in the morning. But concentrating on the train put off taking up the thought of the carbonized body, with teeth as bright as a crushed rat's, that had entered his life from a car in Naples. Even as he put on his tunic after breakfast he held the thought away by finding, and wiping, a dull place on his shoulder bars.

Mascagni lived near the Via Aurelia, far out beyond the Vatican, in a neighborhood of four-story apartment buildings, supermarkets, cafés with spindly chairs, and sickly saplings in earth that smelled of dog piss. His barracks were in the northern outskirts. Rome's exiguous subway system did him no good at all, but he was obliged to make only one change of bus. They had a little Fiat, but his wife kept it. He could get an official car when needed. As today.

Once on the street, the thought of his family was sweet to him, like the taste of coffee fading in his mouth, though he did not dwell much on either. Rodolfo Mascagni respected small, orderly blessings: the smell of his wife's skin, a moment of sagacity in a difficult case, his son's marvelously light and supple shoulder blades when he sat upon his knee, the taste of well-dressed lettuce after pasta. Just before he was given his medal, lying in the dark of a nearly mortal wound on a hospital bed, it had seemed to him that such things were also holy, more reliably so than the nun beside him. The body in the car from Naples came from the cavern of jeers and misery and dismembered creed from which the shot that wounded him had issued. He feared the cavern, but so far this had made him cautious and implacable, not irresolute.

But his mood was not altogether somber this morning. Interesting lines of inquiry led from the burned body. Also, he had thought of a secure place where the American, Stears, could take him for a relatively expensive lunch with something like a day in the country thrown in. Also, he did not have to wait long for a bus.

On the Gargano Peninsula—ethereal of light, nobly crowned with chestnut—Dr. Fausto Calvetto set down his sack of stone and rested. He had not walked extremely far and his sack was light, but his spine, where pain glowed softly all day long, had heated and sparks of pain flew off it; flames flickered from his pelvis to his neck, he felt the shape of his spine like an abscessed tooth within him, and as he sat he hung on to a weary groan lest it fly from his mouth as a yelp. A drop of sweat from his forehead fractured his vision. He wiped it away and looked down at the selected target, the small town of Monte Sant'Angelo. He saw its thrifty, twisted streets, its patches of cloth on clotheslines shifting in the breeze, the stir around its marketplace, and his spine exulted that Monte Sant'Angelo would soon know grief. He looked at his watch. He had some time to wait.

To the east, beyond the chestnut forests, were the Adriatic and the invisible coasts of Albania and Yugoslavia. To the west, beyond sparse plateaus with rare fields and herds of half-wild pigs, were the lowlands around Foggia and, in the distance, the peaks of the Abruzzi. Beyond the Abruzzi, Rome was a little north, and Naples, a little south. The Gargano headland sticks out of the ankle of Italy like a spur. There were fishing villages below him.

And high above him, out of the forest where the grand curves of chestnut trees sparkled at their edges as broad leaves mirrored the sun, a thin, dun-colored mast emerged. Guy wires extended from it into the trees. It was hung with odd protuberances, like ear trumpets, like salt shakers, all of which faced out to sea. It looked frail and rather comic. Dr. Calvetto looked at it with satisfaction and contempt. It was a United States electronic surveillance post, discreetly ignored by the Italian government, officially and vaguely accounted for as a "relay," and in fact set to spy on communications inside Yugoslavia and Albania. The only road to it led up through Monte Sant'Angelo. Dr. Calvetto checked this road, but it was still empty. He moved carefully. His spine had settled to a dull fire only a shade brighter than the coals that scorched his life. With the tip of his fingers he grasped the hem of his sack.

His findings were not extraordinary. This was a chalk-and-limestone formation. No glories of the earth were here, no translucent drops of the earth's chilled fluids, no flowers of marble or jade. Fossils mostly. He did not care much for them, as a rule. But here one did find the fossils of tiny shells, of delicate, frail crabs, of preposterous screw-shaped creatures, creatures like snowflakes, creatures like comets. He was no naturalist. But with their clammy lives extinguished, their smells frozen in rock, their scurryings fixed forever, the dead little animals were transfigured almost into the perfection of stone. Dr. Calvetto studied them with reserved approval.

Now a movement on the road below Monte Sant'Angelo caught his eye. Abruptly, he dropped the sack, groped for pencil, pad, and stopwatch in his pocket, and endured his backbone's savage lunge. He did not need his binoculars. Three vehicles, all khaki-colored, darker than the rock. A Jeep led. He could see it bounce on the ill-made road and he caught the red of the Stars and Stripes. Last came a lumbering military ten-ton truck. He could hear the motors now. In the middle, like a soft, fat larva, was the fuel tanker. Such was the weekly convoy to the surveillance post. He had observed it three times now. The order was always the same. The time was approximately invariable.

The timing would have to be correct, but it was not difficult. The watcher, who would be where Dr. Calvetto sat now, would see the convoy as it rounded the cliff and also see the road behind it. Dr. Calvetto timed it now. The watcher would now alert the forces down on Monte Sant'Angelo.

Three minutes, four hairpin bends later, the Jeep crawled into the outskirts of the town. That would be the second alert. Dr. Calvetto could see it clearly now. He saw a hand wave from the Jeep and a wave from a shop door in return. The convoy had become a part of life. A minute more and it was in the square, circling the fountain in front of the church. Then the convoy turned uphill, changed gear, and bored into a narrow street that became the mountain road.

At that instant, two weeks hence, Monte Sant'Angelo's fate would fall like a bolt from heaven.

Dr. Calvetto had explained the principle of it to his Libyan clients, though he had not then had the method. "The people principally to suffer should be Italian villagers. The immediate reason for the suffering must be something that the Americans are not supposed to be doing at all. A secret electronic installation that spies on Yugoslavia and Albania and has never been officially declared to the Italians serves that purpose well. The Italian Brigadists who take responsibility for the attack will claim to have known this. Yugoslavia has good relations with most Arab powers, you see, as well as with Italy. The United States will once again seem inept, dishonest, and dangerous both to Italian interests and to innocent Italians. I can promise that this operation will take few resources. What is even more, it will fix the eyes of the Americans on a remote and primitive region just before we begin to do much worse things to them in Rome itself. It will really be rather beautiful."

So it would be, and not for strategy alone. Dr. Calvetto, obliged to quip and fawn through days of pain, Dr. Calvetto with a bag of rattling stones for company, Dr. Calvetto who had known neither trust nor love nor a woman's body, now looked down upon Monte Sant'Angelo and foresaw the day in all its detail. His spine reared like a fiery snake in triumph.

Giovanni Stears sat on a terrace a little way outside of Rome from which the peaks of the Abruzzi, cleared by now of snow, pricked the east. They were about as far from Stears as from

Dr. Calvetto in Gargano, though in the opposite direction. Caught in slow eddies of light, the mountains changed fitfully from brown to drab green to granite. Opposite Stears, Captain Mascagni picked up an unlabeled bottle and poured him a glass of purple wine.

"When my sister got married," said Mascagni, "we drank this from one o'clock in the afternoon until just before dusk. There were no ill effects. So it must be very honest. At least no really ill effects. I had forgotten all about this place."

"I would not have forgotten it," said Stears. "It is much too pleasant."

Which was polite but true. This was a farmhouse with discreet indications of resident chickens and rabbits and geese but with a striped awning over its terrace and turned into a country hostelry, straightforward but not cheap.

"I really should not be seen always running in and out of the American embassy," said Mascagni, "and it is not safe to meet in Rome. Here it does not worry me, so long as we travel separately. Yes, it is very pleasant. In a place like this near Rome, you should have lamb." The menu was handwritten and to some extent unnecessary; rich smokes of roasting lamb, sweet fragrances of chicken, high notes of rosemary rose up from the kitchen and floated briefly over the terrace before the breeze shooed them away. The tables were filling up.

"Indeed so," said Stears. "We were shepherds before we were an empire."

"Excuse me for forgetting that you are slightly Roman," said Mascagni. "Your Italian is rather Florentine." *And it is all one to me,* he thought, *if you order mongoose.*

But Stears reverted to the main, and earlier, topic. "An interrogation that savage, disposal of the body by firebombing," he said, "that does not sound like the Red Brigades to me. It's not the pattern. The gasoline sounds like Mafia. Are you sure of the identification? That the victim was the boyfriend of the man in the building site?"

"No," Mascagni said, "not sure. We can only go by teeth, and he was not of the class to have elaborate dentistry. But I am told that the probability is high. And that interrogation technique is not very Mafia either, though I agree that the gasoline is typical. The Mafia have been known to make men eat their own testicles, but they do not seem to be good electricians. There is not much call for that in Sicily. I agree that none of it seems very Red Brigades." He added with no change of tone, "It seems more like what the CIA taught the South Americans."

Stears, who had abandoned ideas of Mascagni's simplicity, said, "I shouldn't think we had to teach them. And I rather doubt that story, though one never knows. Let us assume that the body was the boyfriend. He seems to have fallen into the hands of a particularly vicious professional or para-professional intelligence service. To me that says 'Arab.' "

"To you everything means 'Arab,' " said Mascagni. "It is your magic word." *He is not easy to shake,* thought Mascagni, *but either this is not very real to him or it is much too real. Ever since we have been talking of this, he has held his wineglass by two fingers.*

"I see so many Arabs," said Stears and patted a thick envelope on the chair beside him. "Tell me about the boy."

But then of course, Mascagni further thought, *a bloody Tuscan would probably hold a piss pot by two fingers. Let alone a Yankee Tuscan in an English suit.* He said, "Tell me why a professional or para-professional intelligence service would choose to go to work by the railroad track in a more or less public place?"

"An emergency," said Stears. "Tell me about the boy."

Mascagni told him. It was a simple story and his attention was less than half on it; just as his choice of meeting place had less than half to do with security or even with a free, prodigal lunch. He wanted urgently to fathom Stears, and at the American embassy he had found him all but invisible. He had divined that the Jaguar in the parking lot was Stears's. Expensive foreign cars being rare in Italy, it struck Mascagni as extravagantly lush, at least as much so as a Ferrari would have seemed to Stears. Out of the corner of his eye, Mascagni studied the cobalt-blue paint, the creamy leather no doubt exhaling opulent scents, and tried uneasily to reassure himself.

Mascagni finished. "We seem to come back to Naples all the

time," said Stears. "That's not the old Red Brigades at all. That was Bologna, Turin, Modena, up there. Surely I'm right?"

"Mainly," said Mascagni. "Not quite so much toward the end. In later days one of the four principal groups was the NAP, the Nuclei Armati Proletari, and that was largely Neapolitan and Calabrian. It bridged the prisons and the universities. We never quite found the cornerstone. One suspected some radical professor at the university, but none of the obvious ones would fit. Because of the prisons, the NAP also stretched into the Mafia. In the end, the boundary between the Brigades and the criminals became difficult to see. That's what interests me about the boy in the car, in spite of the electricity. Maybe we have found a Mafioso who can change a plug. I am having the police search the files for leads in that direction. I do not think we have to look for an Arab."

"If all these corpses are from the Sagatto bunch, they're killing each other off pretty quick," said Stears. "There must be resentments. Perhaps resentments we could find and use. I still say Arab, incidentally, and most of them have more resentments than clean underwear."

"It would be very difficult and we have no leads in that direction at all. Arab or not, which we do not even know, it would be absolutely a question of finding the proper man."

Which it always is, Mascagni thought. *And what of this one?* There was the cavern of misery and hate, of poisoned theories and burned bodies and ragged wounds. There was the true world of work and sufficiency and children. And then there was the painted ceiling. Mascagni knew very little of the nobility and the rich, and what he did know, he distrusted. They seemed to him, whether film star or Duchess, figures of ambiguous smiles, floating prettily on their appetites without conscience or seriousness or remorse. He had dealt with a winsome little Baroness once who had let four Brigadist killers use her house and who had taken pleasure in giving him to understand that she had enjoyed them exquisitely in bed. Between the painted ceiling and the cavern, Mascagni suspected an intermittent and hellish treaty. When he had been asked to take into his confidence an American half-Marchese, he had been appalled. General Della Cappella, whom Mascagni revered, had said, "You are completely right. But the Marchese Ugolino-Ferrara is one of the good ones. In the war, when I was a boy, I carried messages for him. Perhaps the nephew is all right as well. Who knows? We do not have a great many choices." Mascagni did not know yet.

"You have brought the complete listing of American installations in Italy?" said Mascagni.

"Yes," said Stears, "it's all here. It just occurs to me that whoever interrogated and killed that boy is not from Naples. At least he has no base there now. He used that railroad gallery because there was an emergency and that was the safest place he could think of. So it is somebody not based in Naples who knows Naples rather well."

"That is not a bad point," said Mascagni. "Four hundred and twenty-six American installations, did you say?"

"Four hundred and twenty-eight," said Stears. "There was a submarine magnetic-field-detection device somewhere on the Isole Egadi that everyone had forgotten about. Maybe they've died of old age there. Also a villa full of paintings belonging to the State Department."

"Dear God," said Mascagni. "And all of these have to be supplied, so there are American trucks and Jeeps roaming around all over Italy. And all the houses where these people live, and no doubt they have children who go to schools. It is a nightmare, Stears."

"That is why we have to look for the root," said Stears.

"Indeed so. And meanwhile the root may be looking at all this," said Mascagni. "Have you begun with your Arabs? Apart from talking about them."

"I have done what I could," said Stears. "There are a lot of sightings. We are too close to the baseline to know what they all mean. Take a look."

Mascagni looked. The waiter moved toward them. Mascagni skimmed the range of the reports. He looked at Stears, surprised. "I find this quite remarkably impressive," he said.

"I would find it more so," said Stears, "if it had any shape. So far it doesn't."

The waiter stood behind them. Stears gestured politely to his guest.

"Certainly the lamb," said Mascagni. "And first an artichoke."

"The roast chicken," said Stears. "With lettuce. Also an artichoke."

The waiter withdrew. Stears said to Mascagni in half-apology, "For me, the weather is getting too hot for lamb."

Damn him, he is right, thought Mascagni.

"The sort of garbage that we know," said Stears, "is which Cultural Attaché is late for the German opera."

Stears sat in the Jaguar while Mascagni drove down the drive in a large brown Fiat, with no marking except the starkness that government cars achieve even in the finish of their paint, and turned with a spatter of gravel toward Rome. Stears turned the key. The day was hot, turning from the cordial bake of midday June to a midsummer oppression. He pushed switches: up went the windows, over came the roof, eager zephyrs whirred out of the dashboard and chased Italy away.

But at the end of the drive he looked right instead of left, to the Abruzzi Mountains and not to Rome. The peaks stuck up into their own ether, framed by a sky thin and clear enough that the air over Rome looked like a dirty river. He turned the wheel toward them, though keeping his foot on the brake. A moment's longing brought back the high plateaus with beeches and oaks in fields of cattle with woolly fur, the long ribs of gray rock and the red roofs of the villages. Mustaches on the men the color of the rock. He had not been there in twenty years. He felt the sun on the walls of Guglielmo Orsini's castello east of L'Aquila and saw Gabriella lie on the roasting parapet and check the distribution of her tan. She used to do that with a severe and critical eye and then roll over on the parapet, whose edge plunged a hundred feet below. One could not say that it was dangerous, but it always made him hold his breath.

And now he shivered and felt tightness in his chest, for he had caught her eye and it was not across twenty years of memory. It was gone too fast to see clearly.

He needed the Abruzzi. He looked at his watch. He had no time. Perhaps he could make calls. An Alfa stuck behind him lost patience, crowded his rear and flashed its lights. He did not have time.

He turned left, away from youth and the clear Abruzzi into a widening highway, thickening air, and a musk of guilt and doubt and lust and pity quite different from a girl's sweet sweat. At that, a thought struck him in Gabriella's voice. It was never simple and sweet. You only tried to make it so—and what I am asking of you now is ten times what you failed me at then. It startled him so much that he pushed memory hard away and thought of business.

His drive was not unprofitable. He thought his observation about the torturer in Naples sound. It would be useful to re-study the data in the light of possible odd absences. He had not had the manpower to have anyone followed beyond Rome, but the data might at least give clues as to what direction someone had started in. The chance of success even in this one far lead was small, but that was nothing odd. In intelligence one lives by rolling bad dice a thousand times, in this case while a whimsical monster eyed the American sheepfold and slavered. Also he thought of surveillance schedules. One could always think of surveillance schedules.

This lasted until he parked on the Via Boncompagni beside the embassy. He opened the rear door of the car to get his briefcase from the floor. On the far seat was a brand-new shoe box from Franceschini. It had grown familiar, for it had been there three days, but it still had power to comment. It contained Marie-Sophie's special sandals. He picked it up; he would have someone mail it from the embassy. He put it down again; he would have to call for the address. He picked it up; his secretary could call. That was certainly unthinkable. He opened it. Marie-Sophie had nice ankles.

All this greatly intrigued a youth in a third-floor office of Air Yemen who spent most of his days peering with low-powered binoculars over an enormous bilious Fernet-Branca sign at the United States embassy across the Via Veneto. When he got back to the Libyan embassy, he reported to Yussuf ben Baghedi, the Cultural Attaché. "He didn't go into the embassy for a long time," he said. "He sat in his car holding women's shoes and putting his hand in them."

Yussuf had been obliged to spend his lunch hour at a dress show where the Roman nobility smiled and clapped at young women in dresses that a sailor's harlot in her doorway in the casbah would blush to wear. He said to the youth, "I have heard of that act. Every one of these people is a pervert." It depressed him that God endured a world so tainted.

C·H·A·P·T·E·R 9

Stears worked late that evening. He was uneasy, but he covered it with work. He spread out the surveillance sheets from four to seven days before, the period of the abomination by the railroad track in Naples. He noted every apparent departure of an Islamic diplomat or embassy staff from Rome. With most of the embassies this was hit or miss—an Egyptian could easily have slipped away—but the net around those of Iran, Libya, Lebanon, and Iraq was passably tight. He found sixteen absences. Next he brought out four stacks, one for each day and each the bulk of a telephone directory, of daily intelligence factual summaries from Washington. Deep within these were abstracts of global diplomatic and high-official traffic. Eleven of the departures were plausibly explained. Two more had been by air and seemed to have been out of Italy. Those he set aside. There remained an Iranian Second Secretary who had gone off in a car and might have done anything, and a Lebanese consular officer who had flown to Naples at just the right time; the third was a Libyan Attaché who had taken a train in that direction and had next been seen sitting morosely in the opera foyer while the rest of the diplomatic corps enjoyed a whole five-hour German treat. He enjoyed this work. The paper, the flat idiom, the times and names and places hid the horrors that might lurk behind them but did not quash the sense of his own quiet, canny hunting. He scrupulously gave the Libyan no special weight.

His last stop was the cipher room. Thence he had the three identities of the Iranian, the Lebanese, and the Libyan Attaché sent to Washington for deep analysis. He added those of the Iraqi and the other Iranian, though they had probably done no more than fly home.

On Thursday mornings Randall Quincy Beebe, CIA Chief of Station, Rome, briefed his Ambassador. This morning, he had first called in Giovanni Stears. He greeted him by raising from his desk the confidential memorandum Stears had written the night before. "Summarize this," said Beebe, "operationally." It was clear in his voice that he was administering a test, but perhaps with kindly expectation.

Stears said, "First, an Iranian diplomat whom Washington identifies as the brother of a Revolutionary Guard was absent from Rome and not under surveillance between ten and eight days ago. If he had spent the intervening time in Naples, for which there is no evidence whatever, it would have been possible that he assisted at the interrogation and murder of a man whose body was found there burned beyond recognition. The dead man was quite probably the disappeared homosexual lover of another victim whose body was also defaced beyond assured identification at a place within an hour's drive of Sagatto. That death probably occurred on the night of Leipzinger's murder. The lover is known to have written to the police identifying that body. There are remarks in the letter that suggest a probability of involvement at Sagatto. The background of both murdered men supports this, if the identities are correct. They were radical left-wing students. One can construct a scenario in which some other member of the Sagatto gang heard of the contact with the police, hence the interrogation."

"All right so far," said Beebe.

"Second," said Stears, "all the same possibilities apply to a Lebanese consular officer who is definitely known to have been in Naples during this period. He had a reason for being there, a commercial meeting, but he was there for much longer than that required. The meeting could have been scheduled for cover. This Lebanese officer is a Muslim and is known to have dealings with Shiite leaders. However, Washington does not see him as an extreme radical, still less as a murderer. But perhaps that's wrong."

"Indeed," said Beebe. "One never knows."

"Last," said Stears, "a man who is an accredited Libyan diplomat in Rome but was once a member of Qaddafi's personal goon squad left Rome during the same period for no evident reason on a train with the principal destination of Naples. The next night he was seen arriving late for a diplomatic function, the German opera. All the other observations apply to him as well."

"Why do you put him last?" said Beebe. "He's the obvious one."

"Exactly," said Stears. "Because he's what we're looking for. He's convenient. And I was late for the opera once. I couldn't find my bow tie and there were no cabs on Madison. I wasn't killing anybody that night. I swear it."

"Well done," said Beebe. "Still, he's a trained killer, isn't he?"

"Oh, indeed," said Stears. "He's at the end of a loose string of evidence and he fits a ready-made assumption. That's the only thing that's wrong with him. But one still has to note that the Iranian's brother is a Revolutionary Guard and that the only one who was certainly in Naples is the Lebanese."

"Suppose two of them were there," said Beebe. "Or all three."

"Why?" said Stears.

"I agree," said Beebe. "Why? But you would assume, would you not, that the murderer in Naples was also the murderer near Sagatto and was probably one of Leipzinger's murderers as well?"

"I wouldn't assume it," said Stears, "but it's something to think about."

"Good," said Beebe. "What are your intentions?"

"Intensify surveillance of the three subjects. Tighten surveillance, human and electronic, on those three embassies. Notify my Italian connections."

A light frost descended on Beebe's eye. "You will consult with me as to the form of that," he said. "And try and avoid the intellectual temptation of assuming that one of these men has to be the link. There may be nothing here at all."

"That was my conclusion too," said Stears.

Beebe looked at his subordinate hard but then nodded sharply and checked his watch. He said, "I'm due at H.E.'s. We may as well go together, Stears. Your business is top of the list anyway."

Beebe had begun referring to Ambassador Buxhalter as "H.E." of late. Since United States Ambassadors are not styled "His Excellency," one was left to guess whether this was irony or anglicism. Irony had support; rumor had it that Beebe had used "Maximum Leader" among friends.

"I would also ask you to note," said Stears, "that exchanging information with the Italians has already turned up three agents on our Roman list who were patently unreliable."

"I did note it," said Beebe. "It is kind of you to tell me twice."

Yet Beebe was in better heart. For the first time since Leipzinger's death a crackle had come back to his eyes. This morning's pinstripe was navy blue and the jacket parted quite dashingly as he led Stears down the hall. The improvement was general to the embassy. People had begun to speak heartily from doorways again instead of gathering to mutter over desks. Water coolers were busier. Visa business was brisk, always a good sign. The wolf had not been seen for two weeks; there were even suggestions that the hunters had found a scent. Perhaps one could soon think again of picnics.

Something of that sort seemed to be taking place outside the Ambassador's formal office. It was a handsome room with French windows open to a courtyard with climbing roses; this was now full of small children, running and shrieking. But the Ambassador was attending to General Brandt Larsen, the Military Attaché, who had gotten there first. Buxhalter mouthed and smiled a greeting. Larsen gave a crisp acknowledgment with his hand. What with the children, it was necessary to raise one's voice.

General Larsen said, "We've got the Libyans locked up, Ambassador. The battleship *New Jersey* has been added to the escort of our surveillance ship in the Gulf of Sidra. That is now an invulnerable escort. The Air Force has begun regular U-2 overflights of the Libyan Desert—the aircraft carrier *Kitty Hawk* is moving in to protect them. She's waiting off Gibraltar now for an escort enhancement. Between that and the satellites, we'll know it if somebody farts out there. We have been able to ascertain so far that there is absolutely no change in Libyan behavior. They're still staying off the telephone. Those boys are having to keep their heads down. The F-111's know their way to Tripoli and the Libyans know they know it. That's the military picture."

Randall Beebe moved swiftly in behind. He said, "And then, of course, we have the economic sanctions. Embargo on Libyan oil. They have had to re-route four of their tankers from United States ports to Canada. And the selective ban on exports hits them on the head tomorrow."

"Yes," said Buxhalter. "Pharmaceuticals, marine propulsion units, and forest products. Why exactly those? Has anyone told you, Randall? Nobody's told me."

"I believe it's a question of what the United States actually does in fact sell to them. That means toothpaste, outboard motors, and toilet tissue. Their middle class is beginning to use it. Most of the stuff they buy is Japanese, Italian, and Korean, unfortunately."

"Oh," said Buxhalter. "It's certainly a message, though."

"Affirmative," said Larsen. "The *New Jersey* and the *Kitty Hawk* are an awesome sight. Don't fuck with a hungry bear." He spoke through a well-set jaw, but absently.

"Really, Brandt," said Buxhalter, "there are all these children here."

Closer inspection revealed that the larger group of children was dark-eyed and black of hair and had the focused, sharky look of the children of the poor. Their clothes were new and stiff. The smaller group seemed to be American, mostly blond.

Beebe said, "The CIA is also making some progress on the

local front, Ambassador. In spite of Deputy Minister Tasso's reservations, I have found unexpected access to certain Italian intelligence.'' His finger slightly indicated Stears as ''access,'' as one might a keyhole or a telephone. Larsen raised an eyebrow.

''I am glad of that,'' said Buxhalter. ''The local front is important too. I should think a battleship might be easier to keep safe than an embassy, in certain respects.'' In spite of Beebe, Buxhalter turned straight to Stears. ''What is going on, Mr. Stears?'' he said.

But a more ominous note had invaded the prattle from the garden: apprehension from the small blond group, ululation from the Latins. Buxhalter smiled at it benignly and checked Stears.

''My little Sicilians,'' said Buxhalter. ''We are learning that Italy is a divided country, Mr. Stears—the north is different from the south. The north is rich and the south is poor. Oddly enough, the north is Socialist and the south is much better in that regard. I don't understand it. It seems the northern part of a country always attracts Communists. My own belief is that it has to do with magnetic influences acting upon the nervous system. At all events, these little fellows here are poor, conservative Sicilian children from the Roman slums and they are going to come here once a week so that they will grow up knowing that America is their friend. Now they are having a treasure hunt and afterward they get a nice lunch. I am sorry, Mr. Stears; I interrupted you.''

''Briefly, sir,'' said Stears, ''there are possible links between any one of three Muslim diplomats in Rome and a pair of murders that may be linked to the Leipzinger murder. The three diplomats are Libyan, Iranian, and Lebanese. A collaboration seems unlikely. It's very far from conclusive and it's also extremely nasty.''

Outside, the Sicilians had encircled the Americans and now began a drive toward the rosebushes. Stears raised his voice and summarized for the second time that morning. He ended, ''I stress it's not conclusive. Not at all. It's not even sure that anyone but the Lebanese even went to Naples.''

''Oh dear,'' said Buxhalter, though perhaps not to Stears. The

Sicilians had backed the Americans up against the thorns and were going through their purses and pockets, not gently. The Americans were screaming.

"Perhaps we should give them the milk when they first get here, in future," said Buxhalter. "That is another reason why they are coming—to get into the habit of milk. The Italian diet is starved of calcium and that is why things are so overexcited here—all that wine they drink leaches out whatever calcium there is. I had a vision of a conservative South buying American milk and being much healthier and calmer for it. That would have been something to base our Italian presence on. Didn't we always know it was the Libyans, Mr. Stears?"

"We thought so, sir," said Stears. "But this does not confirm it."

Two gondolier waiters burst into the garden from the direction of the kitchen and began cuffing and pulling at the Sicilians. Several little Americans were bleeding quite a lot from the thorns. "A proper breakfast would have been the next thing," said Buxhalter sadly. "Not over-strong coffee and sugar rolls. It's elementary. That's very good, Mr. Stears. The State Department will be pleased to have a link to Libya confirmed." He added confidentially, "The Secretary's been wanting it."

"It's very remote even if it's true," said Stears.

"Right now, the Libyans are not going to move," said Larsen. A blond child had unleashed her little handbag and was smashing it to and fro while blood ran down her cheek. She did considerable damage. "Way to go!" said Larsen. "Look at her."

When the meeting broke up, rather literally, it was a little before noon. Stears left the room and the embassy. He found a cab on the Via Veneto, kept faith with it around the Piazza Venezia, and abandoned it in a traffic jam on the Corso Vittorio Emanuele. Not only was it quicker, it would also frustrate anyone following him in a car.

He walked to the Piazza Campo dei Fiori through the small streets and sudden spaces of old Rome to the Palazzo Ugolino. His uncle had been slipping in the last two weeks: twice he had been indifferent and vague; once, in a sleep so deep that Stears had called the doctor. Concern alone took Stears to the Palazzo Ugolino today. He had no energy for other problems. More than at any time since arriving in Rome, he was oppressed by swift, ugly fears darting in from the shadows. They were able to turn on a dime, lighting at will on his own life or terroristic horrors. Real work, the architecture of undistorted fact, would have helped him; prattle at the embassy did not.

He could think of no good reason for the degree of his nervousness. Leipzinger's death and the corpse in Naples were exceptionally nasty, but it was the nature of his work to deal with jagged acts and alarming possibilities. His uncle's weakness was that of a very old man and did not in fact seem critical.

His own life was doing fine. He had seen Gabriella twice since her picnic on his bed: once for lunch like regular people in a small smart restaurant on the Piazza Navona, once for the whole evening and night at his apartment. These were not extreme encounters. One could even have called them "dates"; he had, and she had laughed. In his apartment, they had held hands on his balcony before falling happily into bed. Sometimes in her manner there was an anxious gratitude toward him that he found odd, but it was not menacing. There were patches of unsafe ground between them, but, given the past, that did not seem inexplicable. In his own life, therefore, he was in a state of sexual excitement and affection that should have been almost precisely that of happiness, at least of the moment. He recognized this; it was just that he didn't dare look at it.

Here, near the piazza, the open market within was packing up and he was crowded against the walls by corrugated vans bouncing noisily and smelling of fish or fowl or flower stalks. It cheered him somewhat. In the piazza itself, up against the column at the eastern end, there were still fluttering avenues of hung dresses and a booth festooned in brassieres like a swarm of butterflies. He stood and watched the market like a tourist. Small, sober enterprises were an invigorating sight. The pavement was strewn with vegetable bits and melting, fishy ice. He walked across to the palazzo.

He waited a long time at the door. The furniture finisher

below was boiling horse-hoof glue, which did not improve the wait. When Luigi came, he had the muddy eyes and bungling movements of a stupid man pushed to confusion, but Stears quizzed him sharply anyway.

"I am trying to take care of the Signor Marchese, Signor Giovanni, as well as everything else," said Luigi. And over his shoulder, with even less grace: "I am only one man."

"Does he know that I am coming?" asked Stears.

"I think so," said Luigi. And then, in shuffling, peeved retreat: "Who knows?"

Stears bent to kiss his uncle's cheek. This was still not natural to him; he did it awkwardly and the Marchese moved his head away. Ugolino-Ferrara's eye was bright, but his cheek was unshaved and smelled unwashed. "Don't do that in an American suit, my boy," he said. "You make a fool of yourself. Why have you not come to see me for two weeks?"

"I have come," said Stears. "Once you were asleep."

"And the other times I was gaga? Well, maybe. Maybe."

"No," said Stears. "You just seemed to be thinking about something else."

"Perhaps," said his uncle.

The French windows to the roof garden were closed, but not shuttered against the sun. Stears was too hot in a summer suit, but Ugolino-Ferrara lay bundled in blankets and gowns and smelled of old age and eucalyptus. His face looked foxy today; this was the partisan with a knife behind the door, not the warrior on the hill. He looked at Stears bleakly.

"Have I come at a bad time?" said Stears.

"Yes," said his uncle. "You make me see my condition." He looked at the rat's nest around him, lifted the edge of it, and seemed to sniff its air. "But that time will not change. I shall soon have to choose between being bullied by a nurse and neglected by a dirty oaf like Luigi. I still prefer the latter."

"You could have a young nurse," said Stears. "A pretty one. Just in the morning. Maybe I could find you an American. How about that?"

"Too noisy," said Ugolino-Ferrara. "Is it lunchtime? Are

you staying? I would like you to stay. I will think about the nurse.''

"Yes,'' said Stears.

"Then call Luigi. He should prepare the dining room.''

"That is much too elaborate,'' said Stears.

"Nonetheless, today he shall do it,'' said Ugolino-Ferrara.

The painted ceiling of the dining room was intended as a scene of naval mayhem: two fleets of galleys engaged around the apex of the vaulting, smoke and debris floating off to the sides; disintegration of plaster had by now made the action confused. Oars appeared at odd angles. Over the pantry door, a fellow in fantastic armor sank to a watery grave. A sail emblazoned with the lion of St. Mark billowed high above the table center; some hasty replastering had severed its mast. The ships were mostly gone, though a prow with beak and banners swept down upon the guests and was soon to split the skull of a drowning slave. The slave looked Muslim. Perhaps it was the Battle of Lepanto.

Below this disturbance, Stears, Luigi, and the Marchese Ugolino-Ferrara entered in small, crippled procession. The Marchese led in a wheelchair, uttering running, though not extremely sharp, rebukes. Luigi pushed and protested. Stears picked up cushions and odd bits of blanket as they fell or were thrown from the chair. Two places had been laid at opposite ends of a table for twenty. Communication between them had been blocked by an impressive porcelain object to do with Jove hurling thunderbolts, a creation either stored there or placed by Luigi in hysteria. Rectifying all this gave the soup, far away on the sideboard, time to chill. The dining room was shuttered, dim, and cold.

But Ugolino-Ferrara rubbed his hands and looked around him with innocent, fierce glee. Though the soup now had clouds of congealed fat floating upon it, he rattled his spoon in it with pleasure. "It is really only my damn broth,'' he said, "but here I can pretend that it is food. Yours is supposed to have some mushrooms in it.'' And then, abruptly: "Luigi, I shall have a glass of wine.'' When the glass was brought, he said to Stears, now seated by his side, "Pour for me, my boy. This is a celebration.''

Stears poured with a flourish. It came to him with tenderness and sorrow that for his once prodigious uncle it was an adventure now to eat at table. He sought a topic outside the house.

"I'm working with General Della Cappella," he said. "With one of his officers. He's giving me a lot of help."

"Good. Good," said his uncle vaguely.

"It is a terrible thing," said Stears, "the worst of the Arab terrorists working in Italy against America."

"I knew Della Cappella once," said Ugolino-Ferrara. Then muttered, "I told you that." He began to ferret around in his coverings, and Stears, who was cold in here himself, offered a selection of the fallen blankets. But Ugolino-Ferrara waved them away and after urgent tuggings produced from the chair a folder creased to the shape of his own thin buttocks. He half opened it, showing photographs within. "Take a look at these," he said.

Stears put the folder beside the soup and sorted through it. There was a jumble of photographs, not new, black and white with crinkly edges. There was a field of stubbly crops edged by a high stone wall, with a pair of horses in the distance, plowing. There was a shot of steeper land taken at an awry angle, a tended vineyard with the ruins of a castello behind. There was a pleasant, disheveled villa with Alfa-Romeos and Lancias of the 1950s in the drive and a gaggle of guests, redolent of luncheon. There were barns and machinery. There was more land. It was all vaguely familiar.

"I think I have been there," said Stears. "Long ago."

"Once," said his uncle. "You were a little boy. That is the estate at Borgonuovo. It is my principal agricultural holding, though the house needs some repair. It brings in a hundred million lire in a decent year. These particular photographs are not important—they are just the only ones I happen to have. What is important is that I have decided that the estate is yours. It would have to go to your cousins Claudio and Ottavio otherwise, and they are bankers who have never given me a moment's pleasure. Or even anger. Besides, they have fat children. They will still get something. Do well by Borgonuovo. Enjoy it."

Stears sat back in his chair slowly. "I am overwhelmed," he

said. "It is ridiculous to say 'Thank you,' but I do not know
what else to say. I am truly overwhelmed. I have to tell you that
I am not certain that this is a good idea."

"It abuts on Farnese land," said Ugolino-Ferrara. "You undoubtedly never knew that. You and your bride will own half
the land between Lucca and Montecatini. I should warn you, it
is full of Communists."

"I beg your pardon," said Stears.

"All the villages have Communist Mayors."

"What bride?" said Stears.

"What bride? Don't waffle with me, boy. It is worse than
lying. You have been to the Farnese's villa, you drive with her
all over Rome. She hangs around you at the embassy. Do you
suppose I think you have not been in her bed? You have broken
your promise to me and to yourself. The last times you came, I
could not see you through the dark of my own anger toward
you. That was how I was gaga, Giovanni. But I have begun to
see the light again. I was looking at it the wrong way. You are
an American and so is she. You are going to divorce your wife
and marry your paramour. I do not approve of it, but that is
what Americans do and it seems to suit them. It is a possible
decision, obviously. She is a handful, your new one, but she will
probably be grateful to you and you could do worse. And it is a
pity to see a Farnese as disorganized as she.

"But you cannot do this as an American functionary, Giovanni, no matter how well connected. You would risk becoming
her poodle one day, whether she wants you to or not. It is for
that that I give you the land." He checked Stears's reply with a
finger. "I have thought further. Never underestimate a senile
mind. Your new woman is going to cause a lot of changes, but
then they usually do. So let us have one more. I will adopt you
and you will have the title too—it is foolish to have the land
without it and your Farnese will at least be a Marchesa, your
Marchesa. His Italian Majesty in what passes for our court in
Estoril will not object—I have already ascertained it. If his father had done what I suggested he would still have his throne,
but that is another matter." Now he raised himself from the
mess of blankets around him and held Stears's eye while his

own startlingly filled with feeling. He held it long enough for Stears to frame the idea that it was not unlike having a wolf lay its head on your lap—there was deep, uneasy affection and there were lots of teeth. Ugolino-Ferrara at last saluted him and quietly said, *"Figliolo caro. Caro Marchese.* We have disposed of Sidgewick and all that at last, I think."

Stears said, "I cannot respond to this."

While his uncle spoke Stears had groped for the dimensions of a gift that was priceless and undeserved, offered with clear title, offered with diffident joy, offered with a joy whose existence revealed a blessing that must have illuminated his life for years, almost unknown to him. He felt his throat swell. For the first time he saw humility in his uncle's eyes and that appalled him. "I have nothing worthy to say," he said.

"Say nothing, then," said Ugolino-Ferrara. "Whatever you say now will be stupid anyway. You only have to do it. You have made most of the choice already. I am only giving it an honorable ending." He raised his chin at that and cocked his wrist. He looked like a duelist's second perfectly satisfied as to the arrangements.

"Think clearly, Giovanni," he said. "You are not a trivial man. If you choose otherwise you should leave Italy, I think, at once and forever."

Stears had dinner outside at a restaurant on the Piazza del Popolo. Crowds and cars with open windows eddied past, the cars slow and amiable here—one could have patted their flanks. He listened to the Roman voices—foreign tourists being part of the accent of a Roman crowd. The walls of the grandest square in Rome surrounded him, four baroque churches as toys for God, fountains, noble space, and steps up to the terraces of Roman pines whose upturned feathered arms told one not to take it all too seriously. He was shaken suddenly with the joy of harmony: the city he could love above all others, the woman of his life found again and of Rome, his own belonging, stamped with a title given with love. It occurred to him only at this moment that a second before he had known that Gabriella had not tried to stop her car, his life had seemed to him as intact as it could be and that it had never seemed so since. Held out to him as a gift was the annihilation of time. Take it, and he got instantly all the benefits of a choice that he had run from twenty years before.

C·H·A·P·T·E·R 10

Gabriella Harriman-Farnese did flowers in the morning. The *orangerie* at the villa was a greenhouse now. Roses and orchids sat on graveled tiers. Freesias and gardenias placed small, intense offerings of scent into the air of moss and water and earth and bark. Grapefruit and avocado trees sent down the shadows of their leaves while their fruit hung in the sunlight. Water moved through troughs from cisterns, causing tentacles of emerald algae to clasp and wave. In summer, the high windows opened in slanting panes whose edges reflected rainbows; sometimes larks or swallows flew in and darted across the painted ceiling like frantic messengers between the Farnese ancestors and the ambiguous angels on puffy clouds above. Sooner or later all these birds tired and fell and were swept up by the gardener. Gabriella turned especially to flowers when the decorated surface of her spirit cracked and she looked out on darkness, void, and blood.

But this was not at first apparent. She sat this morning by a tub of gardenia. She was cross-legged, surrounded by small trowels and clippers, the tips of her fingers were smudged with earth; she wore a green cotton skirt that covered the floor around her. She was working bonemeal into the gardenia.

Her hands, at least, did this. The rest of her seemed sunk in torpor. Her gardener was used to this and had trained himself to slip silently about his duties through the underbrush in sandals like a stealthy savage. Her lovely eyes changed their aim erratically from the trunk of the gardenia to the middle distance to the blade of the clipper on the floor beside her; but their pensiveness did not change in doing this and only her forehead, over which fell strands of chestnut hair, furrowed a little in acknowledgment. One hand, not needed for the bonemeal, drifted to the clipper and ran its fingers along the blade, leaving on the index finger a barely perceptible, not even crimson, line of blood.

The sound of a car came up the driveway, then the car itself was visible through the glass of the *orangerie*. She looked up, but, though her body stiffened as she first saw it clearly, she did not follow it with her eye. Instead, she seemed to sink farther into herself; her gaze sank down to her lap and the movement of her fingers in the earth became aimless.

Very shortly, a manservant, wearing an apron, smelling of polish, and embarrassed to be found so, came to the doorway from the villa. He saw no one and said hesitantly, *"Signora Principessa, scusi."* He got no answer at all. He stood on one foot and then the other and then committed to the empty air: *"Signora Principessa, un certo dottor Calvetto desidera essere ricevuto."* (A Dr. Calvetto wishes to be received.) A far-off gardenia shrub spoke in a low and toneless voice, *"Fatelo entrare."* And then more sharply: *"Grazie, Giuseppe, questo è tutto. Andate pure, tutti i due."* The servant and the gardener, the latter evidently with surprise, withdrew.

She had met Dr. Calvetto in Milan, at a lunch party at a publisher's penthouse. Her presence had been her farewell gift to a Brazilian novelist, the guest of honor, for good behavior during an affair of four weeks. She felt, as she always felt when ending a liaison, like a summer house left alone once again: dark falling early in the rooms, a window rattled by a breeze from the lake grown chill. One became conscious of time. On the other hand, she could look forward to days without making up. She could think with relish of her bed, unshared except by novels and a tray.

Dr. Fausto Calvetto was there. He did not catch her interest, though one could not fail to remark him, until after lunch. He took Cointreau. There was bright sun that day. She saw him hold his glass to the light and turn it as though it were the color only he had poured it for, an ugly little man in a strange private glee. She indicated that he might join her, disengaging herself from the Director of La Scala. The party was at the apex of Milanese chic, several planes below her.

He came slowly toward her with a derisive smile, abruptly bent low, and kissed her knee just below the hem of her skirt. Then sat on a stool beside her chair and posed himself to look sideways up at her with a court fool's simper in which a memory of the Director of La Scala's countenance was not quite absent. She laughed out loud. It happened that lunch had been a bore.

"I have amused the Princess?" he said, the simper still in place.

"You have amused me, Doctor," she said. "Are you from Milan?"

No, he was Sicilian. He taught periodically in Naples. He lived in Rome. They talked.

At a certain moment the Brazilian novelist looked over at her, his eyebrows and his black mustache in identical curves of hurt proprietorship. His shirt was rumpled. He looked hot. Calvetto noticed her displeasure. "In such a man," he said, "passion is like the steam off a horse. And very similarly produced. He is for the simple. You are right to send him away."

She flushed, but his eye had nothing of impertinence. His voice could have come out of the confessional from an old, malicious priest.

This had been three years before.

The Gabriella who received Dr. Fausto Calvetto today was not quite the princess to whom the servants had bowed, though she still had smudgy fingers and, on one, a thread of blood.

Calvetto appeared in the door. It had gotten hotter in the last few days and he wore a white linen suit with a shirt of ivory silk. He carried a Panama hat. In consequence of all this, he looked like a comely and urbane man seen through a fun-house mirror. Gabriella received him standing, her hand upon the white caisson of a grapefruit tree, and her skirt shaken into rough order. She did not extend her hand.

"Doctor," she said, "why did you come here?" Her severity was pretense; it was the tone used to a cheeky lover or, at worst, a rash adventurer. Or was meant to be. The sham did not work. Her body was stiff and inclined backward, as though a shrub in front of her had become full of spiders.

Soon after the party in Milan, he had invited her to lunch. Holding the invitation at her writing table, she surprised herself by saying to her secretary, "Accept." It is true that a university doctor has a dignity that transcends his rank.

On the day, discovering at once that she was the only expected guest, she was at first provoked, then amused, then neither. She asked, in the cool and gracious voice with which she exercised authority, why she was here and why alone with him. "I have no one to put beside you," he said. It was neither flirtatious nor fawning.

"You honor me," she gravely said. It was apparent that none of the dancing steps between man and woman, not even their mimicking, was appropriate to the case.

And that that guaranteed no innocence.

In his rooms, the place of pictures or bibelots was taken entirely by semi-precious and unusual stones, none set, sometimes whole and uncut, sometimes as polished facets with the surrounding rock in place. This display intrigued her, though Calvetto's means were not such that they were opulent: the colors and whorls of agate and malachite which, like the patterns in a kaleidoscope, were always just beyond the edge of meaning, the composure of jade and opal, the cold eye of chrysoberyl. He saw her looking at them once and said without his usual irony, "They are all very different from the stuff they were formed of. They were ordinary once, before they knew terrible things.

They changed deep down in the darkness under frightful circumstances. That is real passion. Such things do not happen up here under the sky." Then his voice refound itself and he went on, "Everybody knows that, of course. And you must have much finer things."

She would have despised him if he had hired waiters with greasy waistcoats to serve. He had done no such thing. Lunch was excellent and simply contrived. His conversation seemed always to lead toward the questionable but to turn back from it at a point she could never catch. Consequently, it kept her always in suspense. The lunch passed quickly. When she left, she said, "I have enjoyed this, Doctor," permitting a warmth in her voice and a smile to acquit him of audacity.

Today, Calvetto stood still, smiling with bright eyes. Suddenly he turned his back so that the white suit flickered. He shut the doors to the villa. They were double doors and they shut *click, click,* like scissors snapping; half-noticed sounds of housekeeping ceased and sounds of dripping water, a beetle, and bird wings trapped against the ceiling swelled.

He turned again and came down the three steps, his limp making this look like a merry prance, and came up close to Gabriella. He snatched at her hanging hand and then, moving to exaggerated courtliness and leisure, kissed it. He was Sicilian enough to manage this farce well. *"Cara Principessa,"* he said, "first I wrote to you discreetly in the city. Your Grace did not deign a reply. At the opera you left me with such haste that I had to wonder if the building was on fire. I pine for your company. You're not trying to hide out here, are you, by any chance?" Calvetto's breath was of an expensive mouthwash contending with garlic and very nearly beating it.

"I don't hide," said Gabriella.

"I'm sure you don't," he said. "Look." He reached into his pocket and drew out a soft small pouch. He loosened it and shook four stones into his hand. "Quartz with a flaw of copper sulfate," he said. He was much shorter than the Princess, and when he held it up to her his hand was at the level of his own eyes. "Like a diamond with a purple curtain inside. This is sulfur too, but its own color. It looks like a sun in the rock but it is the blood of volcanoes. Then two lovely marbles, one like jade, one like *oeil de tigre*."

"I am not interested," she said. "Why did you come?"

She had fallen into the habit of visiting Dr. Calvetto, sometimes for no more than tea, not much less than once a week when she was in Rome. These days acquired a different color from the rest, a stronger one. One day she surprised herself by remembering more clearly that she was to have tea with Dr. Calvetto that afternoon than that she expected to consummate a romance without much promise that night.

One afternoon he asked her lightly to do him a favor. Would she take a package to an address on her way home? This, she felt, presumed; she bridled more than a bit and asked rather stiffly where. He mentioned an industrial slum in the direction of the Tor Sapienza on the far side of Rome and an address that appeared to be an apartment far down in the alphabet on the fourth floor. She looked at him for the clue to the joke. Then she looked at him astonished.

"But you will have to change clothes," he lightly said. "I have them all ready." He took from a chair what she had assumed to be some kind of cushion and held out to her a bundle of denim things with a cheap blouse and what seemed to be a pair of shoes wrapped up in it. "You can change here," he said. "It's a dangerous neighborhood for a person like you." It took her a moment to decide whether to laugh or slap his face. Meanwhile he said, "Perhaps too dangerous. Perhaps you should not." This time his eyes did move. A veil of disinterest fell across them.

She undressed then and there, confirming herself by daring him. He watched without apparent feeling, then stepped forward and passed his hand up the inner surface of her leg. She drew in breath and was dismayed to know it, for it marked her horror that she wished he would go farther. For his part, he stepped back as though finding a device without flaw.

As she left in her new clothes, he took a scarf and carefully covered her hair.

She carried out the errand. She resolved to have no more dealings with Calvetto. The circumstances of the episode repelled her.

She went to him at his invitation the next week. He had her recount to him the whole delivery. Her rehearsed intention had been to answer flippantly, but the thing so fascinated her that she could not stop herself from telling every particular. The building had been filthy. She had stepped over two Turkish laborers in a stupor on the stairs. When she knocked at the apartment door she had been let brusquely into a tiny hall and then felt over for weapons by an expressionless Arab. Only then had she been let into another room where there were three more Arabs. One took the package and said, "A message?" Then she was sent away. Behind this new self she had watched all this, fascinated and appalled. For this herself that was not Gabriella there could be no degradation, only experience as bright and sharp as a cut finger.

This must have shown in her manner of recounting it, for Calvetto, who had never more than kissed her hand, now patted it.

"You did well," he said.

She asked, "What was in the package?"

"Explosive," he said.

She opened her eyes wide. He patted her hand again. Then added, "If you had thought it was explosive, would you have dared?"

She looked into the slate eyes and saw that the question was serious and with consequences. So she shivered as she looked at him with chin high and said, "What I do I will do whether it is dangerous or not. I am not a coward."

"I knew that from the first, Princess," he said.

The next time he was dressing her and covering her hair he said, "We need a name for this new woman we are creating, you and I. Have you thought of one?"

She frowned as she examined the contents of a frayed straw shopping bag she was to carry and absently shook her head.

"We'll call her Rosa," he said.

. . .

He still held out his hand toward her with the four stones. He said, "But, Rosa, they are special. They are from the hills around Sagatto. I found them when I was scouting."

"Sagatto was horrible," said Gabriella. "It was shameful."

He did not seem to hear and continued to look into his hand, but with fading rapture. "All quite valueless, but lovely. Just like your Grace."

"I have realized what this really is," said Gabriella. "I will do no more."

He put the stones away and drew the pouch tight. "Squeamish?" he said. "Or scared? Or both? Not arranged to your Grace's liking? Not even to Rosa's?"

"I want no more of this," said Gabriella. Though she was still standing, she had sunk back toward her torpor in front of the gardenia and this made her voice sound supplicating, with no force but repetition. She overtopped Calvetto, but only as a big, puzzled girl in front of a sprightly teacher.

"The Princess is no longer amused," said Calvetto. "Fold up the scenery." He came even closer to her, raised up his hands before her face and made a gesture as of a master of revels dismissing minions. *"La commedia è finita."* He snapped his fingers.

"You shit," said Gabriella, unsurely and in English.

"Sit down," said Calvetto. She did not move and he said. "Behind you." She did not move and he poked her in the stomach, not hard but with stiff fingers. So she sat down. This was on a rough marble slab beside the blank wall of a cistern. Convalescent orchids trailed down from above and the slab was enveloped by boxed magnolia, bloomless and dark. He squatted in front of her with his Panama on his knee.

"Your courage is your beauty, *carissima,*" he said. "It is the light of your eye, the flower of your skin. It is your bearing. It is worth suffering for a little. Lay it aside and you begin to wither. Don't do that to the world." She was not looking fully at him and he reached up and fiercely shook her chin. "What's wrong with you?" he said.

"At Sagatto . . ." she began.

"At Sagatto," he said, "a man was shot without anesthetic

two minutes before he was going to die. I have heard all about that objection. It is quite common in battle for men to be wounded without anesthetic. Are you suddenly frightened that it will happen to you?''

"I said I was disgusted," she said, "not frightened."

"Good. Because next time you will have to hold your ground for a while so others can escape. You at one point and Alfredo at another. You will hold the most exposed one. It is what I came to talk to you about." He patted her reflectively but impersonally on the lap. "It will be quite something. It should be worth a month of lovers for you."

"There will not be a next time," she said. "Please understand that. This is finished. I was willing to be a warrior once. Never a butcher." Her voice was a very fair imitation of her own and she even tried to smile. "Your treatment is over, Doctor."

"Why?" he said. His hands moved from her lap and gripped her knees, not kindly.

"You've tricked me. You've used me."

"Dr. Calvetto has used a Farnese! He has tricked a Harriman! What a crime! And what a stupid lie!" His hands rose deliberately to her breasts and hovered by their tips. He looked her closely in the eye while he caught the cotton over the nipples with hooked fingers and meanly squeezed. Her eyes widened but she did not move.

"Do better than that," he said. "Here is the truth. The Princess was bored. I gave her the opportunity of participating in serious matters connected with political evolution"—he had slowed his voice while he held her—"so that the Princess, who cared nothing for this, could get a sexual frisson out of her aristocratic courage while she shot at people and risked her skin. Now she is bored again, so she has been used. Is that better?" He stuck his head abruptly forward and scrutinized a face that, in fact, was dissolving in affliction. He did not let her go. "Or, perhaps"—he affected revelation—"perhaps Leipzinger counts as a gentleman. A Harriman might know him. Does that make the difference?" He looked at her closely again but now smiled gently and said, "I know you so well, Gabriella. You don't have to preen to me. You don't have to fascinate. Spoiled bitch. You don't have to make an opera of your appetites. Slut in a palace. We know how I see you, don't we? And we know I can forgive you. Just answer me the truth.''

She whispered, ''You are driving me mad.''

His fingers slowly relented on her breasts but stayed crooked in front of them. ''How is that, Gabriella?'' he said.

''I have dreams,'' she said. ''I wake up crying. I scare myself awake.''

''Many women do that,'' he said.

''I am covered all over in blood. Later it is sweat but when I wake it is blood. I am talking to someone and blood pours out of his stomach like the General. Black blood. I close the doors and windows so the servants do not hear me in the night. It is worse since Sagatto.''

''A little stress,'' he said. ''It is common in exposed lives. All of the comrades have to face it. Poor Gabriella! There is so little in her. It is such a pretense. I am sorry for your nightmares.'' He patted her gently on the neck. ''I am the one person who sees you as you really are. It is lucky that I came.''

Gabriella trembled suddenly. He said softly, ''Repeat your lesson, Gabriella. The first one.'' She flushed and lowered her eyes. He leaned forward so that his face was almost touching hers. ''Say it now. Say it because you believe it. Then we can talk about what is best for you.''

From the beginning, she had enjoyed her beauty with him, enjoyed using it kindly. His deformity made her beauty hum within her, and excited her, for in his company her beauty would come to no animal purpose. With him she felt her body like an angel's painted on a vault high over the head of an adoring, afflicted mortal. Drawn on by the asepsis of his eyes, she found it easy, in this immaculate state, to recount to him her traffic with men. This was first in light allusion, then, especially when newly in love or loss, in increasingly compulsive detail. She watched his face closely. There never came the snicker or moistened lip that would have cut this off in her at once. It was an unburdening not to be thought of with any other man and different in kind from the slightly clammy reassurance and rivalry of such memories with her not very numerous girlfriends. In the end it became a pleasure to itself.

She would find herself, elegantly and demurely dressed as she always seemed to be with Calvetto, looking into those slate eyes and recounting in modest vocabulary the failings in technique of a fading lover. The telling was often more absorbing than the event. She found herself once drawing in breath and pressing her bosom to herself as she spoke. Not a worm of salaciousness stirred in Calvetto's face. So that was all right, too. It was like one's own mirror. Like a mirror, he always asked the proper question. His gradual ownership of her crept comfortably over her like warm, stale water. She was much too Roman to find any pleasure, of itself, suspicious.

She whispered, "Only Dr. Calvetto sees me as I am." He nodded and she went on. "That is why he is harsh with me. Other men see only a body to climb on top of, they do not see me, they see only their own lust. That is what they admire and love. They do not care for me, they care only for their loins. Only with Dr. Calvetto am I more than a prostitute on the street. Only Dr. Calvetto cares for Gabriella. Only he can make me more than that. Only he gives me tasks."

"Do you believe that?" he said.

She nodded. He patted her very gently on the cheek. He folded her hands over her breasts. "There," he said. "Now you can take away the hurt I gave you. Take it away yourself. You hide nothing from me. Let me see you do it. There. More, as though I were one of the men who slobber over you, who were all you had before I began to care for you. Show me what you show everybody else, take down your dress top. Do it now. Good girl. It really is quite pretty there, quite pretty, is it not? Is the hurt all gone? Shall I give you some more? I think so. Lean closer. See, I touch you only with my nails. Gabriella is so brave. No, your hands will not go back there. Take up your skirt. Take it up completely. Take those off. Yes, but I do not want them near me. Now let me see. All that so many people want of Gabriella. Almost all she was before I made her more. Put your hand there. You may put your other hand back upon your breast. That must be very nice for you. I will take the other breast myself and this time I do not let go. So Gabriella has pleasure and pain together, does she not? There, show me more. This is how it should be when you are fighting with the gun— one part is wonderful, one is pain. I know what Gabriella needs, I see all of her. Do not cover that, show me. Would she like it if I made her stop? It does not matter to me. If she stops I will take my nails away at once, do you hear that, Gabriella? But she does not stop. It is like that with the more important thing she does for me, with the gun. If she stopped, there would be less suffering but there would be very little else. There, it seems that it is worth it. I know everything that she needs. See, Gabriella, you need not be shy. I make you do it but it is for you. Say Yes! Say Yes. Say Yes again. Ah, Gabriella, I believe you mean it.''

He released her. He stood up abruptly. He looked down upon her shoulders, which were folded over her thighs, all surrounded by the skirt like a limp green leaf. Now that she could not see him, his face changed as though springs had released inside it. The bright malice became wistful, a monkey's wise misery, and even when he hooked his finger under her chin and pulled her face up to look at him his expression was not harsh.

"I shall need you in two weeks," he said. "You will be under orders for forty-eight hours at least. You will be working with Alfredo. Things are moving toward a climax and you cannot desert your comrades now. Roberto died last time and I cannot use his friend. You understand this, Gabriella? You will be ready on the evening of Thursday after next one. You will be picked up in the city."

She nodded almost invisibly and he let her turn her face away. "In a few months, matters may move to a different phase," he said. He began to move, then stopped and drew the little pouch of stones from a pocket. He dropped it on the slab beside her. "These were for you," he said. "I brought them for you."

He walked toward the door, then stopped again and turned— a pretense of casualness, though his audience was not watching. "Another matter of importance," he said. "I have found out that the Americans have imported some sort of special officer to

C·H·A·P·T·E·R　11

Alfredo, the gunman, watched the American convoy. After the climb from the Adriatic up the flank of the Gargano Peninsula to the village of Monte Sant'Angelo, after the sharp turn into the piazza, it moved across the front of the church hardly faster than at a walk. Though only of three vehicles, the convoy was as long as the church and higher than the fountain in front of it. The diesels in low gear drowned the talk in the open shops around the piazza. At this moment the three Libyans, the officer and the rocket team, concealed since dawn on the roof across the square, would be ready to go.

Nonetheless, the convoy was bovine, not warlike. The two American soldiers in the leading Jeep stretched in the sun. One turned around to grin at some clowning little boys. The high, stained bumper of the truck advanced with such stalwart awkwardness that two old men with chins no higher than the wheels completed their daily ceremonious greeting before stepping from its path. The mouth of the alley that led from the piazza to the road farther up into the hills was cool and dark in front of the Jeep and seemed much too narrow for the trucks. As Alfredo watched, the grocer by the alley corner bethought himself and their embassy who is supposed to work with the government against us. He is CIA, of course. Find out what you can about him. His name is Stears. Giovanni Stears. Evidently he has Italian connections. This may be important. He was brought very suddenly from London and we should regard him as a special enemy until he proves himself ineffectual, like the rest. You are the best for this. He might be very dangerous to you eventually. On the other hand, just now the shoe is on the other foot; he will have no suspicions of the Princess Harriman-Farnese, so for now you can be very dangerous to him."

He looked at her closely. Her head was turned toward him and her eyes were open. She neither nodded nor spoke, but he appeared satisfied. He climbed the steps, bobbing and twisting with his limp. He shut the doors softly behind him.

Sometime after he was gone, she rose slowly to her feet and drew the top of her dress around her. She went to the cistern and plunged in her hands, then let them hang in the water. It was almost perfectly quiet and it was possible to hear a swallow brushing across the ceiling and knocking against the glass.

moved a crate of melons and a box of figs a little to the right, out of the way. Alfredo, the leader, would hold his fire until the Jeep and the tanker behind it were in the alley.

Alfredo turned his eyes to the tanker now. It was close enough that he caught a rich smell of carbohydrate as the battery of valves and taps along its side lumbered past and he saw the paint flaking on the cautionary, stylized flames. It came to him with momentary surprise that these vehicles of the imperialist army were by no means new. The smell of fuel made the thought of the rocket bursting within it disturbingly real, and Alfredo felt a slither of nausea in his throat.

Now he looked again at the truck, this time at its passing rear. The Jeep was entering the alley. The moment of attack would be when Alfredo opened fire into the truck's inside. He saw the faces of two young servicemen within. Secure in his invisibility, he made himself see them wholly, for to kill blindly was against his ethic. One chewed gum behind soft and solemn lips. The other considered the church facade with drowsy pleasure and hooked his fingers around the tailgate to lean out and see more. The tanker entered the alley. Alfredo, as always when looking through a gunsight, squeezed up his nerves and braced his soul against the recoil of judgment. He held it, endured it, and relaxed.

He checked the stopwatch.

Dr. Calvetto watched him across the café table. "One could hardly deny that the situation is perfect," he said.

"It is advantageous," said Alfredo. "Are you sure that the Libyans can get onto that roof?'

"Yes," said Calvetto. "The building is deserted at night. As for the American soldiers, they might as well be in bed asleep."

"The enemy's preponderance of force itself produces a sense of security which may be used against him," said Alfredo.

Dr. Calvetto barely looked at the trucks. Instead, he kept his eyes on the black-and-white television set with a cracked grille above the bar in the deep, dim café across from the church on the piazza of Monte Sant'Angelo. The front was open wide and a breeze brought in smells of cured anchovies and sometimes grains of dust. A woman was expounding on the course of a trial in Palermo in a voice that set the grille to vibrating like a blue-bottle at each point of emphasis.

Dr. Calvetto knew that Monte Sant'Angelo had had one previous crash with history. In 1544, a raid by corsairs serving the Turk had been repulsed here after two days of unimaginative slaughter ending with the ruse of pouring barrels of oily anchovies down a scaling ladder to make it treacherous and the intervention of Sant'Angelo with a wind. A frieze over the north door of the church depicted the anchovy incident, though the fish involved looked more like dolphins and were leaping vigorously considering their pickled state. A local sauce was called *di acciughe dei corsari*. Dr. Calvetto took pleasure in the thought that his day would be remembered at least as long. The corsairs with scimitars had been bad. The Libyans with rockets would be a good deal worse.

"Don't look too interested in the Americans," said Calvetto quietly. "Any outsider attracts attention here, though no doubt me more than you. Do you have any objection to the operation now?"

"Only to the withdrawal," said Alfredo. "The Gargano Peninsula is easily isolated."

"Indeed so. I will show you that phase next," said Calvetto. "But remember that there will be total confusion. There will be a burst of gunfire—that is you—and then an explosion and fire. Complete disorientation. It is most unlikely that anyone will see the rocket. Nobody will know what to look for—he raised his hand for the waiter and ordered refills of a tiny glass of dark-brown bitters and a cup of coffee. He took a third bite from a sweet biscuit, changing its shape from a crescent moon to a shark's tooth. Alfredo drank beer without enthusiasm. Calvetto indicated it. "That was foolish," he said. "Beer is not that common here. Another grain to lodge in someone's memory." He continued in the same mild tone, "Many Italians will be killed, some quite cruelly. Fire is not a pleasant thing."

"Yes," said Alfredo.

"It is true that the Libyans will actually fire that shot. It will not be you."

"That is irrelevant," said Alfredo. "The operation is valid or it is not."

He sat in silence, his face drawn tight, but his shoulders slowly sagged as though his self-trial in the faces of the young Americans were consuming him from within. Then his scrutiny began to move—over the wall of the café, over the photographs of the local football team, over the pile of racing papers by the bar; it moved with increasing truculence out into the piazza, where the market had comfortably resumed, and by the time it caught up with the back of the priest's soutane as it disappeared through the church door under the saints, Alfredo's eyes were positively strutting. He said abruptly, "All this Italy must go."

He said it in a mutter, but as though in validation. "These villages moldering like old wedding cakes. Decay, ignorance, and malice under the armpits of Mother Church. Who can think in a place like this? Dear God, a nation admired for its waiters and cracked plaster. I hate these places. That is why I choose to live in the modern proletarian quarter. There the ugliness is stripped open and there for all to see. Capitalism became too greedy in our day, too greedy for its own good. These damned saints and fountains hide the injustice and cruelty of a thousand years in rotting heaps all over Italy. Burn it. Burn it."

Calvetto lightly smiled and said, "Burn quickly, quickly? Before another American can come and snap a photograph? Finish your glass or leave it. We have seen this part."

"It is not the people's fault," said Alfredo. "They are only the poor rubble in which the lies breed. They should not have to suffer. That part disgusts me. But they will always suffer." His gaze had fallen to the floor and his voice came from a throat too small for it.

But Calvetto popped from his chair, walked to the bar and paid. His head was little higher than the counter and its shadow on the zinc top was round and dark, like a waggish loaf of bread. Having paid, he put on his hat and walked straight out. Alfredo followed behind. Under the sun of the piazza he looked at the ground and held himself as though against the cold.

A hundred meters away they reached Calvetto's car, which was an excellent brand-new Lancia with a driver's seat built especially for him. The Libyans paid quickly and well. It was now hot. They had left Rome early in the dawn, before the traffic, when Rome—as Calvetto had proposed with enthusiasm and Alfredo received in silence—recovered a certain classicism, for both marble and the Roman pine, did one not think, were essentially creatures of the dawn and sunset. Thus it had been cool. Their way wound across the high Abruzzi where Calvetto had delighted in the sweetness of the Lancia on its first real outing and the mercy of his seat, in which, for the first time, the shaft did not spin through his spine. They had reached Monte Sant'Angelo at mid-morning—but here it was eight hundred meters above the crinkly Adriatic, which kept early July at bay and allowed Calvetto to enjoy the electric sunroof and the murmur of breeze that made conversation with Alfredo unnecessary. Now, after the café, it was finally hot and the nice-smelling leather seats were sticky. Calvetto therefore had the almost brand-new pleasure of directing the electric windows up, not down, and switching on the air-conditioning. Alfredo noticed suddenly that the car was expensive and added stiff censure to pervasive gloom. Since Alfredo was tall, with a thin neck, and Dr. Calvetto drove very close to the wheel and was short, the effect was of a frog driving a peevish goose.

Calvetto drove west out of town. They formed part of tourist traffic, which would be dense in August but now pulsed lightly. The road wound and was narrow but had been improved and was well-surfaced. Three hundred meters beyond a roadside farmhouse that had been turned into a filling station and marked the end of Monte Sant'Angelo, Calvetto pulled over into a space surrounded by a stone wall and olive trees. Beyond, the road curved again, the farmed land ended, and small flocks of sheep wandered like clouds in the distance over the moor. The road could intermittently be seen looping its way to a higher point, where it divided.

"This is Rosa's part," said Calvetto. "She will protect the withdrawal."

He felt his breath grow tight. Within him Gabriella's glory had been freshly painted by his time with her two days before. Her splendor was all his. It struck him again with awe that he, neuter and marred, had formed such a warrior goddess of vermilion passions. God had made no more of her than a conventionally promiscuous great lady.

He got quickly out of the car and crossed to the stone wall, where he sat. Alfredo followed in due course, but stood. Calvetto indicated the road to Monte Sant'Angelo as though offering it to Alfredo.

"Confusion," he said. "When you yourself have emptied your magazine at the Americans and the Libyans have shot their bolt, you will all run from your hiding places. You will not have been clearly seen. Your car is fifty meters from your hiding place, not much farther for the Libyans. There has been a terrible explosion. A fire is raging. Many are already dead. Some Americans will be firing, no doubt, but these are hardly front-line troops and they will be totally dumbfounded. The car is out of their line of fire, so you have only to fear a wild shot while you are running. It is not a big risk. The two local police, the *vigili,* have not even reacted yet, of course, even if they are both still alive. So far it is very simple."

"It is never simple," said Alfredo.

"However, simple as it is, someone will see four men hurry into a car and rush off on this road," said Calvetto. "That is where your trouble begins. You are on a promontory where only three small roads lead out."

"Exactly," said Alfredo.

"The Libyans leave by boat. They have only to get down to the coast, which they will do long before the Carabinieri from the mainland arrive. They will meet a freighter at sea. Your case is more difficult."

"Yes," said Alfredo, with satisfied gloom.

"There will be pursuit. Perhaps not perfectly organized at first, but probably quick. It will be very difficult for you to shake it off and it will eventually drive you into the incoming forces. This is where Rosa comes in."

"You have said that," said Alfredo. His manner to Calvetto, like the manner of Alfredo's discouraging pupils to himself, never rose quite to open challenge, nor was it ever agreeable.

"She is the ambush. This is how it works. Three hundred meters around this bend, there is a wide area by the road. While you and the Libyans are in Monte Sant'Angelo, two cars with appropriate documents from different parts of Italy will be left there. There will be appropriate driver's licenses and documents as well. It is good to have generous resources. You will go as fast as you can to that point, where you will separate and change cars. Pursuit will no doubt be close behind. The pursuit will come past this very point here where there will be a lady in her car. She is getting out, because she is understandably concerned by all the racket. The lady is Rosa. She has a machine gun. She uses it very well. The pursuit goes no farther. Do you understand?''

Alfredo screwed up his eyes as though seeing it with pain. ''Yes,'' he said. ''That could work.''

''After that, you simply drive away, no hurry. You meet the Carabinieri coming in. They stop you. 'Yes, something terrible seems to have happened—you are not quite sure what.' They have no reason to hold you at all. An Italian Brigadist group takes responsibility, stating a Libyan connection. And that is perfect. It means that, because of American meddling, the famous Libyan terrorists are now attacking Italy, which they never did before. Simply perfect.''

''It will be quite dangerous for Rosa,'' said Alfredo.

''It is her role. It is what she must do. She is equal to it.''

But Calvetto stopped. For warmth and sweetness poured suddenly through him, poured like syrup around his heart and lungs as though the sun-warmed stone he sat on had flowered and embraced him. He found the concreteness of it almost unbearable. Rosa, his Princess, his Gabriella, would touch the stone of this very wall, her thighs might vault it, this stone might stand between scorching bullets and her flesh. He saw, shaded by these trees, Gabriella rise up with her rifle beside the road as the pursuing cars bore down; her danger bewitched him and he felt her courage flow through her spine, her flesh, his bowels. He saw the tints of her skin, he heard the intake of her breath. He had a climactic, racking vision of her body lacerated and bloody with wounds. Flooded with tenderness and excitation, he almost cried out loud at the glory that her life and hazard bestowed upon him. He felt that his face was flushed and observed that Alfredo was looking at him with surprise. Calvetto added quickly, ''It is a fact that she has always been extremely lucky. That is something to count on.''

"She needs backup," said Alfredo. "A second gun. Maybe Maurizio from Naples. Even without his friend, he would be steady enough with Rosa. He has a regard for her."

"Maurizio may not be available," said Calvetto. "I will see."

He walked back toward the car. He felt drained, but sweetly so, and he treasured the splendor of his vision all across the swooping moors to the lowland. For once, he drove in silence.

C·H·A·P·T·E·R   12

Now in July, the feet and ankles on the Via Lucullo that constituted all the view from Stears's office window were, if female, mostly stockingless and in sandals. A pair of perfect calves, heels burnished in Ferragamo crocodile and scorning the street, were visions offering quick joy and speculation. Sometimes they whispered to Stears, "Marchese!" and sometimes, hopefully, "Gabriella!" though none of them turned out to be hers. Within, there was the appearance of a prospering operation. Maps had multiplied, two gray strong-box filing cabinets had been moved in, plus a third full of medium-denomination lira bills, limp but nicely illustrated. The telephone rang constantly, and there were six boxes of pins, in different colors.

However encouraging this scene, Stears was often away from it, stopping, in a manner well short of official, and balanced between professional and merely pleasant, at the offices of various Italians. Ugolino-Ferrara had given him a graybeard high in the Italian foreign service. Stears called upon him once or twice a week like a dutiful young relative and was entertained with preternaturally boring stories about the graybeard's pig-sticking in old Sardinia with Ugolino-Ferrara when a stripling. In the middle of these would come a remark such as "The Minister has been approached by the Tunisian Ambassador. His request was that we should deny the use of Italian ports to United States vessels supplying your ships off Libya. Our response so far is that we do not know that the United States has ships 'off Libya,' merely that they appear to be in that sector of the Mediterranean." These were often delivered with an innocently malicious grin as though establishing a tariff: so many pig bladders, spear strokes, and bleeding horses for one bright nugget.

Friends of his own youth were a more cheerful source, though not yet so eminent. He discovered one, a Colonel of paratroops with whom he could share fairly honest expectations of troop response along with secular memories. Another, who had once been suspected of a calling to the priesthood, turned up at the top of security for Alitalia and knew everything that could be known about traffic through Italian airports. The circle grew. There was involved etiquette here, requiring forty-minute cups of coffee and elaborately accidental meetings. There was very little Stears could ask, but a great deal he could from time to time be told. In a real emergency he would have claims of friendship.

His anchor was always Mascagni. During the week since their lunch in the hills, Stears's and Mascagni's cooperation had become systematic. They now corresponded daily in abbreviated fact sheets, a bit like the records of chess games. The couriers were plainclothes Carabinieri, frequently changed. Personal meetings between Stears and Mascagni had been reserved for crises. Stears had twelve Italian agents on the payroll. Two juniors from his own service, billed as immigration clerks, crisscrossed Rome by subway and cab, bringing in notes and rolls of film and paying out cash. When an agent perhaps had information with brittle facets, Stears would undertake the contact himself. Most telephone calls, limited by Stears's fiat to twenty-five seconds, were from agents at random telephone boxes. Others were long, often from Randall Beebe, complaining testily that General Larsen had testily complained that his four-hundred-odd installations were getting bugger-all defensive help from the CIA—hadn't Stears been given all the room he needed?—and ending, from the mind of Beebe himself, "You know the rules, Stears: you buck procedure, you gotta produce." The last in democratized accent, Beebe being of fine ironies.

Intelligence work, very rarely revelation, consists mainly of assembling patterns tending toward probabilities. It operates best against large entities with slowly evolving aims. In trying to match the activities of diplomatic missions from a dozen unstable countries with those of a hundred Italian extremist groups, Stears and Mascagni were uncomfortably close to applying the rules of Linnaean classification to a firework display.

Progress did nonetheless take place. The Libyans were edging ahead as likely, still unproven, enemies. There was no clear demonstration here; but an increase in courier activity between Rome and Tripoli, the arrival of several unexplained extra embassy personnel who were never seen again, greater movement on the part of the present Cultural Attaché and former tough, and whispers from the CIA's one timorous, low-level source within the embassy added up to more than was evident elsewhere. On Mascagni's side, it began to seem probable that the Italians involved would be found to share connections with grouplets once associated with elements of the major terrorist constellation, the Nuclei Armati Proletari, the NAP, now principally Neapolitan but which in turn had an extremely remote ancestry in the University of Padua. Stears's and Mascagni's work ticked to a slow march; both assumed that their adversaries' ticked to a lively jig.

Even these results took a great deal of work. Stears's lunch, when he was not prowling his friends' corridors, was daily brought down to his desk by a gondolier. By recompense, the gondoliers conspired to make his sandwich much nicer than Mrs. Buxhalter's lunch at the residence. He left work at eight or considerably later, tense, tired, hot, and deserving peace. He formed the habit of heading straight for a trattoria.

Where he stayed this evening until he began to yawn into his plate. At home in Parioli, the elevator's sigh had for two days become the prologue to tense thought.

During these two days, he had not actually seen Gabriella, though it was arranged that they should lunch the next day but one. A telephone call yesterday had not been returned.

Which was a minor irritation; his Gabriella would call because she felt like calling, not necessarily because she had been called. And Italian servants can be casual about messages. The trouble was that time without her was becoming an absence now. Also a hiatus. He had seen her only once since Ugolino-Ferrara's munificence and then not at leisure.

In her absence, uneasy spirits bred. In Gabriella's absence, in his bland rooms, wraiths of his wife Marie-Sophie came out of a hairbrush she had given him, a clock, a formal little note giving her address at a girlfriend's house near Brussels. He was not dishonest enough to deny that it needed only a hard, impatient demand from him for her to materialize with smiles and too many bags at Rome's airport. His marriage was moribund, but he was turning his eye from its deathbed. His eye was fixed on Gabriella as the entry to another life. The need to consummate the future with her was becoming ripe.

So, coming home from the trattoria, he went almost at once to bed. Which was haunted by Gabriella with the slatted sun upon her.

In such circumstances, the more daytime activity, the better. He was pleased to get an unscheduled call the next morning from Paolo Strozzo, one of his better agents and thus assigned to the Libyan Cultural Attaché. Strozzo was calling from a filling station just outside Rome and in the general direction of Naples. Yussuf ben Baghedi had left suddenly by car, but not without Strozzo behind. Ben Baghedi was now buying gas, looking at a map, had visited the urinal, and was fiddling with the fit of his pants, all like a man going on an outing.

Indeed Strozzo would follow, agreed Stears. Strozzo would meet Stears himself the next day. If the Libyan stayed away overnight, Strozzo would call that evening.

Late that afternoon Yussuf ben Baghedi drove back from Monte Sant'Angelo. He had discreetly inspected Monte Sant'Angelo, which he had known in advance through maps, photographs, and Dr. Calvetto's diagrams. Yussuf's intellect, a sturdy, surefooted little beast on its own terrain, had apprehended without doubt or deference that the doctor's tactical plan, though rudimentary, was basically sound. He had made a professional's improvements. As to the larger plan, Calvetto himself had called it "sublimity of purple political theater." Yussuf preferred modesty in others and deprecated such language as inconsistent with simple faith. Still, he could see that it was pretty good.

Soldiering was Yussuf's craft and its exercise always brought him peace. He enjoyed his drive. He could regard the granite flanks of the Abruzzi with respect and it came to him in a flash of generosity that the men of those strong stone villages might be sober men, though infidels and enemies. The meadows here were not fat. It would not be a weakling's country. He liked the bells on the cows. He wondered if they were left on in the barns or taken off and, if taken off, with a buckle or with something else. He liked the sophistication and breadth of view that allowed these thoughts. Yussuf had become conscious of a richness crystallizing day by day around the wellsprings of his life. Its model came each morning when he arose from prayer in his spartan room at the embassy and opened the dressing-table drawer and reached his hand into the cool, deepening billows of his swelling hoard of Italian shirts. The ragged Bedou boy was far behind him. It was not written that a Muslim should not be of substance. Yussuf knew that he was accomplishing his increase with no softening of his manhood or his faith.

He allowed himself to enjoy the road and his Mercedes—it was well known that Colonel Qaddafi enjoyed his Ferrari no end. On the long uphill swings he enjoyed the buffets of wind as he tore past the trucks and his steady overtaking of the Italians' cars. Far below, behind him, a dark-blue Alfa-Romeo sedan, a common model in a popular color, almost kept up with him, as another like it had this morning, going to Gargano—but again not quite, not on the longer hills. The driver had a mannerism that cost him time; he would pull out and then hesitate a moment before giving the car its head.

As had the similar car this morning. Also well back, behind.

And at that, Yussuf's interest settled home with a jolt, like a manhole cover into its frame. There remained a hundred and fifty attractive kilometers to Rome. Not once throughout them did his thoughts budge from a flat, hard focus.

Just outside Rome, already off the *autostrada* on the Via Tiburtina, he turned abruptly toward the dim mouth of an almost deserted multistory parking lot in a shopping center just built and scarcely yet in business. Yussuf had noticed this building before and had found it appealing, though not until now in a definite sense.

The Libyan embassy, not extremely far from Stears's apartment, was well out of the center of Rome, halfway along the broad and pleasant Via Nomentana. The street was much given to convents, monasteries, and other pious Catholic foundations; this was perhaps the reason why the Libyan People's Bureau and the embassy of the Islamic Republic of Iran found it comfortable to huddle together side by side. The Iranian embassy was a cheery sort of place. Dirty, dark-eyed children could be found playing around the back of the drive among heaps of abandoned furniture. Chickens would not have been unexpected. The embassy was in full view.

The Libyans, by contrast, had a dungeon. The villa had originally had high walls; on top of these now soared stanchions bearing barbed wire. The scrolled iron gate had been blanked out with boiler metal. The pretty apertures in the walls had been stuffed with paper bearing, for some reason, the name of a Roman central heating contractor. Dense and gloomy greenery bulged against the masonry. Intruders might feel themselves menaced by large snakes as much as by Dobermans. Three vanloads of Carabinieri sat outside, more than for the whole United States embassy downtown.

The Lieutenant of these saluted Yussuf as his Mercedes was passed in. In doing so, he unwittingly saluted Paolo Strozzo, who was tied up in the trunk. Strozzo had cautiously entered the suburban parking lot a little behind Yussuf's car, just to be thorough. He had intended to ascertain Yussuf's intentions there. He had succeeded: Yussuf had been waiting for him in the shadows. Two hours later, the Carabinieri saluted Strozzo in the trunk of a car again. This time, he was badly mutilated, concealed in a weighted canvas bag, and dead. It was not until September that the body turned up under a bridge in a disused canal in the Campagna—and only then because that September was exceptionally dry.

When he had taken off his rubber gloves and thrown them in the garbage, Yussuf thanked the colleague who had helped him with the spy. The body had been taken away. Yussuf went up to his office. He rinsed his mouth out with strong coffee and washed his face. He copied his jottings made during the questioning onto cleaner paper. Then he sat down to think.

He would need to confer with the Chief People's Representative, formerly the Ambassador. First, he wished to have his thoughts in order.

The man, the spy, Paolo Strozzo, was an Italian, but he did not work for the Italians. He worked for the Americans, for the CIA. His mission had indeed been to keep constant surveillance on the Libyan Cultural Attaché. The Italian did not know anything else. This was while the man had expected to be bullied and let go, and was said in a normal tone of voice.

He was not the only person watching Yussuf, who was watched around the clock. The embassy was also watched. The filling station across the street and the bicycle shop on the corner had been bought by the CIA. This had all begun not long ago and had been intensified recently. He knew none of the names of the others and his contact with the CIA was totally indirect and would not be recognizable to him. He would be willing to try and find out more, sir. He had not yet reported Yussuf's presence in Gargano, only his departure from Rome. He was not to report until tomorrow. This was at the beginning of real fear and was said with increasing rapidity.

Yes, that photograph corresponded with his CIA contact. No, he had worked with the CIA before but not with this man. No, he knew nothing more about him. Yes, he would find out if he could. Just let him go, he'd find out. Oh, God, yes. He did not know the names of the other agents. He would recognize photographs if shown them. He would, sir, truly. Believe me, the Americans do not know you were in Gargano. I will never tell them. These questions had been put repeatedly and got the same answer, between shrieks.

CIA but not American. Italian. Please, please, truly. Italian. Yes, CIA but Italian. Yes, I know one other name—Carlo Danello watches the embassy. No others, I'd tell you, my God, I'd tell you. Yes, CIA officer is Italian. Don't know purpose, no. Did not report you . . . Gargano. Not time. Not time. I don't know. I don't know. I don't know. Voice had sometimes failed here and he had used raised fingers and things like that. That seemed, in digest, to be it.

He had a thought and yelled for Dr. Basenji. He heard the old man jump off his chair and come pattering along. There was a moment of relief when Basenji, whom Yussuf had not seen for two days, opened the door. Yet again, the old suit offered fun. Some vital thread must have given way in the lapel. The buttonhole had split wide open and the blossom and stalk of Basenji's flower, which anyway must have been yesterday's, was hanging limply out of it. Yussuf roared with laughter.

Basenji looked puzzled and frightened. Yussuf explained, discovering in the process a concrete sexual image which itself made him laugh again until he was weak.

But back to business. He handed Basenji some photographs of Stears. He said, "This asshole is called Giovanni Sidgewick Stears. He's a Yank spy but he's mixed up with the Italians somehow. Maybe he hung around Rome once. Maybe you know something about him." He was about to hand the photograph over, but looked at it once more and added thoughtfully, "He looks like the kind of stuffed shirt you used to know."

Basenji took it gently. He said at length, "There is something a little familiar. The name and the face. But it is not recent, my lord. I am not at all sure." He looked from the picture and said cautiously, "Others might know, my lord. That is, if I made a call . . . calls. To friends, persons at the same . . . level. If you thought it advisable."

"Certainly not," said Yussuf.

"Perhaps if I think some more," said Basenji.

"Try it," said Yussuf. He got up. "I shall be with the Chief People's Representative," he said. He flicked Basenji's flower and chuckled another ribald comment as he passed. Sometimes he was quite fond of the old man.

. . .

At the end of the evening, when the sun, even in the modern
Parioli quarter, found marble here and there to transmute to
gold, Yussuf sat again in his office. The Ambassador had agreed
with Yussuf's slow conclusion: that there perhaps was not much
in this. The agreement with the Italian government that Arab
embassies not be watched was still in force. So the Americans
were acting on the sly and would keep very quiet about it. It
might be possible to embarrass them publicly with the Italians
in due course—that would also be enough to unlink any clandestine cooperation. It was disquieting if the man the Americans
had brought in already had a line on the embassy, but Yussuf's
Dr. Calvetto had warned them of that possibility, though without elaboration. Find out all about this Yank you can. Now one
was warned. Now one knew who the enemy was, whom one
should hold in one's sights. Very lucky that Yussuf had not been
reported in Gargano. Nonetheless, Yussuf would clearly be especially careful now, stay in the background, and all that. Perhaps even lead the Americans off on some merry chases to
nowhere. Under the circumstances, the Ambassador considered
this a serious, but not a vital, obstacle to the matter in hand.

Yussuf was congratulated on his quick action.

Now he was back in his office, deep in his fine, small altera-
tions to Dr. Calvetto's plans. It was also clear that special precautions would be needed to keep the three Libyan *guerriglieri*
destined for Gargano well away from the embassy, however
well they were disguised; fortunately there were resources for
this.

In the midst of his work, he heard Basenji's mild step and a
faint scratch at the door.

Basenji offered the photographs of Stears as though he expected his hand to be slapped. "I am sorry, my lord," he said.
"The memory is too faint. One day, I will remember, perhaps. I
am sorry."

Yussuf took the pictures. He said, "Too bad." He was in a
good mood again and he said it almost pleasantly. He went back
to his work. He became aware that Basenji had lingered an
unexpected minute by his desk.

"Ah, she is still a beautiful woman," said Basenji's voice.

"What?" said Yussuf. He saw that Basenji was looking at a picture of Dr. Calvetto's "Rosa" full face and with no scarf and he pushed it quickly away. "That has nothing to do with this," he said. "That's all."

Basenji walked slowly away. Then he stopped abruptly. He said in a murmur, "It is odd to see them together again here."

"What?" said Yussuf.

Basenji turned eagerly, "Now I know who that man is. I know very well. He has aged a little more than she has. But together again on your desk, of all places . . ." Basenji even looked, thought Yussuf, a little malicious when he finished, "when one thinks of the places they were seen together once."

"What are you maundering about?" said Yussuf.

So Dr. Basenji told him.

Dr. Calvetto received the Libyan's call late in the evening. Now he sat in the dark of his living room. His rooms were near the river. On this summer night, the lights of cars poured across the bridges and the streetlights played in the river like phosphorescent fish, but Dr. Calvetto sat with his back to this in the inmost corner of the room. He saw only the light reflected from the polished facets of stones on shelves. These blinked like the eyes of owls and ferrets in a wood; Dr. Calvetto crouched among them.

In his torment since the Libyan's call he saw himself as a twisted dwarf, a cracked, misshapen leather doll.

He told himself now, as he would convince himself by daylight, that Gabriella had known this man when she was a girl; that Gabriella had known many men, even since she had been Calvetto's own; that her pulling back from him four days ago was explainable by events, and that he had shown anyway then, and in purple colors, how closely he still held her.

And he told himself that Stears—as he still held crumpled in one hand the photograph he had snatched from the desk drawer when the Libyan called, when it was still light—was a wandering CIA spy turned up in Rome by chance. And once a youth of Gabriella's circle. And nothing more than the first link by chance in the writhing chain of whole male flesh that followed where Calvetto led his Gabriella.

But Calvetto felt a stirring against the back of his neck and he insisted to the dark: Nothing is laughing because I told her of his presence and steered her to him. Nothing is laughing. But the words fell to the floor like phlegm.

Heaven had denied him everything, so he had taken everything by speed. A limp brings kicks or pity; a caper weaves a spell. A piping voice is despised until it speaks grandly, pirouettes in scorn. Heaven had kept its graces from him and he had stolen every one of them. He disdained Heaven for the ease with which a small, quick finger could pluck away its toys.

In Gabriella he had seized Woman, the last grace denied him, and denied with a cruelty savage even for Heaven. He had seized it with an insolence savage even for himself. Heaven, no doubt, would have yawned consent if even a twisted, loinless, sapless doll had stolen kindness from a servant girl. So he had looked Heaven in the eye and—with a daring that made him shiver—had taken the beautiful, the lioness, the Princess, the sumptuous whore. He would have hated her as another's; as his, he looked upon her stunned by her magnificence. He adored her.

And so he had conquered woman and man at once. He had made jealousy his lapdog. Having subdued Gabriella with his infirmities, he gloated over the whole men she played with. He had followed her passing attachments, followed them on the street, sat at a far table from them on the Via Veneto, followed rapturously one tanned and muscled lout to the beach at Fregene and shivered while the other warmed his loins and belly on the sand. He sought to see if her loves had hairy arms or knotted thighs; he chided her for grasping a waist too flabby, or for letting a balding head thrust back and forth above hers; he longed to know the taste of her lovers' breath. He sought to know the time of her assignations. All this was his. He, a man distorted, had dominion over any lithe flesh that followed after her, for he ruled their mistress.

But he was small and alone, however brave. Heaven was populous and great. If once she turned from him and took to her heart an ordinary man formed whole in his mother's womb with only Heaven's coarse daily gifts of limb and life, then instantly Calvetto would become the pariah. Heaven had easy chances. He listened for its laughter.

He picked himself up, unlocked his hands above his head and raised them toward Heaven. "Back to our game," he said aloud to the dark. He put a smile on his face. Now he turned his hands toward himself like convex mirrors and placed in one the memory of Gabriella's gold and tinted body and in the other, though unseen in the dark, the black-and-white photograph of Stears. He said gently to Gabriella, "Kill him for me, my angel, and we shall be better than before." And then he added, "But this time, my love, I will not force you. If you would prefer it, I shall kill you both together. It will be just the same. I will not force you." He said it with pain and love.

At eleven in the morning the next day, Giovanni Stears sat behind the pages of *Momento Sera* in a café on a street off the Via Garibaldi and heard the occasional whoosh of the espresso machine and the underlying warble of the floor polisher. He waited for his agent. The café was in Trastevere. It was respectable enough to have well-waxed floors and homely enough to wax them under the feet of early customers. This locale, the choice of *Momento Sera* as newspaper, and the canary cotton pullover and brown slacks that Stears now wore, all suggested a quite ordinary Roman whiling away the morning. They hid either an officer of CIA or—the thought drifted in from the shaded and newly watered street—the next Marchese Ugolino-Ferrara. Had Rodolfo Mascagni's wife, who at that moment was buying pork chops two streets away, happened by the café, it would never have occurred to her that two such recondite creatures were drinking coffee there on one spindly metal chair.

Agents, as is well known, are punctual to the second. Stears himself had been trained in the stoical romance of that school. *Z forced his eyes, grimy with fatigue, to focus on the Prague (substitute at will* Berlin, Bucharest, *or* the Finland Station) *plat-*

form. Torn shreds of Berliner Tagesblatt *blew around his feet like lonely puppies. Z saw Dr. Hemelchius emerge, a gray, almost anonymous figure in a shabby greatcoat, through the steam of the locomotive of the Warsaw Express. The station clock moved.* A minute late, *thought Z.* He's telling me he's blown, telling me to run. *He turned away. The chill wind drew water from his eye.* Such was the case in expensive, neurotic espionage establishments beyond the Alps. Here, one got accustomed to waiting.

Now the minutes turned to quarter hours. Even cisalpine punctuality became stretched. The espresso machine whooshed in faster rhythm. The floor waxer was dragged away, though its cord and plug made grabs at the table legs. And concern like a hard small marble lodged behind Stears's brow and the *Momento Sera* grew blank before his eyes.

He paid for his coffee and walked into the street. Though his impression was that he was not under surveillance, he walked purposefully, as though the café had been a holding point and his goal was still ahead. From a corner where there was a tiny shop for glass and silver jewelry he saw a public telephone, not the closest one to the café. He walked to it and quickly dialed the secure number at the embassy where special messages for him would be recorded. There were none. Strozzo, his reliable agent, had neither kept the rendezvous nor canceled it.

He went back to the embassy. He called Mascagni, who was not there. He left a bare report with one of Mascagni's Sergeants whose name he knew.

Had the Libyan remained away overnight, Strozzo would have telephoned a report the evening before.

There was no positive evidence that ben Baghedi was in the embassy; since he lived there and worked in a closed section, days often went by without sighting him.

His scattered surveillance people would call in brief reports throughout the afternoon on arbitrary schedules. He could have sent one of his juniors to find and debrief each of them in turn, but there was nothing sure to be gained by that and there might be harm.

So he waited one by one for the reports, which brought him nothing, well into the evening. Late in the afternoon, Mascagni called, promised support, and suggested a meeting outside Rome at noon the next day.

Stears called Gabriella to change tomorrow's lunch to dinner; his heart lifted a second with the thought that dinners come with nights attached. His heart went back down again; this time there was no answer at the Villa Pamphili-Farnese at all.

He fell into the most detailed and detached work, possible scenarios based on time sightings of subjects until the sun hung heavy. His last stop was the cipher room. This was in a far part of the embassy. He left the building by a back way not for public use on the Via Friuli. This brought him to the Via Lucullo and then around to the Via Boncompagni and his car. The summer sunset was turning the Pinciana Gate to gold, but down in the Via Boncompagni it was dusk.

This, and Stears's unexpected heading, made the clerk working late at Air Yemen miss him completely until he was already in the Jaguar and about to move away. The radio taxi driver waiting near the Hotel Ambasciatore knew his job and could never have caught up unnoticed. He went quietly to a vantage point on Stears's street instead.

Where he had to wait for hours.

For Stears's work had held disquiet at a distance only while it was in front of him, and now he was in a car alone, sealed in and breathing denatured air, stuck in the traffic of the Pinciana. The sunset scorched his mirror, fired arrows from the chrome of cars around him, and turned the windows of a house to molten lead. Qualms seeped and simmered in his stomach. From the moment that he had counted Strozzo as missing, a shape had begun to take place in his mind, the revolting photograph Mascagni had shown him of a skull-faced cinder with lips split open across the teeth. Now it rose in his gorge. He choked it down. Next, trailing concupiscence, tenderness, and increasing puzzlement came wayward thoughts of Gabriella. He saw her as on his bed three days before, stroked by sun, exhaling scent of life and lust, he felt her hands against his chest. And then the vile photograph spewed out again, but now with a transformation. For he saw straight into Gabriella's own nightmare of herself, saw her burned body in the car, wrapped Gabriella's long-ago Ferrari around Mascagni's horror. He threw it off, but it held him long enough to soak his shirt with a sweat that the chilled air turned bitter. It left behind a sense of disturbing, unseemly intimacy: that he had woken with her in her own bad dream.

Now it also occurred to him—while the mirror scalded his eyes, while his shirt froze, while a coven of car horns blasted the air from two ranks of traffic behind him—that when he had seemed to catch her eye that afternoon in the Abruzzi the face had not been Gabriella's twenty years ago but now.

The thought was intemperate and so was what he did. He fought his way off the Pinciana, turned down a warren of streets he had forgotten that he knew, bullied his way across the Piazza Venezia, finally reached the Tiber, and drove off into the Campagna to the villa. Not until he was on the old unchanged road, and the marshy creek beyond the sheepcote had saluted him with the last blade of sun did it occur to him that he had no reason to assume that she was there. He did not turn back.

When he reached the villa, it was dark. He drove slowly out of the drive into the circle in front of the house. He parked in his old place, under Diana, this time without noticing.

Two lamps were on in all the villa. One, like a glow on the ground by the wall before him, came up from below and would have been a kitchen. Another, deeper gold and very faint, was on the ground floor and must have come from the stair hall within. The villa was entirely quiet.

But stone gives light at night, like flesh, and he could see well. The tall arches of the *orangerie* framed the dark glass with silver. On top of its little hill the villa was sharply defined though it seemed weightless, as though a drift of mist had become columns and a dome, and balconies, and a doorway sculpted to the likeness of a shell. The heads of two wistful graces worshiped the jowls of Pope Paul III, Alessandro Farnese. The Jaguar's door crashed. Stears's feet crunched the gravel. To his left was the path to the sea-horse pavilion. He found that he touched the doorbell lightly.

But it rang, just audibly, from deep down within. Preceded first by a distant scrape, and last by footsteps, the front door shook itself, banged its bolts, and opened to frame a servant. Stears inquired.

The man said, *"La signora principessa non è in casa, signore."* The tone was not stately. The tone was somebody torn away from television. But the jacket was smart and the collar, buttoned.

And when would she return? *"Non lo so, signore. Mi dispiace."* Stears turned away. The door closed gratefully. Chastened Stears went to his car, got in, and drove away.

And parked it in the dark of the cypress drive, got out, closed the door with a fingertip, and came quietly back. For a servant left to himself in a country house at night is not that shaved and buttoned. Inside in the dark was Gabriella. He knew a way to get in. He had done it more than once. He would debase his coming if he simply drove away.

He stood under the wall of the house and touched the first handhold. It was an ample ledge and the climb looked no worse than he remembered. He was hardly twenty-one now, but he still had a climber's legs and balance. But his vision on the Pinciana had dimmed and he felt his mettle shrink. He was going to break the law, break his leg, get mauled by a Doberman, be called a fool—all to see a grown woman in a private house who had instructed her servants to have her left in peace? For all he knew, Gabriella was lying in the dark with a headache. To what ledge of exposure does one climb to say, "My love, I saw your face in fire and I have scaled your walls to wake you"? He stepped back.

And then at length looked up. Because to climb one had to be properly aligned for the next handhold, an urn, which became the second foothold after the ledge. And an important one because the third handhold, somebody's breast, was one of the two tricky ones, not well designed for the purpose and dicey if one's hand began to sweat. His hand did now begin to sweat, even as he took the first handhold. The grain of the stone dried it. He pulled his feet up, steadied them, and felt for the lip of the urn.

He reached the breast. His hand was dry and did not slip. His foot steadied in the fret of a stone lyre. His hand moved to the carved furrow of a grace's hair. So far so good. The next hand-hold was his old favorite, the tumbler of a papal key. He would break bones from this height but probably not his neck. Good to remember that while one hooked one's hip around the armorial shield and got such foot purchase as Farnese's nose would give. His heel slid a quarter inch. Then stopped, but he felt it in his stomach and it wet his hands. Breathe deep. Get the other foot up on the shield. Balance with your fingers on a crack. Good. And now—this part was always sickening—lunge!

And grab the parapet. A scrabble and he had it. He felt blessed and great. He had always admired the art of the baroque. Now he looked down. It was nothing extraordinary—he was only on the second floor, twenty feet up—though the footholds looked more daunting from above. But, here as down below, they were less daunting than to be Gabriella's lover and fear to enter her house. He had climbed his way out of more than safe good sense, even acceptable fear; he had climbed through the knot in his own belly and he was ready for Gabriella on her own pure and desperate terms.

For the first time since twenty years ago when he had run away. As, choosing a window now, he could at last admit. Getting in was no problem. He was on a cornice outside a gallery with high windows, most of them open for the summer night. He walked ten feet and ducked inside.

There were four closed doors and one open to a salon. He tried the doors. None were locked. The third was Gabriella's. He knew it first by scent.

He did not see her. He heard her voice say, "I heard you at the front door. I heard you drive away. I had forgotten that you would do this."

He still did not see her face. She spoke from a high-backed chair facing away from him toward the open window. She did not turn her head. Her voice was barren.

He crossed the room. The house was darker than outside and her room was darker than the gallery. He struck his leg against a stool.

She was in a long white nightgown and was facing the wall as much as the window. She might not have moved for an hour.

"A locked door is a locked door," she said. "My wishes should be respected."

He stood with his hand on the arm of her chair but not upon hers. "I felt that you called me," he said. "And now I think I'm right."

She turned to face him then. She looked at him a long time through clear and distant eyes. He had time to think, *This is how she will look when she is sixty. She will be beautiful.*

She said, "Maybe you were right, Giovanni. But I changed my mind and then I locked my door." She touched his arm, but remotely. "I will never forget that you came. It pays all. Now go."

"How?" he said. "Jump out the window? Pays what?" *And what is the title of this piece?* The Duchess of Malfi? he thought but did not say. At a second look, the thought became a hope and he acted on it. He put his arms around her, pushing them past her shoulders, and drew her bosom in its white shroud to his face. "Gabriella," he said. "What?"

And found himself knocked nearly to the floor. His Gabriella had kept her muscle tone. She rearranged her gown as severely as a nun's. "That is poison," she said. "It is horrible, that slobbering and groping."

"You should have told me earlier," said Stears. But that was said with the last hope that this was simple drama, for she had shuddered as she had closed herself within her gown and he added gently, "Do you really mind if I sit down? I had some trouble getting here."

"No," she said. "You must leave." She took a tray with a little soup bowl and a glass with a pearly trace of milk off a small table beside her chair, put it on the floor, then moved the table closer and patted it. "Sit here if you want to," she said.

"I was near Vicovaro since I last saw you," he said, "on the road to L'Aquila. I thought of us at Roberto's place in the Abruzzi. You used to sunbathe on the parapet. That was when I thought you called me, though I did not quite know it at the time."

"They have built a ski resort there now," she said, "and it is very ugly. And Roberto doesn't own it anymore. Not for years. So you see, everything changes and goes away."

"Then I saw something worse," he said. " I saw how you see yourself in the car. The fire. The nightmare you told me about."

"I told you I do not have that very much now. In the days when I did have it, you were not here."

"No," he said. "I know that. That is also why I came now. Locked door or not."

She said nothing. His eyes were down and when he raised them he saw to his astonishment and horror that she was trembling; eyes dry, face rigid, hands clamped to the arms of the chair, and swept by spasms. He said, hearing the hollowness of his own voice, "I am sorry. I should never . . ."

But "It's not that," she said. She reached quickly to her neck and to the back of her gown and arched her shoulders. The gown fell to her waist. She turned half toward him. "Hold my breasts," she said. "Just that. Don't make love to me. Don't talk. Just hold me." She bent toward him.

Her head was on his shoulder. He quickly learned to dread the first contraction of each quaking of her body, though they grew milder slowly. What would bring his Gabriella to this state was beyond his courage to imagine. For the second time in his grown life he felt his throat hot and choked with unshed tears. When she finally spoke, it was in a quiet and simple voice.

"You were right at first in the garden here," she said. "You said we were too long ago and you were right. I thought you could give me now what you owed me all those years ago. And you would. I know that now, too. That's what I meant when I said your coming in here pays all—I expect it's a silly phrase. We were just too young then. But you can't. It's not possible. Things can always be done in their time and then it gets harder and harder and finally they can't be done at all. It was just an accident that you came to Rome, not what I had thought at all. And you have to go. And not see me again."

He said, "Not unless you tell me why. Not after this. I can't do that." He held her face in his hands now and looked at her closely and made himself speak as though it were an elementary proposition. And so it was. After a while she nodded with a sorrowful little smile.

"I'm better now," she said. "Don't ask a woman her reasons. It's usually embarrassing." She began to move out of his arms. He hung on to her, for this was not theater but simple fraud. Her body was cold and stiff, not at all the savory warm weight of a woman whose devils have rioted in her and rampaged away. And the sorrowful little smile was stuck on with paste. She took herself away. She put her gown up around her shoulders. "Thank you, Giovanni," she said.

"I got a little overwrought," she said. She had taken off the sorrowful smile with the corners turned down and put on another model with the corners up. He guessed this one was worldly.

"A woman at my age gets very fond of her youth," she said. "And you had the tactlessness to turn up in Rome. So I was eighteen again for a week. It was fun. Tonight I had realized it was over. That's tough on a woman anyway and then you came bursting in and made me really embarrass myself. That's all."

She changed smiles again. This one was coquettish by design, but it was from an inferior line. It was ghastly. "And I have to tell you, Giovanni, there's another man in my life. Fidelity was never my forte, I suppose."

"Balls," he said.

"Well, maybe once it was, but not for more years than I would like to discuss."

"I don't believe a word of this," he said.

Now the smile left and his own Gabriella said softly, "You have to, Giovanni. That's all. You have to." And he felt an anvil inside him for she had truly gone beyond his reach.

"And now you must go," she said. "See, I'm asking you nicely. Please get up and go. There's a light on the stairs and you can open the door."

He stood and kissed her on the forehead. "I will come back," he said.

"I thought of that," she said. "So I won't be here. I'm going on a trip. Good-bye, Giovanni."

He stopped in the door. He turned in the door and said clearly and with weight, though he was so little clear that he said it with difficulty, "A small man. Deformed. Almost a dwarf. He is part of this. Tell me, my love."

And for all he could hear, she hesitated for no more than the intrusion of the entirely silly. "Now I really do not know what you mean, Giovanni," she said.

Out in the drive, beneath the dark windows, he thought he heard a sound from within as of breath being dragged over coals. He did not dare stay to hear it.

Stears quickly shook Captain Mascagni's hand and then sat down at another café table, this one outside on the beach at Fregene. It was a little after noon the next day. Mascagni said at once, "I have nothing good to say, Stears. There is no trace of him yet." An angry, slithering sound at Stears's back made him spin in his seat; it was only the wind beating the dry palm fronds of the café hedge. He had not slept until dawn. A corner of the awning thrashed intermittently like a snared thrush. The tables were nearly empty and one had blown over. He had driven here across the Campagna from Rome, on a road not far from the Villa Pamphili-Farnese. If he had gone there on the way this morning, all would have been well and the nightmare dispelled with the day. If he had gone there, a situation needing time to heal would have been pushed to ruin. To have dropped off there on the way here would have belittled Strozzo, who had quite possibly died in his service. He would go there on the way back. He felt himself fold his arms across his chest against the wind and desolation.

"What was your contact schedule with this one?" said Mascagni.

"By telephone if something extraordinary happened. Or that evening if the Libyan remained away from Rome overnight. Or otherwise at the time and place where I was waiting for him yesterday. In all cases, the least possible over the telephone."

"And if he had felt it ill-advised to go to that particular rendezvous?"

"Then he would have telephoned later," said Stears.

Mascagni went carefully on. "Sometimes with Italians there are simple, enormously stupid explanations," he said. "A man vanishes and it turns out that he did not have a shirt that he cared to be seen wearing or that some person was chasing him over a woman—something like that. And in our business there is always the possibility of double-dealing. But I do not put much stock in any of that. I fear that something very bad has happened to your man. You are certain of it, I know."

"He was a reliable man," said Stears. "You confirmed that yourself."

"You are assuming that he was interrogated, of course?" said Mascagni. "After that other business in Naples you would really have to."

"Yes," said Stears. "I am assuming that Paolo Strozzo was similarly interrogated."

"I could not know about this *sirocco*," said Mascagni. "Normally there are crowds here, pretty girls with no tops for their bikinis, a good place to meet. Today it is not a very good place." He sighed. He looked cold. Stears had already revised his theory that Mascagni affected morosity. Mascagni, he believed now, was one of those who smells wickedness as others smell bad drains.

"What did Strozzo know of you?" said Mascagni.

"My face," said Stears.

"And perhaps the fact that you speak native Italian."

"That, too," said Stears.

"Native Italian with out-of-date slang, American idioms, and an accent that got lost somewhere between Rome and Tuscany. It is really quite startling, your Italian—but probably a Libyan would not ask those details. Strozzo did not know your name?"

"No," said Stears. "But he could identify a photograph. It is not beyond the Libyan service to have taken some interest in me.''

"Indeed," said Mascagni. "Your Libyans. Thank you for not saying, 'I told you so.' But that is why I mentioned the *sirocco* and the empty beach. You are assuming, I would think, that your identity, or some part of it, is now known to the enemy. It restricts your options. Perhaps you are now even at risk yourself. Do you think you were followed here?''

"No. I took care. I used the usual tricks," said Stears. "I said that Paolo Strozzo was a reliable, ordinary agent. Good for watching outside an embassy, having a drink with a policeman, taking pictures at an airport. He was no guerrilla. I am sure he was not armed. He had a family. I thought I was using him properly. No, Captain, Giovanni Stears is not at risk. The intelligence officer almost never is. For the officer it is really quite impersonal. The dangers we face are a skipped promotion, a less pleasant posting.''

"And why should Strozzo be a *guerrigliero*?" said Mascagni. "This is Italy, not Afghanistan. We are an eminently civilized country. If you should happen to be blown to shreds at a railroad station here, you will probably have an excellent cup of coffee in your hand at the time. And the man who threw the bomb takes his children to the beach and eats at *trattorie*. Please do not think that there is anything irregular about an ordinary little Italian being killed.''

Mascagni appeared to shiver, but it was perhaps only his shirt rattling on his ribs like a sail around Cape Horn. Where it pulled away from his chest, Stears could see the margins of a whorled, lowering scar.

"I still think you should take care," said Mascagni. "Whatever you say, it is not normal for an intelligence service in peacetime to kill an agent, either." He looked beyond the café's clattering fence and beyond the beach where four paper cups pursued by an arthritic straw hat scampered helter-skelter among the bodies on the sand. Many of the bodies seemed nude, though covered with sand over grease; but there were not many, and scattered among them were empty, shallow recent graves.

Stears said, "Naples, Naples, Captain. It is always Naples. That is where they were going.''

"One can go to other places as well as Naples on that road," said Mascagni. "Across to Bari and Brindisi, for example. That could be a Greek connection or even Yugoslavian. Sicily, of course. One can even leave the *autostrada* halfway to Naples and cut across the Abruzzi, though it would not make much sense unless you were going to Foggia. Beyond Foggia there is nothing, or only Gargano. Naples is the obvious guess, I agree. Perhaps we will find some indication that this Libyan was there. Probably we won't. No doubt your man's car will turn up sooner or later." Mascagni's eye settled on the gray sea where a blotch of unhealthy sunlight sweltered. His hand indicated Naples, though in fact the view down the coast ended several hundred kilometers short, at the Fiumicino headland.

The paper cups cavorted over a belly attached to a towel-shrouded head. The straw hat took the easier road, bump-bump across the knees. The towels stirred, the head cursed, and the belly rose up above a twisted loincloth and trudged toward the parking lot.

"I am using other agents," said Stears. "They are also 'ordinary little Italians,' but most of what little progress there has been comes from what they have told me. Now I know what can happen to them."

The waiter came and put on the table a jug of wine, some bread, and two plates under tin covers.

"I ordered," said Mascagni. "It is less noticeable to be eating. Maybe you like this. It is just the thing for a day at the beach. You expect all your agents dead by morning? I think it most unlikely. Your Libyans know that a general massacre would be received quite badly. One missing person can be brushed away by all concerned. Everybody in this knows what is allowed and what is not." Mascagni gestured with his fork for Stears to pick up his own. "Poor Strozzo was that unlucky man. Please at least seem to eat your food. With the beach so empty, this is not a difficult place to watch."

Stears removed the cover, which was as cold as the plate. There was a heap of fried squid. He said, "General Leipzinger. The body without a face in the building site. The boy in Naples. Now this—and it is all probably connected. To put it no higher, Captain, this is already a general massacre on Italian soil. Can't the Carabinieri move a little faster?'' He began to eat. Sand clicked and scraped along his teeth, suffused with the tallow taste of oil grown quickly cold.

"But yes," said Mascagni. "We are beginning to move at amazing speed. I have even brought more reports for you. We know the model of tire used on the terrorists' second escape vehicle from Sagatto. By the width of the tracks, we know that the vehicle was an English Land Rover, the model with the longer chassis. We are tracking down all such vehicles registered in Italy, but that is not an easy job. We have found a barn where they evidently changed cars again. There are traces of blood there compatible with the boy at the building site, so that connection is now clear. The owner of the barn says he knows nothing, which may well be true or almost true. We have found a dental record for the body in Naples. We now know a great deal about these two dead boys. They both had contacts in the Nuclei Armati Proletari in Naples, so we are questioning those people vigorously, especially in the prisons. We are trying to persuade one or two of the judges to give us a little bargaining power with the prisoners. We have ballistic information. Unfortunately it all adds up to nothing. Maybe it will never add up. The police work is being done competently, however. And you, Stears? What are your superiors saying?''

"My Chief of Station reminds me that this surveillance was my idea. The Military Attaché has expanded upon this, noting that, 'we knew it was the Libyans all along.' There is some talk of retaliation, which is not meant to be taken seriously. The main note sounded is caution; it seems easier to be bellicose generally than in particular. The Ambassador is mainly concerned about some sort of open house he is putting on and about not spoiling it. These are early reactions, of course.''

"It is a little cold, isn't it," said Mascagni. He looked around at this and could conceivably have meant the wind. The *sirocco* was increasing; one was chilled and sweated profusely by turns. The sea and the scrub pines behind the beach were now much the same sulfur color and both writhed without direction. A Campari poster, the bottom end come loose, struggled against the wall.

"Anyway, you understand me," said Mascagni. "It is generous of our governments to pay us, you know, when both of them agree that the terrorists, whoever they are, are easier to live with than the actions required to deal with them.''

"The Italian government,'' said Stears. ''At the Quirinale, if you recollect, the United States called for action.''

"Is that so? Yes, I recollect something about satellites. Thank you for reminding me. Now that you have a well-founded suspicion of the Libyans, will you take decisive action?''

"No,'' said Stears.

"Why? I would like to hear it from you. Why does the dreaded CIA not intensify surveillance of their embassy so that not a fly can go through the window unidentified?''

"Because the Libyans—assuming it is they, of course—will expect this and will make use of other resources, safe houses and all that. If the surveillance were at all evident, they would complain to your government. That would make my superiors' position embarrassing, and ultimately my own, and would also end this collaboration.'' Stears used a tone of recital.

Mascagni raised a pedantic finger. ''Why does not Washington make a stern complaint to Tripoli, backed by all those ships floating around out there?''

"Because Italy, a NATO power and a friend both of the United States and of Libya, does not countenance surveillance of friendly embassies. Therefore there was no agent, no surveillance, and of course no incident. But tell me this. Why do I not seek out an officer of the Carabinieri and report this crime to him?''

Mascagni raised his glass and tipped it by five degrees to Stears. ''Do you have any real weapons, Giovanni? May I call you that?''

Stears raised his glass in return. ''Please do,'' he said and his own voice surprised him by its warmth. ''Like the Carabinieri, the CIA does its proper job well. We have knowledge of disaffected Libyans. We steer contacts, often at two or three removes, with sources in Tripoli or at the embassies. It is daily work. It provides a daily trickle, much of it misleading. It is very slow. At the moment we are cultivating a certain clerk at the Libyan embassy. My colleagues have been doing so for two years—he is a very frightened man. In the end there are usually results, but one cannot predict when or in what context. Sometimes the whole puzzle is given to us when we least expect it. It has happened.''

"In short, we wait and we watch," said Mascagni. "The Carabinieri and now the CIA. We react. It is better than acting. He who acts makes mistakes. That is why the terrorists are nearly always caught in the end. And they are caught. Truly they are. Even at the worst time, a few years ago, most of them were caught. In the history books, it will not look so bad. In the meantime, the dead bodies multiply. Do you think we will stop these terrorists before their next performance?''

"If they have nothing planned for a year, then yes," said Stears. "Unfortunately, I do not know their plans.''

"Exactly. Unfortunately, the dead bodies do not just go into the ground and vanish. Each one leaves a little poison behind, a contagion of anger and distrust. How much poison kills a country? Perhaps the Lebanese would know. Italy has taken a great deal already, Giovanni. I do not like to see her take more in another country's cause.''

Stears raised his hands as though in supplication, but Mascagni stopped him.

"I am not complaining to you, Giovanni," said Mascagni. "Sometimes I am beginning to forget that you are American, whatever I said about your Italian. Just consider what I said. Anyway, I see that you did not enjoy your squid. Personally I do not like them very much at the best of times, but it is what people order here. I suspect you do not even want a cup of cold coffee full of sand. Perhaps you should leave first. The government of Italy has bought this lunch. Do not go directly to your car, I would suggest. Walk a little on the beach. Look put out. You have driven out from Rome and it has not been all that much fun. Scarcely even any pretty girls. You have wasted your day off. Good-bye, my friend.''

Stears rose. As he did so, Mascagni's shirt filled with wind and lifted over a scar centered on a spot like a dented drum above the gut. Mascagni saw his eyes waver, covered his breast quickly with his hand and looked away. Stears as quickly turned.

. . .

By now the beach was almost empty. Sand cut his eyes and his footprints filled six steps behind him. Yet whorls of bilious sunlight raced along the beach. Between here and Rome, behind the seaside pines, lay the Campagna; he could see the light pulse on it like lightning on distant clouds. There came to his mind the wind rattling the reeds along the drainage ditches, bending the Roman pines, gusting against the walls of the empty Villa Pamphili-Farnese, hooting in the sea-horse pavilion with a noise he all at once remembered, scattering the pine needles where he and Gabriella had lain. He screwed up his eyes in spite of sharp sand to cut short the vision.

When he opened them, movement drew them. Far down the beach a figure moved toward him, footless on blown sand, ungendered until long hair whipped out. A woman. A boil of sun swept over her, the hair flashed chestnut, the blur lightened to show the form of a woman's breasts and hips. He turned in her direction and his steps quickened before his brain registered what the chestnut flash had intimated, his Gabriella borne to him on magic and the wind, answering his thought, evicting desolation. It was farfetched, said reason, but his blood ignored it and rejoiced, drank the chestnut flash like a familiar perfume, and even reason admitted, as he now walked straight toward the vision, that many rich Romans had seaside villas here. It came to him with certainty that no conflict, no question, no tears or anger could prevail in the face of such a meeting. His hurried foot dug into the top of a dwarf dune and he skipped and stumbled down it. He was much closer now and, believing or not, passionately sought out the face.

The wind dropped a little and even the feet on the sand took shape. Above them was an extremely fat woman, with hair dyed in a hard, bright color in sympathy with skin baked livid by the treacherous combination of sun and wind. Their steps crossed; he caught a scent of flesh and oil and could not fail to see a pattern of rivulets of sweat through greasy sand beginning at the shoulders and neck and ending at the nipples. She trudged sulkily from the beach. She looked in his direction. Her expression was malevolent, but perhaps not meant for him.

C·H·A·P·T·E·R   15

At Princess Dolly Casamassima's villa near Pallanza, the rising sun took a daily path down the hillside to Lago Maggiore. It arrived by way of the Alpine ridges, which it turned to fire at dawn, slipped down the high pastures, plunged down the ravines and rocks above the lake, bloomed in the spray of torrents, and then fell into the crowns of the chestnut trees behind the house. Mist from the lake was still in the garden then; as the sun came down the paths, the azaleas and pomegranates on the terraces and the magnolias by the dock were shiny with dew and the crickets were too stiff to move. When the sun took to the water and the mist began to boil and break, it slunk up through the garden in wet gray coils. Dolly Casamassima's second-best girlfriend, Princess Gabriella Harriman-Farnese, pulled her dressing gown still closer around herself as she sat under a cedar branch on the edge of a marble bench, but continued to shiver just the same. The fits of her shoulders were in contrast to her face, which was calm, though fixed.

She had been on the bench for two hours and, before that, pacing the garden long enough for her slippers to have become sodden with the dew. She had woken in her bed from a dream in which, naked, filthy, and in dread, she had been set to clawing through some pit of rubble and caked blood. Her supervisor was Dr. Calvetto, dressed just as in the *orangerie*. He stood above her and prodded her. "Go on!" he said repeatedly. "See whom you will find!" At each repetition, his face wagged to and fro, but his customary animation had changed to the motions of the most repugnant kind of clockwork doll.

She had just decided to kill Calvetto.

This had come upon her as though, striding, wheeling through the garden, she had churned it up from her own body. It had issued as a gust of rage and fear that she felt tear through her. She could rip Calvetto flesh from bone with bloody nails. This vision left her exalted, weak, cold, sick, and leaning against a tree. Then she had wearily sought out the bench where, insomniac though less distraught, she had witnessed the daybreak on two previous mornings. During the dark, a nightingale had sung from far back in the chestnut trees. As her sweat chilled she even listened to it, though it seemed unlikely that it had been put there for her.

She did not move until the mist retreated to the tops of the Borromean Islands and the first *motoscafo* running out from Stresa drew a straight white line upon the morning. By then the sun had climbed the terrace wall, flooded the lemon trees by the balustrade, and woken an emerald lizard that raised its prudent head, looked around, and gave three twitches of its tail. Gabriella had watched the lizard wake three mornings now and she was moved to smile upon it. The smile touched and left her face as surprisingly as a puff of breeze on still water. But this was not the only movement. Doors within the villa knocked. Soon the smell of lake and cedar was coarsened by coffee and hot milk. The sun was warm upon Gabriella's front by now and she had ceased to shiver, but her face, which had approached serenity through the dawn, became drawn and watchful. She rose abruptly. The lizard scampered along the stone.

She walked back to the open French window of her room, passed through, closed it, and let down the blind. She sat among her dim messed sheets, picked up a bottle from the bedside table, and shook out of it two Valium tablets and then a third, which she swallowed with the abrupt motion of a chicken drinking. She lay down on her side with her knees almost to her chin. While the tablets took effect she lay with eyes wide open, for her sleep had become too strangely painted to enter unprotected. She grieved that the pure and conscienceless dawn had once again become fractured, and a day.

Her decision to kill Dr. Calvetto had spread within her. It met no impediment in her veins. By the time the boat's wake had crawled across the lake, it filled her with peace, for she began to see no reason why, that done, her life should not recover Giovanni Stears and thus harmony and grace. But when the day imposed its bulk, it came upon her that she had looked for none of the details of this and that each would be full of vipers hissing at her all day. She was not good at negotiating corners.

Six hours later she awoke, knowing that the furnace door of a nightmare had been slammed shut behind her, but in this case just in time for her eyes to open. And yet she was on a bed, safe inside her sheets. Circumspect sounds from Dolly Casamassima's maid and a smell of freshly ironed linen were in the room. Her anguish did not retreat, but it turned its head aside. On the terrace outside her window, a footman arrived to set a table for lunch. The footman was cut in strips by her lowered blind; beyond the footman was the terrace wall and far beyond the wall were the wrought-iron railings and iron gate of Dolly's gardens —gate and railings scrolled with dolphins leaping over anchors, hundreds of yards of dolphins playing beside the lake. There was sanctuary in that. Even toy walls outside a toy fishing village with toy boats were a comfort while one lay in bed and tried to let a new life catch hold inside one.

Though her real protection was her cut-and-run from Rome. She had bolted three days before, not a suitcase in the car, the Ferrari sizzling up the *autostrada* without even a destination in its head, finally a telephone call to Dolly from a nasty Perugina restaurant on the *autostrada* outside Prato. Not even her own maid. All this had been after two terrible days alone in the shuttered Rome apartment, beginning the morning after she had dismissed Giovanni and left the villa. All this had been the morning after Dr. Calvetto's note arrived and two hours before the visit it announced.

She had been certain the day Dr. Calvetto came to the *orangerie* that he had already discovered what she had been to Giovanni Stears. Though that had seemed not to be the case, she was certain that his second call meant that her reprieve was over. Calvetto was far from her circle and had known no one in those days, but he had good ears. This theme had intruded into her already overcrowded sleep.

She turned on her back. Dolly had surmised man-trouble—and so had welcomed Gabriella with a merry, supportive leer. Though the linen sheet brushed Gabriella's stomach as she turned, it brought nothing but chill. Dolly was right. The furnace door budged an inch in memory and she saw Stears and Calvetto, like stick figures moved by clockwork, rotate their faces toward each other behind it. She winced, though such nightmares belonged to what would in all probability soon become the past. Her own sex seemed to her to have become a poisoned trap within her. She could have cried out, but she did something more therapeutic; she racked her brain for the name of Dolly's maid, remembered it, and spoke it. Then, "I would like a bath," she said.

She felt better at the thought of it. A day flowed by in hours and the hours had their virtues: the smell of scented bath salts reaching her pillow, the funny shadow of a fig leaf falling on a stiff-peaked napkin outside where the footman was setting the table, her waking desire for lunch. She dared at last to stretch her arms, fold them around an imaginary Giovanni, and rub her tummy against the sheet, where he would be. The surface hid much, if one only let it. And surely the surface could be built out day by day, a bridge over darkness.

So, bathed, a newly ironed linen blouse slipped over her submissive shoulders by the same maid, who had gone out through the gate with the chauffeur to buy it the day before, Gabriella sat at the lunch table. She had the grateful, watery feeling of a good child at the end of a sickness. She paid great heed to her present surroundings, for they were her defense. Calvetto's hooked hands, Leipzinger's cloacal blood, and the dark worm within her could not be in the same dimension as Dolly's summer table. If she heeded one, the other would have to go. Calvetto's murder would intrude, but that would be a quick crimson splotch, like a mouse swatted on the floor. She feared this act, but still, whatever else might be shaky in her, her courage was a solid shoulder to lean on. She watched the fig-leaf shadow, which had moved from the napkin to her plate. She watched her lizard on the wall, who was spending the midday upside-down. Tiring of this, she watched her hostess. This was all colored by three glasses of white wine stirring up the Valium. She knew this, but it invalidated nothing.

Dolly Casamassima was breaking up a bread stick into shrapnel between her fingers and putting the bits into her mouth one by one. Meanwhile, she was looking into the bougainvillea much as though it were a television set. Her sunglasses were up on her forehead. Ever since the first evening, Dolly had dropped her friendly leer and had treated Gabriella with careful gentleness. Gabriella was suddenly swept with gratitude for this and she broke into a smile. She had known Dolly since they were children at Palm Beach Christmases and Dolly was Dolly Biddle.

Dolly barely moved her head but she said, "Feeling better?" between *grissini* bits.

"Yes," said Gabriella.

Right in the center of this woozy peace was the thought of Giovanni, warm arm like warm sun across her shoulder. Life with Giovanni was completely visible right now from this lunchtime garden. Life with Giovanni would be stately stiff napkins with a fig-leaf shadow dropped among them as a fetchingly improper joke. She giggled to herself. A little drunk, but she knew that already. She thanked God that Giovanni, down the years, had taken roads that ended as a spy and not a pin-striped Ambassador. But she had loved her Giovanni's stateliness from the first and she had no doubt that for him to abandon it and climb her villa walls at night to get into her locked room, her locked self, was as rich a present as she had ever had. That would also do to think of while she killed Calvetto.

She was ashamed now that her first intention, when Giovanni came back to Rome, had been a simple job of seduction and use.

She had not worked all the details out, but it had seemed manifest that in a mess like hers a CIA man in one's bed could solve a lot, used properly. *Giovanni could damn well repay her*, she had thought.

What she needed, she had known after she sent him away, was not Giovanni's influence, but Giovanni. And to have that with certainty she would have to put herself on the line once more, not as a fractious child this time but as a woman with a goal. And kill Calvetto.

Giovanni would never know what it was like to look into Calvetto's eyes and see your new fate take shape in them and know that you would follow it. How could he, since those eyes would soon be closed? And with them all the places in herself they led to that she could never have found alone. From now her life would be secure among pretty tables in sunny gardens where one feared only the dead brambles pushing in from the wood, a few more each morning.

Quickly she thought of the harmonious joy of Giovanni's clean-smelling, ardent body, wonderfully grateful for anything new; deep, grateful safety in knowing that, even as he drove and brimmed inside her she could look, if she wanted, into clear Boston eyes that would never let things go, really, beyond control. Nice, for a change. She loved him. She loved herself with him. Principessina Gabriella fresh out of the schoolroom discovering inside herself, to her entranced surprise, enough sex to light up Italy—and all with her pure, passionate American. A park to romp in with safe gates. She sighed.

At which Dolly Casamassima turned from the bougainvillea and cleared her throat. The words "Gabriella, dear, what the fuck is going on?" which had been fully formed in Dolly's head for two days, like a well-rehearsed question to a foreign station master, got their chance to come out. Gabriella looked a bit less shaky now.

Gabriella said, "You remember Giovanni Stears?"

No, she did not. She had not met Prince Casamassima when Gabriella began her grand tour of defloration across Italy, a country which Dolly Biddle had not at that time even visited. She had been safe in Philadelphia. Yes, she knew about it, about Giovanni Stears. *Dear God*, thought Dolly, *that's all this is?* It depressed her to think that she and Gabriella were entering upon another set of years in which one could make a fool of oneself at any moment. There was such a short period in between.

These thoughts quickly uncovered some envy. Her guest had been wandering around at night, sozzling wine and, according to her maid, gulping Valium. She had been talking to herself. She should have looked ungodly. Yet there she was, chestnut hair cascading down, a light in her eyes glowing through her face, the breast holding position within the blouse quite obviously unsupported. *Sex was good for women*, thought Dolly, *certainly for the skin*. Gabriella's advantage probably lay in starting early. Dolly felt the guy ropes of her face-lift twitch within her cheek. Sex might land you in the gutter, but you looked good going there.

She said, "Lots of luck, darling. I hope it works." At bottom she was a kindly woman and she meant it.

"It's going to work," said Gabriella, but she was thinking of Calvetto.

Prosciutto appeared from behind her shoulder, wrapped around ripe figs. She took four of the little bundles; Valium and alcohol had dug a hole inside her. She ate one without waiting. *Prosciutto con fichi* was one of her absolute loves, delicately salty and then lusciously sweet—so much so that a wasp cruised over and hovered above her plate.

She was not especially considering method or theory.

As to theory: that to murder Calvetto would solve her more apparent problems was a given, hardly to be discussed. It was Gabriella's belief that no other person could connect her with her crimes, for so Calvetto had assured her. Absent Calvetto, she could withdraw from them in silence. As for Calvetto, since her fear of his subtlety was superstitious, she easily assumed that he could find a way to betray her and save himself, if that were what he wanted. Or have her killed. He would surely do one or the other. She had never accused him of indifference.

Even suppose that some other person had knowledge of her, perhaps not quite precise, it was still by no means certain that any but Calvetto would lust to destroy her if she merely ceased to participate. It seemed to her obvious to anyone, since it was obvious to her, that there was no clear connection between ceasing and confessing. She might be wrong about that, but she was ready to risk it.

All of this, abstractedly, had been clear to Gabriella for some time. It occupied her very little now.

What struck her was the similarity between Calvetto and the wasp above her plate. He was quick, sudden, venomous, and danced upon the air. She lifted her knife swiftly and trapped the wasp against the plate. She pressed. The beautiful golden wasp lay severed, abdomen from thorax. A drop of ooze was on her plate. She was sure that she could kill Calvetto.

"I thought I'd go swimming a little later," said Dolly. "It's lovely at the end of the afternoon. Anna could go out and get you a bathing suit if you feel like joining me."

"I'd like that very much," said Gabriella. "Thank you."

She ate another prosciutto. It occurred to her that it was pink flesh with dark soft entrails. She deliberately did not drive the thought away.

Princess Gabriella Harriman-Farnese lay on her back at the far edge of the Casamassima swimming-dock without one single property around her. Princess Casamassima, who lay upon and among towels, pillows, creams, magazines, a novel, an insulated glass of gin and tonic and an ashtray both capable of upright flotation, a transparent cigarette lighter, American cigarettes, a can of bug-repellent, a spare bikini, and a large ostrich-leather sack that had held all the other items, found this unnerving. Gabriella did not even have her bikini top to keep company beside her, for she had not brought it from the house. Her eyes were shut and her face, at first impassive. Lying on the stone, she looked austere to the point of violence, like a police photograph. It was true that the stone was warm.

Between the stone and the toasting sun, Gabriella found this a better place to deliberate than any recently to hand. Instead of beating themselves against her skull, her thoughts moved easily from her head into her blood and were tested by her body. Certain things fell quickly into order. Dr. Calvetto would now be a more skittish target than before, for her disappearance would have warned him even if he had not become privy to her and Giovanni. These two thoughts brought a chill to the inside of her thighs and a warmth above them. In fact, Calvetto had perhaps not for a long time been as nonchalant as he seemed. He now saw her always at her own houses, where there were always servants. She tried to frame procedures of disposal involving laundry baskets, luggage, large tureens with a dead dwarf unseen inside, but none readily occurred to her.

Calvetto himself had rooms in an old building by the Tiber. He lived alone. There were balconies and cornices; one could probably wriggle up the stone at night, slip in, and rise above his bed. She tried to bring to memory the outside wall of the house, below his window. This seized her lungs with a deep breath while vertigo tingled her spine.

It was followed by the memory of Dr. Calvetto in the *orangerie*, dressed just as he had been that day and in her dream. In this recollection, the steel garden shears that she had had beside her that day caught the light and flashed. She heard a sound in her throat and saw Dolly look at her with consternation.

She rolled over and dropped into the water. Even Lago Maggiore becomes tattered by the end of a summer day. The surface was chopped by water-skiers and slurped to the wake of a steamer. She dived. The alpine water shocked her skin. She pulled her body against it, straight down. She was a good swimmer. She dived down alongside the old stone courses of the dock, crusted with freshwater mussels and rippling with feathery weed. It was green down here. She swam under the arches, where it was dim and cold. A cloud of minnows moved away from her and she followed them. She felt the water buffet beside her head and a thick, blunt body scorched out of the stone and raced away. A lake trout; she felt the motion on her face. The space lowered as she swam forward. She felt panic grip her lungs, but clamped down on it, made herself flip over on her back and pulled herself farther into the narrowing darkness. Only when she felt her eyes begin to dim did she point herself at the arch filled with emerald light, shoot through it, and rise the silver meters to the surface.

She broke through, put her hand upon the dock and breathed to the pit of her stomach. All around was the sunny summer water, chopped up by pedal boats and skiers, crisscrossed by steamers giving jovial toots, only very slightly spoiled by a Gelati Motta carton just off the dock, waterlogged but still afloat. She breathed again and caught the scent of Dolly's sun cream.

She left in the dark that night.

Depletion and sun put her to sleep early. She forgot her Valium. If she dreamed she did not remember it. She woke in the dark. To wake up undrugged and not hurled out of a nightmare had become unusual for her.

Instead of rage and despair, she became gripped by ordinary terror.

Here lying wide-eyed in the dark was a woman of not much guile who had gotten herself obliged to take a mere first step involving the murder of a wicked and resourceful man whose eye she had to wonder if she could face. Her heart quailed, for it came upon her that from such a place one is unlikely to salvage a whole life.

In such a state, Dolly's decorous and sleeping house no longer seemed a protection but a stone hiatus. She had nearly made a routine for herself already: dawns of horror on a bench, noons of aperitifs on the terrace.

She got out of bed and turned the light on. Though her movements were not extravagant, she was in great agitation.

Departure was at least not difficult. She wetted her face and used a comb. She pulled the linen blouse, still quite clean and with her panties to hand on top of it, out of the laundry hamper. She had arrived in slacks. After a moment of distress, she found her keys. She opened the French windows and walked out. The air was cold and sweet. She shivered.

Her Ferrari was on the gravel at the left side of the house. She was so gripped by the ordinary that she considered the noise of her departure and let the car idle all down the drive in neutral. She regretted the clanging she made with the gate.

Just as she gathered speed down the road, the alpine ridges were lit into a ring of fire by the invisible sun. She did not see it, for she was facing toward Rome. As far as she knew she was alone in the dark with the steering wheel in her hands. Superimposed on the road, she had a vision of Dr. Calvetto. He was smiling and wagging his head, but this time the motion was alive, not mechanical. He was looking her straight in the eye.

C·H·A·P·T·E·R   16

At dawn, a breeze down the river valley from the Apennines came through the woods of the Ugolino-Ferrara estate near Borgonuovo and rattled the window in the bedroom where Giovanni Stears slept. He had gone alone for the weekend there at his uncle's offended second urging, reopening the villa after several years. He had gone for more than his uncle's feelings; to have declined to go would have given fate an excuse to set a seal upon Gabriella's turning from him. The wind woke him, as had the mouse on the tiled floor and as had the thunderstorm soon after—the most blazing flash of which had come just as a small, bedraggled rabbit crossed the wide-open terrace within striking range of the caretakers' cats. Stears woke to jagged thoughts about the concerns in the briefcase full of working notes he had brought from Rome—now lying on a huge and dusty linen chest just beyond the foot of the bed and his toes; about Gabriella's silence. The room he was in had high beams, big windows, and sturdy harmonies; but he barely remembered the villa, and it had given no signs of any inkling that he might be its future lord.

But although it was July it was cool at dawn and the wind had come through the woods; it smelled of leaf and loam, it had mushrooms at the bottom of it, and as it rattled the window, Stears pulled the one blanket up around his neck.

He remembered at that moment exactly when he had last been here. It had been a hunting party in the fall, and he a little boy with his mother. His American father in Switzerland had undergone some particularly shabby crisis and they had been hurled into asylum here. His mother had been the only lady in the house. The wind had come through the woods and carried the yelps from a full kennel and smells of fungus and autumn leaf. His unfamiliar uncles and cousins arrived with mustaches, boots, and guns. He had studied them from halfway up the stairs, his arm around a friendly banister. The rooms had flickered with firelight. The servants had rushed. In the kitchen, he had been allowed to touch a terrifying thing, the head and tusks of a wild boar, to be the next day's banquet. He had gone to sleep hearing the dining room downstairs and the kennel beyond the window, warm with shyness and wonder.

Ugolino-Ferrara had woken him in the dark. He was allowed to breakfast with the men. He sat at the prodigious table by a fire that smelled of kindling. He sat in silence holding a thick, untasted slice of bread. His life until then had rested upon his flimsy parents, blown like leaves through mysterious disgraces, whims, repossessed apartments, and servants who appeared and vanished within a week. That morning, the youngest of his new-found tribe, his face warm with the steam of his first-ever cup of coffee, he had first heard of staying downwind from a stag and first intuited permanence, ceremony, and faith.

Five days later, something had been patched up in Geneva and they had ventured back. The memory of the villa had become a lodestone inside him and, even when its shape had faded, its spirit had remained for years a spot of warmth.

Now, a tattered spy of no very certain country, blown here by an uncle's concern and with a case of virulent documents by his feet, he tasted all this in the wind. He was overcome by emptiness, by a yearning for continuous, touchable things. And, with a groan of longing, for a chestnut-haired bride to wake in simplicity and faith beside him.

Having supplied the wind through the woods, the villa now threw in the kennels, but less generously. From just the direction that Stears remembered, a dog yelled in challenge, not the jolly hysteria of a dozen retrievers this time, but one watchdog with sounds alongside it of a chain. Still, Stears got quickly up and, leaning on the windowsill, looked out. His view was the terrace with tubs of neglected roses, the vines below it where drops of the night's rain sparkled on the leaves, a bright-yellow bus climbing the road up the river valley, and the rear of his own Jaguar, beneath whose chassis a small rabbit had been dragged and partially eaten.

The virulent documents, his notes and Mascagni's over the past three weeks, would go downstairs with him. To re-examine these alone in a new perspective was Stears's exoneration to himself for leaving Rome. Wandering around the house the night before, after the bean soup that an anxious manservant named Bartolomeo had held for his late arrival, he had found a study with a broad oak table. He would set up an office there. But the truth was that his operational analysis had been made before he left Rome and could not be advanced without new data.

His conclusions were thus:

There would in the close future be a terrorist attempt requiring at least light commando strength against a target in Italy. The target would be an American military facility, presumably small. Libyans would participate directly either as firepower guided by Italians or as weapons advisers for Italians, the former more likely. The attack would not come for four or five days but in less than two weeks. The target would be close to civilians and would be one that symbolically offended Italian autonomy. It would be a quick operation, allowing for the dispersal and disappearance of the terrorists if the target were not forewarned and alert.

His reasons were these:

A second small but unexplained group of young Libyan men had arrived in Rome and had been helped through customs by embassy personnel. One individual had much resembled a known instructor at a Libyan terrorist camp. This information had reached him not through Mascagni's Carabinieri, whose eyes for once had been shut, but through the friend of his youth and sometime possible priest, now Chief of Alitalia security— whose people had followed the trainer through the air transport system like a pipe smoker through a powder mill. The friend of his youth had called not from his office but even more discreetly from his house at breakfast, so that the call had had a background of unecclesiastic domestic noises. It turned out as a more cheerful coda that Stears had long ago been to dances with the security chief's wife, whose voice was now overheard objecting to the throwing of bread at one's little sister.

According to the CIA's source within the embassy, the first group of young men appeared to have been spirited away. The second group would no doubt follow; even the Libyans would not wish to use an embassy as a commando base. They would be fanned out to safe houses, undoubtedly outside Rome, probably in the region of the target. This, requiring stealthy logistics, would take a few days.

This in turn argued considerably more force than that for a kidnap or a bombing. Since the Tripoli government was signaling friendship toward Italy and was virtually at war with America, the target would certainly not be Italian. According to the previous logic of this campaign, it would have a connection with the Air Force or Navy, these being the forces that pressured Libya.

It would enrage Italian opinion because that was the whole point.

He had met with Randall Beebe in Rome. Beebe had read his report twice and had said, "All your data suggests that these people have their strongest organization in the South. All the attacks that have actually taken place were in the South. Yet you are dispersing what surveillance assets we have around small bases all over the country. Doesn't make sense. Why?"

Stears said, "Because they have always attacked small targets."

"And always in the South," said Beebe.

"And because they have always attacked in the South," said Stears, "they have always attacked where we are not prepared.

They will see the South as a pattern by now as well and therefore they will change it.''

"They work in the South because that is where their strength is. You admit that.''

"Yes," said Stears.

"Then that is where we prepare for them," said Beebe. "If we had larger resources I would consider your point, but we can't afford it. Overruled on that one. We concentrate.''

"It makes me very nervous," said Stears. "These people have an instinct for making fools of us.''

"Can you prove you're right?''

"No," said Stears.

The CIA had therefore made the following dispositions:

Local police had been asked to report unusual movements of people in large properties associated with Arabs. Results, highly unofficial, would be leaked to Stears. Photographs of known Libyan troublemakers, especially ones now in Rome and even more especially the present Cultural Attaché, had been distributed to American bases. Certain small Southern bases that fitted Stears's profile unusually well had been ringed by the CIA surveillance people. These operatives had also come into possession of photographs of Italians, not legal suspects but connected with certain grouplets increasingly of interest to Mascagni.

Security at all American bases had been increased and a quick-response helicopter crew had been assembled near Salerno, south of Naples. That was Army business, not CIA, and Stears would have wished its position a great deal more central. But Stears had finally found a day to carry off Colonel the Count Stefano Condriani of Italian paratroops to a long lunch at the Bolognese, complete with truffles and an august Barolo. He had found the Colonel to have still fewer political inhibitions than he had guessed. He had dropped mention of these United States Army preparations with a friendly bet that Italian paratroops could assemble a force to react even faster. After the *risotto* with truffles, Stears had ordered his friend the house's speciality, translucent slices of raw meat, fit food for a paratrooper's ferocity.

In short, it could be said that, under Stears and with Italian

cooperation, American posture had turned from bewildered torment to the possibility of counterattack. Not only could it be
said; Randall Beebe had said it.

Randall Beebe had offered Stears a drink. Perhaps as conso-
lation for geographical overruling. "Or maybe you'd prefer
milk?" he had said with a fine, ironic smile. In the conditions of
the Rome embassy, that, Stears thought, constituted invitation
to a club of which Beebe was President, committee, and most of
the membership.

Such were the contents of the briefcase on the linen chest at
the foot of the bed hoped to be one day the *letto matrimoniale*
of the Marchesa and Marchese Ugolino-Ferrara, formerly the
Princess Gabriella Harriman-Farnese and Giovanni Stears of the
CIA.

As a general morning rule, Yussuf ben Baghedi spent several
waking minutes fraternizing complacently with his erection,
then drove from his bowels discomfiting vapors one by one,
then, that finished, ran his hands up and down his chest, through
the hair, communing with the muscle. Thus he brought cheerful
gratitude to God's each new day. This morning he woke
abruptly and awry and dreading the telephone.

The CIA man, Stears, had left Rome suddenly. Yussuf's surveillance team had performed unusually well at first, tailing
Stears without mishap to the outskirts of the city and then at a
discreet distance with a different car up the *autostrada*. Moamar, nominally a visa clerk, was the chief long-distance tail: a
practiced man with a meaty smile and a thick, furry wrist that
could drive a stiletto in a lethal dance, almost a friend of Yussuf.

A friendship which Moamar had tried to invoke the night
before when he had called to report, in a voice of ghastly casualness, that he and his helper had lost Stears. Something about
a rural exit from the *autostrada*, a brow of a hill, a Belgian in
the fast lane.

Yussuf ben Baghedi thought principally in pictures. This
morning he lay briefly in bed picking his feet, for his more luxu-
rious functions had failed. He entertained a picture of Moamar
dying in his own excrement in a prison cell outside of Tripoli,

his face and ribs marked with sinks the shape of interrogators' boot-tips and all with a sound track of fat flies. This distracted him from the knowledge that the principal enemy agent against them, a man who had apparently once unbelievably and literally penetrated Calvetto's most trusted woman fighter, a man so subtle that he could change like a gas from American to Italian to God knew what else, was loose all over Italy a few days before Gargano. And that he would have to report that, sooner or later, to the Libyan Chief People's Representative in Rome.

But forty minutes later found Yussuf drinking coffee and peaceably admiring the fit of his new shirt. The telephone call had come. The lamb that had been lost was found. Moamar had hunted through the night (during which, Yussuf was glad to hear, it had rained brutally) and had found Stears's car at dawn at Borgonuovo, the third small town after the *autostrada* exit, behind the wall of the largest estate outside the town. Moamar had ascertained the number of the car. A barking dog, which had forced Moamar's quick retreat, had even brought the spy to a window.

Yussuf knew from the very first colors that swam into his head that the mental pictures based on Moamar's report would not be cheering. It was, however, still early. He was still in his room, which the new addition of a parlor had turned into a suite, on the fourth floor of the People's Bureau. The storm that had come to Borgonuovo in the middle of the night sat on the hills toward Tivoli like an old wool hat, but there was sun in the city. He allowed himself a quarter hour to admire the improvement of his circumstances. He had already said his prayers.

By the time he was down in his office, pictures of the matter were all jumbled up inside him.

He saw the CIA man's guile, a pair of pale eyes in the shadows; for there was no doubt that, even before Yussuf had begun to watch the man Stears on Calvetto's advice, Stears had already begun to watch Yussuf. Yussuf might never have known this had he not observed an Alfa-Romeo with an awkward manner of overtaking.

He saw the pale eyes now waiting in a lonely house.

He saw the image, rich with squirming flesh tones and with a crimson background that Calvetto's unconcern did nothing to mute, of the CIA man and Calvetto's whorish warrior groaning in their past beds.

He saw the pale eyes in the empty house waiting for their visitor. And here neither Yussuf nor much less the CIA man had any need for imagination at all, for the expected guest without a shadow of doubt was chestnut-haired Rosa, now become Princess Something-or-other and the CIA man's bedmate and presumably his colleague for all these years.

But here Yussuf, too broad-shouldered to fit through the entrance of any intellectual trap, ran straight into another picture set at a contrary angle and which stopped him dead. He had been shoulder to shoulder with Rosa under fire. He knew the sound of her breath, the smell of her skin in terror and delight.

He knew that Rosa was not a traitor. Or had not been then.

A more indifferent man would have denied his own certainty for his own ease. Yussuf sat with his head in his hands and looked long and blankly at the puzzle. The man Stears sat like a spider at its center, but Yussuf could not make out the web. Yussuf was even courteous when Dr. Basenji crept in with the morning mail, for he knew that Basenji possessed subtlety and that subtlety was a gift occasionally of value and not vouchsafed to him.

A last, consoling picture took shape within him: the lonely house, the CIA man, and Moamar and his stiletto in the dark. He looked at that picture a long time, touching it hesitantly with his mind. While doing this he emitted, as was his habit though unbeknown to him, startling and stertorous grunts.

That evening, Dr. Calvetto waited for Yussuf ben Baghedi in the shadows. The shadows were not desolate. They were full of conversation and expensive scent—an evening dress brushed Calvetto's arm in passing. Given the American scrutiny that the Libyan now undoubtedly endured, he could be approached in person only at such cultural opportunities as this festival of German art furniture, held in the winding galleries of the Villa Medici and illuminated, this Saturday opening night, by guttering *flambeaux*. Hence the shadows.

Calvetto was glad of them. He had been bitterly wounded by

his Princess and dreaded that it could be seen. After being revealed as an adulteress to his heart, Gabriella had apparently become traitress as well and turned her back invisibly upon him.

But he retained some pride and it was screwed to one point: Though he made himself imagine Gabriella speak of him with pity, with laughter, with disgust; though he made himself hear her speak thus not merely to the world but to the American Stears himself and to a Stears in the very act of triumphing inside her, still he turned his back as coldly as hers upon the evident possibility of her literal treason. Gabriella could in principle arrive with the police at any moment, and that Calvetto treated as beneath his notice.

Nonetheless, there were mean problems. His wounds had to be picked over. Calvetto's forces were dwindling just as the real battles began. Roberto and Maurizio were dead. Gabriella was not only his soul's jewel but an important piece of ordnance— the loss of which, rubbing more humiliation into his wound, he might soon have to ask the Libyans to make up for. He doubted that he should tell the Libyans why and, picking at the wound again, was obliged to curse the fact that knowledge of Gabriella's cuckoldry had come through that source. He could not even be sure that, in the moment of revelation, he had not let the Libyan hear his pain.

Therefore Dr. Calvetto watched from the shadows for what he had come to loathe: his confederate's bull neck, the liquid, complacent eye, the walk that pushed the Libyan's pelvis before him like a prow. The crowd eddied into this gallery under a lamp conceived as a neon guillotine with a bead of crimson at its edge. Women moved toward him casting shadows with arms like lobsters' arms, hips that swelled like toadstools; when they passed him in conversation their teeth glittered under darkened eyes. Before very long he saw the Libyan. So prepared was he to hate the Libyan's taurine complacency that it exacerbated his mood further to see him approach anxiously and perhaps tired.

The Libyan said at once, "The American, Stears, has left Rome."

"It is a July weekend," said Calvetto. "He has Italian friends."

"Not where he is now," said Yussuf. "He is holed up in an empty farmhouse not very far from Florence. He must be waiting for an agent. God be praised that I have people to tell us this."

"But he has seen no one?" said Calvetto.

"We are being watched," said the Libyan.

"I think not," said Calvetto. "It is probably the furniture." Calvetto had taken up position behind a desk of pure Lucite so that his hand seemed to rest on nothing but the same column of ether that supported an executive ruler and a framed photograph of a blond lady in garters only, no doubt a German executive wife. "He has seen no one?"

The Libyan drew in breath so that his chest all but touched Calvetto's nose. "No," he said. "Your Princess has not arrived there yet."

"So I would assume," said Calvetto, turning away. "It is better if we walk on a little." He felt the hard bulk of the Libyan press against him from behind, yet the bulk was tremulous. Calvetto walked hastily, for he felt within his own shoulders the sprouting wings of a sublime, iridescent lie and did not know whether he dared to fly with them.

Yussuf said, "And who else would he be waiting for, with what we know about her now? Do you not see this?"

Calvetto breathed deep and turned and said, "I do not know whom he is waiting for. If he is waiting for Rosa, it will be a long wait. I saw her this afternoon in Rome and will see her again tomorrow. I prefer to keep close contact with my people just before an exercise."

He looked the Libyan in the eye. Magic in his veins had turned his wounds cool and sweet. He added, and savored it, "But it is most important that you watch this farmhouse carefully. Who knows who may come there to Stears."

"That is good news," the Libyan said.

"It was a foolish doubt," said Calvetto.

He turned again. The Libyan plucked at him; he motioned him to follow. Except for a coat stand conceived as hands reaching through prison bars, nothing striking separated them from the end of the exhibit. Beyond was the roof garden of the Villa

Medici set with statuary and potted trees. People paused here with evident relief to finish drinks and to look down at the lamp-lit Piazza del Popolo and at a slim moon scattering light upon the roofs and pines, but there was room enough. Calvetto led the way to a corner where the light was poor.

"Let us go and see her," said the Libyan. "Let us go now."

"A poor idea," said Calvetto. "Besides, how? She may be out. She may be receiving. I do not know if she is in Rome or in the country. And if we do find her, why have the boys suddenly burst in? She has to be handled carefully, that one. She does not like you very much, you know."

"Tonight I can have Stears killed," said Yussuf.

"Ah," said Calvetto, louder than he would have chosen, for a finger had plucked his spine.

"My man will call just before eleven o'clock," said Yussuf. "He is more than a pair of eyes—he is a serious man. Stears is alone there. Or perhaps there is a servant couple, nothing more."

Calvetto said, this time quietly, "And why do you want to see Rosa tonight?"

"When the criminal Leipzinger was executed, she was not a traitress. I have thought about this and I know it. Not a traitress, whatever else she has been. I would like to see her now."

"Yes," said Calvetto. "But if that is not possible?"

"Then I must believe that she is on her way to Stears, whatever she has told you. He has called her to this secret place. She will go to her old lover because she is a woman. He has called her now because he knows that our plans must be made and that she will know much of them. She will tell him what he wants. You have used her well, Doctor, but a real man can get anything from a woman. That is why he must be killed tonight. Even if she is already with him. If he is killed in front of her she will see where the real strength is and she will gladly come back to us. Do you not see all this?"

Calvetto touched his hand to his face and said, "I had not until this very moment." And then with acid: "Because I see through open eyes. I did not see this genius who had only to offer a woman supper to know everything and yet stood back while we executed a commanding General of his country. And much else. If this is why you wish to rush in upon Rosa, I do not consent. I see her when it is needed. What else do you wish to tell me?"

"The freedom fighters from my country for our two battles have arrived in Italy. Their weapons have arrived. Both are concealed. These are only simple matters, but Libya keeps its faith. Shall I go on?"

Calvetto, though glorying in his flight, heard the dangerous sullenness of a dutiful man. He said at once, "They are the matters in which you are irreplaceable and faultless. Tell me all, by all means. Something else: It has been my intention that Rosa shall kill Stears, for in that case there would be not even a lingering doubt. But, my friend, if something in her actions should suggest that she is under his control, then the strategy toward both of them shall be yours at once. Do we agree?"

"Yes," said Yussuf. "That is better. And do not doubt me. I shall watch."

After leaving the Libyan, Dr. Calvetto took a taxi, but abandoned it near the Teatro Marcello by the Tiber, though his lodgings were on the other side. To walk, for Calvetto, was to move over coals of pain, fanning them to heat at each stride, but the distance was short, the night was pleasant, and his spirit, shy at its resurrection, needed room.

He crossed by the Isola Tiberina, two short footbridges and an island in the middle. There was not much light here. He crossed the narrow square between the Franciscan hospital and the basilica and was swallowed by the dimness. He walked slowly, barely waking his pain. Saturday's late Mass was in progress, but it was not crowded and the voices within were faint. He loved the shadows of churches and the sure sense of his enemy within. But though he smiled at the church doors and the emaciated figures of saints in the dim porch as he passed, the same shyness forbade him to jeer. He walked out of the shadows toward the bright lights of traffic on the Lungotevere dei Alberterschi.

His building was in sight. Though technically in Trastevere, it faced the river and turned its back on the winding, shady streets behind. It was a four-story apartment building, built between the wars but looking older, with small, crowded balconies, stucco, tiled roof, and vines. It made the corner of the Via Titta Scarpetta; his apartment was cool, with windows on three sides. It was neither a mean nor a pretentious place to live.

By the time the elevator shuddered down, then, gasping, bore him upward, his elation at his recovery had become tinged by humiliation at his lapse. As soon as his Princess had turned her back, he had let himself fall into the leaden tread of the pre-scribed world, which could only crush him. It had taken his spite toward the bull-necked Libyan to rouse him to a lie and back into the world of risk and magic where, by means he could not yet fathom, he might still prevail.

He had left by daylight and did not at once turn the lights on now. The river and embankment reflected enough light to see by. He crossed the living room. His displayed stones were heavy on their shelves, though some had facets that glimmered in the night. He stood by the open window. Traffic ran like a necklace along the river beyond the dark corner of the house. The breeze was pleasant, for the room still held a remnant of the afternoon's heat.

He heard the faintest sound within as of a hiss of cloth. It came to him at the same instant that a facet of stone had blinked as though something had passed across its light, and that there was a woman's scent behind his back. And that the scent was Gabriella's.

C·H·A·P·T·E·R 17

Eighteen years before, during the time when Gabriella had shared Giovanni Stears's bed most nights, night had been a movable feast. He had gotten used to opening his eyes upon her hair or (since much of that time had been summer, long before air-conditioning) the curve and flourish of her back with a sheet still lingering somewhere across her thigh. After that he would look around to figure out where they were that morning. A piecrust of molded plaster or ladies half-draped like Gabriella up above indicated the bedroom of a borrowed castle or palazzo. The reflection of wavelets shimmering on the ceiling meant Portofino, down by the harbor, bliss. Cold white light and iron-framed windows were a bland little apartment, the only one they ever had, in the Roman suburbs, gotten on a two-month lease. A morocco dressing case embossed with a coronet sitting on a rickety bidet beside a plastic bucket on whose rim a cockroach stood to applaud turned out to be the Grand'Albergo Turistico in a beastly little town near Verona where the Ferrari had broken down again.

None of this had ever interested Gabriella until eleven o'clock. When he kissed the back of her neck on waking she only made an arching motion like a cat. He used to dress in silence. He got accustomed to breakfast alone. He read the papers in detail. Often he had known from day to day which Italian government held power.

Returning to their room was nice, for by then she was awake and, waking in her own sweet time, woke usually in good humor. They would talk while he sat on the bed. It seemed that she swam out of sleep trailing long thoughts behind her; this was often their most reflective time of day. On many mornings he brushed her hair while they talked, supporting it by a hand on her neck and feeling her warm shoulder and the stiff brush against his palm. Then he would leave again for her to dress. The day did not really get going until lunchtime.

And into one of those mornings must have fallen the seed, and on others must have swelled and taken root, of the thought that ended in the smashed Ferrari. He had sat with his hand between her shoulders and her chestnut hair and had never felt it grow.

So dressing on Sunday morning at the villa at Borgonuovo, he had only to turn his back to imagine her there. The more real her presence, the more frightened he was. He discounted drama now. To climb a villa's walls to be abjured in the dark by Gabriella in a gown as severe as a novice nun's was not extremely far beyond her idea of interesting life, though her voice and body then had scared him. But she was also kind, valued the knife-edge of feeling too much to bludgeon with it, and anyway needed a trusted audience.

It terrified him that she had now vanished for a week.

He saw a woman trapped in tangled metal just at the end of short black tire marks; for this time, too late, she braked. And this time, quick as a snake, a thread of flame slipped down onto the ground behind her. Sometimes at the edge of these images he saw, for lack of any better sense of cause, the little man of the opera as he first had seen him, with his face screwed up as though to curse the sun. He gripped the doorknob, shut his eyes, and drove it from him by main force.

He walked to the stairs. Eight rooms opened off this landing. A smell of coffee came up. One of these banisters must have been the one that he had hugged as a little boy long ago and the revelry must have come through that open door, but he remembered the fact of it, not the shape.

He walked to the dining room where there was bread and jam on the table, by an enormous napkin. He stood by the window. In the village the Sunday church bells had begun, with an unusual silvery and rather sickly tone.

A decision that had been shifting to and fro clicked shut inside him. On Monday when he returned to Rome he would subvert the power of the CIA, abuse his position, gull Mascagni, and have Gabriella found. He felt better.

Bartolomeo came in with coffee.

Moamar, who had trailed Stears, lost him, and found him again at Borgonuovo, did not dare a second mistake. He made sure to impress his assistant, Sidri. "You are worth as much as your eyes," he said. He held his stiletto very close to them. It was just the right size to go through. This rigor did not seem objectionable to Moamar, even had it been applied to himself. Integrity was much the same as ferocity to him.

They lay in the edge of a wood or drove the car, keeping the gate in sight. At night they watched near the wall by the house. At intervals one would sleep or go for food. It was a pity that neither could pass as Italian if he opened his mouth, for either could have been a farmhand from the Mezzogiorno at a distance.

Twice a day, Moamar put together what they had seen and called Yussuf ben Baghedi in Rome. He did this now from the piazza on Sunday morning. He was glad of the church bells' ringing, for they screened his voice.

"The spy is still alone. There are two old servants. They serve him meals but they are rarely close to him. Their quarters are not near his. The dog is on a chain except when the old man walks him. Mostly the spy sits in a room downstairs. There is a French window there. I think he reads. He does this also after dark by lamplight. There is much farm machinery. On weekdays, there must be men to work it. It would be easy to get to the spy at night. The house is not secure and he takes few precautions. I cannot say if he is armed."

. . .

Bartolomeo approached with the coffee tray looking askance as though Stears were a libertine and might ask him to strip. He placed it down at a cautious distance. This was disconcerting, for Bartolomeo was a big old man. He wore a loose black coat this morning, a snowy collar fully buttoned, and no tie. Above this he had a jaw like a metal press. Nonetheless he stood two meters from Stears and ducked his shoulders when Stears said good morning.

Stears further said, "If you and your wife have plans for today, you need not wait on me. Leave me some ham and fruit for lunch. Sunday should be yours."

In which Bartolomeo found something too embarrassing for easy speech. He got out, "My wife cooks well," and retreated. At all events, she made good coffee.

After breakfast Stears walked down the hall to the study past marble busts of Ugolinos. This was a sporting room as well and smelled of gun oil and the dusty feathers of six stuffed wild duck. Baroque Rome was far away here; these Tuscan rooms, assured and square, asked no one to smile at them, and had beams as hale as a boar hunter's spear. His notes were spread on the table. He was staying at Borgonuovo until Monday midday; thus he would see the estate at work. Rome was two hundred and fifty miles, *autostrada* all the way. He would be in his office by late afternoon. Both the CIA and Mascagni had the number here. His Jaguar had been fitted with a telephone.

"And why not go off for the weekend?" Mascagni had said. "Why stay in Rome? Since we have no idea whatever where the next horror will fall, it is quite possible that you are going straight to that place. Anyway, you are beginning to sound terrible. What is this house that you are going to? A nice lady's, I hope?"

"An old relative's house in the Appennini," said Stears.

"Cooler than Rome," had said Mascagni. "Also duller."

So now Stears sat at the broad oak table. The light, which came from north windows, brought grace to the barrels of a dozen shotguns in the locked gun rack, expanse to the tiled floor, and clarity to thought. Stears had spread his own notes to the right, and Mascagni's to the left. In the middle were sheets waiting for new conclusions.

At mid-morning, Yussuf ben Baghedi called Dr. Calvetto's apartment. Since Dr. Calvetto had brushed off all of his arguments at the Villa Medici twelve hours before, this was not easy for him. To be seen as an anxious, garrulous sort of man was distasteful to Yussuf. He had written down four good reasons to call on the back of an envelope.

He concentrated on these so hard that the telephone had rung fifteen times before it occurred to him that it was not going to be answered.

At eleven, Stears took a walk. Without new data, he had no new conclusions. He had added to his collection of misgivings, especially geographical, but these were without remedy by him. He checked the window latches of the study, locked the door, and pocketed the key. Leaving the house, he walked across the gravel. Under his car some hanks of bloody fur remained of the rabbit.

Though the villa and garden had been allowed an absent-minded decline, there was no nonsense about the fields. Maize stalks, hot, green, and odorous, brushed Stears's shoulder and overtopped his head, a gainful jungle laid out in ledger rows. He took a path through the lowest part of the land. To the right, bean bushes sat heavy as hogs. The path was straight and hard. The land rose eventually to the vineyards, angled craftily like entrenchment lines. Where a spur of hillside jutted out, there was an olive grove, silver in the distance and shaped like a slice of cake. The oil would be sold marked "Lucca," and expensive. Only beyond these riches were the penniless and seigniorial woods.

Moamar and Sidri watched from the fringe of them. They had driven the Fiat up a track that led into the woods a little way. By walking back to the edge of the woods, they kept the villa in good view.

Sidri used binoculars. Moamar was proud of his eyes.

"What do you see?" said Moamar.

"He is coming out of the maize," said Sidri.

"Of course he is doing that," said Moamar. "What do you see?"

"Before long he will be among the olives," said Sidri. "Perhaps there is a message for him hidden in one of the trees."

"Which is the reason he came all the way from Rome. Try and learn, boy. This is the first time you have seen your enemy except as a face in a window. What do you see?"

Sidri said, "He is thoughtful," after a while.

"His hands are folded in front of him," said Moamar. "He is scared. What is he scared of?"

"People like us," said Sidri, with doubtful cockiness.

"He looks sometimes at his feet and sometimes at the far distance," said Moamar. "He is not afraid of this place at all." He handed his stiletto to Sidri. "You could walk slowly up to him, say 'Good morning,' and then stick this in his ribs." Sidri looked unsettled. "I am not telling you to do it now, boy," said Moamar. "It could be important later."

His walk had filled Stears's nose and eyes with maize tassel. Among the olives, a stone had gotten into his shoe. He had taken pleasure in the vineyards in heavy grape, a month from harvest, espaliered above soil as clean as a bakery, but it was hot up there. His shirt had been soaked.

Now he had been called to the dining room. Kleenex, a sponge, and a clean shirt had restored his person but not his humor. Sitting at the table, he fidgeted with the knives and forks and then counted the courses to come. It became clear that Bartolomeo's wife believed that an Ugolino-Ferrara kinsman should get a Sunday lunch to think about.

Considerable as it was, his place setting was only a beachhead on the table that had made all that noise so long ago. The tusked boar would have looked down from that sideboard at its guests. The table was lacquered, but only by age. Under it, the grain lived. He let his fingers trace it. Chestnut. It felt like a gunstock. From time to time, the villa's substance reached him.

He enjoyed a vision of the rational. Call Gabriella in the dusk this evening, a glass of Scotch in hand, his fingers dialing a number whose sum was known to be affection. *You'll love the view from the bedroom window, darling. We'll have to do the bathrooms over. I think the butler is insane.* And so forth. Such conversations certainly took place. *See you tomorrow evening, love.*

He would keep this house as he had seen it first. House parties in cold weather, dogs and guns—an Italy far more prized by him than summer and sweet drinks. Gabriella had been a superb shot once. Perhaps still was. If not, he'd teach it back to her.

Bartolomeo came with the antipasto and a small jug of white wine and set them down, coming almost close to Stears. The ritual of service was strengthening him bit by bit.

Roasted peppers and herbs in very good oil, certainly grown here. Bartolomeo retreated.

Leaving Stears with his most baleful image: a sense of life like pictures blown in the wind, gaudy postage stamps of different nations swirling without connection.

He could not remember the first memorable incident of his life, his parents' war-time bolt from Paris to unrationed, unoccupied Bordeaux, but he had picked up scraps of it. They changed in detail but they went like this: Someone's Hispano-Suiza, himself perched on the picnic hamper; his nursemaid, who had been sent out at the last moment for *cornichons* and mascara and stayed out too long, left behind in Paris and never seen again; a whole *pâté de foie gras* surrendered for a tank of gas; Champagne corks fired at a very distant airplane. He had heard these scraps, not as confessions, but as a brave and lean campaign. Joseph and Mary into Egypt. No mascara. No nurse. The beginning of his story.

The absolute substitution of velocity for mass.

Bartolomeo took away the antipasto. He brought pasta mixed with beans. This was country Tuscan.

Stears said, "I was here many years ago, when I was a boy. A little after 1950 it would have been. Perhaps you were here then?"

But this was too much. Bartolomeo said wildly, "I do not remember, sir," and cantered out of the room.

But Stears now remembered better and more darkly. Sitting

in the half-dark on the stairs, then frozen with awe at breakfast with the hunters, he had not at all felt that something new was his, but that he had been shown something denser and richer than he had ever touched and that circumstances dictated he would not be given. He had known it also in the kindness of Ugolino-Ferrara's hands waking him in the dark. They had held kindness for an orphan.

Stears's father, who would have faced prison in the country whose secret wars Stears fought, had bequeathed his son the metropolis of exile, the capital of flimsy choice, Geneva. They lived in furnished apartments, not only out of convenience or need but as though self-expression required removals, taxis, and subleases.

He had had within one year a folding bed, a bed with mirrors and mauve lights, a place on a sofa, and a huge, lugubrious Swiss-German thing with carved bears and two broken feet.

In his father's house one was merry about clan, country, and family. One was embittered about almost everything else.

It would have been nice if Bartolomeo could have said, "I remember when you came. You wore a cap. You liked the dogs."

Instead, Bartolomeo brought the next course. It was rabbit, which gave Stears pause. He tasted the red wine. "Ours!" said Bartolomeo abruptly. Stears took it as the provenance of the wine, not as accusation of theft.

When his mother had gone down to dinner here that night (brothers, cousins, uncles, the boar, and she), she looked unfamiliar; she looked mussed and happy. It was for that reason he had gone out and sat upon the stairs to listen. He knew what he was listening for; he had seen it in the driveway in the embrace of mustached hunters in the rain, he had heard it in Ugolino-Ferrara's voice calling greetings, instructions, advice, and imprecations in the hall.

On the way back to Geneva on the train he had sobbed through the Simplon Tunnel. "Addio, bella Italia," he had cried. The Italian customs man was charmed. His mother had no trouble getting her currency through. She laughed about this later with the bright laugh he was familiar with, which shut off as quickly as a tap.

And at the end of youth, Gabriella lost, his parents dead, Italy abandoned, and America briefly tried, he had returned to his true home: Geneva.

Bartolomeo arrived with fruit and cheese. Bartolomeo seemed to have had some kind of effervescent news poured into him, which was boiling in his mouth.

"My wife was here at that time," he said. "She knew your mother as a little girl, sir. She was born on your grandfather's land, my wife."

"She has the advantage of me then," said Stears. "I was never there." Bartolomeo fled the room.

But Gabriella had not been lost then. Gabriella had been abandoned.

He had abandoned Gabriella in the hospital on the second afternoon with the knowledge that he wanted nothing to do with an intensity of feeling great enough to have brought her there.

And that because her act had been foolish and ill-judged and exhibitionist and savage and hedged with a half-child's half-belief in its invulnerability, he had been able to treat it with a disdain he knew it did not deserve. And so, escape with excuse, velocity substituted for the densest of all mass, a woman's, straight across the Alps.

He felt the far-off tiger's growl that he had heard in the dark of his mind at the Villa Pamphili-Farnese lift the hair on the back of his neck.

Coward and fool. *Vigliacco e cretino.*

When Bartolomeo came back, Stears did not acknowledge him. He was looking fixedly out of the window and his hands gripped the arms of his chair. This although Bartolomeo came with the cook's grace note, a frothy *zabaglione* with a scent of Marsala and lemon, as much at home with the rest of the meal as a canary in a henhouse. It must have been the cook's sudden, mad ambition, for Bartolomeo had to bring a special spoon.

Late in the afternoon, Yussuf ben Baghedi found the situation unendurable. He had called Dr. Calvetto twice more, each time without an answer.

It began to dawn on him that he had missed a beat. Had he gone to the Chief People's Representative immediately upon learning of the spy Stears and The Woman, his position would have been secure. Instead, he had been browbeaten by Dr. Calvetto. Now he felt no choice but to hang on.

But the thought grew in him as the day went on of some irreparable disaster unknown to him but already accomplished and dragging him down. He was accustomed to action, not doubt. He could not find Calvetto. Calvetto had not tried to find him. His link with Moamar was not as close as he would have wished. Gargano was coming closer by the hour. By degrees, the idea of Stears's cunning had swollen in him almost to the supernatural.

At eight o'clock, Moamar would call and he would have to give him orders.

In the late afternoon he did something that in terms of security was desperate. He ordered his car, a plain one with Roman plates. He was going to Calvetto's rooms.

At the door of the embassy, he thought again. He went back to get a pouch of keys and burglar's tools.

Just before dusk, Stears went into the garden. He walked to the end of the graveled path, past the marble benches stained by dead leaves, to the surround of cypresses. Beyond, the maize was dark by now but the olives above it shone like pewter. He looked at the woods behind them.

He turned back to the villa. Its square mass rested on the countryside softened by evening; to Stears it represented now an act of pardon too big for him to look at. He took a different path on the way back, toward the other side of the house. It led to a low enclosure of orchard and kitchen garden, in the territory of the servants' quarters but prettily laid out. The stone wall came just above Stears's shoulder. Fig trees were trained on it.

Bartolomeo was there, up a peach tree on a ladder, looking like an ill-balanced vulture, for he was still in his black coat. Below him was his wife in a Sunday dress the color of an artichoke and somewhat the same shape. On her right hand, Stears thought for one astounded moment, she wore a catcher's mitt. This was not quite the case, it was a cushion. Bartolomeo was dropping peaches to her one by one. There was a crate beside her. But it was not that simple either. Bartolomeo was giving the peaches twists and shortfalls, lobs and shots—the peach removed gently from the bough, concealed in his hand, conveyed through the leaves, then flying through the golden light toward the cushion, making a quiet thump when it connected and getting surprisingly earthy comments from the *zabaglione*-maker when it did not. None were impossible for her to get, all kept her on her toes. Stears also heard a sound he took at first to be the ladder grating against the bough; it was Bartolomeo laughing.

Stears went to bed a little after ten. He read briefly, then turned out the light but did not sleep. He had come back to terms with the house. He thought he knew now which room had been his that time. He was not going to sleep soon. He slipped out of bed. To turn a light on would have made him feel foolish. There was enough light in the gallery to see the doors.

He was sure that he was right. This was a small room with one window and a narrow bed. He stood over it; it was covered now with a dust sheet. Just so Ugolino-Ferrara must have stood in the dark that morning—and must first have handled his gun, for just now Stears recalled the exact smell of strong soap and gun oil. He stood and had a sudden vision of himself on the pillow and of all the twists and turns that had brought him here and thus. He quickly lost it, but he stood until his feet grew chilled upon the floor.

He went back into the dark gallery. A dim bulb was left on at the end of the hall below, but its light barely reached the top of the stairs, closer than his room. Such was his state that it seemed to him that by the third banister from the top he could see his childhood's shadow still waiting on the stairs.

The shadow moved and rose.

It moved toward him. Later, he remembered thinking for a heartbeat: At least it is not a little boy. The shadow stopped at the top of the stairs. It turned away from him.

Stears's mind, pulled by the scruff of its neck out of meditation, landed staggering as intelligence officer. He sidled closer to the wall.

The figure in the hall was passing into darkness. He thought it hesitated by the door to his own room and then passed on. Stears moved closer to the stair-head and added his outline to the frame of a large painting. He heard a click, as of a door opening.

He would have heard burglars moving about downstairs. The intruder had considered his door and gone on to the next. It was a fair choice for someone who did not know the house and had picked his room from outside by his face at a window.

The intruder would not have needed to enter the house to know that he was here. It was possible that he needed to ascertain that Stears was here and no one else. Presumably, then, he would try all the rooms in turn. It would be a good idea to identify the intruder. Perhaps not worth a confrontation.

The door faintly caught the light as it reopened. The shadow came out and back toward him. Unless a Negro's, the face was blacked. Without hesitation, the intruder moved toward Stears's door. Stears tried to recollect the state of his bed. He had not thrown the sheet back. There was possibly some hump of covers in the dark.

The figure was now just within the faintest spill of light. One dark hand settled on the door latch. One hand ended in a gleam that was neither glove nor flesh.

Stears spoke to himself the word that he had kept at bay: Assassin. He was in bare feet and pajamas. He was cold of a sudden between his stomach and his neck. The assassin opened his door.

There were no telephones upstairs. Even were he to call Mascagni, the nearest Carabinieri force would be in Lucca, thirty kilometers away.

There were guns downstairs, in a locked rack.

His taste in pajamas ran to navy blue, but his face and feet were pale. Still, perhaps he could stay ahead of the assassin, who would soon begin to search. If he were cornered, the contest would be between an equipped, trained killer and an unarmed man.

He broke for the stair-head. Though the inside of the stairs was darker, he took the banisters to break up shadow. Light increased as he went down, but was still extremely dim. His back felt scalded. He had not identified the weapon. An image came to him with horror of the study door locked, the key cozy in his pocket up above. It was not so. He had latched the windows this evening, not the inside door. His feet reached the hallway and he turned for the study.

A voice spoke behind him. It was low and questioning. It was not extremely close. He ran. The voice came loudly, now above running feet. The voice was Arabic.

The gunshot was terrific. Stears dropped behind the pedestal supporting the head of an Ugolino. The study was two doors away. He saw a young man with an open mouth come quickly toward him holding an automatic. The automatic was not steady. There was another voice from upstairs and feet on the stairs. Stears rose up and lifted the marble head, threw it with extreme force in the direction of the open mouth, and hurled himself the opposite way toward the study door. Assorted, tremendous noises marked the long, long time during which he found the door handle, got back to his feet, and plunged inside. He thought, put his hand outside the door as into a mastiff's mouth, and brought the key in. He locked the door. He had confidence in the stoutness of *quattrocento* construction. Outside, the dog had begun to bark. He found the light switch.

There were feet and voices outside the door, which shook to kicks and poundings, but seemed unimpressed.

If he survived this attack he would have to take account of the fact that he had been marked for death by the Libyans even before he visibly took any definite action against them. This made as much sense as finding a meteor aimed at him, but analysis would have to wait. The times required a gun. At close quarters a shotgun is the surest weapon, as six stuffed duck would have agreed. His case was not yet hopeless.

It had seemed to him that the gun rack was more decorative than extremely strong. He got the poker from the fireplace, put its end between the frame of the rack and the lock and pulled with his full weight. The rack was stronger than the poker and so was he. The poker's end was bent double. Outside the door, voices had stopped.

Grating noises began in the lock of the door. His own key

popped out and fell upon the floor. The grating noises grew longer. He saw that there was a little space between the gun rack and the wall and was able to force the doubled end of the poker into it. He levered. The poker bent, but the space widened. He was already scanning the boxes of shells, looking for four-shot, or, still better, two.

The dog was suddenly barking much louder. He could hear its chain flailing in the dark outdoors. He pulled on the poker again. The butt of a Beretta was now half out of the rack. He pulled a third time.

A shadow appeared against the window. The glass broke, a point of fire took its place, the room filled with a gunshot, and splinters were close to his face. He heard himself wail. The second man had gone around outside and Stears was too far from the light switch. He dropped to his knees, which put the back of a leather sofa somewhat between him and the lethal window. He could reach up to the butt of the Beretta now, but it was stuck. A second shot blew a hole in the sofa. Horsehair puffed into the air. He pulled on the Beretta with all his might. The barrel bent, but the rack pulled away from the wall. Three shotguns rattled down upon him and boxes of shells thumped on his head.

The study door swung open. The black-faced man stood in it, holding an automatic with a protuberance. This time, the automatic was perfectly steady and there was no pedestal or sofa between Stears and it. As the shot came, Stears held a gunstock in front of his face.

The man shot again, but for some reason he had jumped away from the door now and was shooting down the corridor, not at Stears. And his automatic had a silencer and the shot had been loud. Stears stuffed shells into an over-and-under. He rose, swung, and fired at the darker figure behind the dark window, once and twice. Something screamed and fell. He threw himself over the sofa and loaded again. He seemed to have a Churchill in his hands. There were sobbing noises in the corridor and then a scrabbling. He crept from the sofa toward the door. He had no fear of missing, only of not shooting first.

Opposite the door, a man in blackface leaned against the wall.

His shoulder and cheek were swampy with blood and flesh. He raised the automatic. Stears fired and the man's chest and throat dissolved. Another figure, like a collapsed, ungainly bird, lay on the floor farther up the gallery, a little closer than the place where the marble head lay cracked upon the fractured tile. A shotgun was not far from the body. Being a cheap farmer's gun, the stock had partially separated when it fell.

Bartolomeo was as large and awkward in death as in life and perhaps as shy. His arm was around his head, but this did not conceal the leaking crater in his skull.

There was no doubt whatever that Stears's intended assassin had been an expert shot, even after he had been taken by surprise and wounded. This judgment would have pleased Moamar, had he been alive to know it, for his weapon of first choice was the stiletto.

Mascagni said, "You are tormenting yourself, Giovanni. Perhaps you should have expected surveillance, but not this. Surveillance would not even have mattered—it would only have confused them. And what should you have done? Asked the assassin to kill you quietly so as not to wake the staff?"

"Perhaps," said Stears.

"Ma va' ffa'n'culo," said Mascagni mildly.

"I should have been armed," said Stears.

"Armed and asleep?" said Mascagni. "If you had not heard the assassin come up the stairs and if he had not gone into the wrong room first, you would have been dead, armed or not. It was your ears that saved you, my friend. Ears and reflexes. You did not do so badly. Of course, this changes things."

Mascagni had said this in the early morning at Borgonuovo. The sun sparkled on the vine leaves, and a mist clung to the woods. Bartolomeo's widow sat blank-eyed among village women, with her hand still covering her mouth. Festive flashbulbs popped all over the house, as though Leipzinger's party had moved here from Sagatto.

"I suppose one must say that it is a pity you killed them both," said Mascagni. "I gather they have no identification."

"I killed all three," said Stears.

"Stop it," said Mascagni. "Do not borrow other people's evil."

The telephone at the house had been cut by the assassins. Stears, with the shotgun still in his hands, had discovered this just as Bartolomeo's wife had crept into the hall, given a shriek of terror and then a rising howl of grief. He had used the radio in the Jaguar, raising first a U.S. Navy facility, then the embassy, and finally, at two removes, Mascagni. Behind this, sitting in the night in the scent of leather, he had heard the wailing rise and fall within the house.

Now, eight hours after Mascagni had first arrived at Borgonuovo, Stears was in Randall Beebe's office.

"I'm not sorry they did this," said Beebe. "They tipped their hand, gave us a murder both we and the Italians can use in different ways—and we didn't lose anyone. Still, why, Stears? Why?"

In moments of deep thought, Beebe had the habit of running his fingers over his tie as though the answer were among the polka dots, in Braille. He went on, "The geometric answer would be that you are thought to know something that no one else could know. That is when one eliminates. Do you?"

"No," said Stears.

"It is not a simple question. Play with perspective." Beebe showed how to do this with his hands: it was much like patty-cake. "The point is how it looks to them. Some action of yours. Some specific target of surveillance. It's a subtle business." He looked at Stears hopefully, but Stears's hands were not playing. "You look tired," he said.

"I had a restless night," said Stears. Just south of Orvieto, he had opened his eyes at the thumping of the steering wheel to find the Jaguar heading for the mountainside.

"Yes, of course," said Beebe. "Go home. Get some rest. You may need it. Think about it that way. It occurs to me that we should assume increased urgency on the opposition side. Something coming up, perhaps."

"That thought had occurred to me," said Stears. "And Lucca is by no means in the South of Italy."

"That was a special case," said Beebe.

. . .

He walked to the embassy the next morning. The thought of lunch with Ugolino-Ferrara hung over the morning like a cloud. The increasing urgency, in which he thought Beebe to be entirely right, almost cheered him. On the Via Veneto, the sidewalk cafés were serving breakfast, cappuccino and rolls, with bright glasses of orange juice on American tables. The embassy was four blocks down. Stears's eye caught the back of a newspaper and was held for a second by letters in a headline too far away to read. He was on the next block before he knew consciously that the letters were *H* and *F,* spaced as in Harriman-Farnese but probably not that at all. The paper was *La Repubblica,* which would be waiting in his office, so he did not need to buy it.

He bought it at a kiosk on the corner.

Nothing on the back page. The paper must have been folded.

He turned the pages until the pedestrian light turned green and he was carried along over the curb. He bumped into someone's back and creased the paper.

He found it in a ghetto of late news. It was principally the picture of the remains of a car, scorched and sheared with boulders around it. The report was terse and sketchy.

A body presumed to be that of the Princess Gabriella Harriman-Farnese was recovered early this morning from a wrecked car in a mountainous region near Frosole. The car, a Testa Rossa model Ferrari registered to the Princess and frequently driven by her, had evidently left the road and plunged into a ravine, where it was partially consumed by fire. The cause of the lugubrious event, to which there were no witnesses, is unknown, according to the Polizia Stradale. The Princess, descended from prominent Italian and American lines, was thirty-five years old. An inquest will be held.

There was a photograph of Gabriella too, but it was smaller than the car's.

He never remembered reaching the embassy that morning or going to his office. Later he discovered that he had evidently answered the telephone there and given instructions to an agent. About mid-morning, the telephone rang again. This time it was

Randall Beebe's aide. He was to report to General Brandt Larsen's office on the instant. An emergency. Stears got up and moved the chilled acid inside him in the direction of the elevator.

Beebe was already there. Embassy people were moving toward the office as to the sidewalk opposite a fire. Stears shut the door behind him.

Larsen looked at him. "I can see you've heard already," he said. "That's where it is." He tapped a pointer to the Gargano Peninsula. "A U.S. Army facility at Monte Sant'Angelo. Very small outfit. It appears all hell has broken loose."

The telephone rang. An aide answered it.

"Rocket attack on American troops," said Beebe. "It seems a fuel tanker was involved. Not nice at all. That's all we know now."

Stears strove to recollect the last few days. He looked at the map, then looked Beebe in the eye and said generally, "According to Randall, it must be a false alarm."

Beebe flushed. Larsen said, "What the hell do you mean?"

"Gargano's not in the South," said Stears.

C·H·A·P·T·E·R 18

Once again Alfredo watched the convoy crawl across the piazza of Monte Sant'Angelo. He had the same stopwatch, but this time his rifle was real, not imaginary, and Dr. Calvetto and the glass of beer were memories. His thoughts, gloom brightened by self-righteousness, were much the same.

He was crouched on steps going down to a basement entry near the mouth of an alley off the piazza. It was dim there and the square, in full sun, was unnaturally bright. The military trucks passed café tables supporting aperitifs like precious stones, past flower stalls burning with crimson and blue, fish on heaps of diamonds. The wristwatch of the American soldier in the back of the truck sent out pinpoints of pure light.

Alfredo kept his eye on it as he unwrapped the rifle and put it together. This took eight seconds. The lead Jeep had entered the piazza twenty-six seconds earlier and would be at the mouth of the alley leading to the hills in twenty more, give or take a couple. The tanker was ten seconds behind the Jeep. The Libyans were in place. Alfredo cocked the rifle and forced himself to look at the face of the soldier he was about to kill first. Twenty-two seconds to go.

The soldier was an Alabama boy called Charlie Pugh. His first training had been in infantry antitank tactics. His eye had been following a swift or swallow darting and turning over the piazza and then shooting suddenly up as though on rubber bands. As his eye was pulled along the roofline on a height beyond the piazza he saw part of a pointed sticklike object with angular bulges appear suddenly above a cornice and move quickly, as though passed from hand to hand.

He saw it for only a few seconds, but he needed a third of them to know what it was: a U.S. Army LAW antitank rocket or its Soviet clone, an RPG-18. By no lawful possibility whatsoever could it be on a civilian roof above the convoy.

First he shouted. Then he pointed.

Alfredo saw the soldier lean out of the truck and saw the wristwatch on a stiff, outstretched arm. The man was shouting. He could not see what he was pointing at but he knew exactly what was there. He could see movement begin within the truck.

He put the rifle quickly to his shoulder, breathed deep, and shot. He did this while calamity welled within him.

Charlie Pugh, shot in the chest, fell out of the truck.

He fell twenty meters from a table occupied by Tomaso Magnolo, a schoolteacher. Magnolo saw American soldiers jump out and run for positions around the truck. On the roof that the Corporal had been pointing at, three children seemed to jump up from behind the cornice and start fighting over a toy. The toy had a wide barrel. Magnolo threw his chair back behind him and ran for the café. Just as he was halfway there, he felt the breath of an enraged angel scorch over his head. He saw a flash from the corner of his eye.

The rocket hit the tanker in the rear chassis with such force that it slewed it through an arc of twenty degrees in the middle of the piazza. One wheel with heavy tire soared up and hung above the square like a spectacular soccer punt. It hung above a deepening collective scream and a movement of people toward the edges of the piazza. The tanker driver immediately turned on the foam extinguishers and jumped out. He had a hand-held extinguisher as well, but the back of the tanker was burning from deep within and he could see catastrophe on the way.

The Americans were sending heavy fire to the Libyans' roof.

An officer was running from the Jeep, past the tanker. Alfredo stood in the mouth of the alley, shot at him, and missed. He ran toward his escape car. He saw an American turn toward him. Something blunt hit him unbelievably hard in the knee, which collapsed under him. He found himself sucking on a stone of the piazza and sobbing. This was Alfredo's first lesson in being shot.

The back of the tanker sent up a fountain of flame which turned suddenly into a white-hot balloon that rose over the square. It passed the wheel, which just then came down and went bounding and smashing all the way to the church. Out of the white center, pieces of jagged black metal transported themselves instantly to the sides of the piazza where they clattered down upon people, sometimes covered with charred flesh. Roofs and windows disintegrated. A breath of hell hung over Monte Sant'Angelo.

Many American soldiers had been thrown to the ground by the blast, but some, sheltered by the truck, kept up their fire on the Libyans. These were seen to be leaving the roof. After a moment they were seen scampering down a short outside staircase and then were lost to view. The Americans did not know the village well and, though they had given a good account of themselves, were leaderless and stunned. Their Lieutenant had been close beside the tanker when it blew.

Alfredo saw the Libyans run out of a little archway, as planned. They were not extremely far from him and he held up his arm to them for help. The man he knew to be their leader looked at him, raised his side arm, and took careful aim. Alfredo tried to move, but used the wrong knee. It squirmed under him like a caterpillar and he screamed for that at the same time as for the second bullet, which hit him in the back. The Libyan aimed again but an American had seen them now and opened fire on automatic. The Libyans ran out of sight. Alfredo's eyes went dark.

That was the end of the firing.

Monte Sant'Angelo was covered with a stinking, roiling cloud. All around the square small fires had begun to burn in windowless, roofless buildings. Sobbing came from everywhere and was broken by screams like bright short flames from the grievously burned. At a café immediately opposite the tanker, very bad things had happened. A man was found to be scorched fast to his seat as though by an inexpert cook. The head of Saint Angelo above the fountain had broken off and a thick mat of smoldering flowers was pasted against the church wall. Mangled fish turned up in broken cars, in the telephone kiosk, in the lap of a burned and weeping waiter, as though in strange memorial to the day of the corsairs. A screaming of higher pitch began from a window above a grocer's store. It seemed that a child was stuck in a burning room.

Thanks to Corporal Pugh, Monte Sant'Angelo beyond the piazza was not devastated. The town's ambulance and fire engine, both its doctors and two of its policemen were in condition to give help. Within an hour, many of the fires would be out, the square full of filthy water, the faces of the dead covered, and the worst wounded placed on stretchers and drugged. The American installation on the hill quickly sent such help as it could. Medical helicopters and Carabinieri arrived.

Alfredo felt that something pressed against his mouth. It was hard and bitter, but he sucked at it. He lay at the bottom of a deep, dark pool of pain and the sensation at his mouth stopped him from drifting on into utter blackness. Sometimes fear floated over and nuzzled his neck. Then his hand, far away, tried to tighten over the shape beneath it.

As soon as he did that, he became the subject of a property dispute. The American soldier standing over him had thought that the terrorist was dead—there was a bog of blood and mess in the small of the terrorist's back—but when its hand moved on the stone of the piazza and its mouth opened on the dirt, he realized it wasn't. He called over to the other Americans. This brought one of the two local policemen, who had just entered the square. Though there was devastation on all sides, a body with foreign troops standing over it seemed compelling.

The American soldiers knew neither who their attackers had been nor whether this was the beginning or the end of the attack. To most of the Italians in the piazza, the Americans appeared to have leapt out of their truck and assumed the offensive before anything else happened at all. Italians not originally in the piazza came into a scene of horror involving American soldiers without any apparent enemy whatsoever.

Under these circumstances, Alfredo, alone, scrawny, sprawled on the ground, with a rifle a meter from his hand, was the only starting point for comprehension. He was like a terrorist poster fallen over on its side.

The American installation under the antenna array on the hill was designed to eavesdrop on the Balkans, but it had little contact with the village below. The chestnut forest cut off the view. Although preceded by Alfredo's single shot and then the rocket, the explosion of the tanker, which came as a white glare through the trees and then a jolting concussion, seemed to come from everywhere and nowhere. With the Lieutenant dead and the Jeep wrecked, it was some time before a soldier in Monte Sant'Angelo used the undamaged radio in the truck to call the base. The Major there, with no information but the light-arms fire after the explosion, had by then already sent what he could —a light ambulance, a Captain, and two Jeeploads of men, most of whom were radio technicians. After the call from the Jeep, the Major sent the first message to United States command headquarters in Naples, using terms not surprisingly shaken.

This convoy took about a quarter of an hour to get out of the compound and down the hill. It was the first outside force of order to enter Monte Sant'Angelo after the blast.

It was this second convoy's report which was being digested in General Larsen's office at the embassy in Rome at the time when Giovanni Stears was invited to augment his knowledge of Hell for the second time that morning.

In an Italian helicopter, Stears sat bowed in silence with his arms around his middle. The voices and body smells around him at the outer edge of consciousness were Italian, not American, and this gave him a comfort he half recognized.

The summit of Gargano was below the helicopter, then beside it. Monte Sant'Angelo was beneath them. The ventilator began to give out burned and bitter air. General Della Cappella of the Carabinieri, who had laid his braided cap on his lap, suddenly

took a small comb from his pocket and began urgently to comb
his hair. Captain Mascagni, sitting across from Stears and behind his Chief, looked up, startled at such emotion. General
Della Cappella realized what he was doing and put his cap
fiercely back on his head.

This was a staff helicopter of the Carabinieri. American
medical and command personnel were coming from Naples,
not Rome. No American diplomats were coming to Monte
Sant'Angelo.

"We are taking the position," had said the First Secretary at
the United States embassy, "that the target was not American
military. American personnel merely became entangled in an act
of Italian domestic terrorism."

"Fully agreed," had said Randall Beebe. "CIA concurs."

"That is total crap," had said General Larsen.

"It will do until the perpetrators put out their communiqué,"
said Beebe. "Which of course will tell everybody that they were
shooting at us. Might give us a whole hour. I wonder what
they'll call themselves this time."

"That is not certain at all," said the First Secretary.

"Balls," said Beebe. "There is one small bright spot. There
is currently no American television news team in Italy. By the
time they get to Gargano, the raw meat should be gone. Let us
be thankful for cutbacks."

"They'll buy Italian tape," said the First Secretary.

"Then try and be an Italian if you see a camera," said Beebe
to Stears. "After all, that's your special skill."

Stears had therefore to hitch a ride with the Italians and was
the only American civilian in Monte Sant'Angelo.

Since the attack had been over before it was reported, much
less suspected, neither the existence of the American quick-
response helicopter three hundred kilometers away south of Salerno nor the ardor of Stears's paratroop Colonel had been of
the slightest effect.

The present helicopter settled down into the piazza. Two
sharpshooters got out first, crouched down, then everybody
stood aside for General Della Cappella. Stears, whose eye had
passed vacantly over the false scenery of the Abruzzi sparkling
in the sun and cows contented in the meadows, now observed

that they were back in the authentic world of ash, fire, and death. He retched at the new air through the ventilators, then made himself breathe deeply. Mascagni looked through the windows and murmured to him, "I always used to see you in such nice places, Giovanni. They are getting less and less nice."

Out on the Adriatic, the young leader of the Libyan rocket squad could see the smoke rising from Monte Sant'Angelo halfway up the Gargano headland. The fishing boat carrying the three Libyans out to sea was still close enough in for him to make out the road twisting up the hill, but the trees were just a wash of green. His legs flexed to the motion of the boat. It ballooned through a light swell. Fans of spray blew from the bow and sparkled on the gunwales. The boat's planks were freshly painted blue outside and gold within, the engine sang freely, and the hull met the waves with a sound like deep, easy breaths. It was a situation to feel grand in.

The dirty smudge on the horizon was the freighter that would take them back to Libya.

The leader's legs flexed awkwardly, for he was not a seaman. There was bile in his throat. He watched a helicopter making angry, angular dashes low above the sea. It was too far away to tell whether it was American or Italian. If it turned straight toward them now, it would reach them before they gained international waters. Their boat, however, was like all the other fishing boats, of which there were several dozen on the sea today.

Not only was there bile in the young leader's throat, there was anguish in his heart. He was a captain who, by throwing all his faith and courage into every test, had become accustomed to the taut joys of achievement.

It was conceivably not his fault that an American soldier had apparently seen something before the strike; the roof they worked from had been inspected by Yussuf ben Baghedi, a senior man. Under the circumstances, hitting the tanker prematurely and incompletely was conceivably excusable.

But he had let himself be panicked at the end and he had not made sure that the Italian on the ground, Alfredo, was dead. He should have made sure and died himself. To that there was no argument. If Alfredo lived, the spine of his own life was broken.

The freighter trudged the horizon, dark as a prison hulk.

Like many Army men, Colonel Strindling, the ranking United States officer now present in Monte Sant'Angelo, did not like the CIA. The CIA could be expected in situations that a straightforward officer would give two medals to avoid. He found the CIA man he was dealing with now, called Stears, more unsettling than most.

He had been watching Stears whenever possible. The man had arrived from Rome with the Italians, had identified himself to the officer in charge of the medevac team, and had ignored Colonel Strindling. That "ignored" was not quite the word was what made the man so unsettling. His examination of the piazza was unhurried and precise. He talked to Italians, especially to civilian survivors, which he appeared to do with ease. He found a local to take him to the roof the terrorists had used and stood for several minutes looking down from it. He went into the field hospital that the Italians had established in a building on the piazza and spent some minutes there. He spoke to American wounded being taken to the helicopters. Colonel Strindling saw that they appeared to talk to him with perfect naturalness although his expression was bleak and although young American soldiers abroad are usually shy in front of notable American civilians.

The time came when Colonel Strindling observed that Stears was walking toward him, deviating exactly one foot around the rotor of a helicopter that had begun to wind up. He thought for a moment that Stears was going to walk through him, but he stopped at a perfectly correct distance. He looked at Strindling's shoulder tabs and uttered "Colonel," as one might say "orange crate," or "wood pigeon."

He then said, "There has been a communiqué. Responsibility for this action has been taken by a group named the Aurora Rossa, the Red Dawn. The Red Dawn is the group that murdered General Leipzinger." He said this as though dropping a package at a door.

Colonel Strindling took in breath to speak. Stears spoke instead. "There were three terrorists besides the one who was captured wounded. I believe there were eighteen American soldiers and an officer. If the terrorists had been overpowered and captured by our men in hot pursuit, it would have fully restored American credit. Apparently this was not tried. Is there a reason?"

Colonel Strindling spoke of lack of vehicles, disoriented men, the officer's death.

Stears broke in with no change of tone. "The Italians now believe that the terrorists escaped by sea. We do not know if they are foreign or not. We are dependent on the wounded gunman, who may never talk. After he is moved from here, it will be difficult for the CIA to get access to him. He will be protected by Italian law. I think that is all we have for each other, Colonel."

He looked Colonel Strindling full in the eye and left. Only then did Strindling see what he had been groping for since he had first laid eyes on Stears. He said to himself, "He doesn't look like someone who's flown in to look things over. He looks like the people it happened to."

Alfredo now lay in a room off the lobby of the less damaged of the two pensions on the piazza. He had already changed ownership several times between the Americans and the Italians. His circumstances had improved slightly with each switch. So had the rank of his captors.

As well as being shot, he had briefly experienced humanity, also a novelty for Alfredo. He had floated up out of his pool of dark pain to find himself turned over on his back, on white sheets, smitten by the light. His body grated with pain. Through his brain bolted hard, bruising phrases—*Taken by the Fascist Enemy, Interrogation, Failure of the Mission*—but these were as though projected by a cruel light from another room. This was before he had been placed under full guard in a separate room. He had been among bodies unconscious, whimpering, or whose eyes were blank with incidents they could not incorporate. He felt that these people and he had drifted together out of the dark pool. Among his victims, for the first time in his Armed Struggle for the Proletariat, Alfredo felt a thread of fellowship.

Now he was attended by a doctor and two nurses. Officers of

the Carabinieri, even a General, came in and out and stood beside his bed. A priest drifted in and looked at him hungrily. For a time there was a civilian there in the background; after this man left, somebody murmured "CIA." No less than four Carabinieri commandos with submachine guns protected Alfredo's sickroom. When the door opened he could see that the large room outside had been turned into a field hospital for civilians, presumably awaiting ambulances, but these received far less individual treatment. It occurred to Alfredo that the Fascists believed that an armed attempt to rescue him might be made on the road and that he was being kept for a military ambulance helicopter. This thought, which was correct, was quickly eroding his sense of being a part of a general suffering. His suffering was heroic and special.

On the other hand, he undoubtedly was suffering and they were beginning to question him.

He had been asked about the nature of his group, the size of the attacking force, the names of its participants, its escape route, and its purpose.

He remembered now, though not quite clearly, that the leader of the Libyans had been the last to shoot at him. He understood that the purpose had been to silence him. This made him bitter, but it was a dark and exalted bitterness to do with the Harsh Destiny of the Revolutionary and it hardened his will instead of undermining it. He hoped to return the same favor to the Libyan one day.

He had given his name only as "Alfredo," and his profession as "Revolutionary." Nothing else.

Though the tone of the questioning so far was tentative to the point of barely exceeding polite interest, Alfredo showed courage in resisting it. His mind was not clear enough to trust itself. He suspected that he was badly hurt. He was alone among his enemies. Every mention of capture by the Fascist police, in his circle, included references to "torture" and "interrogation": endlessly repeated, this had become a fact equal to and independent of the fact that Alfredo knew several people who had been to prison, none of whom had been tortured and two of whom had gotten married and begun families there. In the theoretical part, much the larger, of Alfredo's brain, he was about to be flayed.

This courage, and the fact that he was the center of attention, served to waken that ravenous beast, his self-importance. At the very beginning, the Alfredo who had risen from the bottom of the dark pool was discernible, though only in mild voice and lowered eye. By this time, he had progressed to answering with bantam defiance and with a voice like a loudspeaker running on poor current.

The American who had been there earlier had come back. He was silent as before. This time, however, he did not stand at the rear.

There was a lull in the questions. The American leaned forward, looked Alfredo carefully in the face, and said quietly, "Why did you do this?"

It was surprising enough that Alfredo was taken aback, but he quickly rallied.

"For the Liberation of the Italian People," he said. He spoke louder than he had spoken yet.

The American had come back with something in a cloth which he now deftly unwrapped. He leaned forward and quickly but gently dropped it on the white sheet over Alfredo's breast. It was black and ended in slender extremities pointing up from the bed. It sat on the sheet like a dark lily.

It was a charred hand severed jaggedly at the wrist. The fingers were slender and the nails were long and even. On the index finger, a gold wedding band was soldered to the skin.

"Consider the question," said the American.

The scene until then had had something of an Adoration, the Italian faces, gravely concerned above uniform collars, all considering the body on the spotless bed. Now a wind of abhorrence blew through it. A nurse moved before anybody else. She was a plain woman of quiet movement but she grabbed a towel and took up the severed hand like an overboiling pot and threw it all from the room. She turned on the American as though he had bloodied an altar.

"*Barbaro!*" she said.

"*Sì,*" said Stears.

Ambassador Buxhalter said to his First Secretary, "You were wrong about the bake sale, Henry. It would have served a purpose. I felt it as soon as the helicopter landed in Castel Sant'Angelo. There was palpable hostility there from the very first. I can hardly condemn it. Those people suffered a terrible thing."

This was at the embassy. The helicopter that had carried the Ambassador to and from a commiserative inspection of stricken Monte Sant'Angelo was just now rising from the roof on its way back to Naples. Its Navy colors had been polished for the day. It looked like a flying eggplant. The demonstrators outside the embassy were stirred by its flight into holding their placards high and jumping up and down on tiptoe as though being almost sucked up by the rotors. Two days had passed since the disaster. Monte Sant'Angelo still stank of smoke. There had been placards and shouted slogans the evening before, but the demonstration had begun in force that morning.

Henry Halston, the First Secretary, raised his voice. "*Monte* Sant'Angelo, Ambassador. *Castel* Sant'Angelo is here in Rome. Yes, there was hostility. There will be more."

"I knew that," said Buxhalter. "*Monte*. The trouble with the State Department, Henry, is it forgets that nations are people. If all the United States forces in Italy had spent two days baking cakes and selling them on the streets—as my wife suggested— and I had brought the proceeds to the town of Monte Sant'Angelo today, that hostility would have melted away."

The demonstration at Monte Sant'Angelo had been unpleasant. A few stones had sailed out from behind the placards. A tomato had hit the helicopter's gleaming door four-square. In the immediate vicinity of the Ambassador, who had been quite unmistakably affected, things had been a bit more civil. The demonstrators, in fact, had not seemed to be from Monte Sant'Angelo.

"No doubt," said Halston, with a buttoned little smile.

Buxhalter looked at the smile. "I ran for the Senate twice," he said, "and I won both times. I used campaign stunts that would have made me far more ridiculous in your eyes than cake sales, Henry." Buxhalter walked toward the window, from which the tail of the helicopter could be seen disappearing in the sky, and said in its direction, "An opinion that would have troubled me less than you can imagine, Henry."

Halston looked up sharply, but Buxhalter turned and said, "Did you know that the Mayor of Monte Sant'Angelo was a Communist? Just think, this morning I kissed a Communist with a mustache. Tell them that in Wisconsin!" He shook his head in disbelief. "To tell the truth, I rather liked him, the poor fellow."

Buxhalter, at the window now, was driven back by a howl of *"Assassini americani! Assassini militaristi!;* this must have been meant for the helicopter crew, Buxhalter being civilian and singular.

"You are due at the Quirinale in an hour, Ambassador," said Halston. "From what I hear, taking a cake might not be such a bad idea."

Buxhalter sat down weightily at his desk and sighed. "What is the main problem over there, Henry?" he said.

"The main problem is beginning to be the relationship of the United States and Italy and of the United States bases in Italy. Even before Monte Sant'Angelo there was public enmity, and now there is an outcry. With any luck, the Foreign Minister will not choose to get too far into that today. The immediate problem is a rolling gun in the CIA here called Giovanni Stears. He has been organizing surveillance of Arab embassies in a manner that we are committed not to do. And heaven knows what else. The Italians are furious. That will be their lead-in, Ambassador. Stears.''

"A rolling gun?'' said Buxhalter. "Stears? He always seemed quite sensible to me.''

"CIA," said Halston. "And an arrogant son of a bitch as well. He rolls, all right. Ask Beebe. He also behaved offensively at Monte Sant'Angelo.''

"Did he?'' said Buxhalter. "I should have thought it was difficult to be noticed there at all.''

"It's not entirely regrettable,'' said Halston. "I should advise you to use Stears, Ambassador. It's a little bit unfortunate that we never told the Italians officially that that installation existed to spy on the Balkans. They knew, of course, but now they can say they didn't. That seems to be fueling the demonstration more than anything else right now. The more the Italians talk about Stears, the less they can talk about that.''

"The Italians do not know how to humanize disasters,'' said Buxhalter. "Girl Scouts. Rotarians serving coffee. Blanket round-ups. I have noticed that they have no talent for it. A bake sale would have shown them the way.''

Mrs. Quist called Stears at home that evening in the still hour of the Parioli night when papas have long since driven home from work and then reissued toward dinner parties with their nicely scented wives. Unlike any other Roman district, Parioli is quiet all evening until the brief hour of car doors shutting, tinkling laughs, and the somber good-nights of doormen. This silence was bad for Stears. The telephone in his apartment almost never rang. Now when it did so, the sound made him freeze as though only the accumulating weight of death and horror around him could have tripped the bell.

He did not recognize Mrs. Quist by name. But then the rough-sawn and angular voice brought to memory a silk shawl of dragons, nicotine fingers, the fountains of the sea-horse pavilion at the Villa Pamphili-Farnese, and, for a racking second, Gabriella's warm body under the pines. Mrs. Quist had been their bridesmaid more than she knew.

"The worst part of these situations," Mrs. Quist said, "is that one never knows what the relationship between people really was and so one never knows what to say. One can be foolish or embarrassing. You have been on my mind all day and I am going to risk it. I think I am desperately sorry for you and I believe I ought to be. It has always seemed to me that at these times people should treat lovers and mistresses just as they treat widows and widowers, but they never do." And then, by way of explanation: "There are advantages to status. The American Academy is terribly established. I called the Buxhalter woman and made her find out your number at home and give it to me. I supposed that even spies had telephones. Is there anything at all that I can do?"

There was not, he said. All that had been in Mrs. Quist's old manner, though a little ragged around the edges. And then he heard over the telephone a rattling exhalation of smoke as Mrs. Quist whipped her voice across hurdles of delicacy and said, "Apart from Dolly and me, there's not going to be a cat at the funeral, from what I hear. She didn't really have anybody, our Gabriella, in spite of all. There's some mincing cousin somewhere, a Prince Something-or-other who goes around with priests. And they're treating it as, you know, it doesn't look as if she tried to stop the car, and the bloody Catholics are treating it as though it was black magic. They're burying her as though they were ashamed of her. I think we ought to go to the funeral whether they want us to or not. I dare say she was more yours than that Prince's, no matter what the hell you were doing to each other. I didn't mean that. I'm sorry. Dolly Casamassima said she was talking about you and nothing else. Oh, damn, this is awful. Will you come? It's tomorrow at one o'clock, I've found out. It's a little church on the Via Appia. I guess they'll cut the priest's tongue out afterward."

He didn't answer. Mrs. Quist said, "Are you there?"

"Yes," he said. "I can't. I can't go."

He heard breath rattle sharply in. "I didn't mean to disarrange your day," she said.

"Things are worse than you realize," he said. "I think they are worse than I know. The embassy is almost under siege. I do not think that Monte Sant'Angelo will be the end of this, and that was bad enough. I can't go anywhere. I have to stay."

"I think you have other reasons," said Mrs. Quist, "that I do not want to know. I suppose I am sorrier for you than ever. If you need me, I am here. Perhaps I was embarrassing after all."

"Believe me," he said. "You weren't."

Stears sat in Randall Beebe's office. Three days ago the letters *H F* had pulled his eyes to *La Repubblica*. Three hours ago, he supposed, his love had been buried. His eyes now were still able to observe that a sandbag filled the bottom half of Beebe's window and that broken glass below it indicated that it had been put there none too soon. The demonstration was worse today. Beebe's office was on the second floor. Stears's brain, though in the state of shock where thought exists only in fine-grained black and white, still functioned well. Beebe's office still existed and Stears was in it. His present was apparently not much affected. The future and the past were gone.

He had just entered the room. Beebe had motioned him to a chair. He sat in silence.

"Apology," said Beebe, "is something the Company dispenses with, thank God. When we shut the lid there aren't stray fingers out there waving good-bye. Officially, you've been a disaster, Stears." Stears was alone with Beebe. Though it was late afternoon, the light was poor, what with the sandbag. The white polka dots on Beebe's tie stood out crisply.

"I accept the apology," said Stears. "If you mean that Monte Sant'Angelo could easily have been secured and that I had advised it." There was a whiff of tear gas in the air, the political counterpart of bad drains. It was very faint; only a single canister had yet been fired.

Beebe said, "The left-wing press has come up with a name for you: Carnefice, the butcher. Fortunately, they don't have a real name to put with it. As a matter of interest, when you were dealing with the Germans, did you go about throwing severed limbs at people?''

"It never came up," said Stears. "And when I dealt with the Arabs before that, they frequently did it themselves."

"Concentrating our resources in the Mezzogiorno was logical. As it happened, it was wrong," said Beebe to his shirt cuff. Then he raised his eyes and looked at Stears. "Something we really try for in the intelligence business, Stears, is nicknames in the press. The little bastard didn't talk, either, did he? Still hasn't, has he?"

"No," said Stears. "He came close. Opinion was not with me. He sensed it. That was that. Now he's under the protection of the law of 1977 with access to lawyers in a comfortable hospital. Maybe he will make a deal one day and maybe he will not."

"So," said Beebe, "you had calculated all the odds." For a moment Stears found himself held by Beebe's eyes which, above the polka dot and the snowy collar, turned suddenly intrusive and bright—an old tomcat's eyes opening at a sound outside. Then Beebe reclined into the jacket on the back of the chair and said, "It might have worked." An object—it sounded like a bottle—borne up by a yell outside struck the wall not far from the sandbagged window. Beebe gestured toward it. "Instead, you gave us this," he said.

"That's not worth an answer," said Stears.

"No," said Beebe. "Nor would it be interesting. The United States was being pecked to death by sparrows here. I was allowed to try for a strategy of aggressive cooperation with Italian security. It involved you and then it depended on you, which has turned out to be lucky, though it was far from the intention. It has resulted in an escalation of violence that threatens the political viability of American installations here. It's a short-term problem, in my judgment, but a dangerous one. So we're running for cover. Which leaves you. You're the aggressive policy. The tallest sunflower is the first to be cut. We're repudiating all your actions as irregular and unauthorized. I have already signaled that to Washington and what is heard in Washington is ultimate truth. We may leak *Carnefice* to the press with your name on it in the end—it's the kind of thing they'd love. But not until the Italians have calmed down. Still, you're out.''

"Then I can leave Italy," said Stears. And felt the light change inside him to uniform gray on dull, straight edges. It was a relief to get rid of the last colors of the sunset.

"That was arranged," said Beebe.

"Good," said Stears.

"However, I am changing the arrangement. You'll stay."

"Why?" said Stears. "Plain malice?"

"Yes," said Beebe. "An old Roman custom—exhibit you in chains for a while. Repudiating your actions was our best card with the Quirinale. So the more the better, it seems to me. We'll give you some low-level duties. Put somebody in over you. Really make the point. They'll appreciate it for what it's worth —ceremonial humiliation."

"I have other arrangements of my own," said Stears. "I have decided to leave the Agency."

Beebe smiled. "Good. I'm delighted. Because the timing's perfect. If you give formal notice now, you're still in for six months, aren't you? That's the contract. So we really will bust you out in public. It won't even look like acting. It's your own fault, Stears."

Stears rose without reply. Beebe quickly spoke again and put his palms hard on the desk under rigid arms. "Because I detect insufficient penitence," he said. He bore down on his arms, an old tomcat getting up stiff-legged. "A lack of penitence," said Beebe, "or I'd have let you go." He looked Stears full in the face. "As though you might be more out of control now than before. I felt it while we were talking. So I said to myself just now, 'He might as well stay. Seeing as the assignments we'll give him can't possibly lead to trouble. Seeing especially that we've disowned him in advance.' "

Stears took one step back toward Beebe's desk and cursed himself for doing so. Beebe went on, "I even thought about that ice-cream man we let him play around with. That Mascagni. Maybe there's insufficient penitence there, too. Of course, I can't know anything about that. Doesn't concern me."

Stears said quietly, "Are we talking double cover? Special assignment."

"Good heavens, no," said Beebe. "Repudiation pure and simple. Inside the Agency as well as out. Straight from the bottom of my heart. Since you raised it, I'd love to have your resignation."

"You don't get that much," said Stears. He turned toward the door. From the street, an ululation sounding like "Carnefice!" came through the sandbag; he had heard it before but had not realized that it was peculiar to him. This being Rome, perhaps he should pick a balcony and take a bow. In the gray landscape of his spirit, small, savage creatures began to creep out of cracks and group.

He left Beebe's office and headed down stairs and corridors to his own. His ears rang with the thunderclap of time, eighteen years of hiatus since he ran from Gabriella's hospital room ended by his return. The grinning director standing by the cobwebbed camera had seen the cast finally reassembled: "Take two. Gabriella's death. Let's get it right this time."

Down on the Via Veneto, Giuseppe Stompano had racked his brawny lungs getting the cry of "Carnefice!" taken up by the mob, but his main concern was his feet. He was a Sicilian wide boy, and he was obsessed with shoes. Two days of almost constant duty working the demonstration in front of the embassy had given him an insight into the sudden prevalence of creamy, thick-soled American boots in Roman shops and their advantages over his narrow, spiffy shoes. He felt the pavement at every step now and it seemed to be topped with broken glass. So he sat down a while on the sunny yellow cloth of an outside table at the Grand Hotel Excelsior's café, pushed the table settings aside, stole the flower for his buttonhole, and sneered at the waiter. Order had broken down.

Which had not been easy to achieve. The American embassy was not well-positioned for mobs. It faced the Via Veneto in front and side streets otherwise. Though the junction of the Via Veneto and the Via Bissolati just in front of the embassy's formal entrance made a miniature square for a crowd to build in, it was not large and some determined traffic still pushed through both the streets. It had been necessary to keep a reserve of crowd boiling around the youth slum on the Spanish Steps four or five blocks away and keep funneling its energies to the embassy. This in turn required "speakers," musicians, food, subsidiary causes for indignation, toilets, and mob leaders. The whole organizing capacity of the Nuclei Armati Proletari, such as was left of it, was giving its best to this end. Stompano was a mob leader. Before getting "Carnefice!" going again, he had incited the first tear-gas attack from the police, rallied his troops to face it, and rotated the incapacitated to the rear. As instructed, he had taken the appearance of a camera with the colors of the American CBS in front of the embassy as his cue. It was hard work to keep morale up and channeled. Ask any good infantry Lieutenant.

Stompano had shown early talent managing crowds at village prizefights. When in prison for car-stripping, he had done well in two cell-block riots. Afterward, he had been recruited quietly into the Nuclei Armati Proletari. This had class, what with its old revolutionary agenda, and earned manly respect through its connections with the gangs. It could put a man in contact with a *capo* on one hand or a professor on the other, just like the Christian Democrats. The police, as far as was known, still looked on Stompano as a hoodlum without political pursuits, which made him well suited to a job like this. He was not well known in Rome.

Lounging on his table, he looked down the dress of a foreign woman eating at one of the tables just inside the Excelsior, caught her eye, and made indecent motions with his hips. But he was not really so blithe. He knew that this business had real political terrorists mixed up in it and maybe even imported killers. Such people scared him. He intended to give them no chance to disapprove of his work. He got up onto his sore feet and began to walk the block to the fringe of the crowd. Then he changed direction. It was time to check on the Spanish Steps.

He also knew that this demonstration was due to turn much uglier before long. People he had known in prison were being brought from Sicily and Calabria tonight. Real rough stuff was coming down. And even that was only a diversion, it seemed.

． ． ．

Nobody called Stears that night. The Parioli silence settled in with the dark. By nine o'clock it drove Stears from his apartment. Out of the silence came the thought that the flesh that had breathed on his sunlit bed two weeks before was boxed and denatured in the dark, in a place he did not know, tended by nobody who cared for her. Back in the silence, accusation, with all the time in the world, waited to speak.

For the special barb in his grief, beyond his love's death, beyond her death in the shape of her own nightmare, was that only at Borgonuovo two days before had he recognized the vulgar cruelty of his old response after eighteen years of blindness. And all those eighteen years, when he could at least have told her that he saw it, now waited to jeer.

He walked fast on well-lighted streets in the direction of the railroad station. The Via Salaria took him near the Piazza della Repubblica. He went into a simple eating place, half-tavern, half-trattoria. He chose it because it was crowded. He ordered the first pasta on the menu and a bottle of wine.

It was better here. It was rushed and loud. He sat with shoulders bowed and played with his knife and fork while he waited for his meal. His ear occupied itself with strands from conversations here and there. He took momentary solace from the waitress's flank as she stood beside him to serve.

There was a television above the bar. When he began to eat there was a soccer game, but then the news came on. He was immediately given a grandstand seat in front of his own embassy, waist-high to the mob. The demonstrators swirled, he was breathing down their necks, their elbows were in his eye. The camera pulled back. Stears realized that he was looking toward Beebe's window. A head jumped up in front of the lens. It had spectacles and hair plastered with sweat upon the forehead. The lips with pimplets emerging from the half-formed beard suddenly opened wide, splitting for a moist tongue. It yelled "Carnefice!" straight into the restaurant. It did it again. Then shut its mouth with a look of work well done. Under the television, the barman made espresso. At his table, Carnefice, the butcher, swallowed bread. The camera turned to the Marine guards standing rigid behind Italian police. Stears's attention tugged as the camera turned and, as it turned back, tried to retrieve the detail that had caught it. A face. But it had sunk back into the circus cavorting above the bar.

The demonstration was replaced by a panel of persons discussing its meaning. Evidently it meant nothing good. Stears knew at that moment that he had little interest in what it meant, that his return to Italy was over, and that, whatever intemperate outlawry Beebe hoped he would be fool enough to commit, he himself was through.

He sat with his empty wine bottle and coffee cup with dried foam until his waitress began to look at him oddly.

He walked home. It was near midnight, but in summer Rome is a late-night city; the streets were as busy as before. In a while even Parioli would know its hour of cars with merrily slamming doors, but not yet. His apartment building's marble lobby spilled light onto an empty sidewalk. He went in. His eye was caught by the mailboxes. He had not looked in his for two days himself and his servant was not reliable about doing so. It did not matter much. Few people wrote to him there. The day of Gabriella's death, Ugolino-Ferrara had sent him a letter with a distinction of feeling he had rarely met and with the salutation *"Caro Figliolo."* In other days, notes from Gabriella had been there. This evening, that almost made him shun it, but he stopped and unlocked it nevertheless. There was one small, cheap envelope. It seemed to be addressed in pencil. He was surprised to see that the name on it was really his.

He was at the elevator before he looked again, and the handwriting, though coarsened by a blunt pencil, made his hand freeze. He was so shocked that he opened it slowly, not even seeing the elevator's door open and then close. He fumbled with the flap. In it was a piece of paper covered with small squares, the kind used in Europe for every kind of notes and odds and ends and jottings. On it was a drawing, not very skillful and probably done in haste.

It was a little sea horse and, over it, a coronet.

Now he banged at the elevator's button and the door opened patiently again. He pressed his floor four times and looked again at the drawing and the envelope.

He had not seen Gabriella draw four times in his life but he knew her handwriting past and present. Not well organized, she had often to make do with a pencil end. What he held was in Gabriella's hand.

Unnecessary to doubt, he realized as the elevator slowed. The sea horse, for sea-horse pavilion, meant nothing except between her and him.

As the door opened, he was hit by a sickening doubt: Italian mail is not reliable. He looked closely at the postmark. The day before yesterday. *Good going, letter!* He was almost carried off again by the elevator, but stuck his elbow in the closing door. Posted two days after Gabriella had died.

Posted, his front door commented, by a different hand.

This knocked him into the first chair in his entry hall, beside the gondola jam after Canaletto.

But if posted by a different hand, why ever done in the first place? He tried to picture Gabriella with a pencil composing a taunt to reach him from the grave, but though it caused a freezing in his spine, it was entirely unconvincing. Four pages of furious abuse in such a case, perhaps. Not this.

Now he grew calm. Postmarks had something else beside a date. This one had "Marsciano." The place was not familiar to him. He went to his Michelin *Italia* and looked Marsciano up.

It turned out to be a small town not very far from Perugia. It was close to the *autostrada,* one hundred and fifty-three kilometers from Rome.

The Jaguar, he decided on the way to the door, was going to do them in an hour or maybe less.

He summoned the elevator and let it open before he turned his back on it. Gabriella had no villa or castle in that part of Italy that he had ever heard of. He seriously doubted that she was a long-term guest at the Albergo Moderno (twenty-two rooms, private shower and W.C. in two of them, Visa and Diners Club —but not dogs—accepted).

It did not seem useful to drive to Marsciano and stand all night in the square. Better to call Mascagni.

And say what?

Now he sat down in the apartment's best chair, pulled a

notepad onto his lap and took a silver pencil from his pocket. That Gabriella had been discovered as a corpse and buried struck him only as a subsidiary problem. In this his trade thought suddenly for him; in intelligence, burned corpses are suspect even without cause.

An hour later, he left the apartment, this time more calmly. His best tools were at the embassy, and at night he could use them without constraint.

As he left the building into the summer night, there rolled upon him the whole sweet consciousness that Gabriella was alive in it, alive for him, that the world had changed again. He was suddenly overwhelmed, rigid with sexual excitement. This abashed him until all at once he laughed.

On the morning after her recorded death, Gabriella Harriman-Farnese sat on a straight-backed chair in a bare bedroom. At this same time, though she could not have known it, Giovanni Stears, in bitter mourning for her, was alighting from a helicopter in Monte Sant'Angelo.

The door to her room was closed. Wasps cruised through the open window. There was a peach orchard outside, neglected and overgrown. Fallen fruit fermented in the high grass and wasps wavered in and out of it, all a little drunk. Beyond that was a stone wall. She had not been told where all this was, but she guessed, rightly, that she was in the hills of Umbria.

Dr. Calvetto had brought her here the morning after she had failed to kill him. He had heard her and turned around at just the last moment in the dark at his window. Had he flinched or begged, she would only have brought down the knife more cruelly. In the event he had faced her like a hurt, sly child. "In the back, your Grace?" he had said. "You kill me from the darkness, from behind?" Her knife had wavered. She still, at that moment, had thought she could do it, but she had been wrong. These memories would not grow indistinct, for now she had to recite them to him minutely whenever he came to her room at night. It was the last thing they did.

Now Gabriella took a canvas packet from the box and opened it. Inside were the parts of a disassembled gun. Her hands moved quickly and surely. This was her assigned task at this moment. The pieces snapped together. The gun grew between her hands as quickly as a fisherman's imaginary fish. Within ten seconds she pulled the last piece, the magazine, into place. But this did not quite work. It did not snap shut. She tugged at it and frowned, and then, moving even more briskly, reduced it all again to bits and started over. Still the same fault. This flaw aside, what she had in her hands was a modified Uzi submachine gun built almost entirely of plastic. Such a gun, compact anyway, could be gotten past most screening devices, though it could not be recommended for a lifetime of use. Gabriella took it apart again, this time dismissively, put it back in the packet, and dropped it well to one side of a heap of three similar packets, raising dust on the floor. A wasp knocked clumsily against her forehead, suggesting an embarrassed hiccup, and she brushed it away with her hand.

She could hear voices, raised but unintelligible through closed doors, from the room across the corridor. One was bluff, protesting on the edge of anger. The second was tenor, by turns placating and mocking. Probably Yussuf ben Baghedi, the Libyan, trying once again to persuade Dr. Calvetto to allow her to be killed. She had heard him do exactly that the evening she had come here with Calvetto. Such a waste of time, she felt. Calvetto was four times a match for him. She was sure of that. And Calvetto would never give her up.

Now that she had surrendered to Calvetto, anything whatsoever could happen to her at any second, as she had been made to see already. In this state, where not the thinnest membrane stood between her and terrible invention, she was entirely cleansed of dread. The dead brambles had absolutely ceased to crawl at the edges of her mind. At her stomach there was a constant elation, sweetness on one side, sickness on the other, changing but never quite unmixed. It was the same feeling as in the first days, when Dr. Calvetto had begun to send her disguised and renamed on errands she knew nothing of, when she had quivered in the discovery, and the distress could be folded up with the pretense. Though that had been like a sharp, occasional breeze, and this, like a submerging river.

The sweetness in her stomach grew, turning definitely toward sickness. It was cold, though less than the chill last night when she had seen the dead woman's body with her own rings put into her car, almost a part of her, and the engine started one last time. "Push, Gabriella," Calvetto had said. "You must make it move." She pushed with all her weight and the wheels began to turn. The ground sloped toward the drop-off. She was close to trotting behind it in the dark when his arm pulled at her waist. "That is far enough, Rosa," he said. "Gabriella will soon be gone." Her car had bounced down to the edge. Its chassis caught on the brink too late, as though it had seen at last. Calvetto put her into his car. She heard the explosion from below and saw a flicker of orange light climb out of the ravine. Calvetto touched her face. "This is our wedding night," he said.

In the room he had said, "And what are your embraces with other men, compared to ours? You looked in my eyes to kill me and could not. I looked at death and it did not strike. That is truth beside that trivial business, is it not? Soon you will do that for me with some man and I will tell you how it seems to me. There are no secrets now between you and me."

The voices in the nearby room stopped from time to time. She became aware that a third voice then began, almost too low for her to hear at all, much less understand. It came to her that it was a radio. After one such pause she heard the Arab's voice raised in dismay. "Alfredo!" she heard him say and then, "Not dead!" And then, in rage, "The little bastard!"

This did not concern her. She took a fifth packet from the case. This gun assembled perfectly. She put it together and apart four times each, her hands never resting. Not a hesitation. It was the best one of all. These plastic guns, it had to be said, were not of the standard of the Purdy she had had when she was Princess. She played with the thought that this one might be given to her. She did not know if she were going on this fight, nor where it would be, nor what it would be about. Evidently it involved rapid assembly of a gun in a tight corner.

. . .

Two days later she had a shorter task, the assembly and oiling of a half dozen ordinary submachine guns made of steel. They had arrived in a crate. She supposed she had all afternoon to do this. Her hands moved methodically but paused from time to time and rested, even rearranged her dress. Her fingernails were oily, but not much battered.

Footsteps came upstairs. Her door opened and Calvetto came in. Seated, she looked up at him, though not by much. He looked at her with reverence, as though at a sunset.

"These are all right," she said, pointing to the three weapons already assembled. "I have tried them very carefully."

He nodded. "There are almost enough already," he said. There were still three in the packing case. He tapped it with his foot.

He said, "When you finish this, you should come to the kitchen and eat. I will have to shut you in your room later—there are people coming I do not wish to explain you to. Perhaps you will be fighting alongside them one day, perhaps not. But I will not do that before I need to. It is a nice day for my sweet Rosa at the window. Probably I can have supper with you late, alone. We did not do that last night." He smiled and looked at her a long time, up and down, breathing more deeply. Then he frowned and stepped forward briskly. He took her left hand. "Be careful of your nails," he said. "I do not want them spoiled. Be careful." He squeezed her hand rather harshly and pushed it back upon her. "*À bientôt,*" he said in spiky French. He walked to the door and closed it behind him. It remained unlocked.

"Come," she said to the door. "Come by all means. I shall be at my best tonight."

A buzzer rang in the house. It was the buzzer connected to the gate in the wall, and soon, after Calvetto's quick footsteps going down the stairs, the gate opened and the grocer's van came in. It bounced up the drive.

She drew her face back from the window. She had secrets from this house now.

When the grocer's boy had come the day before, she had been in the room beside the kitchen. It was Calvetto's vanity not to keep watch upon her intently, nor to lock her door. She saw from time to time his eye upon her, adoring and complacent at once. In her deepest self she knew it saw the increasing apathetic grace of her movements, the growing perfection of a soulless face.

There was writing paper in the room.

Calvetto went for money.

For ten seconds her spirit lay too sick to move. It took her ten more to make her little drawing, which Giovanni could never doubt and only Giovanni could understand, and to write the address. She heard Calvetto's steps returning.

But chance had blessed her. She needed only a moment to cross the kitchen, press the envelope into the young man's hand, look him in the eye and murmur, "A favor to a lady. Mail it for me, please. Silence, understand. Quickly, hide it." There was never a doubt. He would have died to mail it. She was proud of her Italians. But, sitting at her window, she dared not risk a wave or a conspiratorial smile that might be intercepted.

She took another gun from the case and went through the drill, but her movements halfway along stopped. Her lungs drew breath in all the way at the thought of her revolt, her sea horse and coronet. Princess Gabriella alive again, only for Giovanni Stears!

For to run from Calvetto was only to run to more humiliation. If she couldn't kill him he could take her back, and she couldn't kill him. To be taken by others from Calvetto would never erase her abjection nor the pictures of it in her mind.

To be taken by Giovanni was an entirely different thing, for she could tell Giovanni about these things one day and have them put in place and forgotten in another life. And Giovanni's was her rightful bed and none of this would have happened if it had stayed so.

She owned her victory already, for her message could not be stopped and just having sent it was enough. She could enjoy it whenever she wished. She had thought about it already. She had decided to tell Calvetto what she had done when she was most defenseless and he most lofty, the next time he came to visit her at night. She shivered at the glory of her revolt and at its consequences.

She heard the grocer's van start up around the stables at the back of the farmhouse and shortly she saw it rollick down the drive. It must have been a big order.

Stears drove into the Via Veneto. There were demonstrators around the embassy even in the middle of the night. They seemed divided in spirit. The larger group had gotten some candles and apparently a clergyman and was eddying on the far side of the street. From time to time a candle or a placard was raised up on high in the manner of mild, safe exercise. The rest were wide-shouldered boyos with muscular necks given to rushing out in the street and bullying the traffic. Stears aimed the Jaguar at one; sentiment communicated itself and the yahoo flinched aside. The Marine guard at the embassy muttered, "Way to go, sir," as he saluted and passed Stears in.

The embassy was still. Corridors were lighted at their corners, dim between. The demonstration faded into city noise.

There were maps and photographs for him to look at. Italy, a NATO power, is mapped and photographed from satellite by the United States almost as thoroughly as Russia. Stears could quickly know the neighborhood of Marsciano as thoroughly as a local crow.

Which might be of very little consequence. Gabriella might have stopped there only to post a letter.

There was more for him here than maps.

He could call only one thing certain: that Gabriella wished him to know that she was alive. Nothing else—what had happened in between, her present state, her needs, her wishes, danger—could be assumed.

But a place to start was the bare possibility that had come to him in the armchair at home; that Gabriella was in some way part of his own world, the secret one. If that was the case, he thought, the classified files here should give him an inkling by dawn. At least with a little luck. He thanked his earlier luck, the high-security clearance that his cryptic role in Italy had required.

Ambassador Buxhalter looked at the Chief of the Visa and Immigration section as though at an exemplary son. This was in the Chief's little office off the visa hall in the consular building, where rows of clerks at desks were agreeably attended by clients, though it was not much after nine o'clock that morning. "You say new applications have been down by only twenty percent through all this fuss outside," said Buxhalter.

"Twenty-one percent," said the Chief of Visas. "Still." He was a large man in a chalk-striped suit who seemed to have some extra tissue like foam padding under his jowls and vest. A terrible mistake in Islamabad balanced against pleasant manners and membership in the Knickerbocker promised him a life among visas ending with a Second Secretaryship in Paraguay if all went well and in Burma if it didn't. His cheeks were starting to blossom with Scotch whiskey.

"This is the finest thing we do," said Buxhalter. "When I enter this room, I hear it rustling with the wings of hope. It's a great thing to know that real Italians are not put off an investment in an American future by that dirty rabble outside."

And indeed a United States Visa section, with its appearance of selling a desirable and inexhaustible commodity, is a heartening place for an American diplomat. There were smiles of satisfied customers going out, past the large, polite Marines frisking the hopefuls coming in.

"You may have heard a saying," said the Ambassador. "When the going gets tough, the tough get going. That's meant for you, son. I'm seeing the *Times* man in my office in a few minutes, and that is what I shall say."

"I'd say it's meant for you, Ambassador, and I'll bet the *Times* knows it," said the Chief of Visas, who kept a firm eye on a Paraguayan future at all times.

But the feeling was general that Buxhalter had done well. The embassy could have become a beleaguered, humiliated place. Buxhalter had trotted back and forth through the gardens, visiting each building in the embassy compound in turn, giving a fresh-cut rose to a typist here, a platitude to an assistant consul there, a hand on the biceps to a Marine. The effect had been excellent. The *Times* man would find a spirit of adversity, with jokes. It had become a point of honor to cancel nothing. A luncheon had been held as planned for some Italian alpinists on their way to Denver. Robert Frost readings progressed. World

War II veterans from Brooklyn met their former enemies in the
Bersaglieri. Even the weekly encounter, due this morning, between embassy children and Buxhalter's Sicilians—whom Randall Beebe had almost avuncularly named "the Pests of
Palermo"—was to take place as usual in the Ambassador's
courtyard garden. To everyone's great relief, the little Sicilians
were accompanied these days by an escort of teachers from
some special school.

Today began well for the embassy. *La Repubblica* and the
Osservatore Romano both rumbled with responsible musings:
America's arrangements with Italy were of long term, and hasty
reassessments should not be made. The demonstration today
was certainly smaller, though the rough element in it seemed to
have grown.

Across the gardens from the consular building, on the top
floor of the embassy itself, Stears looked down on the crowd
from the landing outside the classified files. He was unshaven,
sleepless, anxious, full of an urgency both morbid and carnal,
and absolutely unsuccessful. If Gabriella Harriman-Farnese had
walked through the secret world, she had walked on printless
feet—though her forebears had left tracks the size of woolly
mammoths'. There was nothing remarkable whatsoever about
Marsciano or the countryside around. He would go to his own
office, see if any of his past responsibilities now demanded his
presence, and then drive to Marsciano.

He avoided the elevator. Bristles scraping his collar always
made him feel that he had spent two weeks in airport lounges,
unbathed. The main staircase, not much used, descended in a
stately semicircle past windows onto the Via Veneto and the Via
Friuli. The Roman police kept a formation like a pie slice pro-
tecting the grand main gates and another by the more secure of
the two motor entrances on Via Friuli by the side. Right now a
small bus was going in there with childish heads in the windows
—presumably the Pests of Palermo and their keepers. Immediately inside both entrances, United States Marine guards
checked for appointments and weapons; the Carabinieri did preliminary checks outside. The Carabinieri had two blue vans with
flashers in reserve down the Via Bissolati.

Among the placards below—ASSASSINI, SPIE—he saw one good old CARNEFICE. Only ten hours before, he had taken refuge in a restaurant with a television on a dying planet. The thought made the present case seem better.

Coming down by the stairs, he crossed the ground floor of the embassy, right by the anteroom where Gabriella, golden in her ostrich-leather dress, had invited him to her version of a picnic. Deeper into the building, just before the stairs down to his basement, he found himself in the path of a wave of snickering, tussling children driving on toward the embassy courtyard garden. He stepped aside. The wave carried with it a man and woman teacher, respectively bearded and straight-haired, both familiar by now and looking like social workers anywhere. He hoped that the embassy children were absorbing the vocabulary of the little Sicilians; it would liven up diplomatic parties down the road. The third adult was a young priest, trim and olive-skinned, also somehow familiar.

He went down his stairs. The priest was a television priest, he thought. Something like that. He had seen him only yesterday.

He opened the door to his office, unlocked it and went in. An alarm had begun to ring somewhere under his ribs, but it had been ringing for this and that most of the last four days. Still. He had seen the priest for one second last night among the demonstrators on the television in the trattoria on the dying planet. The alarm was replaced by a fist around his intestines. That priest was no priest—not then nor ever before. That priest's face, even in his state last night, had plucked at his memory.

And now opened it. The face came from those memorized four years before, when he had dealt daily with the Arab world.

He reached his desk at a run, picked up the telephone and ran his finger, cursing, down the list of internal numbers to that of the officer commanding the Marines. He dialed. A secretary answered.

"Where is he?" said Stears. "Quick."

"Captain Matheson is away from his desk. May I ask who's calling?" the voice sweetly said.

"I'll be there," said Stears. He broke for the door. A chirp came from the telephone. He picked it up again. "Tell him he's got a PLO guerrilla trainer in the embassy garden with the children. Find somebody. Find a Sergeant." He was down the corridor and leaping for the stairs when he heard a momentary burst of automatic fire. "Oh, dear Christ," he said out loud. He kept no weapon at the embassy. Halfway up, from the opposite direction, he heard a howl from the street and a sound like a shower of bottles of warm Champagne. As he reached the top, the embassy alarm let go like a banshee.

In the garden, it was very quick. Today's arrangement was a nice breakfast, to be followed by a showing of *E.T.* indoors. There were smells of sausage in the garden. The breakfast table was in front of the rosebushes and covered with a white cloth. A big bowl of punch sweated in the outdoor heat. The punch was pink and the top was all sparkling ice with two little flags stuck into it. A gondolier was arriving with a carrot cake. Two others stood behind the buffet. The eight American children were already present. With them were two embassy mothers, a young man from the USIA, a Marine whose child was present, and two Italian girls from the typing pool. The Third Secretary was also there, smiling brightly, like someone not staying long. Since the fiasco of the first encounter, adults had been generously supplied and the program was not wholly unsuccessful. There were very tentative friendships. There was some exchange of language. For the little Americans there was sexual education, so far theoretical. Nonetheless, as a party it was a lot like a football game.

The Sicilians came into the garden through a door beside the Ambassador's offices. The three adults were behind. They shut the door. The American grown-ups were behind the breakfast table, except for one mother who walked forward to greet the Italian woman. Many days later, she said that the woman had looked different this time, as though on drugs, but this may have been invention. The priest, a new addition, turned to shut the door. He stayed with his back turned for some seconds and perhaps hunted in his jacket, but this was not conspicuous. When he turned around again he had an object in his hand.

The object produced a burst of fire. A window into the embassy disintegrated. The priest said loudly, clearly, and in English, "Everybody keep still." The man and woman teacher reached into their handbag and jacket and openly, but very quickly, assembled guns.

The Marine was a deep-chested young man with a ruddy face and china-blue eyes, now utterly confounded. He ran suddenly around the edge of the buffet table toward the Italians. The woman raised her gun as she locked the magazine in place, but the priest was faster. He fired another frugal burst straight into the Marine's chest. Such was the Uzi's rapidity of fire that the chest was turning bloody before the man fell.

There was complete silence for a second and then a possessed screaming from one mother and one child as though both were on the same switch. The Italian woman, cradling her gun, walked up to the mother and slapped her extremely hard. The screaming stopped. "America makes war on civilians and murders children," said the woman. "The soldiers of Italy and Libya do not." This was theatrical. She was a young woman, but with lines in her throat.

There was a hiatus. The American children were blank-eyed with terror and several had their hands in their mouths. The Italian children were also paralyzed but it could be seen that several of them still stayed close to the teachers. The woman had little hands with white knuckles holding her skirt. Nobody went near the priest.

All this had taken two minutes.

"We are serious people," said the priest. "You will listen and do exactly as we say." He had to speak loudly, for the alarm had since begun to ring. He was not disputed. The gondolier had been holding the carrot cake all this time at an increasing angle. Now the whole thing slipped onto his feet.

The events in the garden had not set off the embassy alarm. When Stears reached the top of the stairs he saw two Marines heading the opposite way, toward the entrance. The demonstration outside had suddenly gone mad. Parties of roughs had begun swinging at the police and driving back the line. Three bottles sailed out of the crowd and became Molotov cocktails. One was still burning in the entrance of the consular building while innocents, visa applicants, anxious tourists, and the like, struggled away screaming, some slightly hurt. One bomb had bounced off the wall and another had lodged in a window, which was fortunately sandbagged. Down toward the Via Bissolati, the Carabinieri vans had started their engines and their flashing lights. There was traffic milling, and everything smelled of gasoline and tear gas. Several café awnings had been pulled down and were flopping in the street.

Inside, attention began to swing toward the garden. Stears found the Captain of Marines leaning over a telephone. He looked like someone who had been knocked down from behind but was now recovering. Stears gestured to him to put the telephone aside and told him about the priest. "Jesus H. Christ," said the Captain. Stears told him about the burst of fire. "I heard the fucking fire," said the Captain. He picked up the telephone again. "Tell the Eyeties to handle it," he said. "We got worse."

Stears, the Captain, Randall Beebe, the First Secretary, an aide to General Larsen, and some others converged from different corridors to the principal entrance to the garden at about the same moment. It was shut.

It opened. An embassy waiter, one of the gondoliers, came out. The man was shaking and his eyes rolled in his head. In his silly costume he had a mild, weak-chinned face, now white, and looked like a sad clown brought for the children's party. Stears looked in horror at his shoes, which were covered with a reddish goo. Beebe shook the waiter. "What, man?" he said.

"They have guns with the children," he said. "The teachers and the priest. They have killed the soldier. They send me out to tell you." His teeth began to chatter. The stuff on his feet is only cake, thought Stears, thank God.

"Tell what?" said Beebe.

"You are to go into that room," said the waiter and pointed to the door to Buxhalter's anteroom. "They talk to you through the window there. Already they shoot the glass. If you have any weapons, they shoot." He ended miserably, "Maybe they shoot the children. I think they take them anyway."

From the window of the anteroom the scene had at first the look of some elaborate pantomime frozen by photographic flash. Naturalness, however, was not restored. The priest's Uzi was pointed straight in the window. The teachers covered the American adults, who had been rounded up in front of the table. Guns pointed over the children, though not at them. The children were frozen stiff, like rabbits in a headlight. The Third Secretary turned to look at the Americans inside, but a motion of the woman's gun pulled his face back as though a string led from the muzzle to his chin.

The woman spoke. Her voice carried easily through the broken glass. "This is a joint military action of the Italian and Libyan Proletariats," she said. "You will see that it has caused only one casualty. Its purpose is to dramatize the American occupation of Italy and to take hostages for negotiation. We require immediate safe passage through the embassy to our point of entrance." She had a habit of swaying back on her heels when she declaimed so that her throat tightened and her breasts pointed straight at her audience like weapons.

She went on, "The members of the embassy and the children will come with us. You will make no report to Italian authorities for thirty minutes. We have police-band radio and we will know if you infringe this. If these demands are met, the children will be released shortly after our successful departure from the city. We are teachers. You may count on this. Otherwise the consequences are on your heads. Raise your hands to signal that you have understood this. Now."

The first hand was Randall Beebe's. It went up above shoulders that seemed thin and bent. Stears felt his own rise. It was barely connected to him. In his head a record turned very slowly, scraping his skull. *I should have recognized that man last night*, it played. *I could have stopped this*. All the hands were up.

The woman said, "In two minutes we shall open the door and go back through the embassy the way we came. All embassy personnel will evacuate that route. If we see anybody in our path, we shall assume that it is an armed person. The guards at the motor entrance must place their weapons visibly on the floor at least six meters from them. They will stand with their hands up as we pass. They will be careful to do nothing to alarm the Roman police. Is there anything that you did not understand?''

Beebe turned to the Captain of Marines. "Do it," he said. He looked around at the others. He said, "Comply." He said to Stears, "Stay with me." The Captain left.

Now the woman turned and spoke quietly to one of the mothers, who flinched as though struck. She shrugged, motioned her male colleague to come closer, and went herself toward the American children. She herded them into the center of the garden, two by two. She did not handle them roughly and they went like stuffed animals. The Sicilian children made way silently and did not quite look at them. The teacher with the beard jostled the adults along. The priest went to the door and looked at his watch.

Nobody had noticed that Ambassador Buxhalter had come into the anteroom. Stears heard his voice from behind and jumped. Buxhalter said, "They have to take me instead. Tell them, Randall.''

Beebe answered without moving his head. "It would not be helpful, Ambassador. Anyway, they won't.''

The priest had opened the door and gone through. The bearded teacher prodded the adults along. The children came next, followed by the woman. The garden was empty except for the breakfast and the dead Marine, whose cap had parted company with him. The flags on the punch had fallen over into the ice.

Buxhalter, it was realized, was now at the French windows that led from this room to the garden.

"What are you doing?" said Beebe loudly.

"I'm going with them," said Buxhalter. He looked small and old and very frightened. "I brought these people here and I'm going with them now."

Beebe said slowly, "I beg you not, Ambassador. It is a gallant gesture, but it would not be helpful." And then: "Anyway, you heard what they said. They'll take you for a commando chasing them.''

Buxhalter went through the door. He resembled a discouraged child as much as an adult. He turned and tried a smile. "I don't think anybody would take me for a gunslinger, Randall," he said. He crossed the grass. He hesitated at the open door and then, just as his back disappeared, seemed to break into a trot.

"Dear Christ," said Beebe.

Distantly, outside the front of the embassy, all hell seemed still to be loose.

C·H·A·P·T·E·R   21

Buxhalter disappeared from view. After him came tear gas. It seeped out of the sky, waited for the children and one forlorn act of chivalry to be gone, and took possession of the garden. It settled on the dead Marine. It licked through the broken window into the anteroom, carrying rancor and dread.

Beside Stears a woman reached a nail into a pack of cigarettes, lit one unsteadily, and held it to her mouth as though suspended from it while she looked through the broken glass. She was Buxhalter's secretary. She said quietly, "They'll kill him."

A telephone rang. Stears picked it up. Shortly he said, "Thank you," and put it down. He spoke to the room. "That was Captain Matheson. The departure went smoothly. The embassy children and adults were made to lie on the floor of the bus, it seems. The Ambassador is with them. There was no trouble with the Italian police."

The room by now was rather full. A woman Stears recognized as a cipher clerk was crying quietly and now began to speak at the same volume. "Smoothly," she said, "no fucking trouble." She said it several times. At each repetition Henry Halston, the First Secretary, made an agitated movement with his feet.

"Call the Italians," he said to no one in particular. Then: "I shall call the Italians." In between, he had remembered that he was now in charge.

"No," said Stears. He said quickly. "We should do exactly as we agreed." Beebe looked at him sharply and then nodded.

Stears said more loudly. "This is Italy. The children will not be hurt except by accident. I am sure of that. Let's not cause the accident."

Beebe jerked into motion. "Right," he said. He looked at Halston. "We lost this round, Henry," he said. "Let's play the next. Don't tie up the cipher room. The CIA needs it. Where's Larsen?"

"In Naples," said General Larsen's aide.

"Lucky bastard," said Beebe. "Signal them down there, secure codes. Stears, come with me."

On the way out he said to Stears, "First things first. What's the status of Arab surveillance?"

"Discontinued yesterday," said Stears. He took in breath and formed the words, *By your instructions,* but left them unsaid.

Beebe, who had closely watched his face, said, "At my instructions. Thank you, Stears. You believe it about the kids?"

"I believe it, yes," said Stears. "I do." And then: "I saw that priest last night on television news, just for a moment. He was using the crowd to take a good look around. I had memorized his face in my Middle-Eastern days, you see. He was out of context. But I could have stopped this."

Behind them came a woman's anger and a sound that could have been a thrown ashtray; voices boiled up after it.

"People," said Beebe. "Easier without them. When do we call the Italians? Ten minutes?"

"Seven now," said Stears.

"You should have recognized the priest. I should have listened to you and widened our surveillance," said Beebe. "This is the worst thing since Teheran. Trashing an ashtray is rather mild. Better than trashing yourself, though."

"How nice to be needed," muttered Stears to himself.

Magic and sacrifice are of God. He who walks unarmed to sacrifice walks with a burning sword. When Yussuf ben Baghedi learned of the precise circumstances in which the American Ambassador had been added to their haul, he felt a flux of superstitious dread. He had assumed in the beginning that the strike force had netted the Ambassador through healthy violence. Now he sat in Calvetto's car a little distance from the old dovecote—of thick stone, round, windowless, and six meters in diameter—that was to serve as jail and watched the adult captives herded toward it. Buxhalter teetered and blinked like an old tortoise thrown into the sun. One of the Italian girls had taken him by the arm. Yussuf heard the whole story. Buxhalter's condition, which had struck him as droll at first sight, now spooked him stiff right in that spot where a man walks alone under the desert night. This was a tender spot in Yussuf.

But he could not articulate it in a way that seemed up-to-date. An American Ambassador was worth a 747 at least, presumably. Calvetto at any rate had no doubts. He sat at the steering wheel; his legs vanished under it and his torso was not large, so to Yussuf he appeared to consist of a madly grinning head.

"It is magnificent, is it not?" said Calvetto. "To think of the pain and time we lavished upon Leipzinger, and then this Ambassador falls into our hands like a fruit! If I were the Americans I would go home in sheer discouragement."

"Yes," said Yussuf.

"We will strengthen the initial demands in the communiqué. We will demand the departure of all United States military units from the Mediterranean before negotiations begin. That will make them fear an endless process. Also I think we shall not contact them until tomorrow. Let them begin to turn upon each other."

"Yes," said Yussuf.

Calvetto looked put out. "Do you not see, man," he said, pointing at the hostages now entering their prison, "there goes America's power in Italy."

Whatever the case, they had already acquired the first characteristic of captives: their clothes had become completely inappropriate. Entering the ammoniac gloom of the dovecote, a young woman tripped in her trim skirt and smart high heel and staggered like a heifer. The young man from the USIA stopped to put out a hand to her and was prodded with an Uzi. There were nine in all: five Americans and four Italians. Calvetto and the Libyan were well out of sight in the car. A Cultural Attaché has a position to keep up and Dr. Calvetto was not unknown.

"We are playing such a high game now," said Yussuf. "Have the grace to get rid of the woman."

"You are a bore about this," said Calvetto.

"We should be serious men, you and I," said Yussuf. "We are rectifying the injustice of history. That is not a thing for unclean hands. An honorable man does his work and goes home to his women. He does not pollute his work with harlots. With treacherous harlots who have to be bought with stolen corpses stuffed into cars. That is unholy work. We are soldiers, not ghouls. No good can come of this."

Calvetto's mouth had set into a line. He tapped the steering wheel in cadence to his answer. "The Americans will try an undercover response. They will do this while they are negotiating. It will be led by this Stears. And who will step up to kill him but a supposedly dead Italian-American Princess who will turn out to have been, as you would say, his whore. The Americans have a phrase for it. 'It will be a classic.' "

"I do not see it," said Yussuf.

"I faced her down in her moment of greatest passion," said Calvetto. "I can do this too. Let me enjoy my morning. This is an unusual feat for a professor. As was that."

"We have much more to do," said Yussuf. He should not even have been here. He should have been in Rome, reporting this triumph himself to Tripoli. These, in addition, were his last hours of easy movement. It had to be expected that American surveillance, crippled for the vital period since Monte Sant'Angelo, would now be revived, even if in rickety form. He went around with Calvetto now as though they were two burglars with an indivisible swag.

In the event, such was his unease that Yussuf got no farther than the farmhouse that provided their operational headquarters among the alcoholic wasps. He called Dr. Basenji, his threadbare clerk, as errand boy out from Rome. This required caution, since Basenji was not privy to the operation. At the summit of his life's work, during the days that would lead him to glory or extreme punishment, Yussuf had to juggle the security implications of his Italian ally's eccentricity and the administrative demands of the work. This was another burden laid upon him.

He therefore received Basenji with the spite that he deserved. The old man brought sealed, encoded (more work for Yussuf!) traffic and was given more to take back for transmission, along with such less delicate material as Yussuf's stale linen. Yussuf made a point of neither rising from his lunch while his clerk was there nor offering him refreshment.

"This man was a Councillor before Libya was renewed," he observed loudly to Calvetto. "Now we can afford to use him as a taxi driver." Rather carried away, he said to Basenji, "Little fingers that break seals get cut off with scissors, you know," and other jollities. He told Basenji to remain on duty all day and night and ignored his polite departure.

He would have been startled to learn that, however scalded with humiliation, Dr. Basenji whistled on the drive back. He was a cultivated man; he whistled Mozart, from *The Marriage of Figaro,* and in his brain the words ran under it. The pretty Umbrian villages sailed above him on their hills. And the words and music repeated and repeated: *"Se vuol venire/ alla mia scuola/ la capriola/ insegnerò."* Dr. Basenji arrived back in a good humor. He did not exactly know what his master was up to, but it had the look of the precipitous and he dared suddenly to hope that his downfall might not be far away. Dr. Basenji was not quite Figaro, but his heart was darker.

In the middle of the afternoon Stears stood in a corner of the platform of the Rome underground under the central railroad station. There was a grimy firehose coiled there and a scent of urine. The ceiling groaned and shook, oppressed by trains above. After the embassy, sick-hearted and bestrewn with broken glass, after the narrowing options from Washington, after the increasing coolness of the Italians, such a place was drearily fitting. This appalling day had so far kept at least a memory that Gabriella still breathed its air. Down here even that paled. He waited here for Mascagni at Mascagni's suggestion.

He did not, therefore, smile when Mascagni, arriving, said, "Really, Giovanni, it gets worse all the time, the way we meet. Last time at least we had a helicopter. Now this." And Mascagni, anyway, seemed on edge. He continued, "On the other hand, this will probably be the last meeting."

"You're pulling out?" said Stears. He said it with not great warmth. "That's the reason for this hole?"

"Caution is the reason for this hole," said Mascagni. "Also I could get here quickly. It is always something when one can find a use for the Roman metro. When you asked to see me, I came, so I am not pulling out. General Della Cappella has not told me to. But there is a big deliberation at the Quirinale this evening and I think I know what will happen then. As you do, Giovanni, do you not?"

"Tell me anyway," said Stears.

"It will be decided that Italy must be firm—that is how cowardice will be made to seem courageous. That Italy cannot allow American interests to dictate Italian policy. That the matter of the hostages will be handled strictly as an Italian police matter, with no American participation whatsoever. Why should we tell you how we are dealing with a civil kidnap case? As to the bigger things, the demands that these people will make any minute now, we will accept most of the ones that affect the United States here so that we can be self-righteous and strong about the ones that affect our own politics. The Greeks and the Spanish placed tight restrictions on your forces and the sky did not fall, so why should we be more generous?"

"Yes," said Stears.

"And at that point, Giovanni, I do not know what you and I could do. Especially since you are almost a nonperson now."

"Especially since you know what I must do. Do you not, Rodolfo?"

Mascagni looked away. "Tell me anyway," he said. "For now you can still at least speak to me in confidence."

"You know that the CIA cannot permit a hostage negotiation that may cripple the United States in the Mediterranean to take its course if we can help it. We have to take action. Whatever Washington says to the Quirinale. In this matter, I am the CIA."

"Yes," said Mascagni. "And it has been a bloody business

already, has it not, just in the prologue? Is this why your people made you a nonperson?''

A metro train had entered and now got under way again. Its windows were open and a line of heads ran by.

"I am not sure," said Stears.

"It might be wise to find out. I wish I had not seen you throw that damned hand, Giovanni. It affects my memories of you."

"I need to know," said Stears, "what I can expect from you if we are forced to take hard action undercover. Help? Information? Nothing? Or hindrance?"

"I cannot tell you now. My loyalty is to Della Cappella, not to you. When I know what has happened in the Quirinale, when I have talked to him, perhaps I can answer you usefully. By then we will have heard what these murderers choose to want. It depresses me that what you will ask of me is likely to increase the chance of bloodshed. Understand this well—while the children are missing, I will take no risks."

"I told my people," said Stears, "that even the Brigadists would not risk them. Was I right? "

"I think so," said Mascagni. "I have known most of the worst people in Italy, but I have never met a child-killer. For the grown-ups, it is very different, though."

"As many Americans as Italians, and the Italians are my people too," said Stears.

"To say that, my friend, you seem to leave Italy very easily and for great periods of time—just as you do America, I understand. Still, I will gladly give such help as I can give." The headlight of a metro train, headed north, twinkled in the tunnel. Mascagni pointed to it and said, "That is my direction. Do we have more to talk about now?"

Stears shook his head. "When we do, there will be decisions," he said. "Decisions and no time."

The train stopped. "Agreed," said Mascagni. The doors opened. "Good-bye, then," he said, and walked ten meters to an open door.

The train brought him slowly back, by an open window. Mascagni's head passed just below Stears's. Mascagni fluttered his hand.

"Arrivederla, Marchese," he said. And, raising his voice at the lengthening distance as Stears stared at him: "Everybody talks too much in Rome."

Early that evening, all the children abducted from the embassy turned up in a locked barn outside a village forty kilometers from Rome after a telephone call led the police there. Their masked chaperons had left shortly before.

The effect of this at the embassy was that the broken glass disappeared from the floors, telephones were no longer watched like ruthless gods, and, during a quick discussion of logistics, Randall Beebe was heard to laugh. In the event, the children were delivered by the Carabinieri in a bus with a heavy escort.

By this time, the demonstration, which had lost cohesion soon after the kidnapping, was effectively over except for some baby-faced Danes with placards about something to do with seals. An evening breeze had come up to sweep away the tear gas, though it still hung in corners of the embassy. There was a cautious movement to remove some sandbags and open windows.

It was learned that the bus that took the captives from the embassy had been driven quickly to a locked garage where there were two closed trucks. The children had been put in one and the adults in the other. A new man and woman drove the children away. They were soon out of the city and then they were in the barn. There was lemonade and cake.

"They were scared of Mr. Buxhalter," said the oldest boy, eight.

This was during a sort of debriefing session according to Montessori. The mothers, Halston, Beebe, Stears, a nurse, the chaplain, and an Italian senior police officer were there. So was the *Times* man, who had found Buxhalter engaged elsewhere, and had been thankfully collared for this happier occasion. What did he mean, scared?

"You've got to get it down smooth when you pull a caper like that. Mr. Buxhalter was extra. It scared them. I could tell. Is Mr. Buxhalter undercover, sir?"

Randall Beebe leaned forward and very grandly patted the

boy's knee. "Come and see me when you're a little older, son," he said.

The youngest girl identified their captors as Eskimos, but this seemed based on shaky data.

The Italian police report was terse. The Americans were not invited to interview the Sicilian children, though these, presumably, could have picked up more. Stears made this suggestion quietly in Italian, but the officer, who was standing with him at a window, began to talk of something else.

The children, when found, had seemed remarkably calm. There turned out to have been a sedative in the lemonade.

One of the mothers began to quake with dry sobs when this fact came out. "I kept seeing a jug of lemonade in my mind," she said. "But it wasn't sedative in it, it was poison."

"It wouldn't have been. Not in Italy," said Stears.

The dead Marine's child was a little girl who was now under special care. There was discussion of a fund for her.

All this, for a little while and to some degree, cloaked the fact that of the adult hostages, there was no news. Even the *Times* man forbore to mention this until he was back at his own desk.

Late at night, Calvetto finished writing the communiqué to be issued the next morning. He read the phrases, deliberately barbarous, in a soft voice to himself:

> Immediate Release of Proletarian Captives from the Battle of Monte Sant'Angelo; Withdrawal of all Imperialist Air and Naval Forces from the Mediterranean before Negotiation; Immediate Trial for Murder under Italian Law of all United States Personnel at Monte Sant'Angelo; Total Repudiation of Fascist Militarist Base Agreements.

And so forth.

He stood outside of himself and looked at himself shyly. A simple room, cups on an oak dresser by the wall, a wooden table, a lamp, a pen. Himself the frail scholar, cheated of his frame at birth. And developed out of this, driven by nothing but his will, forced by a courage that would crack the chests of ordinary men, a message to make Presidents afraid. If all went precisely well, and all would go precisely well, some slight version of some of these demands would be met. In such a case, Calvetto would have jostled the strident Generals, shifted the great fleets, touched nations. Even God would have to make arrangements. He allowed himself no crowing yet, but still his spirit looked at him with a smile close to tears. "Not bad," he whispered. "Not bad at all."

He capped his pen. He placed a ruler across the two pages to be typed, copied, taken to Rome, and delivered by taxicab next morning. He went to the window and looked out, breathing the summer night and the sweet fallen peaches. The moon made the garden wall silver. A village away, His Excellency the Ambassador lay in fear and darkness on a dirty floor. Calvetto chortled right from the bottom of his spine. *In a tangle of bodies around a bucket, Excellency! How goes it, Excellency?* He laughed again, a sound surprisingly loud in the night. He scolded himself for it, but one should not be too solemn. "Not bad," he said again. "Not bad at all." And then, barely in a whisper, "Excellency, would you rather be Calvetto now?"

He shut the window, turned, and left the room. His feet were light on the stairs and carried him straight to Gabriella's door. Tonight of all nights, he knew that he deserved the crown he had won.

Consequently, when he lifted the wooden latchet of her door tonight, his face did not wear the grimace which, though it seemed a sneer, was nothing but a seizure of self-doubt. She sat in a chair by the window. He smiled, warm with joy and love.

She rose upon his entry. She wore a cotton country nightgown to the floor. It made him shiver with delight—his Rosa, created by himself. He touched it gently and ran his fingers over its grain.

Then he spoke. "Take it off now," he said and held his breath, for this act, though the simplest, was his greatest joy. Her hands lifted its hem. It rose and fell upon the floor. "Pick it up!" he said sharply. As she moved and bent, stretched to lay it on the bed, he watched the shadows move across her limbs and form and murmured, "Oh, Rosa, Rosa." His head came to her breast. He walked around her, feeling her body's heat.

He sat down in the chair. He said, "It has been a great day, Rosa. I will tell you about it soon." He stopped, overwhelmed not only by passion but by domestic bliss: his, the queen of women, before him in this simple, comely room. "You may speak if you wish," he said. She shook her head and smiled into his eyes. He felt it far within him.

He said, "Get the blindfold, my love, and bring it here." He watched her go to the chest and her haunch tighten and her breast dip down as she bent to open the drawer. "Kneel," he said when she brought it back.

He tied it at the back of her neck, carefully lifting her chestnut hair behind and tucking it over her nose. He drew her head upon his lap and cushioned it gently. He sighed from the bottom of his lungs. His hands ran over the shapes of her back and down her thighs. He said, "They are almost gone, the little bruises. Shall we put them back or let them go, white as snow? Rosa is blindfolded. She knows nothing until it happens." Her skin seemed flushed with warmth tonight, to the glory of this day. He would have liked to bury his face in her hair, but held aloof. "What shall it be tonight?" he said. "Shall I sting my Rosa or watch her make music of herself? Tell me what you think and we shall see."

She spoke in the voice he revered, the rough throatiness of noble Rome. "I sent a message to Giovanni Stears," she said. "I sent it while you were getting money to pay the grocer for his cabbages. Giovanni knows I am alive. I am not yours ever again. Not even now."

Yussuf the Libyan, resting badly, oppressed by theological dread, was wakened at the other end of the house in the night and had a hard time getting back to sleep. He had a disturbing impression that he had heard a cry in Calvetto's voice. Not really very likely, he assured himself. At any rate it did not come again. Most probably a rabbit or a cat.

C·H·A·P·T·E·R 22

T he comfort of the children's return departed from the embassy with them. That night it was a place of harshly lighted rooms off dim halls; of anxious footsteps and voices edged with apprehension, indignation, and excuse. There was trash from snatched meals. Stears stood watch in his office, where the basement window was still sandbagged and old tear gas hung around like skunk. From time to time a cipher clerk brought messages to his desk. He considered them, arranged them, and replied to the few sensible enough to ask answerable questions. His position within the Roman station of the CIA seemed to have been revitalized by default into its original uncertainty. Beebe had reclaimed him as his right-hand man. It meant little.

For the poor embassy was not only battered and ravished but also in disgrace. The cable traffic from Washington, first hysterical, had turned peremptory. Uncle was on his way in the form of a member of the National Security Council and an aide to the Joint Chiefs of Staff, both on a 707 already in flight from Andrews Air Force Base. Uncle would shake his stick no doubt at the foreign bullies if they showed their faces, but Uncle would have time for lectures about loose living abroad and how one gets oneself into such a mess. Amid the general ire, Stears's earlier fallen state was scarcely different from Beebe's or Halston's or Larsen's now; in fact, it was less conspicuous.

So far as he knew, he was still a wet dog to the Italians.

Lacking time to go himself, he had called the graybeard Under-Secretary at the Foreign Ministry. The graybeard's aide had responded to his name with what sounded like a seizure. There had been mutterings offstage in the voice, but not on the subject, of pig-sticking. The Under-Secretary was not available.

No communiqué had been received from the terrorists.

At close to midnight he picked up his ringing telephone and heard Captain Mascagni's voice, though Mascagni used no names.

"Meet me in twenty minutes on the sidewalk near Tulio's," the voice said. "Okay?"

"Yes," said Stears. Mascagni hung up. Stears's hand had written "Tulio's" on a scrap of paper; his brain now stumbled around it. He recollected in time that Tulio's was a trattoria six blocks away where he frequently ate lunch. *I am too tired to trust myself*, he thought.

Now he guessed that Mascagni was calling from the Quirinale, which would put Tulio's in between them. The Italian cabinet emergency meeting was probably concluded. He logged himself out, estimating an hour's absence. He walked down side streets from the back of the embassy, by the Via Lucullo and the Via San Nicolò da Tolentino. Here and there were scraps of placards marking the dispersal of the mob. His eye caught a "CARNE——" torn along a ragged line. His embassy seemed to have littered Rome with its blowsy anguish.

Still, the night air and the streets soothed his brain and let him see beyond these dismal imperatives to the lovely urgency of Gabriella's need. Tomorrow he would somehow climb out of the rubble for long enough to care for her. It made him hang on to his strength and wakefulness like a miser. Near Tulio's, he could just see Triton on the fountain of the Piazza Barberini. Much closer, he saw Mascagni in the shadows. Not far from him was a large Lancia with a uniformed driver dimly seen in front. Mascagni's stock seemed to have risen.

Mascagni gestured Stears to the rear door. Stears got in, followed by his host. In the far corner, a monumental shape in military cap jolted into motion, nodded twice, and extended straight toward Stears a hand that took his as though burying it in cement. "My two brave young officers," said a voice like a barrel rolling on a cellar floor, "who were to go to where the sniper was and kill him. We are at a pretty pass now, are we not?" The car picked up motion away from the Piazza Barberini. A tiny Fiat tore past it in low gear, moaning like a terrified rabbit.

"Pass or cliff, General Della Cappella," said Stears. A street lamp shone full on Della Cappella's face. Whatever the voice, the regal jowls looked cheesy with strain and in the eyes there was the look of a shaky *generalissimo*. Stears braced himself for trouble. It was only the lamplight, perhaps.

"Very good," said Della Cappella. "I come from the Quirinale. I am not a pimp and it is not my custom to pick up people off the streets to talk to them in darkened cars. That may tell you how popular you Americans are with the politicians at the Quirinale this evening."

"We have some complaints of our own," said Stears. "Terrorists roam the Italian countryside at will. That, after all, is the problem."

Della Cappella made a large, sad gesture. Lamplight fizzed on gold braid. "Once upon a time I carried messages for your uncle. One had to be cunning to live then as well. Incidentally, Deputy Minister Tasso says that you are about to be dismissed by your people. Mascagni says not so. Are you worth talking to, Mr. Stears?"

"My duties are informed liaison," said Stears. "I am still carrying them out. That anything I say or do can be repudiated seems to be an open secret. Perhaps you should judge for yourself, General."

"Good," said Della Cappella. "Because there are things that have to be said and cannot be said." He drew in breath. "This is the situation in a nutshell."

Italian public opinion would not allow further spilling of Italian blood. Sanguine torrents—so the General's oratory, gathering steam in spite of himself, presented it—had so poured already as to make the Italian heart weep. The consummate priority was to get the Italian hostages out unharmed. Until that point, the Carabinieri would offer no forceful action and would make very sure that the Americans offered none themselves. The Italians out, the game could change.

"They won't let the Italians out," said Stears. "The Italians are the ace."

"But they also cannot seem to persecute Italians," Mascagni said, "unless forced to by the Americans."

"We will offer the terrorist captured at Monte Sant'Angelo against the Italian women hostages immediately," said the General. "As soon as we receive their demands. They will undoubtedly accept. It will make them seem chivalrous and they cannot enjoy having someone who knows about them in our hands. There will be a quick exchange. It will not be entirely easy, for he will have to go to another hospital. They will want him flown out of the country. But it can be done."

"Then you're half out," said Stears. "Two waiters to go."

The point then would be for Italy to behave with craven complicity, to bound forward into adultery with its principles around its ankles so that a quid pro quo from the Brigadists would be impossible to refuse.

"And if by any chance it works," said Stears, "perhaps you get your waiters. They know they can get more Italians if they want. Most of our Americans will probably still be alive. Then what?"

Ah, then the lion would wake. Would wake in certain circumstances. If joint American-Italian intelligence had gotten any promising line on the terrorist lair, then the Carabinieri would go in feet-first, perhaps with American units as well. The Italian heart would warm to such a vindication; the terrorists once visibly crushed, the Italian intellect would see at once the injustice of their cause.

Stears said, "You're asking the United States to hold unilaterally firm in negotiation while you get your people out and then join you in active measures at the risk of our own hostages."

There was silence. They were going west on the Via Nazionale. In front of the Piazza Venezia, Trajan's Column stood floodlit. This was just the way that Stears had driven, bullying the Jaguar and scaring Fiats, on the evening that he had rushed out to the Villa Pamphili-Farnese to see Gabriella for the last time. Then Trajan's Column had been enveloped with the sinking sun. He remembered and quickly shivered.

Beside him, Mascagni sighed. "No, Giovanni," he said. He touched Stears's arm. "Because the United States will do that whether we ask or not. You Americans do not negotiate with terrorists. We are asking you to cooperate fully in gathering intelligence against these Brigadists but to make no use of it whatsoever until our people are safe."

"That is what you wish me to take to my superiors?" Stears said.

"There is something more," said Mascagni. "There will be a terrible temptation for you Americans to make use of any information you can find, as soon as you find it. We have to know that such a thing will not happen, that you will not act prematurely. You yourself must guarantee that."

"That is preposterous," said Stears. "I have told you what my position is."

"That is not what I mean, Giovanni," said Mascagni. The hand touched his arm again. It was determined and shy. "I know you can not dictate their plans. But you can tell us what they are."

"The honest broker," said Della Cappella. "That was why I, who carried your uncle's messages, could say this only to you."

Stears turned away. Above them, on his side, was the Quirinale. As he looked, a batch of its lighted windows went dark. He said quietly, "For men who are not pimps, you may have missed your calling."

The hand fell from his arm. Mascagni's eyes were on the floor and he rubbed his palms together. *That was almost how I first saw him*, thought Stears, *when I spoke of his medal*. Della Cappella lifted up his arm as though to ward off a blow or to strike one. Then he said, "That is unjust, but I will not argue for my honor. We asked this because yours is above question, not to impugn it. With your word, I will go outside my Minister's wishes and permit American cooperation. Without it, I will seal you out—and make no mistake that that is what the Quirinale wants. I believe that such would be a disaster and an insult to you as our allies. I do this because of your family and because of what Captain Mascagni believes of you. Do not call him foul names.''

"If I spoke in haste, I had reason to do so," said Stears. "Take me back, please. We will not talk further now."

Nearly back, on the far side of the Piazza Barberini, he motioned to Mascagni to have the car stopped. "Far enough," he said. And then: "I accept that your purpose was serious. I know the things that you have accomplished, General. I am honored to have Captain Mascagni's trust. What you ask is impossible, but I will go a certain way toward it. If I come to know of an intention on our side that will risk unnecessary bloodshed, I will see that you have time and means to prevent it. That is a promise. If you accept it, you must stand ready to help us destroy these people who have murdered our men and our commander. Do we agree?"

General Della Cappella looked sadly down the empty street. Before he spoke a cat had jumped out of a garbage can and ran across the street into a basement window. "Yes," he said.

Far to the north, in a military hospital under the shadow of the Alps, Alfredo the gunman lay in post-operative convalescence. This was the third day after his wounding at Monte Sant'Angelo. He had endured exploratory surgery two days before. He would thereafter owe a certain use of his legs to a distinguished Army surgeon who pinned his spine back together. It had taken five hours.

This was the first night after the operation. The pain was great and he was heavily narcotized. He drifted in and out of a kind of sleep. Both a nun and a Lieutenant of Carabinieri attended him. The room was lit at their end, though around Alfredo's bed the light was dim. The Lieutenant read a paperback. The nun sewed.

Alfredo, however, lay in raven darkness that slurped and wallowed like an oily sea. A flame began far beyond his feet and spouted sulfur, then ran around him, encircling him from head to toe. It lit the pain in his back. Invisible mouths screamed beyond the flame and their voices drifted over the dark.

Something sprouted from his groin. He saw it as a black bud. Then it opened as a sooty hand whose fingers seemed to sniff the air. They sniffed as though searching, the hand cocked this way and that. Then, when the fingers pointed the way straight up his stomach toward his throat, the hand began to limp. Charred crumbs flaked from the wrist. He arched his head to escape, but his body was cut in two. The thumb groped across his flesh. He could not move.

Behind it he saw Dr. Calvetto, waggish as in the café at Monte Sant'Angelo, between the flame and the dark. He understood at once. The life was to be choked out of him in the night so that he would never speak. The hand made the vague, ferocious gesture of a lobster's claw and he began to mew.

The Lieutenant of Carabinieri wrote down the words as best he could. Little bald man, little bald man—*"calvetto, calvetto"* —no! could not be mistaken, though the rest was wanderings. The nun put her hand on the shoulder of the scrawny, broken body on the bed. An old man of twenty-six with skinny legs. Her touch was safer than more morphine and it quite often worked. Alfredo quieted.

The Lieutenant immediately telephoned Captain Rodolfo Mascagni's office in Rome. He called at a time when Mascagni had left long before for the Quirinale with General Della Cappella and had not returned. Mascagni's Sergeant, who had had one full night's sleep since Monte Sant'Angelo, could make no sense of "little bald man," if there was any to be made.

Just before Mascagni got back, one of the Corporals, who had a ragbag sort of mind, recollected that *calvetto* might also be a name, specifically the name of the only person not a local who had been at the village café in Sagatto the night General Leipzinger was killed. That would be Dr. Fausto Calvetto, a left-wing intellectual journalist of some stature, former doctor of geology of the University of Naples. He had left Sagatto peaceably just before the raid.

It was already known that "Alfredo" was the schoolteacher Guido Callucci, for a colleague had recognized his photograph in the paper.

. . .

Now Gabriella's door was locked. The dawn reached in through her window and painted it with a stripe of rose. Just before that, the dawn had turned the dew on the peach trees silver. Gabriella sat by the window in the nightgown she had shed for Calvetto in the night. She could jump through the window without much damage, but there was a young man standing among the peach trees with a machine gun, and another, she knew, watching from the wall. This regime had been installed the day before, but the young man among the peaches was new. She had slept a little in the chair. Now that she moved, her shoulders and her thighs stabbed her. They would be blue from Calvetto's frantic and forsaken rage, but after a little while the hurt was dull and not absolutely unpleasant. Nor, in any case, important. The effect had been all she had promised herself. The gathering dawn gently erased the stripe upon the door and set about waking up the wasps.

She had failed to kill Calvetto at his window by the Tiber. She would have failed last night or this morning or at any other time. But that, she knew now, was foolish and should never have been asked of her, even by herself. She had used upon Calvetto the incantation that she should by rights have always had to hand, a man of her own not for caprice or capture or sport but held by loyalty and love. Touched by this, the demon Calvetto had burned up like a paper doll. Sitting by the window she felt almost embarrassingly bridal, even if she was sitting beaten up in a cell.

It was true that this left Dr. Calvetto, the Red Brigadist, unaccounted for. By the time the young man in the peach trees had begun a country dance with the wasps that cruised around his knees she heard Calvetto's step upon the landing and the key turn in the door. He came himself, alone. Paper doll or not, Calvetto was never a figure of fun for long.

He looked as though held together with piano wire that would hum to a breath. His limp made a small right angle with his step as when he was most afflicted. He was freshly shaved. He wore a white suit and a hyacinth blossom was embossed upon his tie.

He bowed minutely while his eyes glared. "Your Grace is a prisoner of the Aurora Rossa," he said, "the People's Army. You will be tried by the People's Court when there is time to do so." He smiled a dry smile, but his lips quivered around the edge of it. "Or perhaps the People will let the Italian government try you. They are better equipped for long sentences, which I think Your Grace would not enjoy."

"You may sit down," she said.

His eyes met hers and burned. He said, "You were never wise, were you?" He had a paper in his hand. He said, "Since you are so anxious to send secret billets-doux to your innamorato, it seems wrong to deprive you of a chance. This is the communiqué of the Aurora Rossa. This is the copy that goes to the American embassy. They will get it in no time at all. Would you not like to add a little something, a trace of scent, a lock of hair, that only he will understand? Then you will have a good chance at being rescued. Understand, that is a chance you badly need. There were always people here who wanted to see the end of you."

She put out her hand. He gave her the paper. "A pen," she said. He gave her one. She turned the paper over and drew, taking some pains this time, sticking her tongue between her lips. She gave it back.

"A coronet and a little fish," he said. "A sea horse. How pretty. Like an expensive dinner plate." He folded it. "You were never wise. Either he will see you for what you are and turn from you or he will come alone and you will see him die. The latter is the intention."

"Not wise," she said, "nor stupid. I am not a little woman to protect her hubby. I do not have to. He will know how to come. Your head will be my wedding present. I'll have it set."

"Pretty sentiments, too," he said. "The antique noble style. We'll see."

He left. He locked the door behind him, turning the key until it grated.

She believed what she had said. Believed now that the only way for all to be wiped clean was for Giovanni to destroy Calvetto, not necessarily bare-handed. She believed it, but she had acted precipitously even for her. The note was gone now. The pain in her shoulders and thighs was surpassed by a sharper pain in her stomach. The next days would not be gentle. "Giovanni, dear," she whispered to the window, "you owe me this one. Don't screw up."

C·H·A·P·T·E·R   23

Heat of August rolled off the buildings behind Stears's back, wavered on the hills above Marsciano, lay on the lowlands beyond the river. A minute after parking at the end of an hour's flight up the *autostrada* and into the hills in an unfamiliar car, Stears's hands still tried to shake. He felt this, as he had felt the dissolution of the ground beneath him when he turned over the Aurora Rossa's communiqué and saw Gabriella's mark, through an empty space of exhaustion. He stood against the railing of the bridge and watched the water. The heat on his back and the stream beneath unknotted him a little.

I am here, in the place where her first message was postmarked, he thought. *That's all, and nobody knows even that but me. A market town on Saturday. That's all.* The river ran below him, surrendering the last of mountain brightness in a few boils of foam, mostly smooth and green. *Prisoner or whatever she is, she will not be in the main square waving, may very well not be here at all.* The sign on the bridge caught his eye. The water beneath him was the Tiber, of all things, going home to Rome. *My Roman is a prisoner of the Etruscans. If I thought she was a prisoner purely and simply, I would not be here alone.*

He turned around. The glare from the town's main buildings smote his eye. Sun lanced off the grilles and chrome of cars and baked truck fumes almost into syrup; two significant highways went through the town. The Saturday market was ahead of him; it was mostly aprons, glasses, pots and pans. Away from the river, he could not see the limits of Marsciano, though it was not large. A picture of alleys behind streets, steep lanes of mossy steps, courtyards with heavy gates filled his head and made his quest hopeless and absurd. *You're no good like this,* he thought. *Sit down and watch. Even for the sake of watching. Find a pattern. Doesn't matter what.*

He found a café on the market piazza and sat outside. Heat flowed from the pavement up his spine. In his state of sleeplessness it was seductive and nourishing, like the iced-milk Ovomaltine he ordered, realizing he was famished too. It was clear why Marsciano would be attractive as a base: it had too much traffic for strange vehicles to be noticed and too many shops for gossip to start quickly; it was near one *autostrada* and not far from another; it gave way to mountains with remote farms.

The heat gave a sense of intimacy with all around, with the bare arms and white underarm of the waitress lifting trays, with the bodies on the sidewalk behind his back, each with its passing envelope of sweat. He felt alone and exposed, stripped for once of an armor of circumspection lightly worn and hardly noticed.

His intelligence would not admit that Gabriella was simply a prisoner, let his heart try as it might. There was no mention of the Princess in the Aurora Rossa's demands, no ransom set, no boast. A prisoner might have found a way to send the first scrap of paper, but terrorists so casual as to let prisoners write postscripts and comments on communiqués to governments would not stay in business long. And besides, what she had done since he had come to Rome now settled toward a macabre pattern. She was calling only him. So she was calling him into the shadows and how deep into the shadows he could not know.

He got up and walked back toward his car. He was now more interested in the farms around Marsciano than the town itself. Marsciano fitted as a base, but he doubted that it was either the operating quarters of the Aurora Rossa or the place of imprisonment for the hostages—which might not even be close together. For that, he thought, either a big city or the country. He had decided that much on the drive, but he had foreseen Marsciano as small enough that he could easily ask around about unusual orders at shops or odd strangers. Marsciano was too busy and too big.

And even there he was pretending that he had his usual property of plans and options. He had come because he had to come and could only come alone, however doubtful this foray, in itself, might be. Or turn his back a second time.

Captain Mascagni and his best Sergeant, both of whom had freshly enjoyed five hours of undisturbed sleep, stood in the hall of Dr. Calvetto's apartment above the Tiber on Saturday morning. Two Carabinieri troopers, with guns and nothing to do, stood outside on the stairs. The door had not been answered, but they had not required a key. The Sergeant, who had worked on crime before he rose to terrorism, had pointed to small marks beside the lock. "Someone has been here first, Captain," he said. "I don't think there's anyone inside." He had jiggled the door and it had opened.

Mascagni was therefore on the telephone. "I want forensic people," he said. And then, remembering it was a Saturday at the start of August: "Find a judge and keep him happy. We'll be needing warrants for days."

He looked around the apartment, not for minutiae yet, but for its soul. He had seen a photograph of its owner by now, a man against whom the case was still not only circumstantial but diaphanous. It had seemed the photograph of a rich, wise monkey, antic and sad.

He had the impression that the rooms had been empty for much more than hours, perhaps several days. The building was plain but pleasant. The apartment was not opulent, but prosperous for a journalist and academic. There were minerals and semi-precious stones, probably of considerable value, but then, as well as journalist, the man was a geologist of sorts. No revolutionary posters or such junk. No people. It took Mascagni a moment to realize this, and when he did, the rare stones, arresting in themselves, chilled him: in all four rooms there was not one painting or figure or photograph of a human face.

That was not quite true. Mascagni, still the soul-hunter, opened the top drawer of the dressing table. Nothing there but silk handkerchiefs in thick profusion. He left the bedroom and went to the desk at the inner end of the large living room. He opened the top drawer here, for a man's heart may have its shrine in either place.

There was a photograph there of a striking woman, whose face was familiar though he could not place her at once. He picked it up. Right underneath it was a photograph of his American colleague, Giovanni Stears.

In the hills the roads were dry and narrow and smelled of goat. The hills drew Stears in. The Alfa quivered on rough roads that veiled what they had in store ahead and locked themselves up behind. He had two more places to go to. Time was running out. In the circumstances, he could not be absent for vague reasons from the embassy for more than a long afternoon.

Before he bolted, Stears had withdrawn the military reconnaissance plates for the Marsciano region, stuffed them into an envelope, and carried them off illegally through the prevailing chaos. He had those. He had the best car from the embassy motor pool, a fast Alfa-Romeo coupé. He had started the Jaguar's engine before reflecting that it would be the most conspicuous car in Umbria. In the Alfa's glove compartment there was a nicked and stained Beretta .38 in an oily holster. He had taken it from Borgonuovo, along with the eight rounds he had found with it in the drawer. It was the first weapon he had ever issued himself in his working life and it looked stiff and surly, he thought, as though snatched from retirement.

The cicadas screamed like a burglar alarm that nobody was going to turn off. The reconnaissance plates on the seat beside him were covered with stony dust. He had picked out properties that had walls, that had no near neighbors, that had outbuildings, that were not on dead-end roads. So far they had also had open gates, children in the yards, and dogs of ostentatious amiability. The next property met the basic criteria well. It had a wall enclosing an orchard, and barns enough to hide a fleet of vehicles. About a kilometer away, on what could possibly be its land, was some sort of small circular construction; a water tower or a silo, he supposed.

Yussuf the Libyan walked through the fields toward the dove-cote heavy in thought, a gentleman farmer inspecting difficult livestock. His boys were competent. Prisoners, easily trained to a bucket, were less trouble than a stableful of mules. When they were watered or fed, two Libyan boys with machine guns stood in the shadow within the door. The provisions were carried down only under cover of night. Escape of signals from a win-dowless stone building were hardly likely. It was almost beyond imagination that their whereabouts were even within conjecture by any adversary, and evacuation to a second hiding place could be begun within minutes. Yet Yussuf was punctilious to a fault. He felt that minute care for the details firmly within his grasp might persuade Heaven to see to the ones that were sliding queasily beyond him.

Within hours of their first communiqué, the Italian govern-ment had proposed a preliminary exchange: the Italian women for the Italian Alfredo. Yussuf had felt obliged to acquiesce in this. They had more prisoners than they could easily handle in a crisis. Alfredo's capture alive had been a frightening reverse. Yussuf had reason to believe that the young Libyan officer who had let this happen was now approaching—oh, how yearningly, respectfully approaching!—death in a prison outside Tripoli. Once a Western government began to negotiate, it usually went on. And it would be fun to watch the American women see the Italian women freed and the noose drawn a little closer around them. The mechanics of the exchange would strain their re-sources still further, but nonetheless Yussuf was pleased.

He tried to bear this in mind while he had the padlock to the dovecote opened and the boys took up position in the door. He slipped a linen mask over his face.

The place stank like a ferret's cage but he did not much mind that. Under the August sun even thick stone had become heated, stifling, in fact, but, as chinks of lichen-colored light up above plainly showed, there was no danger of asphyxiation. The hostages blinked piteously in the sudden glare. That was excellent; dazed prisoners are easy to control.

The trouble was that he had to look upon the face of the Ambassador, the willing sacrifice. Each time the door was opened he dared to hope that Buxhalter would be asleep, or at least have found some activity to engross his interest. Yussuf would look away from the quarter the Ambassador had been in last. But it drew him like an abscess every time and he would find himself looking into that face as harmless as a tortoise's, those feebly blinking eyes, those cheeks falling in a little every time, the collar preposterously sprouting straw. He would pull his gaze away like a cable snapping and then scream abuse at some other prisoner, in this case a woman whom he had surprised hiding her face at the bucket. He felt his stature slipping, even among his boys. He went out into the sun every time feeling that he had been poisoned. He took the mask off.

The third property had the highest wall. The sun on it was fierce and suggested dark within. One tree branch heavy with fruit leaned over it as though to pull one in, but the gate was high and closed. Beyond, Stears could see only the roofline of the house. It seemed deserted. He hesitated to stop the car. He had had no such thought in front of the populous and noisy places he had seen thus far.

Therefore he stopped a half kilometer down the road on the tire-scuffed ground beneath a tree. He spread a motoring map ostentatiously on the roof. He stretched. He got out his bright-green Michelin. Vacations were beginning and these hills were slightly scenic. He looked around. He could see a wall around a house.

He could see a track going up the hill on the far side of the road from the house. Higher up, one would get some view over the wall.

And could be seen. One would perhaps be known.

Then it came to him with the freshness of simple certainty that, under the familiar Borsalino hat he now took from the back seat and put on—how suitable in this strong sun!—only one person in Italy, with binoculars or not, could recognize him for sure at a distance. And if she, who would know him by the tilt of his head, by his step on the path, by the fit of his coat, merely knew that he had come, then some part of a spell was already spoken. And that if he could know that she was there, then it was nearly cast.

So he walked to the track and up it, taking the exuberant strides uphill of the casual sightseer who is not going far. Certainly no stealthy creep. He had left his binoculars behind as an unaffordable luxury thus in full view. He looked only up. He had fixed his eye on a knob beside the track, seemingly at the right elevation. When he got there, he turned suddenly, enjoying the view bought with his deep breaths.

No movement. No sound. No curtain pulled aside. And not deserted; though the place was ill-kept, the shutters were straight and the drive was not overgrown. The doors of old stables had been taken off and there were vehicles within, most visibly a truck and a smaller van. He thought he possibly saw, and without binoculars could never know, something move quickly behind a peach tree. He swung his gaze here and there.

He saw what he had not seen earlier, a doorway set into the wall halfway to the far side and just visibly open. It would be difficult to see it from the road. He thought again of the Beretta in the car, of stealthy steps, of a place perhaps almost deserted, of swinging open a door and seeing Gabriella within. Or even of finding a plain and sleepy farm of no further interest. He thought of the movement behind the peach tree. There had perhaps been none at all.

Look carefully, he told himself.

The round structure across the fields was shaped like a beehive—a granary of sorts, he guessed, not a water tower. There were two men in the fields not far from it. He looked back toward the house.

The largest vehicle in the stable was a closed delivery truck. In most lights it would have been visible barely as a shape, but the present angle of the sun picked it out rather clearly, together with its neighbor, a smaller van. Such delivery trucks, according to all the children, were what had been used to carry both them and the adults after the switch in the locked garage. The children had seen little. Even the older ones knew some car models, not dumb trucks. But the oldest boy had remembered that the truck for the adults had been brown.

And so was this one.

He dared stay no longer. He lolloped down, still the energetic sightseer—suspicious probably; identifiable, he thought not. When he was halfway down, a man appeared, walking to the house from the direction of the granary. He could get no easy view of him and dared not go back up. The man seemed preoccupied and looking at the ground.

Stears raced the sun back to Rome. It was still above the hills when he broke through the traffic of the Raccordo Anulare, the circumferential highway, into the city. It was after five, but August was loosening the rush hour. He was at the embassy before six. He took his time walking through it; he needed to deduce what enrichments and recombinations of power had affected the embassy since shortly before lunchtime. There were several diplomats he did not recognize and, worse, several new young men apparently in the CIA. Idioms of the Beltway prevailed. He felt ominously that muscular zeal had come into a fragile and perilous grotto that he barely understood himself.

He found Randall Beebe. Beebe looked subdued. "Where the hell have you been?" he said, but only as salutation. And then: "The Italians have reacted to the communiqué. They're setting up a preliminary exchange of the women for the little man you threw bits of bodies at. Their women, of course. I made the point that our people shot the little bastard first, so he ought to be ours, but they do not see it that way."

"Their women," said Stears. "Only?"

"There is an intimation," said Beebe, "that if we withdraw all our ships immediately from the Gulf of Sidra and get the fleet out of Naples on a course for the Atlantic overnight, we might get ours too. In fact, we are sending the battleship *New Jersey* to within main-gun firing position on Tripoli, so I guess we won't."

"Dear God," said Stears.

"Quite," said Beebe. "Damn lot of good it's done so far. The exchange will be at a small airport, probably sometime tomorrow. Their boy has to go straight to another hospital, so he's leaving the country. Probably Tunisia, maybe Algeria. It's being worked on now. He will arrive by Italian military helicopter. The terrorist guards and the women will arrive however they arrive. There will be a hospital plane that will take the wounded man and probably the terrorists off to wherever they go. The Italians get the girls."

"I see," said Stears.

"We observe," said Beebe. "We get that much. You are in charge of that, quietly. Organize it with your ice-cream man. Another thing. That doodle on the back of the communiqué, did you see it?"

"Yes," said Stears.

"We are the only ones that got it. Does it mean something here? Like three fish with the Mafia? A Sicilian message?"

"I have no idea," said Stears. "Ask the Mafia. This observation tomorrow, we're not going to try anything funny, are we? There seem to be people here I don't know."

"There are," said Beebe. "Nor do I. No. Certainly not yet."

Stears went toward his office.

On an intelligence analysis he had, with a high degree of probability, discovered an operational stronghold of the Aurora Rossa. There was the circumstantial evidence of Gabriella's first postmark. The property would serve the purpose. There was the truck, apparently corresponding to that used to transport the hostages and of a type not to be especially expected on a farm. And there was the disparity between the air of that farmhouse and an Italian working farm.

There was room among the outbuildings to hold the hostages. The windowless beehive of heavy stone came into his memory. Unpleasant, he thought, and not really likely because too far from the house, but possible.

It was all distinctly unproved. He could have found the deteriorating property of an old woman who used a brown panel truck to take what she had to market.

And how, in the name of God, could he explain that he had found it?

He needed movement in a situation now frozen. He needed movement to see, movement to speak. And movement might itself crush what he was bound to save.

He needed Mascagni. Mascagni was the only lever he dared use. And he did not now know how to use that. He went into his office and shut the door.

Mascagni evidently needed him. He had called three times during Stears's absence. Stears called the Carabinieri barracks.

Mascagni said, "I have urgently to see you, Giovanni. We do not need a car in the dark this time, but I think not your embassy either."

"The Hassler-Medici, then," said Stears. "I am in no mood for subways. The lobby. I will buy you coffee. I will even buy you dinner."

"Ah, Giovanni," Mascagni said, "no spy can afford that at the Hassler. Perhaps not even you. But coffee, yes. I will see you there in half an hour."

"So," said Mascagni as he sat, "we are back to nice places. I do not often come here." He smiled but his smile was tentative. "You were gone all afternoon, Giovanni. I am glad to have found you in the end." There was question in his eyes, but as offer more than as demand.

"They are restaffing the embassy under our feet," said Stears. "It is a turmoil and not the best place to think. I'm sorry I missed your call."

"Ah, yes," said Mascagni. Question faded.

"The exchange," said Stears, "tomorrow. I was not told much about it. That is why we are here, I suppose."

"It is evolving," said Mascagni. "It is the diplomacy that is the question. Our part is rather simple. Yours is almost nothing. I am truly sorry for that. I do not like to think of those two young women staying there."

"Nor do I," said Stears.

"It will take place at a small airport not far from Latina. About forty minutes from here. It is one we can close off for the day. At least that is the thinking now. Don't worry. I will keep you up-to-date."

The waiter came. Mascagni went so far as a Campari soda. Stears, who had wrestled sleep in the nice armchair during the three minutes he waited for Mascagni, stuck to coffee.

"Do you know a Dr. Calvetto?" said Mascagni.

"I heard the name this morning," said Stears. "He was emerging as a suspect; am I right?"

"He has emerged a good deal since then. But you do not know him at all?"

"Certainly not," said Stears truthfully. "Who is he?"

"A journalist. A university professor. This and that. Perhaps the link we always sought between the universities and the NAP. Probably the man who had General Leipzinger murdered. And you do not know this man here under any other name?" He gave Stears a photograph. It was of Calvetto.

"Ah," said Mascagni, "I think that means a little more to you."

Stears said slowly, from an armchair suddenly removed from the Hassler-Medici to a precipice's edge, "I have seen him. Literally that. At the opera, I think. If I seem surprised it is because he lodged in my memory."

"He would, I think," said Mascagni. "But there are odder things about him, Giovanni. In all this man's house there were no portraits. No wife, no child, no lady love, no father. No Lenin and no Pope. No mother. This is an Italian, Giovanni, think of that. And yet finally there were two photographs. Hidden, as though too private to show the world. One was this." He gave Stears a photograph. "You see something very much like it when you shave, I think. And one was this lady. One lying on the other. The photographs, I mean."

The armchair tilted on the precipice. He had a sense of struggling in it while Mascagni's mild, anxious eyes looked on unblinking.

Stears said, ruling his voice, "This Calvetto is all you say he is. You believe that?"

Mascagni nodded. Then said, "But surely you know her? She is your national."

"The Princess Harriman-Farnese," said Stears.

"Right," said Mascagni. "Your dead national. As of five days. And your world, Giovanni. The world of an Ugolino-Ferrara."

"I knew her indeed," said Stears. "But mainly long ago." He found his voice was not much above a murmur, as though fearing to be heard.

"But these are not pictures of long ago," said Mascagni. "They are pictures of now. I have seen you in that suit."

"And therefore inexplicable," said Stears. "Unless this: I was this man's enemy, though I did not know it. Maybe she was too. Perhaps a symbol. An American Princess in Italy. It makes some sense. At least it is all I can imagine." *Dear God,* he thought, *now I see. Dear God, blind everybody else.*

Mascagni seemed to become small and intensely sad. "Stears," he said, "I had believed that I was with you on a difficult and dangerous hunt. Now I believe that I am in the dark and that I do not even know the difference between my friends and my enemies. Do not leave me in the dark."

Stears said, "I am certain of nothing that you need to know. Nothing has changed in how I stand to you. You will not fail for the lack of what I know."

Mascagni watched him. "That is all you will say?" he said.

"Yes," said Stears. "Our next business is the exchange, I think."

"Yes," said Mascagni. "That at least is not altered."

The airfield waited. A Lear jet sat unmanned at the end of the runway. Stears had walked over to it and found it all filled up with a white, strict bed and four cramped seats, like a mean lodging. It smelled of kerosene. It had just arrived from Cyprus and had been refueled.

Stears had slept. After a night haunted by witches the dawn had brought some mercy. Asleep, he had been made to face what, awake, he had pushed from his mind: the little gate open at Marsciano had tittered and whispered that it was a baited trap. And set by whom? By the dwarf, or by Gabriella while the dwarf looked on and crowed? In daylight he hung to faith that Gabriella, no matter how far she had consorted with the dark, had called him with the sea horse in the name of what was purest in her, carnal passion, had called him as her mate. On that, unless wholly corrupted, she would not call in bad faith. And wholly corrupted she was not.

All around, the land was flat and dark green, Rome's ancient malarial marshes filled and farmed. It was quiet, except when insects cruised by an ear. Well to the east, edged mountains defined space. The air was of drainage ditches and fertilizer. Stears's shirt was plastered to his chest. He kept a wary eye on some sort of horsefly near his arm. When he touched his hair it was damp. There was warm dew on the Lear jet. The pilot and the medic had gone into an iron-and-concrete shed to drink coffee. There was no air-conditioning there, as Stears had quickly found.

The runway was ringed by a circle of disconnected points. There was a Carabinieri bus with some men standing beside it, rifles casually held. There was a clump of cars belonging to Carabinieri officers, among them Mascagni, and close by two cars from the Italian foreign office. The Councillor from the Tunisian embassy had come with two subalterns shaped like pears. There was a dumpy, camouflaged ambulance. Quite separate were Stears's Jaguar and three other embassy cars. Of the four other CIA men, one was a junior who had already worked for Stears and of whom Stears approved. The other three were new men with expressions of the well-scrubbed paranoia more peculiar to the Secret Service. These groupings failed to suggest a common cause. Stears and Mascagni had shaken hands rather formally.

One of the CIA men gave an oath close to a yelp and slapped his face. The horsefly fell. Unaccustomed to the CIA, it had assaulted trained reflexes.

A rattle grew upon the air. From over the mountains came a drab helicopter, heavy body suspended from its blades like an excessive bug. It maneuvered above the field, blowing damp heat around. It settled on the grass. The rotors sighed, clicked, stopped. The officers got out and stretched. Alfredo the gunman had arrived.

People moved hesitantly from their strongpoints toward the

helicopter, as to interesting carrion. Inside it, Alfredo lay upon a cot with frowsier bedding than the Lear's. Bottles were connected to him here and there, though there did not seem much flesh to stick hoses into. When he saw Stears's face in the doorway his eyes widened. One of the new CIA men elbowed his way in, checked Alfredo's face against a photograph, and grunted to his colleague, without reference to Stears. Stears found himself beside Mascagni, who looked at Alfredo and murmured, "Not very much, is it?" and then drew aside, as though trespassing on former intimacy. People disengaged from the helicopter and trudged back across the grass.

Time passed, copious and damp. People slapped and rubbed themselves in turn. A terrestrial sound impinged; above the maize, the roof of a Fiat van was seen coming swiftly along the road to the airfield. The road being blocked to all others, this was necessarily the terrorists and their hostages. The van bucketed onto the field. It seemed irresolute and wandered to and fro until it picked a point forming a rough triangle with the helicopter and the Lear. Here it stopped abruptly. Its flat face inclined forward and then looked doggedly at Stears.

And Stears, forgetting that he was soaked in sweat, felt suddenly cool and coiled. For the van was the match of the one he had seen yesterday at Marsciano. *So I know where she is,* he thought, *and probably where they all are. Let's get this over with and go.*

Two young men, both with sulky, gentle faces and big dark eyes, got out, encumbered with rifles that clacked and scraped on the doors. One leaned back in, apparently to reemphasize mightily a simple instruction to those inside, but ended with a farewell wave. In his other hand, he held something small and square. The other addressed the company.

"The young women are in the van unharmed," he said. "One Fascist officer may come forward to verify this. The women will leave the van as our aircraft becomes airborne and only then, or it will be much the worse for them. Now we wish to see the patriot Alfredo." No megaphone had been provided and the voice was shrill.

Mascagni walked toward the van. The helicopter crew entered their machine; before very long Alfredo was brought forth upon his litter. His bottles swayed on a rack above; he looked like an unsightly centerpiece. One terrorist walked over and spoke to him, quietly, with no visible emotion. Mascagni looked into the van, spoke, listened, and came away. He nodded to the boy outside and moved toward Alfredo.

The crew of the Lear walked across the airfield from the shed. The medic looked over Alfredo's devices and gave assent. Alfredo began to be carried toward the Lear. The terrorist who had spoken to him started to follow, but Mascagni took his arm and shook his head. Mascagni beckoned to the boy by the van; he came, seemingly without reluctance. He was still carrying the small square something in his right hand, definitely not a gun. Seeing that no one was now near them, Stears wondered vaguely why the girls did not just get out of the van on the other side. It must have been hot in there.

It took time for Alfredo to be installed. There must have been an awkward movement; Stears heard one faint yelp. But it was done. The Lear's crew installed itself. The engines gave two shuddering whines and settled to a burble. The steps were still outside and the door was open. The terrorists looked agitated for a moment, but Mascagni reassured them and then pointed them toward the Lear. They had about two hundred meters to cross, out in the open. The one with the little box in one hand took a firmer grip on it.

About halfway to the Lear, his companion made a sudden movement, half-turned, and raised his gun. That this happened, there was no doubt. Stears, who was closer than most, saw surprise and fear or pain in the boy's face, not aggression. Perhaps he was badly stung. At all events, for a moment he raised his machine gun very much in the direction of the three CIA men twenty meters from Stears. Their response was instantaneous: three long-barreled automatics now pointed at the two boys. The second terrorist, who had barely taken heed until now, brought up his weapon wildly. There was a shout among the Carabinieri troops and clacks of metal. The second terrorist now swung and faced them, in firing position and with horror on his face. The Lear pilot goosed his engines, no doubt from nerves.

Everybody should now have counted to twenty. Everybody should have gone back and started over. Either might well have been done.

But at this moment, the Fiat van, which had ceased to be the center of attention, began to shake violently from within. A door flew open so hard that it rebounded. The two girls, who had sat so quietly, came crawling, staggering out, falling over each other, faces in terror as though the van had bloomed in vipers. Mascagni, apparently at once equally appalled, screamed at them.

The face of the boy with the box now turned to rage and humiliation. The next stage should have been tears. Instead, he abruptly raised the box and moved his hand.

Where the van had been was now a tower of orange flame. The Jaguar clanged like a gong as something hit it. The blast heated Stears's face, though it did not knock him over. The two girls appeared separately in positions possible only for rag dolls on the ground some distance from the van, which was now a tangle of chassis on burning grass.

Everybody began to shoot at once. The boys shot running in the general direction of the Lear. The first one went down in twenty meters. The second was in a fair way of making it, though moving as though with a shattered leg. The steps of the Lear had been drawn up and the door slammed shut before he fell for the last time.

The Lear wound up like a banshee and started forward. Guns followed it, but sense prevailed. By the time Mascagni and the dumpy ambulance had gotten to the girls, the Lear had curtsied with its tail and risen delicately, elegantly from the ground. The girls looked unlikely ever to move again.

Stears got into the Jaguar, started the engine, and moved off so hard that he all but buried the back wheels in the ground. He bore down upon Mascagni so that one of the troopers raised his gun again. Stears stopped by Mascagni and threw open the passenger door.

"Get in," he said. Captain Mascagni looked at him hard and then did so. "Shut the door," said Stears. And then: "We are going to these people, you and I. There are not so many now."

Mascagni nodded slowly. "Then I was right," he said.

"I do not know what you thought," said Stears, "so I cannot tell. But I will tell you all now." They were on the access road by now, accelerating hard.

"Very well, Giovanni," Mascagni said. Even in the Jaguar's air-conditioning, his face was wet.

C·H·A·P·T·E·R   24

The day after Gabriella's door was locked, her shutters had been closed, pulled tight by a twist of wire. Easy enough to break open, but the boy in the garden would know. So she sat alone in the closed dusk, disdaining the electric lamp and entertained by shafts of pure light that rotated through the room by day and lit the half she sat in. That was all she saw of the outside except when a shadow of a cooing dove bounced up and down the bars of light like a monkey on a stick or when once or twice at night the silver headlights of a car whipped across the pitch-darkness on striated wings.

Early that morning she had heard all the voices: the chief Libyan booming and barking, some of the young bullyboys snapping and goading, a plaintive little protest from some Roman girl, and then a long coy threat from Calvetto about explosives in a van and good behavior. All this in the courtyard. Then car doors, an engine, and the gate opening and banging shut.

She herself felt peace moving through her, up her spine like the light dispassionately gracing the floor. She had no doubt left that events were now in motion that would either resolve the distemper of her life or blow it all to pieces. Giovanni being blood to blood a part of this with her, she hoped for him but was not in a fright. Conceivably they were both going to die, but she did not think so.

Consequently when, about late morning, commotion broke out in the farmhouse again, she sat back in her semidarkness to enjoy the interest of it. A real brouhaha this time! The big Arab bellowing like an ox and banging the furniture, doors slamming, the boy crashing around outside, more engines.

Then, announced by his key, Calvetto.

"Get out," he said. "We're leaving."

"Fin de la saison, Docteur?" she said. *"Déjà?"*

"You have less to laugh about than anybody alive," he said.

Yet Calvetto was becoming as brittle as an overbaked meringue. And running around as he had been on his lameness had made him pant, sweat, and moan. She mentioned this.

A half kilometer beyond the airport roadblock, Stears stopped the car at a filling station. Mascagni, who was short of change, made a telephone call to the provincial Carabinieri barracks in Perugia and waited on one foot and then another for the Commander to call him back. Stears did not stop the engine. Mascagni, as staff officer of General Della Cappella, ordered a light screen of Carabinieri observers placed around the northwest quadrant of the environs of Marsciano. This, he was told, would take at least half an hour to put in place and maybe more. He ordered the assembly of an assault squad to stand by. He also ordered a watch for and tailing of any brown delivery truck exiting that region. He promised intermittent contact and further instructions through a radio/telephone frequency available in Stears's car. He revealed obliquely that this was to do with the American embassy incident and with the Monte Sant'Angelo outrage. He mortgaged his career by claiming General Della Cappella's authority for all of this.

He got back in the car. "I have done all you asked because you asked it, Giovanni," he said. "Fortunately Perugia is within the Roman division of Carabinieri. In Milan or Naples I could not have done so much. Surely you want to call your own people."

"I no longer know them or trust them," said Stears. He motioned impatiently for Mascagni to shut his door.

"Then tell me all the story," said Mascagni.

Mascagni shrank into the Jaguar's leather seat, where the points of contact were disorienting after a government Fiat's, and hugged his arms over his chest while he listened. While Stears talked he drove with precise ferocity, granting each other vehicle the absolute minimum of room it could survive with and then consigning it to whatever misery the Jaguar's passage required. He evidently remembered the rural roads. Mascagni at first ventured advice, which was not acknowledged. Then only as they oppressed a car bulging with family on the outskirts of Frascati did he put in, "There's a new *autostrada* here, Giovanni. It bypasses Rome. You couldn't possibly know about it." And got a nod in return. This was seignorial driving, he supposed.

Meanwhile Stears talked. Mascagni listened. His policeman's mind registered notes of further questions needed, objections to be lodged; but in the background he saw his image of the painted ceiling come to life, the cold, ambiguous smiles of its figures become wistful and even afraid, their hands reach for and slip past one another's, while their eyes still contemplated calmly the unearthly irresponsibility of their acts.

But the first thing he said was, "This brown truck—was its back door the kind that rolls up and down or the kind that opens like double doors? It is important for identification on the road."

It opened like doors. Stears had noticed that humble fact. Mascagni could have patted him on the arm had he not needed his own to ward off a petrol tanker by his cheek. It took fortitude for him to operate the radio and report this to Perugia.

At Monterotondo, already north of Rome, he said, "We have to realize that the situation is in fact extremely bad. That airplane probably reported to somebody as soon as it left the ground. Perhaps that was why it was so anxious to take off. These terrorists have done everything right so far, so we can assume that they have excellent communication. They cannot know that those boys at Latina are dead, so they must act as though everyone is now coming to get them. If they are as good as they must be, they have already had time to get out. We will find that brown truck sooner or later, I suppose, but they may be too cautious to use it or even cunning enough to use it as a blind. This is not the ideal control center and the situation is as unstable as it can be."

"I think I will be able to find them," said Stears.

Mascagni unbolted his arms from his chest, for they were on the *autostrada* now and were merely going very fast. He did not speak at once and when he did he spoke quietly. "With at least half the terrorists I have known it did not make any sense that they were terrorists. Why does one lawyer's son stick to his books and another become a murderer sniping from attic windows? Why does one doctor's daughter get married and love her children and another throw a bomb at people waiting for a train? I never found that they had been much different as children. I think we have to imagine that this lady of yours is already a plain and simple terrorist and murderess and is quite willing to murder you, whatever she may once have been. She has gone with vicious people. The fact that you have obviously screwed her again since you came here makes no difference whatsoever. Fucking and bombs go well together, I have found. Probably she spread her legs to get information from you—it would be more fun than reading the paper. Now she hopes you'll come back for more so she can kill you. I am speaking crudely because the truth is crude. And I am your operational colleague and nothing else."

And to my shame I thought of all that too, thought Stears, *much of last night. But there is truth above logic in the flush of skin and there is truth in a cry held in the throat in a darkened house.* He said with conscious detachment, "There are sentiments of a certain kind that do not entirely change. That is important to remember."

Mascagni looked pointedly away. In the world of the painted ceiling he thought nothing less so. A world in which a young girl could buy a Ferrari and use it to blood herself like a savage in the name of love struck him as very far from love and very close to the world in which one evidently immolated stolen corpses to play amorous games. In his mind he began to detach himself from Stears.

The radio squawked. Mascagni listened closely. "Did you hear that?" he said. "Perugia has found a truck to match yours. It is traveling rather fast toward Todi."

"Can you get unmarked cars around it?" said Stears.

"It is certainly the thing to try," Mascagni said. He used the radio. The response was plaintive. Mascagni used the name Della Cappella again. "Perugia will have to bring in other commands," said Mascagni. "Let's hope there are not many brown trucks around. I told them that one of them might have an Ambassador in the back. It impressed them, I think. The trouble is, if that truck has anything to do at all with these people, it must have left before the observers were in place to be anywhere near Todi now. I was afraid of that."

"We shall soon find out," said Stears.

Calvetto stood still in the light of the doorway as she belittled his state, but seemed to darken and vibrate. He said, "Get dressed. Get that damn nightgown off." Gabriella sat and looked at him. "Quickly," he said.

"Then leave the room," she said. "You presume."

He backed through the door and banged it. She got up and drew the latch of the shutter. She doubted that anyone had time now to object. The twisted wire vexed her fingers. She hit the frame with the heel of her hand and the old wood abandoned the screws, swung lackadaisically half open and squeaked to a stop. A thrush moved farther into the nearest peach tree. Gabriella blinked a little in the light.

She stood by the mirror. The nightgown off, her bruises were tending to aubergine with a trace of green; it was not becoming at all and she would restrict Giovanni's ardor to dim rooms for a while. She sighed. It was nice to think in such short terms. She dressed with what was to hand. The blouse seemed loaded with association. She recognized it as the one she had taken from her bathroom at Dolly Casamassima's before dawn so long ago. She frowned at this. Her chestnut hair hung down, long and unkempt. She snatched up the kerchief blindfold that Calvetto had enjoyed so much and wrapped her hair up tight. Rosa stood there, severe and primed. And Rosa might well be needed one last time today. She felt an arousal that she did not quite acknowledge. Quickly, both with memory and eye, she searched the room for scissors, sharp nail file, knife, even cruel-pronged broach to hide inside her dress, but there was nothing of the sort. Clearly, she would have to improvise if the moment came.

She went to the door and opened it. Calvetto stood outside. *"La tua Rosa,"* she said, and looked him a long moment in the eye.

He made her go into the courtyard. Everyone was there. Only two of the bullyboys seemed to be left. They had guns dripping off them as usual. The big Libyan was haranguing them in Arabic. There was a small brown truck, the sort that carries newspapers or milk. One of the boys opened the back of it for a moment to check the latch and she saw that it was full of people. One of the boys got into the cab while the other opened the courtyard gate. The truck started, then stopped in the gate. The boy gave the big Arab a preposterous military salute and jumped into the other side of the cab. The truck drove off fast.

The Arab, now with an automatic in his hand, turned toward her with such a look of baffled rage that she missed acutely the feel of any sort of weapon against her flesh. He pointed her toward another vehicle. It was a Volkswagen camper and Calvetto was already getting into the driver's seat. The Libyan hurried her up with the muzzle of his gun. She got in. The Libyan pushed her to the middle of the three rows of seats, then clambered in behind. Calvetto was alone in front.

She found herself next to a small, dirty old man, blinking foolishly and somehow familiar, who was already in the van. She looked at him in surprise, then remembered him and her manners at the same time. "My dear Ambassador," she said in English. "What a pleasure." She recollected him as rather dull.

But much to his credit he bowed as he could and tried to smile. "Princess," he said indistinctly. "Quite a surprise." His smile was completely toothless. He used false teeth and lacked them, she supposed.

The Libyan said in labored English, "You must not talk, sir, please." And then in Italian: "I would shoot you with pleasure, you whore."

The van started, gained the gate, and turned in the opposite direction from the truck. The Ambassador looked up the road the way the truck had gone, but it was already out of sight.

Stears and Mascagni left the *autostrada* just north of Todi, where the Tiber ran beside the road. "We must be very near that truck now," said Mascagni.

"Yes," said Stears and did not slow down. Mascagni looked at him questioningly, then said, "It is true that this car is conspicuous, and there is already a Lieutenant in charge of surrounding that truck, and we have other things to do."

"I think so too," said Stears.

"And although this radio has the frequency that the Carabinieri cars normally use, the last thing we want is traffic on that particular frequency. I am sure that the truck has a set. I hope the Lieutenant has thought of that."

"Maybe it's a truck full of artichokes," said Stears. "Then perhaps not."

"There is most certainly that," said Mascagni. Off the *autostrada,* he had stiffened up his arms again.

And thus took some pleasure in guiding Stears around Marsciano by roads he could not have known.

Perugia had set up a command post. They were directed there by radio. It turned out to be a grazier's cottage off the road to the target and two kilometers from it. A command vehicle, a slab-sided truck with antennae swaying in the breeze, had been parked in a stone-walled paddock, though the cottage had a telephone. The couple of the cottage had declared a holiday and were sitting in the window with a jug of wine.

A Major Lamprezo was in charge. He exchanged salutes with Captain Mascagni and gave Stears's hand an uncertain shake. "We have been in contact with General Della Cappella," said the Major. "He compliments you upon the original interpretation of his orders." The Major looked at Mascagni sideways; but he was a Carabinieri officer, and thus a policeman with a soldier's heart, and too swept along by an almost military operation to stick on points like that. "Here is the situation," he said. He looked doubtfully at Stears and then at Mascagni, who included Stears with a gesture. The Major had newly brushed his uniform everywhere that he could reach it.

Three brown trucks of appropriate type had been shadowed. This had been a nightmare. One had just unloaded furniture: unfortunately it was nowhere near the other two and those cars could not be reassigned. They were headed back here. The first truck had two unmarked cars up with it and a Polizia Stradale car half a kilometer behind. The second truck had only one car, but a Polizia Stradale car was closing fast.

This valley had been under observation for forty-five minutes. All had been completely ordinary during that time. Observers, going carefully around by another road, had reached the hillsides over the target sixteen minutes ago. The farm seemed deserted.

Indeed, thought Stears. He said, "How many vehicles are there, and of what kind?"

This was some talking on the radio. A car, it seemed. Perhaps it was a dark-blue Lancia—it was hard to see. A tractor. A wagon for the tractor.

Stears nodded. "Then I think it is deserted," he said.

Mascagni sighed and said, "I see absolutely no reason to wait longer."

"The assault squad has still only six men," said Major Lamprezo. "More are coming in."

"Two boys with water pistols should do," said Stears. The Major looked sad.

"We will take the trucks after we take the farm," said Mascagni. "But the cars must be alerted now. One odd movement and they go in. Do not be quite so cavalier, Giovanni. There could still be somebody there."

After a blast of ferocity—the gate slammed in, assault rifles waltzing, stun grenades slapping through empty rooms, an appalled cat bursting out of the cellar—the Carabinieri commandos stood in the courtyard smoking. Captain Mascagni had congratulated them—"Bravo, boys, bravo! A performance to remember!" If there was irony in his tone, it was taken in good heart.

"Now the trucks," said Mascagni. "This frightens me much more." The command vehicle had come up. He went to it, spoke to the wireless operator through the door, and reached in for the microphone. In the sound of wasps and doves, which would not be invaded by the worst result, he gave precise orders. He sat on the steps with head hunched and listened to the radio. After a time he gave Stears a single heartened smile. He listened some minutes longer, leaned forward twice to grab the microphone, and then got up more somberly.

"The second one was carpets," he said. "It was the first one, as we thought. It went perfectly. That Lieutenant should be a Captain tomorrow. The Polizia Stradale blocked the road in both directions. The terrorists found themselves looking down at rifle muzzles from two meters on both sides. They gave up. The hostages are all right—ours and yours. But it is not entirely good, Giovanni. They are not all there. There is no Ambassador and no Dr. Calvetto and no *guerrigliero* of any rank. The terrorists in the truck were just boys. And no Princess, either holding a gun or facing one. It is far from over yet. I think we search the house now. A little more slowly than those heroes."

"I will take the upstairs," said Stears.

The stairs creaked. It was curiously innocent. The steps were of plain wood worn to silver. The frill of a muslin curtain moved in a breeze. Beyond a sharp scent of gun oil hanging in the air around one empty closet, its recent use had left the house untouched and, like a veiled face, disturbing.

The third room had been Gabriella's. Her scent hung in it, faint but true, and more of her skin than her perfume. There was a nightgown on the floor. He picked it up and held it, compressed it in his hands. He sat on the bed, though she, it seemed, had not. Whatever distance was between them now seemed as thin as a membrane. The window shutter was open, its clasp askew. He looked through it, and saw the hill path he had walked on two days before and the knob he had stood by; it was all just above the highest spray of peach. One shutter on this floor, and the attic shutters, had been closed. She cannot know I came, he thought, and his heart contracted not in fear of the outcome, but in fear that she would feel abandoned now. He left the window and looked on every surface for a message to him, even drawn in dust. It seemed easily expected.

Mascagni brought it, and it was not in Gabriella's hand. A

sheet of paper with writing angular as witches' hats. "In the kitchen, Giovanni," he said. "This is the doctor's own writing, I believe. I think the doctor was in haste."

Stears took it to the window. He read:

> The Aurora Rossa and the Libyan People join the Italian People in their sorrow at the events at the airport of Latina precipitated by the aggression of the Imperialist CIA. The Aurora Rossa requires the surrender of the CIA agent Giovanni Stears as redress for this crime. If this surrender is forthcoming, no action will be taken against other American prisoners of the Aurora Rossa while on Italian soil.
>
> No quarrel exists between the Aurora Rossa and the Italian People. The Aurora Rossa will of its goodwill release the two Italian citizens still in its keeping against the promise of the Italian Authorities to cease pursuit of units of the Aurora Rossa. The Aurora Rossa will bargain separately with the United States Government. The Italian authorities will use the CIA agent Stears to carry their response to this.
>
> The Fascist Stears will obey the instructions below and find further instructions where stated. If he is accompanied or followed, another hostage will be killed—he may guess which one that will be. The Carabinieri should note that other hostages are in various places where their fate can be decided within a moment. After the release of its Italian prisoners, the Aurora Rossa will respond to any pursuit by selective execution of its American prisoners.

> IN THE NAME OF THE ITALIAN AND LIBYAN PEOPLES

Otherwise, it was not signed.

There was a sheet of instructions underneath it.

"Good," said Stears.

"Do not pretend to be stupid," said Mascagni. "It is not good at all."

But Stears had spoken not out of bravado but for simplicity. A simplicity that, now a little more than an hour later, when he was driving alone up a steepening road toward a lethal rendevous, still existed at the center though not at the edge.

An hour had been all the delay that could be afforded if the enemy's suspicions were not to be raised. What could be done in that time had been done.

Many kilometers away, an Arab boy, pining for the courage that had left him all alone, sat beside a radio with a Carabinieri interrogator by his side. "My colleague is holding a revolver to his balls," Mascagni had said. "I do not think he will say anything foolish to our friend Calvetto."

That was the wedge: that the enemy believed he held six lives at the end of a radio wave and that in consequence no move against him could be more than a bluff.

Now Stears was in the mountains, in the massif that splits the lowlands around Marsciano on one side from those below Spoleto on the other. He was crossing the top of it. This road would be shown only on large maps; the Jaguar's wheels thumped and crunched on it as though they were boots. A few aspens grew in the protected bends, and across the ravine a single chestnut rose from a fissure. But the roofs of the only village were far below. There were no walls in the short grass and even the smell of sheep was faint.

He had collected the second and final instructions from the base of a crucifix on a mount a hundred meters above the road. That was five kilometers back, before the turnoff from which this road took off across the highlands. They were in the same hand as the paper at the farmhouse. Walking down from the mount, he had seen that this segment of the road could be watched from far away and that cars shadowing his could be easily noted.

Calvetto would assume that Stears could communicate from his car or perhaps that his car carried a signal to be followed. Calvetto would be right. Calvetto also believed that fear for the hostages would force pursuit to stay far behind. From the moment Stears was in Calvetto's hands, Stears would be mute. No one knew what vehicles the terrorists were using or how large a force remained to them or how it could be divided. Since the attrition of late had been considerable, it was assumed that the terrorists were few, including or not a Princess of doubtful virtue. Still, Stears would be swept away.

Thus Stears, the only person whose approach would be permitted, had to try to control, or at worst confuse, the situation sufficiently to safeguard the life of the United States Ambassador while the Italian commando forces, already loaded into two helicopters in the valley, came in behind. Stears would give that signal. The moment the beacon was switched on, the helicopters, with a goal supplied, would leave the ground toward it. Or so he had agreeably been told.

His weapons were the radio beacon and signal for attack that the Jaguar did indeed now carry, and the Beretta in his coat. Both depended on the gun being held against the groin of an Arab boy sixty kilometers away.

The road began to dip. The summit of Monte Martano was to his right. He had been given small landmarks but not the distances between them. He could not frame in his mind how far down the hills his destination lay or what it looked like. Up here the wind blew over the grass. He began to fear the valleys.

In Mascagni's mind this operation was not going to work. Stears knew that very well. In Mascagni's mind Stears had become all at once a man taken by a vulgar trick, even a buffoon with plaster horns. But chance had dictated that he could buy time, serve as a blind; and if an American Ambassador died through the mistakes of a dead CIA man while Italy captured the terrorist chiefs, Italy was not much harmed.

He passed the second-to-last landmark, a roll of rusted wire abandoned and grown over to the right side of the road. The next would be a fork with a torrent to the left. He did not know how far. He was to turn right there. The road pitched down now. When he got there, Calvetto had written, he would know the place.

Dr. Calvetto, Yussuf, and their two prisoners now occupied a building of stone under the wall of a narrow valley five hundred meters below the plateau of Martano. It had been built for the wintering-over of sheep. It was gray, low, and sprawling. Its stalls would easily have held all the hostages if necessary, and its barn, the various vehicles. After two decades of disuse, even the human quarters still stank of tallow. Set against the rock, it was difficult to see from any distance.

Calvetto sat outside, in full view of at least the stretch of hill road that descended the valley, a man taking rest on a sunny bench. Over his head, nailed hastily above the doorway, was a slender radio antenna with a wire leading inside. It was incongruous, but also difficult to see.

Inside, in what had been a primitive kitchen, were Yussuf and the two prisoners. Yussuf and the radio sat comfortably on the window bench, Yussuf with a carbine across his knee. Given the lack of furnishings, the Princess stood. The Ambassador had apologized and then sat weakly on the floor.

This was one of four properties acquired by the Libyan embassy for this operation. At a third, the hostages had arrived almost exactly on schedule fifteen minutes ago. Young Moamar had reported on the radio. There had been strain in his voice, but that was forgivable and Yussuf was pleased with him. Though their situation was deteriorating, they still had strengths, and Yussuf respected his own skill and courage.

Fifty meters away, on the far side of the combe, was a small torrent. It was almost unheard from the house, but it drowned quiet noises. Thus Calvetto did not hear the Jaguar. Though he looked up frequently, he did not see it until it had descended some twenty meters from the point where the track became visible from the house. The surface was such that it moved as though it had sore ankles. Calvetto watched it a moment and then lowered his head. His hidden face settled into resignation and loss. When he raised it, anger had overcome it.

Now he moved of a sudden, like a frog. He stood in the open door. "He has come," he said. The Libyan nodded and got up. He said to Gabriella, "Unluckily for you." He said this over his shoulder with satisfaction as he attended to the radio. The Jaguar was now about a hundred and fifty meters away. Its driver had presumably seen the buildings.

The Libyan spoke to the radio. Moamar answered after a few seconds, beginning with a gasp. "What's wrong with you?" said Yussuf. "The difficult part's over. Get a couple of them ready to talk. One of the women and a diplomat. We may need them and we may not." He said to Calvetto, "Get her out there." He motioned the gun at Gabriella to point her to the door. "Go on, fish bait,'' he said. Action always made him close to affable. As she passed him, he had a thought. He reached up, ran his fingers over her head, and pulled the scarf off.

Stears saw her with joy and dread. He was too far away to see her face, but as she came through the door, her body half-turned back in a swirl of her highest anger, lit by her hair. *However she got there, she's not theirs now,* he thought, and his fingers drummed on the wheel in celebration. *Now I know it.*

Everything else was as bad as it could be.

The terrain was narrow and steep. Helicopters, just possibly, could fidget their way in close by. There would be no grand charge. The place would not be easy to see, except from immediately overhead. The stone buildings would be difficult to rush —though this was less unexpected.

There was worse. The mountain rose steep behind him. Though the beacon to summon and guide the troops apparently did not lack for power, there had been considerable worry whether with such topography it would surmount the hill. "Pray for a little open space," the Carabinieri technician had said. Since leaving the plateau, the voice radio, for a fact, had failed. He turned the beacon on. He had been told it would take twelve to fourteen minutes for the helicopters to arrive.

He drove slowly a little farther. He could see Gabriella's face now. Her eyes were upon him. He felt chill and hollow with the thought that he was bringing nothing, or nothing that would serve. The small man beside her would be Dr. Calvetto. He seemed to urge her back into the door, and she, to refuse angrily. A larger man stepped out and dragged her in, bouncing her off the door frame. Perhaps the Libyan Cultural Attaché. There were two of them at least then. Not a surprise.

All I can use is time, he told himself again. *Do not get close until just before they should come. Then do what you can. If they come.*

He stopped the car some distance from the house. Such caution would be expected. He got out on the far side of the car. He felt the Beretta in his jacket pocket swing, without much enterprise, against his side. He called out, "I am Giovanni

Stears. I have a response from the authorities to your appeal. I have seen the Princess Harriman-Farnese. Now I must see the Ambassador of the United States." He said it from full lungs. They were more trustworthy than his voice, he thought. Two minutes gone.

The Libyan helped Buxhalter to his feet. "You must come," he said. Buxhalter moved slowly toward the light. The Libyan went behind him holding the gun, not on Buxhalter but beyond him. Gabriella looked through the door as they passed. Giovanni was standing by the car. I have nothing to help him with, she thought. Not even a stupid pin. She felt her hand taken. Calvetto had crossed the room. He held it in both of his. She heard the Libyan's voice outside. She pulled her hand away as from a toad but Calvetto pulled at it like a fretful child, though what seemed to be in his face was malice. "You chose wrong," he said. "There is still time. Say it. Look!" He pointed out of the door. She heard Giovanni's voice in the daylight and then the Libyan's in answer. Calvetto spoke quietly but it drowned the other voices in her ears. "Look! Two ordinary men. Shouting at each other. Yours will die, but there is no other difference. Two pieces of flesh that were born and grew like horses. Yours would not even be able to transform himself, and I remade both you and me. Acknowledge it, Rosa!"

She looked down at him. "Abortion!" she said, but a hand inside her chest had gripped her breath. "Two-headed calf! You are a madman. You drove me mad."

"Yes," he said and raised his face, grinning but eyes turning moist, to hers. "I did. He wouldn't. You'd be nothing but yourself."

The hand inside her clutched again, but as in a spasm. Then her chest grew calm and sweet. She said quietly, looking at his face, "I am more sick of you than death itself."

He turned away. "That will come soon then," he said.

She could hear the Libyan's voice now. It said, "We do not have all day. Your Ambassador will listen to our prisoners' voices. He knows them well by now. He will tell you they are in good health. Then you will come forward and surrender as you promised or the woman will die." He came in, pushing Buxhalter in front of him, guiding him carefully through the door.

Five minutes gone. The air above him was still, though there were grasshoppers at his feet. Stears had assumed that he, knowing the sound he listened for, would hear the engines sometime before them. But the torrent, closer to him than to the house, strained out just such noise. It was becoming irrelevant. It did not seem likely that it would take the Libyan long to get a response; Mascagni's colleague would worry more about a delay. Stears had no idea whether the former hostages, recaptured over two hours ago, were still to hand to talk to on the radio. Buxhalter could consume a couple of minutes doing anything. Then that was that. He would have no choice but to go toward the house. Be searched and disarmed. He did not think the Libyan would make mistakes. Between him and the house, there was a rock offering some cover and in the Beretta's range. It was of no value whatsoever unless he could get the Libyan out of the house alone. And probably not much then. The Libyan had a carbine. He did not know if Calvetto was armed.

Two more minutes had passed. Buxhalter came out. The Libyan stood in the doorway, not touching him. Buxhalter opened his mouth but Stears could hear nothing. *This is absurd,* he thought. The Ambassador drew in breath like a man bellowing in a high wind and Stears was reached by a sound thin as reeds and muddy. *He's lost his teeth,* he realized. Buxhalter seemed to say, "Our people are all right, Mr. Stears. There seems no doubt of it." He was pulled back into the door.

From it, the Libyan said, "Now come forward."

Eight minutes had passed. He came around the car. He walked slowly. He kept his hand away from the Beretta. The sound of the torrent receded. The noise of grasshoppers rose. No motors in the air. Perhaps it was anyway too early, but he had a grinding certainty that the beacon had not been heard. He passed the sheltering rock.

Calvetto pushed out beside the Libyan. He seemed to be capering against a gale, in such a state that in real life he surpassed the grotesque of Stears's imagination. He looked at Stears with so much malice that Stears blinked. "Fool," he shouted. "Now we have you all. Blundering oxen. You and the ones we hold far away. Shall I have one of them killed? To show I am able? Will you listen to it before I kill you? I have all the choices."

"You have nothing," said Stears. He stopped still. He locked eyes with Calvetto, though it was like holding acid, and strove to watch the Libyan at the edge. "Use your radio," he said. "Ask your gangster the name of the Carabinieri officer beside him. Ask him the make of the gun in his side. He was captured three hours ago. Listen to your hostages laughing at you. You know their voices. All you have is troops around you. You are—" And at that, seeing the Libyan step quickly back and his eye move toward the doorway, he drove his hand to his pocket, pulled the Beretta out, and, as the Libyan turned again, fired three shots into the doorway and ran toward it himself.

The Libyan stumbled through the door, pushing Calvetto in front of him. Stears saw the carbine barrel glint inside. He heard a crash from the room. Then a bellow of "You harlot!" Then an eldritch shriek. And then a shot.

When the Libyan came back through the door, Gabriella threw the radio at him. It hit him in the face. He rocked. She was off balance too. He recovered, eyes bulging, roaring at her. Calvetto was crouched against the wall. The Libyan tried to raise the carbine and moaned in pain. He took it in the other hand and raised it toward her breast.

Calvetto screamed, "No!" He came from the wall as though falling. He ran toward the Libyan. He spread his arms wide to plead or to assault. He passed in front of Gabriella. The Libyan's shot hit him in the chest.

He spun and fell. The Libyan looked at him as though he had fallen from the sky. Then, mouth still working in rage, raised the carbine again.

A voice beside him said, "Why?" He turned, bewildered, saw Buxhalter's dirty, appalled face and for a second it seemed to him that righteousness itself had spoken. He opened his mouth to explain himself. He heard a noise in the doorway on his other side. He turned again and saw the muzzle of the Ber-

etta three meters from his ribs. Stears fired. He fell. The carbine
scraped along the floor.

Calvetto lay on the floor. He made a mewing sound. Gabriella, who had half-fallen against the wall, looked down at him.
Calvetto's hand moved toward his side in slow jerks. His fingers
groped in his pocket and brought out a linen pouch. The draw-
string loosened and out of it fell scarlet and sulfur stones, like
blood and bile. His finger stirred them on the floor. "These were
for you," he said. "The night that you betrayed me." His voice
faded, but his eyes held hers, the last of their antic mischief
gone, black and sad. "Keep them with you now," he said.

His eyes still held her face. He whispered, "You would have
come back to me." Her mouth shaped *sì*, though no sound came
with it. He smiled. She stepped away. *"Maledetto!"* she said
with an indrawn breath. "Evil!" she said aloud.

Calvetto still smiled, though his breath labored. His hand
scratched in another pocket and came forth. What it held this
time also was colored and bright, lapis lazuli on one side, *oeil de
tigre* on the other, silver between. With failing strength he
turned it in his hand. "Then no one else," he said. From the
jeweled grip, the barrel of a miniature revolver, scarcely longer
than a hornet, pointed up at Stears.

Gabriella screamed, "Giovanni!" But Stears had seen already. He swung the Beretta at Calvetto and fired into his side.
Then, looking Calvetto full in the face, he fired again.

Calvetto shuddered. His head lifted toward Gabriella, but
then fell back. Now it faced out of the door toward the summit
of Monte Martano. His eyes traveled up it and beyond to where
a crescent of thin cloud was lit by the earliest glow of evening.
A bubble of blood formed over his lips and burst. He spoke
toward the sky in ruin and hatred. "Coward!" he said.
"Cheat!" He shook and was still.

Stears heard a voice say, "You had no choice, Mr. Stears. I
am your witness." And realized that the voice was Buxhalter's.

Stears went to Gabriella. He carried her to the seat that the
Libyan and the radio had vacated. He felt her shudder and
clench against him as on the night of horror at the Villa Pamphili-
Farnese, felt her mouth, lips tight-closed, press his neck. But

this time she softened; he felt her breast begin to move as though ice were breaking in it, found his neck wet with tears, found it being kissed. He took her face in his hands and kissed her mouth. She sniffed damply and briskly shook her head.

"I'm sorry," she said. "I seem to do this to you all the time. Are there really people all around?"

"There are meant to be," said Stears. "There just don't seem to be."

Buxhalter's voice said, "Mr. Stears, quickly!"

The Libyan was moving. He was crawling on the floor like a dog with a broken back. He was crawling very slowly toward the fallen carbine. Stears eased Gabriella from his lap, took two steps, and picked it up. The Libyan looked up at him through stupid, haunted eyes. When he spoke, air whistled in his chest more loudly than his words. He said, "Only for myself, sir. Only for myself. You do it now, please. Do not let me live. I am a diplomat, sir. They have to take me home."

Buxhalter hugged his arms around his chest. "I have never seen a man in such a case," he said. "I also saw him with the other prisoners."

Stears threw the carbine out of the door. Its barrel spun in the light. Gabriella shivered where she sat and her face was waxy again. He put his arm around her and raised her up. She followed him through the door, heavy and awkward against him. The light outside hurt but the air smelled of herb and pine. A little louder than the noise of the torrent was now an alien sound, a clattering whine. Quite far off, a helicopter dipped and circled as though searching.

Gabriella pulled him down on the bench outside and gripped him hard, looking him closely in the face. Her breath was acid. "Leave me," she said, "and go away. I am poisoned and I will poison you."

"No," he said.

"That last thing," she said, "that Arab. Everything around me is like that."

"We can be what we should have been," he said. "There is still enough time. Do not let people like this destroy us. What we did ourselves was bad enough."

Her hands were less clenched but she looked down as she

spoke. "I thought that even this morning," she said. "But these things will not leave us. They will not leave me."

"Live anyway," he said. "Live as we should have. Try. Nothing is very pure or very easy. Try. Have you anything better to do?"

"Do you trust me that much?" she said.

"Yes."

Damp, with unsteady breath and chilly skin, she put her arms around his neck and said, "Then I will. Whatever happens, nobody will ever have tried so hard." After a minute she said, an edge of her own angular voice appearing, "I suspect that my days as a reputable Princess, at the very least, are over."

"You can be a Marchesa," he said. "I'll tell you about it."

"You see," she said, now pulling him toward her, "a comedown already." But her voice did not quite succeed in carrying that and, before the helicopter's nearing clatter overwhelmed it, she said again, "I said I'd try, Giovanni, and I will."

About the Author

Frank O'Neill is a native of Charleston, South Carolina, but spent his early years in England, Switzerland, and Italy. After Oxford, where he learned to steeplechase, he was briefly a wine merchant, but quickly reverted to his first love, writing. He now lives in New York City and Brevard, North Carolina.